DEVOTED

Alice Borchardt

Introduction by
Anne Rice

A SIGNET BOOK

SIGNET
Published by the Penguin Group
Penguin Books USA Inc., 375 Hudson Street,
New York, New York 10014, U.S.A.
Penguin Books Ltd, 27 Wrights Lane,
London W8 5TZ, England
Penguin Books Australia Ltd, Ringwood,
Victoria, Australia
Penguin Books Canada Ltd, 10 Alcorn Avenue,
Toronto, Ontario, Canada M4V 3B2
Penguin Books (N.Z.) Ltd, 182–190 Wairau Road,
Auckland 10, New Zealand

Penguin Books Ltd, Registered Offices:
Harmondsworth, Middlesex, England

Published by Signet, an imprint of Dutton Signet,
a division of Penguin Books USA Inc.
Previously appeared in a Dutton edition.

First Signet Printing, September, 1996
10 9 8 7 6 5 4 3

To Howard James O'Brien

ACKNOWLEDGMENTS

My heartfelt thanks to:

Mary Jane Selle, for her careful typing skills;

Joyce Bell, Barbara Dawson Smith, and Arnette Lamb, for their inspiration and belief;

Susan Wiggs, for constant encouragement (not to mention nagging);

Jennifer Enderlin, for judicious editing;

Michaela Hamilton, for her vision;

Lynn Nesbit, for taking a chance in a risky business;

Anne Rice, for all her devoted encouragement and support; and Karen O'Brien, for turning a first draft into a manuscript.

But most of all, thank you to my beloved and patient husband, Clifford Borchardt. Truly all my life's joy is in you.

INTRODUCTION
by Anne Rice

The publication of my sister Alice's novel, *Devoted,* is indeed a cause for celebration! Seventeen years ago, when my first novel, *Interview with the Vampire,* saw print, Alice's name appeared—as it does today—in the dedication.

Now, Alice draws us into her own marvelous book, leading us into the irresistible atmosphere of the Dark Ages, into a vivid and deliciously violent realm of battle, love, and tragic entanglement. Her rich and musical prose invites us to forget the present and to trust ourselves entirely to her splendidly realized vision of *Devoted.*

As a writer and a sister, I'm overwhelmed with pride and happiness and downright glee. But am I surprised at the depth and power of Alice's book? No!

Only two years separate us as sisters, and Alice, the elder, was without doubt the first great storyteller to ever hold me in thrall as a child, mesmerizing me with her tales of fantasy, adventure, and the supernatural. As children, we shared an entire dreamworld stocked with wondrous characters, feeding each other the endlessly intricate plots day in and day out, as we acted the parts of various persons or simply vied with one another to describe the latest imaginary events of our heroes and heroines.

Alice was a guardian angel, a muse, and a frightening spellbinder. If we found a piece of chalk in the backyard, it was the bone of a dead pirate; indeed, a whole cemetery of pirates lay buried beneath our house. Bits of gravel had to be dinosaur's teeth—it was perfectly obvious when she examined the fossils taken from the concrete sidewalk. Rain tapping on a tin roof was Morse code from another planet, and the dots and dashes had to be patiently recorded for hours.

The top branches of the tree in our front yard gave Alice a perfect vantage point to shoot down invading enemies.

My first trips to the library as a child were with Alice, where our father introduced us both to written tales that were sometimes as exciting as those we made up ourselves. How we loved those huge fragrant hardcover books on history, archaeology, the fall of Rome, the Lost Children of Mu, or the legend of Atlantis.

It was with Alice that I sat in the front row of the neighborhood theater, terrified as *The Mummy* crept across the screen, or as Errol Flynn put an end to the evil Basil Rathbone in *Robin Hood* or *The Sea Hawk*.

Nourished on words, lulled to sleep by the bedtime tales of our Irish Catholic parents, aunts, and uncles, we grew to love storytelling as much as we loved running or jumping or swimming.

It is no wonder that two writers should emerge from those early years of eager telling and listening, in rooms filled with volumes of Dickens and Robert Louis Stevenson, or Edgar Rice Burroughs and G. K. Chesterton, where the radio nightly incited us with the eloquent narratives of Hercule Poirot, Boston Blackie, the Shadow, or Terry and the Pirates.

Of course, contrary to what other kids said, we did know the difference between fantasy and reality. But we also knew the most precious secret of all: that reality matters not if you cannot dream; and that all dreams are rooted in truth and speak the language of truth as they unfold in all their splendor. If you're to be the heroine of your own life—to use David Copperfield's lovely phrase—you'd better be able to see that your life is a damned good story.

That Alice should be a natural writer, that her words should so spontaneously unfold into gripping tales, that her characters should come to life so readily—none of this is a mystery to this younger sister who spent her entire life trying to catch up with Alice as she bounded into past and future worlds, opening this one ever more brilliantly to the little kid following behind her.

Surely *Devoted* is only the first of Alice's novels to delight us; surely it is only the first story from her pen, which will take us back into dark medieval forests, and onto treacherous battlefields, and into the shadowy chambers of ages past, where curses are uttered and hearts welded together forever. Alice is as comfortable in a ninth-century cathedral as she is on a Viking ship, or trudging the barren terrain of another planet. Unfailingly accurate, whether she is talking about the shape of a sword or the words of a witch's spell, she has a cast of thousands to reveal to us.

I can't wait to read the next installment of this marvelous tale.

And Alice, what about that werewolf novel you've been teasing me with all these months? I know you've finished it. Where is it? When may I read it?

I'm proud to say congratulations, good luck, and "a job well done" to my sister dreamer, sister writer, sister eccentric. In our heads we were always going where no one had gone before. Isn't it fun that those crazy O'Brien girls—Alice and Anne—are now getting to share their bizarre stories with anyone who wants to read them?

Keep the faith, fellow explorer—my sister, my heroine. More books! More stories! More battle scenes! Nobody writes those battle scenes quite like you do!

Chapter

1

FRANCE, CIRCA 900

THE horse was lathered and nearly spent. The animal was big, rough-gaited and more used to the plow than the armored man and the woman it carried.

They were in the open and the Vikings had fresh beasts. It was at least half a mile to the wood, but they wouldn't make it, and he'd depended on making it. In its darkness, he could lose an army.

He slammed his heels into the bay's flanks. The horse tried to go faster, willing to the end. Its armored rider heard the whiffing breathing increase its speed. He felt the strain of powerful muscles under his thighs. But the bay staggered and fell back into the same steady but exhausted gallop.

No use, the warrior thought. The horse would die soon, even at this pace, and leave them at the mercy of the two following. Better to pick the time and place himself.

A river lay on his right, broad and glistening like a lake in the dwindling afternoon sun. The thin band of trees and brush along its banks would give the girl some cover for her flight.

"When we reach the trees, I'll pull up and turn. You jump off, run! I'll go for the closest one. I think I can kill him. If they get me, keep running until you have to hide."

The warrior didn't know if she understood him. She was probably one of the camp slaves and only God knew where she'd been captured. The only time he'd heard her voice was when she'd screamed a warning that he was about to be surprised and killed by a pack of them while he was watching the camp from cover about a mile away.

Four on foot and five mounted. They'd all come at him at once, but the scream was enough. A second later he'd been mounted and turning to face them.

He'd killed the first to reach him with a straight thrust through the throat. Then the bay reared as he'd been trained to do when one of the footmen seized his bridle. After a slash, the man screamed and dropped away.

He was no match for them; no match for their numbers. He ran and realized the girl who'd screamed was running too.

Heavily armed as they were, the girl was faster. She sprinted toward him, her mouth a grim line, hair flying. He'd known the warning was no accident when one of the footmen gave chase, knife in hand, reaching for the streaming dark hair.

He'd turned and slashed at the pursuer. Seconds later there was a weight behind him and her hands were around his waist.

He spurred the warhorse to the best speed he could muster and they were clear, the chase pounding behind them. The footmen dropped back first. The horsemen hung on longer. The bay wasn't fast, but had the stamina of his plow horse ancestors. His pursuers used up their mounts trying to catch him, falling away one by one until only these two canny horsemen were left. They'd hung back saving their horses, knowing the bay carrying a double load couldn't outlast them.

They wanted him. He'd killed enough of them to ensure that. But most of all they wanted his weapons and armor— the Frankish sword of tempered steel with its ruby pommel and the chain mail byrnie he wore.

The closest one to him was armored in boiled leather, carried only an axe, and rode a scrubby piebald.

The second, trailing farther back, wore a quilted jerkin and carried a heavy two-handed broadsword strapped to his back. He rode a black.

He slowed the bay. The shadows of the trees were upon him.

The one with the axe was only about twenty yards behind. The other, the man on the black, was about a hundred.

He pulled the bay to a halt and felt the woman's weight fall away. From the corner of his eye, he saw her dart into the trees.

The one with the axe lifted it, swung it around his head with a scream, and charged.

The warrior crouched, head by the bay's neck, drew his sword, drove his heels into the animal's flanks, and prayed they both had enough in them for one more effort.

The bay thundered forward like an avalanche and hadn't quite hit his stride when he crashed into the piebald. The two stallions rose screaming, hooves hammering at each other, breast to breast.

The axeman raised his weapon, teeth bared, to strike him down. The piebald's head snaked forward, biting at the bay, exposing its throat to the warrior on his back.

With one swipe he cut the piebald's throat. The horse gave a ghastly, almost human scream and reared up, blood spraying from its neck, then went over backward like a falling tree, carrying the axeman down with him, under him.

The man on the bay drove the knife-pointed rowels of his spurs in to the hilt on the flanks. The tormented animal slammed forward over the still-thrashing piebald and the man on the ground, the big hooves trampling everything. The bay came to a stop a few yards beyond the fallen horse and man, trembling in every limb.

The man on the black reined in his horse about fifty feet away. He studied the two still upright, then the pair on the ground. They were moving, but wouldn't be for long. The horse's legs kicked ineffectually. The head of the leather-armored man was strangely distorted, blood leaking into the dirt and trampled grass.

A breeze was blowing from the river, and the long grass whispered softly in it. The rider on the bay was exhausted. The other could take him now with ease. His arms were like lead and the spent animal under him would barely be able to walk, much less run. The only reason he didn't drop the sword was that his hand was cramped around it, frozen into a claw.

"Come on, friend, if that's what's in your mind." He raised the sword slightly.

The other was still looking at the pair on the ground.

"If you think it's worth it," the man on the bay said.

Evidently the other didn't think so, because he turned the black and rode away.

The man on the bay sat quietly, feeling the wind from the river drying the sweat on his body, watching until the black was a dot moving over the green distance. Only then did he realize that the girl had returned from the cover of the brush. She'd slit the throat of what was left of the axe-wielder, and pulled his body from under the dead piebald. She methodically stripped the corpse. When the woman finished, she handed him the axe, but kept the knife she'd used to do the throat cutting, and tied it to her belt. He dismounted, took the bridle of the bay, and began walking. She followed, slinging the dead man's possessions, bundled in the saddle blanket, over her shoulder.

It was almost night when they reached the forest. Long shadows, velvet and silent, stretched out from the trees. The sky was a black opal with a scattering of stars.

Beyond the wood and the darkness lay Chantalon, his city. He wouldn't try to travel the trails by night. No one could cross this wilderness in darkness.

A hut was just past the first big trees in the wood. It was not so much hidden as reclaimed by the forest, covered with vines, behind a growth of brush and saplings. Constructed of woven branches, twisted and plaited into a cone, the smoke hole in the roof showed stars.

He led the horse in with him and searched the dead leaves and dried grass of the interior with his sword to be sure it had no nonhuman tenants, then blocked the door.

He was nearly falling with weariness, but before he lay down, he unsaddled the bay and loosened the bit, leaving the bridle in position. If they were found, he might have to leave quickly.

"A fire?" the girl said.

"No. It's too dangerous. Go to sleep."

He heard the soft rustling of her body in the straw as she curled up on the other side of the hut. That made him more happy than anything else.

She stank of unwashed humanity and other smells more disgusting. She hadn't been particular about stripping the dead man and she and the bundle she carried were sodden with gore. He lay down beside the stallion, still armed and wearing the byrnie. The hard knot of fear in his belly relaxed, but didn't untie itself. The girl had cut the dying man's throat with one sure stroke. She was ready with that knife and didn't fear to use it.

His fingers curled around his sword hilt. He pulled it up across his chest, clutching the scabbard with his left hand. The feel was comforting.

He woke once in the night, smelling the dawn. It was very quiet. Outside, the mist must be rising from the river, dampening the air. Ever since he'd come to Chantalon, that faint, moist scent and the pervasive cooling of the air signaled the coming of morning to his awakening consciousness.

Someone was crying.

The sound raised the hair on the back of his neck as he recalled old stories of this forest and the things that lived here. He remembered the girl and understood. Still, it was possible that a search party might be out after them. From the camp of those human wolves upriver. And there were other dangers lurking among the trees—gangs of thieves and outlaws.

"Shut up," he growled, "if anyone's nearby, you'll bring them down on us."

She grew quiet, but he heard her deep gulping breaths in the silence. "When we reach the city, I'll find some way to send you home," he whispered.

She laughed, a low ugly sound. "I was their slave, I was their whore. Do you think my kin would still want me?"

"Probably not," he said. He was surprised at his own brutality, but it was likely enough true. Even if he could find her people, and if they were still alive, they'd probably only count her as another mouth to feed. If they were a family of rank, she'd be an embarrassment.

She was still crying, muffled whimpering sounds.

"Stop it," he whispered. "You're not the only woman it ever happened to and you couldn't help it. There's no sense crying over what can't be changed."

She spat back at him like a cat. "That's what people cry over, things they can't change."

His eyelids were falling, his body craved rest. Even death seemed preferable to the exhaustion that dragged at his flesh. "Lady," he snarled in a low hoarse whisper, "I'm defeated by your logic, but shut your mouth, leave off whining, and let me sleep."

She was silent then. He had only a few moments to be thankful. Sleep closed over his mind like a rising tide of black water, bearing him into dark, untroubled depths.

Chapter

2

*D*READ lay like a stone in her chest when the first gray light awakened her. Another day she had to face, to survive in an existence that was one long torment. Then she remembered where she was, what had happened, and most of all blessedly, mercifully, that she was free.

Her body, curled protectively in on itself, relaxed. She rolled on her back and extended her bare legs over the bed of dried grass, feeling only that exquisite relief that comes when pain ends.

Her mind could hold only one thought: It's over, oh, God, it's finished, I am free. She lay, dazed with sleep, basking in the knowledge.

He snored, not loudly but as a young man snores, a soft buzzing noise accompanying each exhalation. She remembered tormenting him in the night with her grief. Foolish grief. She no longer felt it, only joy.

A stealthy movement in the grass brought her to her knees with a jerk, fear tensing every muscle in her body. She looked around the hut wildly. But it was only the horse trying to crop at the dried stalks of hay on the floor. The fear still held her though, muscles taut, eyes wide, peering into the half-light inside the hut, listening.

For all she knew, some of those devils might be outside, creeping up to surprise them. This joyous sense of freedom, of release, might be only an illusion. In moments she might be dragged back to slavery. This thought was unbearable; she had to know. She crawled quickly to the narrow door and peered out through the chinks in the laced branches.

The world outside lay in that misty, gray silence between first light and sunrise. She could see, but not clearly.

The hut stood concealed in thick brush near a small meadow. Something moved in the tall grass, something large and dark. The breath caught in her throat and her heart gave a terrified bound, and then, in the same moment, her practiced eye recognized the long muzzle and the slender curve of the neck—a deer feeding in the early morning stillness.

A shadow detached itself from the trees and flew on silent wings past the hut and into the forest beyond. An owl. She relaxed. They were more alert guardians than she, and would have fled any nearby human movement.

She turned back and looked at the warrior. He slept on his side, one hand on the sword hilt, head pillowed on the other arm. She smiled into the darkness. It is that way when fear is one's bedfellow and sleep does not come easily. The last sleep is the deepest, because the mind fights against the body's vulnerability. In the end, the spent flesh wins. Even fear wears itself out, and sleep becomes a sodden coma not even the dread of death can pierce. Well, let him rest, no need to wake him.

She straightened up and weighed the matter. Would they pursue them? The warrior's gear and horse might tempt them, but they would wait until after sunrise. They disliked moving about after dark, especially near the forest. Dangerous fighters that they were, they still did not have things all their own way. Some raiding parties had met with bloody ambushes near the trees. They wouldn't bother about her at all—a worthless slave, a drooling idiot who babbled to herself in a strange tongue, so filthy that she turned the stomachs of all but the hardiest.

She moved silently out of the hut. So quiet were her movements that she didn't disturb the doe who stood, ears lifted, watching her pass.

The grass was waist-high and drenched with the morning dew. Her single worn linen garment was soaked by the time she reached the water's edge. She stripped it off and slid silently into a clear pool near the bank. The light was brighter, the water an icy shock that chilled her to the bone. Then she grew used to it and was warm.

She had no soap, but made do with fine sand that every footfall stirred from the bottom, picking it up in handfuls and scrubbing her body with it until her skin burned.

Next the hair. She took the knife, found a suitable branch, fashioned a rude comb, and used it to tear the knots, burrs and tangles out almost viciously. Then she formed two braids, one on each side, and fastened them across the top of her head to hold the long fall of the rest of her hair back.

The sun was rising now, its golden light sifting through the treetops. She stared down, caught by the reflection of her nude body in the still water. The dark-haired girl that looked back at her seemed remote, untouched, not herself at all. She'd wondered, in the last few months, if she had truly grown as repulsive as she wished to appear to the men of the camp. But no, she was not. It was almost as though she'd never been captured.

The reflection was herself as she'd been a few months ago, a slender girl of eighteen years. The reflection was an illusion shattered by the touch of a finger in the water.

The marks on her body were truth. Raw patches of skin on her back, still unhealed, torn by the whip. Sores on her ankles and wrist burned into her flesh as she fought the ropes that tied her. Purple and yellow bruises where the hands of some men held her down so others could have their will of her.

The sunlight was dancing on the water now, blinding her. It was her misfortune that she hadn't known how to bend, only fought back until she was broken.

She scooped up the dress from the bank and began washing it, thinking about the warrior in the hut. He'd turned and risked his life to save her, and then, when he believed himself cornered, tried to give her at least a chance to escape. This told her more about him than the praises of a thousand tongues.

The dress was clean enough now, as clean as the pitiful rag was ever going to be. She wrung as much water out of it as she could, remembering his offer to return her to her own people.

Her people, her true kindred, ah, that had been the terror worse than the grinding labor, worse than the blows, worse than the use of her body against her will.

Merchant ships sailed upriver to the camp. She had watched, sick with fear, as men and women were chained. Wives torn from their husbands' arms, children from their parents, and driven like cattle into their holds, to be sold away from all their own kind, losing all they loved and knew forever.

She had known that if she were dragged away, loaded like a piece of merchandise into one of those ships, she would die. She could die, willing herself into darkness. To do so was one of the many strange skills of her people. A thing she had been taught. But it hadn't happened; none of the merchants thought her worth the price. She risked being killed, treated as a thing of no value to be crushed and discarded. Yet she had taken that risk, embraced it gladly, rather than lose her people.

Oh, God, why had she allowed herself to be tempted away from them? She vowed silently that she never would be far from her brothers and sisters again. Those of her spirit, those she loved. She pulled the wet garment over her head and belted it with a strip of leather tied at the waist, then started up the bank, thinking that between the heat of her body and the sunshine, the dress would dry soon enough.

Reaching the top of the bank, she looked out through a screen of young trees across the ravine, and into the open country beyond. Still no signs of pursuit, and he must be sleeping, else he would be out and about as she was.

Should she chance her fortunes with him? Would he want her? Then she smiled, remembering her reflection in the water. Yes, probably he would. In this savage world there were far fewer women than men. Not many young and beautiful ones.

He would of course not know all that he was getting, and might not like it when he found out. Still that could be dealt with when the time came.

The horse whickered softly. Oh, Lord, she had forgotten the poor beast and reproached herself for forgetting. She went to the hut to bring him to water and such forage as she could find.

Chapter

3

WHEN he awakened, the door to the hut was open and sunlight shone through the smoke hole in the roof. The horse was gone!

Christ, no! he thought, leaping to his feet. To lose his horse here, now, might be death. "A curse on that wretched drab!" he hissed, diving through the doorway.

The bay was grazing in the clearing beside the hut.

He relaxed, but turned quickly to look out into the open. The rolling countryside basked green and gold in the morning sun. The only movement was a gentle tossing of the high grass in the soft river breeze. Thank God for the horse and the emptiness of the plain.

"I thought I'd give the poor creature something to eat. Did you think I'd stolen him?" The voice came from behind him.

He spun around, drawing his sword as he did. She stood beside the hut, watching him gravely.

He stared back open-mouthed, sword forgotten in his hand, because she was beautiful. She'd washed everything, body, dress, hair. She wore a ragged linen shift, but its dilapidated condition didn't disguise the fact that she was lovely.

She took one small step toward him, watching him with wary eyes. The sunlight caught her hair. It shimmered, thick, black as some polished stone—jet. Her eyes were blue, not the gray-blue of ice, but the clear crystalline blue of a summer sky. Her skin reminded him of cream in a jar, thick cream, tawny with its own richness.

His first confused thought was that it couldn't be the same woman. His second, how could they be such fools as to abuse so glorious a prize?

She didn't draw any closer. Indeed there was something in

her eyes that told him as clearly as if she had spoken that if he made any threatening move, she was ready to run.

"How do you feel?" she asked.

Ignoring the complaints of his stiff muscles, he straightened slowly from the crouch he'd dropped into at the sound of her voice. "I feel like a man who's slept all night on the hard ground in his hauberk, clutching a sword in his hand."

She nodded, but looked less wary. "You need something to eat." She pointed to a flat rock near the door of the hut, where there was bread, cheese, and a wineskin.

He fell on the food, wolfing it like a starving man. He was nearly finished when he realized he'd left little or none for her. "I'm sorry," he said awkwardly. "It's just that this is my first meal in two days."

She nodded again. "You did the fighting. I had something before we left the camp yesterday."

She was saddling the horse. He pointed at the remains of the meal.

"Where did that come from?"

"The man you killed," she said, tightening the saddle girth, "he was carrying it."

"Who was he?"

She shrugged. "I can't say, one of the hangers-on; there are many of them cringing at the feet of the strong ones in the camp, eager to snap up any scraps that fall from their master's table. Jackals, even by their low standards."

"No one will be in any hurry to avenge him?" he asked.

"No." She shook her head. "Now the first one, the one whose throat you cut, was called Ragnar. He had kin in the camp. They might follow."

He stood up, handing her the wineskin, saying, "If they do, they'd best be ready for a long ride and a hard fight."

He mounted the horse. She handed him the rolled bundle looted from the fallen man and he slung it from the saddle bow, then offered her a hand to pull herself up behind him.

She hesitated for a second, looking up at him as though she wished to avoid his touch.

He sat still, pretending he didn't notice her hesitation. Not out of kindness, but shyness. He didn't know what to do or say, what word or gesture would ease her discomfort.

She took his hand firmly and swung herself up behind him.

She rode with legs dangling at the big horse's flanks, not astride as she had the day before, one arm wrapped around his body, her shoulder against his back.

"You're of good birth," he said.

She laughed, the brittle, ugly laughter of the night before. "That may be," she said, "but I am what . . ." She hesitated. "What I've become and dead to my kin; it's better so."

"How long did they have you?"

"How long is any time in hell?" she answered.

He didn't question her any further. They rode in silence. He cut through the forest, picking his way among the many paths and trails.

It was near noon when she smelled the spring. "I smell water," she said.

He started at the sound of her voice. "Smell water?" he asked. "How can you smell water?"

"It's among the things I can do," she said. "I forget others can't." She pointed to a cluster of beeches among the long aisles of leafless trees. "There," she said.

He turned the horse in the direction she'd pointed. The spring lay amid the beech trees crowned yet with the golden leaves of autumn; they formed a ring around a smaller grove of ancient oaks within. The water bubbled out from the foot of a giant oak and flowed over a boulder forming a pool at its base.

The chill of autumn hadn't yet touched the velvety grass that ringed the pool and small white flowers still bloomed, stars amid its emerald lushness. Looking up at the gnarled yet still green branches of the oaks laced above and the rough, mossy boles of the trees that surrounded them, he wondered if this place ever knew winter at all, or spring for that matter. It seemed timeless, nestled in the breast of its enormous guardians.

She slid down from the back of the horse, walked over to the pool, and drank, cupping her fingers under the flow.

He dismounted and led the horse to drink. "Any more food?" he asked.

"Some bread and a little wine in the skin," she said.

"Take it for yourself."

She did, soaking the hard loaf in the wine and eating it with her fingers. When she was finished, she washed her hands in the flow of water, then pointed suddenly at the boulder. "This is a holy place."

His eyes followed the movement of her finger and he saw the face. Dappled with broken sunlight, old as time, and crusted with lichen, it looked back at him. The artist had used the natural features of the stone to suggest the nose and mouth, but the eyes were clearly delineated, open and looking into his own, wide and sure. Just a few lines suggested hair and a beard.

She opened the wineskin, pouring the last mouthful into the swirling water at the base of the rock. "It does no harm to have friends," she said.

He signed himself with the cross and stepped back. "I can't think I'm a welcome guest here," he said.

"Who are you?" she asked.

"A bishop. Owen, Bishop of Chantalon. It's my see."

She began laughing. This time her laughter was clear and fresh as the water flowing at her feet. "I'm in the arms of the church."

He didn't answer this, but walked to the stream, knelt, and drank almost defiantly, then looked up at the face on the rock only inches from his own. The eyes, those large, calm eyes stared back tranquilly as though in welcome, and he imagined he could see in the quirk of the rude mouth something like a smile.

She was standing beside him, her leg near his arm. The ragged shift was torn and his eyes followed the arching curve of the calf up past the knee and to the thigh. Her skin was lightly browned by the sun, and covered with just the faintest golden down. In a flash his awareness of her womanhood was as intense as pain.

She saw the movement of his eyes and the expression on his face. She stepped away from him, looking amused.

He stood and backed away from her. "Don't laugh," he said, "what I feel here at this moment is no laughing matter."

The smile faded from her lips and her gaze fell from what she saw in his to the grass at her feet. "Am I that much of a temptation?" she asked.

"Yes, you and this pagan place. We might be the only two people left in the world and you're very beautiful."

She stretched out her arms and looked at her hands, then down at her body. "Still," she said.

"Still," he echoed, "fair as a morning in May."

The sun went behind a cloud and the grove darkened, becoming in a moment a place of threatening green shadow, the tree trunks looming black around them.

"You'd take their leavings?" she said, contempt in her voice.

"Don't scorn me," he answered quietly, "or you'll be on your back in the grass and I'll show you how happy I'd be to take their leavings, as you put it."

She went to one knee beside the stream and dabbled her hand in the water. "No," she said, "not here, not now."

The sun came out again as the cloud passed, and sparkled in a prismatic aureole on her black hair. She turned to face him and the light caught the transparent blueness of her eyes. It was as though he looked into the reaches of the sky.

"No, the ravisher gets nothing," she said.

He felt the tension in his body flow out, seemingly into the cool earth at his feet, anger and desire both ebbed away. "No, that is true, the ravisher gets nothing, nothing worth having. Come, let's ride, we have a long way to go before nightfall."

When they were away from the grove and among the leafless trees of the autumn forest, he shook his head as if to clear some darkness from his mind. "That place, those trees," he murmured.

"Sometimes," she said gently, tightening her arm around his waist as if to comfort him, "sometimes it happens that the lord of such a grove will play a trick on an unsuspecting mortal who intrudes upon his solitude too rudely. You made no offering. You should have."

He looked back uneasily at the tall-crowned beech trees. "I am of another party," he said.

"Still," she answered, cautioning him, "it shows respect. You were a guest. Do you insult your host?"

"So he shamed me?"

"Only a little," she said. "You didn't do anything."

"Only because you had the good sense to prevent me."

"The shame is not yours alone," she said.

Startled by her reply, he turned his head, trying to see her face. It was in profile, looking away from him, eyes downcast, her cheeks slightly flushed.

"Why, what did you do?"

"I tested you. I wanted to know if you despised me."

"Despised you? I . . ." He tried to answer but realized he didn't know how to put his feelings into words. What did he feel for her? Admiration for her courage and overwhelming desire to possess her physically? These were not thoughts he could readily express to a woman. She was silent, waiting for his reply.

"No," he said at last, "I don't despise you. There are things in the world, forces before which we are all powerless. Things, they happen in ways that . . ." He floundered. "Sometimes we pay the price of being what we are, where we are, and you're very beautiful. Yesterday, but for your scream, I would be feeding the crows."

"Now Ragnar is," she said, her voice filled with hate. "It did my heart good to see that. Why did you turn and save me?"

"I can't say why. Why did you scream and save me? These things happen so quickly in a fight it's difficult to judge them, in cold blood, afterward."

"It's true, I only knew we were both against them, allies unaware. We hate them."

They were deep into the forest now and the path had narrowed to an almost invisible track hemmed in by tall trees. Even though it was autumn and many were leafless, they grew here so densely that a thick tracery of branches blotted out the sky and kept the sun from reaching the shadowy trail they followed.

"Yes, I suppose I do hate them," he said. "Or it may be that hate is too small a word for what I feel. Three times they've come. Each time when the crops were green and standing in the fields. Three times sailing upriver to plunder and destroy. Each time more cities and people fall into their hands. Desolation is everywhere. There is nothing along this river but the smoke of burning and the stench of death. The river is their highway and all who live here pay tribute to them or . . . they die.

"All the rivers of Francia belong to them—the Seine, the

Marne, the Oise. They sail everywhere a navigable stream flows. I have not heard of a one they don't rule. Not a one along whose banks they don't spread fear and destruction.

"From the north they come, more and more every year. And, like the north wind and the frost, they wither and blacken all they touch. Three times the lord of Chantalon, Count Anton, has bribed them not to attack. But there can't be a fourth. We have nothing left."

"That's the way of it," she said bitterly. "They return and keep on returning as long as their price is met."

He nodded, guiding the horse onto easier ground. The trail widened—they were approaching a clearing.

"We are picked clean now," he said, "and there is no more. We must fight, fight or die. Perhaps, fight *and* die."

"Better that way than live as I lived. It's why I screamed," she said.

It grew brighter, the trees were smaller, second growth. Thick brush flourished in the sunny spaces between them. But the feeling of safety that had followed him from the grove into the deep forest diminished. The going was easier, but he kept the pace of the horse slow, his eyes scanning the underbrush around the trail anxiously.

"Ride astride," he ordered.

She obeyed without question.

"Both arms around me." He rapped out the command.

Again she obeyed, but this time asked in a low voice, "Why, what's wrong?"

They were almost in the open. He pulled the horse to a stop.

"What is this place?" she asked.

"It used to be the monastery of the Holy Cross. Now all that remains is this ruin."

He peered into the clearing. The remnants of the monastery crowned a low hummock in the center, surrounded by fields that still bore the mark of the plow. A scattering of stone blocks laced with blackened timbers, already thicketed with weeds, marked the place where the church once stood. It was silent, with no movement near the ruins. Even the forest around him was quiet in the windless doldrums of the warm afternoon. Yet something was wrong. What?

A thin curl of wood smoke rose from the broken rafters of the church, black against the sky.

The bay snorted and pawed the ground.

He had time to shout, "Hold on!"

His sword came out of the scabbard with a whistling hiss. One of them was ducking under the horse's belly, knife out, ready to gut him. Owen jerked the bay to one side with a hard pull on the reins and slashed, catching the knife owner across the spine.

He screamed and leaped away, spraying blood from a laid-open shoulder.

A weight pressed on Owen's left arm. His cheek burned, gashed by the knife of another standing on his left stirrup, reaching for his throat. The horse spun wildly as he lost control, trying to hack at his second attacker. He was blinded as fingers clawed at his eyes. Suddenly the weight was gone. He had only a glimpse of a ragged body with the face of a demon going down, the girl's dagger in his throat.

The bay bucked, nearly unseating its riders. The men on the ground scattered in terror of the flying hooves.

Owen turned the bay back toward the deep woods, spurring savagely.

One of them was in front of him, an arrow notched in his bow. Owen pulled the bay's head over and rode the man down. Then they were away, the powerful horse gaining speed with every bound.

He felt the girl's arms clinging desperately to his hauberk and sword belt. She was thrown against his back with every bound, but he kept the bay at a hard gallop until he reached a place where the high forest canopy shut out the light and the ground was clear of low growth and shrubbery or anything that might conceal another ambush.

He slowed the horse to a trot, following another winding trail as quickly as he could for at least a mile, then pulled it to a stop. "I should have known better," he said, "but I thought it would shorten our journey."

"Better than what?" she answered. "Your cheek's bleeding. It's dripping on my hand."

"Better than to try to reach the road that way. They hang about the ruins like ghosts preying on the living."

He dismounted and helped her down. They both examined

the big bay for injuries. Finding none, they looked at each other. The fingers of her right hand were torn, but not badly.

"I grabbed a fistful of that mail shirt when I went for his throat. I got him with my left hand. I'm not that good with a knife. I was lucky, but I lost the knife."

"Lost it to good purpose," he said. "I think you killed him."

She was pale and shaking. "I'm no fighter," she said. "He was going to cut your throat."

He was tense, his eyes still darting about, scanning the terrain around them. It was reassuring. Everywhere the trees stretched away like pillars of some giant hall until they were shadowed by distance. The ground was carpeted with brown leaves that rustled underfoot. Here and there a shaft of sunlight cut through the branches arching above, a ray of golden light in the shadows around them.

She sat him on the trunk of a fallen tree in one such finger of brilliance and examined his wound. A neat slice, like a half moon, on one cheekbone.

"Not bad," she said judiciously, "but it should be stitched. It will leave a scar."

He smiled, his white teeth gleaming. "Then I'll be a little uglier than I was. A few scars become a man; others know he isn't all talk."

She stepped back and studied him dispassionately. He called himself ugly, but he wasn't. Brown hair with a slight curl, soft and very fine, cropped short around his head. A thin face, high cheekbones, large dark eyes. The eyes were too intense, tortured almost. He was tall, but the body was wiry rather than powerful. Nature had gifted him with a cat's grace and lethal swiftness, rather than the raw power of a bull.

She found some cobwebs and used them to stanch the bleeding, sticking the edges of the wound together. "Not so ugly," she said.

"Undistinguished then," he said. "My mother used to call me her little brown mouse. I should have been more talkative. My father wouldn't have destined me for the church."

"That was your father's choice?" she asked.

"I was a bishop before I could shave," he answered, "and counted myself lucky. I was Gestric's fifth son and had little to hope for."

"It wasn't a happy choice?" she asked.

"No, not for me." He didn't explain further.

She sat down beside him on the log. "I'm still shaking with fear. Who were they? What did they want?"

He laughed shortly. "I carry a fortune on my back, and then there's you."

It was true. The heavy shirt of densely woven mail was a rich prize. The links were tightly set, not loose as in some cheaper ring mail, each small, thick circle hammered flat and double riveted, painted black against rust. His sword belt and baldric were plain, undecorated, but of the heaviest leather, ox hide, a triple thickness sewn together. The sword itself, the weapon of a nobleman. The cluster of rubies set in the pommel were but a little adornment for the blade that constituted the real riches. It was one of those made of tempered rods of steel woven together while white hot, then shaped with files and sharpened to a razor's edge, burnished until it shone. Such weapons and accouterments were coveted everywhere.

"Yes," she nodded, "then there's the horse and me."

"As to who they are," he said, "they are the outlawed, the hungry, those driven to despair and violence by the times we live in."

"You'd help them if you could?" she asked, surprised at the compassion in his eyes and voice. "I'm not so kind; they tried to kill you. Are you sorry I put the knife through his gullet?"

In answer, he took her face between his hands and kissed her. The powerful fingers on her cheeks were hard and callused by the handling of horses, tack, and weapons. But the kiss was gentle as the brush of a bird's wing, a restrained exploration of possibilities.

She didn't struggle or resist, but obeyed his will as she had when he ordered her to ride astride. He controlled himself. She yielded to the power, the strong grip he had on his own passion, with trust. His hands fell from her face and traced the outlines of her body under the shift. She closed her eyes and rested her head on his shoulder.

He explored with his touch her animal self. She had seen him move his hands over the big horse's legs, searching for injuries with the same cool intensity. He wished to know her in all senses. She quieted under his hands, relaxed.

He drew away. "No, how could I be sorry. Most of them are beyond help. I do what I must to go on living." He took her hand, led her back to the horse, and helped her mount behind him. He started the bay at a fast walk, looking back over the trail toward the abbey.

"In the Viking camp you paid the price of being a woman. In that place," he said, voice tinged with bitterness, "I paid the price of being a man."

She rode astride, one hand holding the thick sword belt, the other resting against his iron shirt, her cheek on his forearm.

"Some of the captured women killed themselves," she said. "I didn't. Others yielded and learned to love their captors. I wouldn't do either one. I knew I would escape. Death is forever; to learn to love the hand that crushes you is a shame not to be borne. Pain and slavery will pass. I believed this and it kept me alive."

"We're alike in that, I think," he said. "When I was fifteen my father sent me to that place, the ruins you just saw, so that I might learn the duties of a churchman. And for five long years those walls imprisoned me. It was a life whose every waking moment I hated. Only in dreams and thought could I seek freedom, and it was everything to me."

"You're free now," she said. "What am I?"

"I'm not completely free. I'm still Bishop of Chantalon. But I'm free enough to be happy. Aren't you happy now, here with me?"

"Yes," she answered slowly and cautiously, "but I might be unhappy if you constrained me."

He gave a snort of laughter. "Constrain you? I've seen you use that knife twice and you survived how many months in that camp unbroken? I'll sing a requiem for the man that crosses, much less constrains you."

She began laughing. "I am unbroken, am I not? That's true, sullied by sin and dishonor, but unbroken."

"Are you testing me again?" he asked. "If so, don't bother, I have a short way with sin and dishonor both. They're conundrums for the saints and I'm not a saint."

"Your flock must find you an odd prelate," she said.

"I can't say," he answered. "A man ordained at nineteen and anointed a bishop at twenty needs to show restraint. Think I want my priests and people laughing at me behind their hands? I preach as little of sin as I can, being burdened with my own. And my people have enough problems without talk of hell and damnation. I can't think God so cruel as to judge them harshly and I refuse to judge others at all, you included."

"Oh," she said softly, "did you suffer so much?"

He was surprised at her perception but answered it.

"Yes, I did. I can't think it achieved the end to which it was inflicted. But I did learn a certain humility and compassion for the pain of others. You were not broken, they didn't have you long enough. I wish I could say the same for myself."

"Then you were conquered by it?" she asked.

"I don't know," he mused. "I may have been. It depends on what I do now about the city, the count, and you."

Chapter

4

*T*HEY reached the stronghold at dusk. It was called Reynald's Hall. A scattering of tiny villages grouped around a fortified position placed in the center of a shallow, marshy lake. The outer and inner circuit walls were of wooden stakes on an island of rammed earth and stone in the center. A narrow earthen causeway led out over the water and to the island through big wooden gates in the palisade.

The hall itself, the inner keep, was of stone, two stories, squat and windowless but for archers' slits placed for the convenience of the defenders.

When he passed through the gate, Owen dismounted and led the horse to the stable. A few voices called him by name. She sat, still on the horse, eyes lowered, very shy, conscious now of her tattered dress among so many people and their curious stares.

Owen helped her down and stabled the bay in the outer circuit with the horses of Reynald's men at arms, making sure, even before he greeted his host, that the animal was watered and fed.

The big horse stood, head in the manger, munching contentedly, while Owen curried him. She ran her hand along the sleek flank and patted one giant shoulder.

"A faithful friend," she said. "Has he a name?"

"No, I bought him a few months ago from a man who told me he was gentle and battle trained."

"Yet you have not named him," she said.

"Horses die in combat more often than men do," he answered. "It's easier to forget a thing without a name. I've learned to guard my affections."

"I know," she said softly, "you've never asked mine."

* * *

Reynald came into the stable. He was a short man, hard, and built like the stump of an oak. He was as roughly dressed as the rest of the men in the yard, as Owen himself was under his expensive armor. His feet, like Owen's, were fitted with heavy hobnailed boots laced high to the calf.

The sun was gone, its last glow leaving the horizon. The stable was dark. Reynald carried an earthenware lamp with a wick set in fat. The yellow light flickered on the satiny flank of the horse, and the weary pair at its side.

"Ah, Owen, or should I call you My Lord Bishop? Did you reach your father's home? What news?"

"No, I didn't, and all the news is bad," Owen answered bleakly.

The older man frowned, the look on his face turning to one of calculation. "Not here then, in the hall when we're alone. Who is with you?" he asked, raising the lamp.

She stood at the bay's withers, chin lifted proudly, very conscious of her beggarly appearance. Owen met her eyes and saw the dismay in them. How in the hell could he explain her to Reynald?

It turned out not to be necessary; the older man drew his own conclusions very quickly. "Oh," he said, "you've found a friend. That was due to happen soon. May I ask the lady's name?"

"Elin," she said, looking down at her muddy feet and ragged dress. "We've had a hard journey."

Owen took Elin's arm and conducted her to the hall where Elspeth, Reynald's wife, greeted them both. She kissed Owen on the cheek, but her aristocratic brows lifted and her eyes widened when he introduced his companion. She was used to wanderers and strays, but this one was more battered than most. Yet Owen treated her like a lady and obviously expected her to be accepted as such.

Elspeth was too kind and hospitable to disappoint him. She led her away to be bathed, dressed, and fed. In due time. she received reports from her maids about the marks on Elin's body, and was duly horrified; then was further informed that Elin was mannerly and well spoken. Her heart was filled with pity for a gently bred girl reduced to such a condition, so she set herself to remedy it by giving Elin such clothing and small womanly comforts as she could spare.

Reynald led Owen to his own room on the second floor beyond the gallery of the great hall. Besides the square box of a bed, it contained a low table and a few chairs—big comfortable armchairs painted red and ornamented like the bed with gilded spirals and curlicues, cushioned with goose-down pillows, red, like the chairs, and embroidered with gold. Owen collapsed into one of them, sinking into the comfort of the padding.

Reynald lifted a bronze lamp from the table. It was cast in the shape of a dragon with a dozen heads; each head held a wick. He lighted only six of the wicks, but the high tongues of flame filled the room with light. Then he poured Owen a cup of wine from a gold-embossed flagon.

The cups were silver, but matched the design of the jug, the leaves and tendrils of a fruiting grapevine. Each cluster of grapes picked out with cabochon amethysts.

Owen ran his finger over the violet stones absently and then said, "Wealth, it draws them as carrion does flies. I saw their camp, they'll stay the winter."

"You're sure," Reynald said, taking a seat opposite Owen.

"The camp is fortified on an island, as is their custom. And also, after their northern custom, has stout longhouses and a hall. They have not come raiding this time, but to stay." He drank deeply from the wine cup and Reynald re-filled it. "Wherever I rode, I saw death. Nearly met my own in creeping up so close to that cursed stronghold of theirs. And make no mistake, it is a stronghold with a stout wooden wall strong enough to repel any attack even our combined forces could make. They hold not only the island but the countryside around it. All along the river nothing but abandoned villages, burned-out farms, the owners either mur-dered or in flight. The leaves are falling. It will be a terrible winter."

Owen drank again and set the cup on the table, covering it with his fingers, and shaking his head when Reynald tried to refill it. "No, I haven't had a full meal in days. It's been a week since I dared lie down unarmed."

In truth, the wine was making him dizzy and the flames spurting from the dragon mouths of the lamp were blurring before his gaze, blurring not only from exhaustion, but with the tears starting in his eyes. He let them flow down his cheeks, small rivulets in the wood smoke and grime that covered his face. Reynald was an old friend and Owen trusted him with his grief.

Reynald listened, chin on his fist, dark eyes fathomless in the lamplight, as Owen continued.

"A few towns, like Chantalon, bought them off and paid a bitter price. Those that managed to get in some kind of harvest will probably survive. The ones that didn't—famine and disease . . . and death, death everywhere."

"Your father?" Reynald asked.

Owen closed his eyes. "I can only hope. I stripped myself, sent him all my people except those too old and weak to travel. But I never reached his lands. I don't know. He's a strong man and a clever one. If anyone can ride out this storm, he can. But he's too far away to be of any help to us.

"When travel became too difficult, I turned back. I have responsibilities here to my own people. The rest pushed on. I hope they reached his land safely. But that's all I have, the hope, no certain knowledge."

"Four kings since Charlemagne or is it five? Strange," Reynald said, passing his hand over his brow, "I can't remember."

"Not so strange," Owen answered. "They are lost among a host of others who wanted to be king, and none of them were able to keep the peace in this realm. They multiply like locusts, and like the cursed insects, each tried to eat up the substance of the other."

"Ah, yes," Reynald said. "First the pious Louis who spent his life embroiled in quarrels with his brother, Lothar, while the Northmen were at his gates. His son, Charlemagne's bald-pated grandson, was a little better, or so they say. He noticed the Viking bastards were with us, and even managed to fight them a time or two. But his son was a weakling and his grandson, the fat Charles, a coward.

"Do you know," Reynald continued, tapping Owen on the knee, "I am old enough to remember when the fat Charles bought off the Vikings in Paris. I well recall my father scratching to pay the sums his minions demanded. They say all the fat king ever worried about was being crowned emperor . . . like Charlemagne. He got his crown and has gone to impress the devils in hell with it, leaving only chaos behind him—chaos and a weak-minded son."

Reynald leaned back in his chair and steepled his fingers, looking down at them thoughtfully. "We're alone," he said flatly. "They say there are two kings, Odo, the Count of Paris, and Charles."

"Two kings," Owen said, "and both worse than no king at all. Odo, once the strong defender of Paris, buys off the Vikings now, while Charles, descendant of Charlemagne and son of Charles the Fat, cowers at Reims. Men call him not Charles the Great, but Charles the Simple, Charles the Fool. Everywhere the Vikings take and take. Our wealth, our lands, our"—his face became a brief mask of fury—"even our women." Owen smiled a bitter, ironic smile and shrugged. "But what's that to us? They'll spend what strength they have quarreling with each other so that the winner may lord over a wasteland. We'll probably be long dead when the issue is decided."

Reynald cupped his chin with his fingers and scratched the gray stubble on his cheeks, deep in thought. From below, a babble of voices and good cooking smells signaled the approach of the evening meal. The news of Owen's arrival would have spread like a grass fire through the little community. Few people traveled these days.

Occasional large, armed parties braved the hazards of the road. And the odd individual, bolder and perhaps more foolish than most, relying on stealth, traveling by night or along deserted paths and byways, arrived at the farmstead.

Each traveler brought tales that started a spate of rumors, making Reynald's life difficult. He'd found the best way to control the spread of these stories was to strangle them at the source, seating the stranger at his own table and steering the talk in directions least frightening to his people. But given the prestige Owen enjoyed, he realized they would hang on the boy's slightest word. The best course in this case might be to hurry him to bed, then on to the city in the morning, giving him as little opportunity to talk as possible.

This shouldn't be difficult, Reynald thought. The young man looked as travel weary and exhausted as anyone he'd ever seen. Owen was sitting, head back, eyes closed, the traces of tears still on his cheeks, body limp against the cushions of the chair.

Reynald reached over and slapped his knee. Owen's body jerked. He awakened abruptly and stared around wildly. Between the wine and the warmth of the room, he'd already fallen asleep.

Reynald, seeing he'd have no problem in dealing with him, gave a quick laugh. "I'm a hard old man to keep a tired young one from a meal and a bed. But before you sleep, give me your opinion, I value it."

Owen pulled himself upright, blinking away the sleep from his eyes. "I'm sorry, my thoughts, you wouldn't like them."

"Life is not governed by what we like and don't like. Good or bad, your opinion," Reynald said.

"Very well," Owen replied sadly, "since you ask, I can be no less than honest. This place will fall. Defend it if you must, but get your women out to Chantalon. The Northmen are gorged now with the rich pickings of the Champagne country, but winter has only begun. All that protects you now is the forest. It is a hard march and a dangerous one through the wood, but in time they will make that march, and on to Chantalon.

"The city may stand. I and the people will defend it, whatever the count does. But that horde will roll over this place like the tide over a sand castle. You are alone; so am I. Count Anton is too old. . . ."

"Too drunken and cowardly," Reynald supplied the rest of the sentence.

Owen lowered his eyelids. "He is a kinsman of yours, and so I did not wish to say it, yet it is true, and no less true for being unspoken. Anton will do nothing to stop them, and whatever I have to give, must be given at Chantalon."

Reynald stared morosely at the dragon lamp on the table, then idly lit the wicks on the rest of the fanged mouths as though hoping the increased light would drive out the darkness Owen's words brought to his soul.

"They are like wolves," he whispered, half to himself, half to Owen. "First they attack the weakest of the herd and fear the strong ones. Some, at least, will break their teeth on me."

"That is as it is then," Owen said with a sigh of resignation.

"Yes, I will hold to what is my own," Reynald said.

"And the women?" Owen asked.

"I'll send them to the safety of your hearth if I can, and if there's a threat, I'll know when. Speaking of women, does the lady you brought here accompany you to the city? The Lady Elin, I believe she said her name was."

Reynald's eyes were bright with curiosity.

Owen rose from the chair. "If she wishes. Once, and then again she saved my life. Of her I will not speak. I'm in her debt. What she tells you of herself is all you will hear."

It was a stiff, formal speech. Reynald asked no more questions. He knew his man: prying any further would get him nothing and only make Owen angry. He found Owen a room alone under the rafters and paid his people extra to heat a bath for him. For the first time in weeks, the young man slept unarmed and in comfort.

Chapter

5

*M*ORNING was gray at the window when he awakened. Outside he could hear the steady tapping of the autumn rain. The small room was in deep shadow, but he saw her sitting on a clothes chest in the corner, staring through the narrow embrasure at the sky.

The room was chilly, but Owen, wearing one of Reynald's bed gowns, was warm. He sat up.

"Have a good sleep?" she asked.

"The best in weeks," he answered.

"May I go with you to the city?"

"Yes."

She sighed with relief. "Good, I was afraid you wouldn't take me."

"Why?" he asked.

"A wife or a woman," she said.

"I have neither wife nor woman, and I owe you that much."

"So cold and owing?" she asked.

"It's a cold morning," he said sourly, "you're in my bedroom. I wish you were not."

"Afraid of talk?" she asked.

"No, there'll be talk no matter what we do."

She stood up and walked toward the bed. She was dressed in a white linen undergown with a blue overdress. The black hair was pinned up and netted.

Even in the dim morning light he could see how beautiful she was. She had not attained her full growth and was still a little bit coltish, but she would be a big woman, a real armful. She moved with dignity and presence. A lady every inch.

"What then?" she asked impishly.

He looked up into her eyes.

"Oh," she said, turning gracefully and walking back toward the window, "you're a man of honor."

"I struggle in that direction, yes. You're making it difficult."

"I don't mean now. I'm no one and nothing to these people but they showed me every courtesy and kindness. You must have spoken well of me."

"They're kind people and good," Owen said.

"Yes, but without your words, it would have been the kindness of the kitchen and the hospitality of the stable. But that's not what I came to say." She reached the window and stood in the narrow shaft of growing light. "This place will fall. Did you tell him that?"

"Yes, if it's any of your business and it's not, I did. This"—Owen pointed down—"is his. He wants to keep it. He's too old to begin again and too brave to run away."

"I was captured in a place like this," she said, then was silent as if lost in some black memory. "My kinfolk, my . . ."

"No!" he shouted suddenly, filled with fury. "Don't tell me what happened to your people, I can guess. Haven't I seen the results of their brutality often enough?"

"I want revenge," she said.

He stood up beside the bed and laughed. The boards of the floor were cold under his bare feet. "Revenge? Great God, woman, that's like wanting revenge for a storm or the river in flood."

"Why?" she asked fiercely. "You're going to fight them. I could be a part of that fight. I want to be part of it."

A dizzying wave of rage swept over him. He wanted to strike her, strike out at something. Had she not been across the room from him, he might have. But as it was, all he could do was shout and he did that.

"My heart is sick in me. Winter is coming. Twenty-three springs have I seen and that's all I ever will see. What I'd give to believe I'd live to watch the trees leaf out, the earth turn green again. You come to me, to my room, all beauty and grace tempting me, inviting me, as plainly as a woman can, to take you to my bed. First, my lady, you had best hear what I have to offer you." He leaned forward and stretched out his arms, his face a mask of fury and despair. "Oh, yes, come, my sweet, come die with me."

His arms dropped to his sides, his anger faded, leaving bitterness and disgust in its wake. "Now go away. Reynald's servants will be up soon. I wouldn't have them find us here alone together."

She was still standing by the window, hands folded, looking calm and composed. "How fond and skilled a lover you are," she said. "Your offer sounds so irresistible."

"If you do join me," he said, walking to a basin and filling it with water from the ewer hanging on the wall, "you'll never be in a position to claim that you were won by honeyed words and cunning lies."

"Chantalon is a strong city," she said.

Owen splashed water on his face and dried it on a linen towel. When he spoke, his voice was quiet and matter-of-fact. "Chantalon is a marcher fortress with a wooden wall, whose lord is an old, drunken, lecherous coward. My bishopric was bought and paid for by the men my father sent to help garrison it. Now those men are gone. Because I, fool that I am, sent that same force to my father's aid when these raids began. They were the city's only hope. Now there's nothing between the city and the Northmen but the courage of its citizens. They have that, I grant it, but few weapons and no skill."

"I can give you other allies," she said. "My mother was a woman of the old people. I'll go to the woods . . ."

He rounded on her. "Folly, what folly is this? By God, I knew there had to be a catch somewhere. You're a witch. Get out of my room and take your stupidities and superstitions with you. I don't know whether to laugh or just have you whipped around the city at the tail of a cart."

She went white. "That is," she hissed, "the basest of ingratitude," and started toward the door.

She spoke the truth and he knew it. "Wait."

She turned and stood still, facing him.

"Forgive me. It's strange," he said, "you're the first to offer me any help at all and I requite you with threats and vile words. But I can't believe in your powers. Besides"—he smiled and held out his hand to her—"it is as I said once before, I am of another party."

She took the hand tentatively and gazed at him solemnly. "You didn't hear me out. I make no curses, cast no spell. That isn't the sort of help I offered."

She was standing so close to him now he could smell the scent of the perfumes and unguents she'd used the night before in her bath. The large, clear eyes were beautiful, even washed to pale gray by the shadows of the room. He wanted to slip his arm around the soft linen fabric of the dress and draw her close, that she might warm away the cold dread, the fear that seemed to have settled in his bones. She reached up and touched a tendril of soft hair that curled at his ear.

"So soft," she said.

He smiled ruefully. "I know, it's one reason I go clean shaven, I can't grow a full beard."

Her fingers fell a little lower and brushed his cheek. His arm did go around her waist then. She stiffened slightly, then relaxed. "You want my help and you want me." She spoke the words slowly, spacing them, wonderingly. "Whether you believe in my 'powers' as you put it, or not, why not take that help? Does your God command that you be led like a beast to the slaughter? I won't believe this. How would your death help your people? What of them? If this count is as much a coward as you claim, then you are all they have."

His arm tightened and he drew her closer.

Someone rapped on the door. They flew apart. The door opened. It was one of Reynald's serving men. He held a tray with bread, wine, and cheese for Owen's breakfast, and a basin of warm shaving water, and some towels hung over his arm. He studied them impassively, but Owen saw the gleam in the man's eye as he filed away this particular tidbit of gossip. Every wagging tongue in the district would have him and Elin coupled before nightfall.

"Shall I return later?" the servant asked.

"No," Owen said coldly.

Elin lowered her eyes, her cheeks flushed. "I was just leaving," she said, as she swept through the door.

Owen breakfasted on the contents of the tray, thinking of Elin and her strange offer. She was an unusual woman. He'd seen enough of her on the journey to know that. Also, a big also, he wanted her.

He walked to the mirror, lathered his face, and began to shave, remembering with a sense of embarrassment and chagrin that he had shown her the full depths of his fear and despair. Yet she hadn't turned from him.

Then on the other hand, he was a bishop. The life of a bishop should be an example to his flock. So Bertrand told him ... with a whip in his hand. "From those to whom much has been given, much will be required," so said Lord Abbot Bertrand. Lord Abbot Bertrand, sole ruler of the monastery of the Holy Cross. Lord Abbot Bertrand, into whose hands had been given the task of training the future bishop of Chantalon.

Bertrand!

Owen struck the edge of the basin with the back of the razor so hard he chipped it. Bertrand! God, how he hated the man. Hated and it was years since he'd been under his hand.

He should never have stopped at the monastery to look at the ruins and try the road. The place still brought him ill luck.

He had thought it all behind him. He no longer woke in the night and, finding himself in darkness, began to scream. He had overcome that last remaining curse a year ago, not long after news of its destruction by the Vikings reached his ears. He'd imposed a fast of two days on himself as a penance, because his first reaction when told of the event was joy.

His hand shook so badly he was forced to lay the razor on the table beside the basin.

Owen had no memory of leaving the place. His first awareness of freedom was when he'd been shocked awake by his mother's voice. She had been screaming, screaming at his father. The shock was that she screamed at all. He had never in all his life heard her or anyone else, for that matter, speak in such a way to Gestric. Normally they treated each other with punctilious courtesy. If they quarreled, it was behind locked doors, and then rarely raised their voices.

"My son, I sent him my best son, a boy who never needed more than a gentle word of correction and look what he returns to me."

His father's exculpatory murmur in reply was even more astonishing. "Clotild, my sweet . . . I don't know what I can do."

"Do?" she answered in a voice hoarse with rage. "Do? There is nothing you will do. The damage is done. He may die. Months of imprisonment in a cell without light or warmth, not even the sight of another human face or the sound of another human voice to comfort him. . . ."

"Clotild, please . . . he is my son, too."

"Your son? And did you carry him in your belly for nine months, then suffer the torments of hell to bring him into the light, nurse him at your breast? But for the love that little-regarded boy bore him, his courage in defying Bertrand, my son might be dead. As it is, his bones show through his skin, his eyes stare at me without recognition. Me, his mother, the first face he ever knew!"

"Bertrand," his father whispered venomously.

"Bertrand!" his mother's voice was the scream of a bird of prey. "I'll drag Bertrand to hell with my two hands, and give him to the devil alone."

She was not a demonstrative woman. He'd never known till then how much she loved him.

Gestric's voice pleaded in reply. "Clotild, what would you have me do?"

Then, in a voice stiff with hatred, she dictated her terms to Gestric, who must have promptly dictated them to the count, and Bertrand.

His mother brought him home and guarded him like a lioness while he healed and regained his strength. After that he was ordained and became bishop of Chantalon. He avoided Bertrand and never so much as rode near the monastery again.

Bertrand! Bertrand spoke for the Church and the Church spoke for God. Was God like Bertrand?

No!

He threw the razor into the water, wiped the lather from his face, and stared into his own eyes in the tiny mirror. What was God? Was there a God at all?

For a man of God to take a woman, one of God's anointed to take a woman, was an evil thing. Women were vessels of corruption. So says Bertrand, he thought, and how much of anything Bertrand taught you do you now believe?

He finished dressing, belted on his sword. All that could be seen through the window was the sky. And all that could be seen of that sky were gray clouds heavy with the winter rain. Yet somewhere there must have been a rift in those chalcedony shapes because the sun shone briefly, the dust motes in the air dancing in its light.

Owen stood quietly looking at the rectangle of gold on the floor. He spoke into the silence, the emptiness, and the sunlight. Answering his own question, he said, "Nothing, nothing at all."

Chapter

6

SHE was waiting in the yard in front of the hall. Reynald gave him an escort to the city, and found a mount for the girl. A gray mare almost as coltish as she was and spirited.

The escort consisted of three men nearly as rough and dangerous looking as the thieves who'd attacked him. Their weapons looked as though they'd seen some use as agricultural implements before a visit to the blacksmith's.

Elin rode astride, trusting to the length of skirt and heavy linen stockings to preserve her modesty. She seemed to enjoy being mounted on her own horse, and impatient with the ploddings of the escort. She colored and broke into a laugh when the gray-bearded leader, with a sly smile on his lips, urged his horse to a gallop and the rest followed suit to avoid being splashed with mud. She paced Owen, her face wind-flushed, smiling brilliantly.

The road was no more than a muddy track between the dripping trees, deeply cut by cart wheels. Above, the clouds were beginning to thin, showing long scarves of blue. The sunlight came and went. The wind in their faces was crisp and dry, the first chill of winter in it.

She rode beside him unspeaking. The alliance she'd offered was in good faith; he had no right to be ungrateful.

"It will be colder tonight," he said.

They had slowed to a trot. She pulled her horse to a walk and he fell in beside her. She frowned and looked down at the splashes of mud on her stockings.

"Please don't think I am always so ill-tempered a man," he said, making a fumbling attempt at an apology.

"Flog me around the city at the tail of a cart," she said reproachfully.

"I wouldn't do that," he mumbled.

"All beauty and grace," she said, her eyebrows lifting.

"The beauty and grace were probably what brought flogging to mind," he said. "Some men rut like stags, others stand by and watch enviously."

They were riding knee to knee, his foot almost touching hers. His large dark eyes were compelling, the torment in them poignant. "You have no right," he whispered, "to be so beautiful and there for the taking. And I . . . I have no right to take you."

"You're tinder and catch fire at a spark," she said. "The fire in me is a cold one that burns at the marrow of my bones."

She looked away sadly at the wet black tree trunks of the woods, at the gray sky. "You expect—" she said hesitantly.

"I expect," he broke in.

Her hands were resting on the saddle pommel, the reins lightly held. He lifted one slowly and kissed the palm gently.

"I expect nothing," he said. "Why don't you try me, see what I can earn?"

He released the hand. She drew it away, a look of astonishment on her face. "You are," she said, "surprising."

"A pity. I'd hoped to be endearing," he said.

"That, too," she answered.

His eyes fell from her face to her body in one sweeping glance that made Elin feel as though he'd stripped away dress and shift and taken her naked body in his arms.

She continued staring at his face, powerless to look away. Then that look faded from his eyes and was replaced by one of objective intenseness. "Are you a Christian?" he asked abruptly.

"One surprise after another," she said, turning her face away then and staring at the escort riding ahead. "If it's necessary that I be a Christian, why then I'm a Christian."

"And a follower of the old gods?" he asked.

She shrugged as though the matter were unimportant. "I think I may be both Christian and follower of the old gods. Who is to say that I may not?"

" 'A man may not serve two masters; he will love the one and hate the other,' " Owen quoted.

She laughed. "A man might not but a woman can; women

do it all the time. They love their fathers, then their husbands no less, and then their children."

"It's not the same thing," he protested.

"Why not? I gave the old gods respect, my worship to Christ."

"They were demons; they are demons," he corrected himself.

"Why are you so sure of that?" she asked earnestly. "Who can tell? They might have been angels sent to foreshadow him and teach a wild people how to worship."

"This is a duel," he said.

"And you are losing," she said, laughing.

"No," he said, but he was grinning now. "I'm not convinced. I still believe what I believe. Christ is my liege lord and I must keep His commandments. I was called to serve Him and must be loyal. If I had been called to serve an earthly lord I would have given him all my trust, my obedience, my love. Being in the service of the eternal God I can offer Him no less."

Owen no longer smiled, his face was somber, his eyes sad.

She was silent, the only sound the clop of the horses' hooves in the mud and the faint whistle of the wind through the barren branches of the trees. From far away came the distant elfin music of a flock of geese on the wind. When she spoke her voice was nearly as soft as the faraway calling of the geese.

"I make no curses, weave no spells. As you are my lord, so will I obey your Lord's commandments. All that I will do is what a good wife does for her lord, bring my kinfolk to your side."

"Who are they?" he asked.

"The people of the forest," she said quietly. "The people of the old gods."

He knew those of whom she spoke so casually. They still existed on the fringes of the settled world, keeping to well-defined paths in the wilderness. He was sure the grove where they had stopped to drink was one of their places. Many stories were told about them, some pleasant and amusing, others darker and more sinister. Yet all those stories were in agreement on one point: they never fought or engaged in any kind of violence. How could they help him?

"I thank you for the kind offer," he said, "but . . ."

"They know things," she answered. "If my family had heeded their warnings, we'd have been away and safe but . . . we waited too long.

"Oh Lord, if they had only listened to me. I came to tell them to flee. I left the band, abandoned my mother's kin to warn my father's. My uncle, fool that he was, patted my head and treated me like a child. He was like Reynald, stubborn and sure of his strength. And so . . ." Her eyes closed, her face twisted with pain, but then, resolutely, she pushed the memory away.

"They know all the secrets of the forest and the plain. They know when the Northmen march, the direction, and their strength. You're a soldier wise in the art of ambush and surprise. Think what you could do with such knowledge."

She left it at that, whether out of wisdom or distraction he didn't know because they were riding out of the wood and she saw the citadel of Chantalon.

The fortress was built on a bend of the river. The inner keep was walled, the outer guarded by an earthen bank strengthened by a wooden palisade. Below and around it, the fields stretched out, brown now with the stubble of the harvest, crosshatched with belts of green trees that served as windbreaks for the farms and villages. To the right and left of them, the forest marched away into the distance.

He pulled his horse to a stop. "My home," he said.

"It's very beautiful," she said.

A ray of sunlight shone down from the cloud rack above and burned the cold gray stone of the Roman fortress to rose and gold. The town surrounding the fortress glowed in the warm light, a multicolored brooch bright with enamel work and set with precious stones against the mantle of the brown fields.

So they came to the city.

About a half mile from the city gate, he said, "Ride side-saddle."

She complied, throwing her leg over the high pommel of the saddle and straightening her skirts. "Why?"

"They will all be looking at you. Have a care for what they see," he cautioned her.

The first sight of the city was a blur to Elin as they passed through the double gates of the palisade.

The main street, a cobbled ramp, was lined with tower houses stonewalled on the lower floors. The upper parts were of wattle and daub, reinforced with stout timbers. Some were roofed with thatch, others with brightly colored tile. The narrow street ran upward through the Roman gate into a square—the city's heart.

The cathedral stood at the end of the square. The bishop's palace beside it backed up to the high stone wall of the fortress.

Old Anna, his housekeeper, stood in front of it, a tall, grim-faced hag with her gray hair pulled back in a knot at the base of her neck. She was a strong woman, though a little hunched now with age. She wore a single garment, a brown linen gown belted up nearly to her knees with a leather strap.

Owen dismounted, lifted Elin from the saddle of her horse, set her on her feet, and brought her to where Anna stood at the top of the steps.

"It's about time you got back," Anna said to Owen. "There is trouble."

"Is there ever anything else?" Owen replied.

"Ranulf wants you. He's in back at the stable. Who is this?" she asked, fixing Elin with an intimidating stare.

"Elin," Owen said.

He was reluctant to say more. The men of his escort were standing at the foot of the steps. They were looking elaborately unconcerned and he was sure they were drinking in every word. The bishop bringing home a woman!

Anna understood his reticence yet she couldn't help remarking, "So you have awakened from your dream and begun to lead the life of a man."

Owen stiffened on his dignity, but before he could think of a suitable retort, Anna forestalled him, taking Elin by the hand and speaking to the lingering men at arms. "Go to the tavern and refresh yourselves. Don't get so drunk you can't ride."

"I will pay the score," Owen said.

The men grinned cheerfully at him; one, indeed, had already begun drifting away in that direction.

Owen went down the steps and turned into an alley beside the building, leaving Elin to Anna's mercies. It was probably a cowardly thing to do, but women understood these things better than men.

Anna led Elin into the hall, turned, and placed her hands on her hips, studying her intently. "You're no peasant," she commented, "but do you understand this kind of a household?"

"I do," Elin said, a small smile on her lips. "My father had eighteen manors and nine children. I was the eldest girl. My mother was a cripple. I can cook and clean with one hand while the other holds a baby and two more crawlers cling to my skirts."

"Well and good," Anna said. Then she added, "Reading, writing, the household accounts?"

"Yes," Elin said, "and birthing children, cows, calves, sheep, and horses. I have walked behind a plow a time or two and always helped with the reaping."

"The perfect woman for him, not so highborn a one that she would never think to lift a hand"—Anna's eyes narrowed—"nor so lowborn as to be a gaping, gawking innocent. You'll be a blessing to this household."

Elin's smile grew as she looked around at the hall. It was the sort of place she understood.

Long, narrow, and windowless, it was dark even in the daytime. An attempt had been made to brighten it by whitewashing the stone walls and painting in a lined border of red, but the paint was already flaking away, showing the gray beneath.

A trestle table, with benches on each side, ran the length of the room. Anna limped over to one of these benches and sat down, facing the big fireplace where the cooking was done. A pot hung over the fire giving out amiable bubbling sounds and an aroma of roasting meat.

"Have you hurt yourself?" Elin asked.

"No." Anna gave a sharp bark of laughter. "I'm old, my bones grate and grind against each other. My ankles swell now when I'm on my feet too long."

"Let me see," Elin said. "There are tonics for old bones

and it's possible to bind the ankles and support them against swelling."

"Are you skilled at healing then?" Anna asked.

"Yes," Elin said, starting to kneel and look at the ankles.

Anna caught her arm. "No, there is one here who needs your services more than I do. Denis the bowman lost a leg in a skirmish with some brigands this summer. The stump has never healed properly. He is upstairs now with a fever. Also, unless I miss my guess, when your husband is finished talking to Ranulf, you'll have another worry on your hands."

She rose and began guiding Elin toward stairs that were supported by heavy beams set in the stonework leading to the upper story of the house.

"Come up and I'll show you the rest and we can talk while you look at Denis's leg. My girl, I won't lie to you. Your husband is the only one who even attempts to keep order here. If you remain, you'll soon have many and heavy responsibilities. I'll get you an apron to tie around that dress."

Elin was following her up the stairs when Anna turned, a speculative expression in her eyes. "I suppose it's as well not to look a gift horse in the mouth but how did Owen come to—?"

"It's as well," Elin said, cutting her off, "not to look a gift horse in the mouth."

The house had a large walled courtyard in back, stables, and beyond that, a garden that ended where the ground dropped steeply off near the river.

Ranulf was coming out of the stable. He was a tall, blond, handsome boy with long-lashed blue eyes and skin as soft and fair as a girl's. The look of relief and joy that spread across his face when he saw Owen striding across the courtyard was very unsettling.

Owen greeted him with an abrupt, "What's wrong?"

"Count Anton," Ranulf said, "or rather Gerlos."

"What's he done now?"

"No sooner were you gone, than he came with five of his men and demanded a wagonload of grain and five barrels of wine. He said you owed them."

"I don't owe the count anything," Owen snapped.

Ranulf looked on the verge of tears. "I know that, so I made excuses and treated Gerlos to a fine dinner and quite a bit of the wine the count wanted. But the next day they were back. So I made more excuses and served them another meal. I got them as drunk as I could."

"And?" Owen made an impatient gesture with his hand.

"Yet they returned, this time the count came with them." Ranulf lowered his eyes. "They wouldn't accept any more excuses. I promised faithfully that I'd send the wheat and wine. Gerlos said he'd cut my throat if I didn't. So Denis and I found the worst of everything, loaded it into the smallest cart, and sent it. But yesterday Gerlos was back, cursing me and talking again of throat cutting, demanding more. I can't fight him."

Ranulf raised his eyes. There were tears standing in them, tears and bitter humiliation. "I'm sorry not to have been a better steward but . . ."

"Hush," Owen said, putting his hand comfortingly on Ranulf's shoulder. "No one expects you to fight Gerlos. If he returns, I'll deal with him."

Just how, I don't know, he thought. This was a worry. He hadn't expected the count to turn on him this quickly. But then he looked up, smiling coldly, at the wall of the fortress towering above his garden. Anton was never a man to let sentiment stand in the way of profit. With Owen gone, one way or another—the seat was vacant and could be sold to another candidate. Bertrand, for instance, who must now find time hanging rather heavy on his hands since the burning of the monastery.

Ranulf cleared his throat, drawing Owen away from his thoughts. "My lord," he said timidly, "my cousin, you know my cousin, Elfwine."

Owen knew her. A slender blond girl with, Owen judged, a completely empty head, but an appealing body and a beautiful face. She was Ranulf's woman, the cousin business was a polite fiction between the two of them.

"She"—Ranulf looked torn between pride and shame—"she's with child." Ranulf licked his lips nervously. "Her people, they're angry."

Her "people" would be. Those "people" included her four large brothers and her even bigger father. They'd been patient enough when he first took up with her and looked the other way. Now it was a different thing. They expected Ranulf to acknowledge the child and provide for her.

There was a timid sort of resolution in Ranulf's eyes. "The lady is ... the child is mine. I won't abandon it or her."

"What is it," Owen asked, "do you wish to leave me?"

Ranulf was shocked. "Oh no! But there are those who say ..."

"Bring the girl to my house. She'll be welcome and Anna can use some help."

The expression of joy on Ranulf's face was beautiful. He seized Owen's hand and kissed it, then ran off, calling back over his shoulder, "I'll go get her now."

Owen stood smiling indulgently at his retreating back, pleased to have made him so happy. In addition, he felt rather glad Ranulf had decided to remain as part of his household. It would have strained his now slender resources to have settled him elsewhere.

Owen's loyalty to Ranulf was absolute. He would no wise ever abandon him, for it had been Ranulf who rode to his mother and brought Clotild back to fetch him away from the monastery when Bertrand's behavior passed beyond simple cruelty and approached atrocity.

He sighed heavily and went into the church to pray. The church was locked and empty. The count's men went where they liked and took what they wanted. Nothing was sacred to them, not even the house of God.

Owen entered by a side door, through the bell tower, past the scriptorium, and knelt at the altar rail. He found he couldn't look at the stiff wooden Christ that hung over it.

He buried his face in his hands. This news about the count presaged disaster for him. There was no way he could appeal to Anton—the man was a debauchee, loyal to no one and nothing but his own interest. And his bastard Gerlos, gotten on one of the count's troop of women, when the count still thought of women, was only too happy to be a tool of that interest.

He was alone now, without his father's men or Gestric's strong backing. Gerlos would test his strength.

All he had was Elin and Elin's shadowy friends. Still that

was something. He'd understood the thrust of her argument the moment she had spoken. But he couldn't take advantage of what she offered without some fighting men, and he had none.

His head fell lower until his forehead touched the cold stone of the altar rail. It was afternoon and the church was growing darker. The high narrow windows, at the best of times, let in very little light, and in the late afternoon it became a vast, dim cavern filled with brooding silence.

When he entered the monastery he had had faith. It was a simple faith that consisted of fulfilling a contractual obligation. A lord expected certain things of the men of his household, others of the coloni and freeholders who worked his lands. So it was with God. He was God, therefore, He had certain expectations of His dependents, mankind. A wise man fulfilled his obligations to his lord. A wise man did the same with God.

Bertrand destroyed that faith, but without putting anything in its place. And now Owen was face-to-face with a remote, unknowable abstraction. A God he had not chosen, but who had chosen him.

The choice had been made clear last winter, after the second time Count Anton bribed the Northmen. The count's exactions had been harsh. Harsher, Owen thought, than would have been necessary to collect even such a large sum. Privately, Owen agreed with the whispered rumors that the count collected half again as much as the pirates demanded and used the rest to fill his own coffers. But he turned his face away and pretended he suspected nothing. He couldn't afford to offend Anton.

That morning he'd ridden out alone, but for two of his hounds, to hunt on the marshy river delta. The sun was over the horizon, its light a golden path on the water. It was not yet cold enough for frost, but the air was chilly and sweet, refreshed by a salt wind from the sea. He was at peace with the universe and himself. Until he was drawn by the howling of one of his hounds.

The infant was newborn, the cord coiled like a white worm on its belly. The tiny arms and legs still moved spasmodically. He knew at a glance that it was beyond any human help. The crows had been at it. The mouth was a shriveled black hole, the eyes empty scarlet hollows staring up at the sky.

He finished it with his dagger and dug a grave. Then he vomited until his stomach knotted, until he was dry, retching, and lying limp on the damp ground.

The eye of what God looked on that and did nothing, nothing but send his eyes to see?

That Sunday he rose to thunder reproaches at his congregation. He looked at them. The large uncomprehending eyes of the children stared back, eyes too large for the small faces. The women were thin and pale. The beards of the men stood out against skin gray with privation.

The hand of God struck him and darkness entered his soul. His tongue froze in his mouth. He couldn't utter a sound. Ranulf, seeing that something had happened, seated him in his chair and led the people in prayer.

The next day he took what remained in the church treasury and such altar vessels as the count had not already extorted from him and had them melted down. With the money they brought, he bought wheat from one of the merchantmen that sailed up the river to trade and used it to feed any and all who came to his door.

Still the darkness remained with him, bad on the cold gray days of winter, but worse on those fine clear sunlit ones. The contrast between the beauty of the earth and the bleak emptiness within his own heart was all but unendurable.

He ceased to eat, to pray, or visit the very discreet older woman he had visited before.

Whispers began to follow him wherever he went. When a few of those whispers reached his ears, he decided he must speak with God again. But now he did it in a new way.

He went to the church alone, armed and wearing his sword, and spoke as he would to an earthly king.

"I am your servant. I failed in my duty to you and have been punished. All that is clear to me. But if you don't lift this curse from me, they will begin to think I'm a saint and we both know that isn't true."

It seemed that very day things became better and gradually he began to live as he had before. But he understood the duties that were required of him and began to work hard to fulfill those obligations.

His tenants and coloni were surprised at his industry that summer. He eschewed hunting, disposed of his hawks to Reynald because they ate too much, and rode out only to put meat on the table. A necessity everyone understood since livestock could not be slaughtered indiscriminately. Ultimately he resumed his visits to the lady.

He raised his head from the rail and realized it was time for him to speak. Not to do so would be to seem to lie to God, the God he'd discovered in the marshes, and that was not to be thought of.

The gloom of evening was darkening the empty church and the horn-shielded lamp that burned in a cage before the high altar was casting strange shadows that crouched around him.

He stood up and looked at the figure of Christ on the cross, nearly invisible in the half-light above the altar.

He reached over and put his hand on the hilt of his sword and spoke to this incomprehensible liege lord.

"If the woman will have me, I will take her. I am your priest and my people's, but I am a man and must live as a man."

A voice answered in his mind, a voice so clear he started and looked around, searching the darkness for the speaker.

"Is there necessarily any difference?"

His hand slipped from the sword hilt. That had almost the force of command, a clear order. Go forward!

Chapter

7

*H*E'D wear his skin out with bathing, but he enjoyed the feel of being clean. Elin had even managed to ease the discomfort of the big house's cold rooms, settling him in front of the fireplace with two screens canted around the tub to keep out drafts. She'd scented the bathwater with rosemary.

She knew how to cook, too, seasoning Anna's unimaginative stews with some spicy herbs and accompanying it with a little delight composed of dried apples cooked in cider, cinnamon, and nutmeg, and topped with sweet cream.

He'd returned from the church to find the household well in hand. Anna sat in an armchair before the fire, her feet soaking in a concoction of Elin's, eating her dinner from a plate.

Elin was in Denis the bowman's room upstairs. He felt a quick flicker of anger when he saw her sitting on the edge of the bed dosing the injured man, but it faded when he realized that Elfwine and Ranulf were in dutiful attendance. He completely forgot his irritation with Elin when he realized Elfwine's condition. Ranulf had mentioned she was pregnant, but hadn't gone so far as to explain that any loud noise or sudden shock might cause her to become two people.

During dinner he found Elin had fed and settled one of Elfwine's brothers in the stable. "I promised," she told him, "three linen shirts for summer, two woolen and a heavy mantle for winter, a beer tankard with each meal, and as much as he could drink on feast days and his saint's name day. I hope that was not too much. He thinks he's a rich man."

"No doubt, by comparison, he is," Owen told her. The

youngest of five brothers, Owen wondered if the man had ever owned more than one shirt to cover his nakedness and that probably worn to a rag by each of his brothers before it passed to him.

"His name is Ine," Elin said.

Ine was strong as an ox and quiet as a stone. He was as towheaded as Elfwine, with mild blue eyes. He filled Owen's bath with scalding water and left him to soak himself in comfort.

Owen let his body sink deeper into the bath and rested his head against the back of the tub, letting the hot water lave his neck and dampen his hair.

Ah, and after the bath, Elin. He closed his eyes. Let's see what I can earn, and thought of Gisela with a smile. Over the years he'd thought of her in many ways.

First with bitterness and anger when she married one of his father's servants, then in grief and guilt as Bertrand tried to teach him to hate the sins of the flesh. But now at last he smiled at fleeting beauty and treasured memory.

As the last boy, with four girls between him and his nearest brother, he enjoyed the luxury of a room of his own. Gisela, one of his mother's maids, awakened him every morning. He was just thirteen and beginning to feel his manhood.

One warm summer day she came in and found him lying on top of the sheets in a state of erection. Scarlet with embarrassment, he promptly hid himself, but she only smiled, and seduced him within a week. It seemed an eternity at the time.

After that morning she no longer awakened him with a rough shake but sat on the edge of the bed stroking his body gently through the covers. Each day she took increasing pains and the caresses that began on his back and chest became more lengthy and intimate. She no longer had to awaken him at all. Soon his eyes opened before the first light of day and he lay quietly anticipating her coming. When his body twisted and turned to receive the ecstatic pleasure given by her moving fingers, not at his will but hers, when he offered himself to her in absolute trust, she slipped into bed and joined him.

She was never a passive partner. "Put your hand there, little mouse. Ah, now do this." She taught him all the "sacred spots," she called them, on a woman's body that will rouse her to cry out with pleasure.

He was an apt and ardent pupil, intoxicated with the delights they shared.

"Gently and slowly, little mouse. Would you have power over women, my sweet one? But give them this burning joy until faintness overcomes them and they will be at your feet."

He sat up quickly, water splashing over the sides of the tub onto the floor and looked down with a laugh. It seemed his body remembered Gisela as well as his mind, and was equally pleased with the experience.

He stepped out of the tub. The fire on the hearth warmed him while he dried off with a linen towel, then pulled on a heavy woolen bed gown, and went in search of Elin.

She was in his room, kneeling naked on the wolf skins in front of the fire. Its light turned her creamy skin to amber. She was drying her long shimmering hair.

He closed the door, dropped the bar deliberately, and turned back to her. She knelt facing him, head thrown back, breasts upright. Her thighs were parted slightly, the fire behind her glowed on the tight curly mount between.

The satiny skin was blue with bruises here and there. She was marked by the fingers of other men—on the arms, the breasts, the thighs.

Desire blotted out everything. There was only the woman, the fire, and lust so great it cramped his loins with pain.

"You could have barred the door," he said.

"Why," she asked, "against life? I think that would take a stronger bar and a larger door. The cold stone slab of a tomb. I am not yet ready for that. Besides, even they were not always cruel ... pike men."

Fury and desire shook his body. He advanced on her, and grabbing a handful of hair, he pulled her head back until she looked straight up into his face. "What daughter of a bitch wolf are you, to tell me this at such a time?"

She twisted her head, indifferent to the pain of his grip on her hair, showing him her back. The fire picked out the scars slicing across it from waist to neck.

"Oh," she said, "there are ways. The other is tied hand

and foot in the sun, salt in your mouth. In time, and no long
time, you'll do anything to be released and more not to have
it repeated. Believe me, I know."

He stepped away from her, took off the gown, and knelt
naked on the wolf skins. She slid slowly down on her back
and smiled up at him as he spoke angrily.

"They take that as they take everything. But is a woman
a walled city to fall to fire and assault? I could give, I would
give, not simply steal."

The smile left her face. She stared up at him somberly. "I
thought by now I'd bear the weight of your gift and you'd
be gone."

He shook his head. The dark, fine hair fell around his thin
face. His lips came down to meet hers softly, as they had in
the forest, that same restrained exploration. He rose and
went to the table, saying, "Rest, you'll bear no weight until
you wish."

He was in a dream. His youthful scurryings were furtive
and sometimes hurried. But this slow dream, this passion of
the flesh, of another to do with as he wished, was the best
of all.

He had asked Ranulf to find some good wine. He had—a
white, light and fragrant as the flowers and herbs that
bloomed among the vines.

He drank deeply, until he felt the blush of the wine in his
skin. She was on her elbow looking at him. He brought the
cup to her and lay by her side. "Here, drink. I would share
this with you."

She did, as deeply as he had, her eyes brightened with delight. "Oh, it is good."

"So," he said, kissing a drop from one corner of her
mouth, "are other things."

He brushed the dark hair aside from one ear and nibbled
the lobe delicately. She had expected him to be quick, not
rough or harsh perhaps, but finished with her and rolling on
his stomach to sleep. But no, and she should have known at
that moment in the forest, when she had taken comfort in his
nearness, that this was his way. He was no different on this
night than he had been then.

The strong hands moved down her back, she closed her
eyes.

"Please," he asked in a low voice, "put your arms around me."

She did. He was lean and hard, skin surprisingly warm, almost hot to the touch. She opened her eyes. His face was close, his eyes were looking into hers, his lips curved in a half smile.

"Your skin is hot, have you a fever?" she asked, a bit alarmed.

He was amused by that, laughter sparkled in his eyes and broadened the curve of his lips. "Desire does that," he said.

"My skin is cool," she said.

"I know. I hope to warm it," he answered, lowering his mouth to her breast, and easing her down on the wolf skins.

The fur was long and soft under her back, the wine was making her a little lightheaded, and the movement of his tongue on her flesh did bring a delicious warmth with it.

She sighed, closed her eyes to better enjoy it, and cupped her breast with her fingers to help him.

He turned his attention to the other and the pleasure grew, peaked, then died away.

Her eyes opened. "Is that all there is to it?" she asked.

"No," he said gently, "it isn't. Shall I do it again?"

"Yes," and she cupped both breasts with her fingers, offering them to his kisses.

This time the pleasure grew and grew, flowing downward between her legs. His lips caressed her stomach, moving down. She opened her eyes and raised her head, surprised. "Will you kiss that?" she asked, pressing her knees together.

"That is the sweetest caress of all," he said, parting her thighs with his fingers. Her breathing quickened with astonishment and a little fear as his tongue probed inside her.

The strong hands were on her buttocks, the gentle pressure of his fingers seemed to draw her open to his searching. His dark hair brushed her parted thighs with its cobweb softness.

Then he found what he sought in her warm darkness. Her fear faded and astonishment grew as a tide of heat flowed up through her body.

He felt her back arch and heard her soft cry and drew away. He waited a few breaths then tickled that one particular place again gently with the tip of his tongue, then drew back.

She caught at his head with her legs and made a whimpering sound deep in her throat. The room misted away around her.

Again and yet again tantalizing, not satisfying. Her flesh was more than hot now. It seemed to burn.

He sat up.

"Oh," she whispered, "a sweet torment."

He lifted the cup from the floor beside the rug. She drank as in a dream, leaning on one elbow.

He took it from her. This time he caressed not just with his lips, but with his hands.

She offered him her body now, her nipples hard, stiff under his mouth. When his head fell lower she parted her legs to welcome him. Again he probed that sweet wellspring of delight.

He raised his head, brushing her inner thighs lightly with his lips. "I am a guest," he said, "and will not enter unless invited. Do you invite me?" he asked, kneeling between her legs.

"Oh, yes," she breathed. "Oh God, yes."

He meant to enter slowly, but she caught him with her legs and drew him in greedily.

It was as though a shaft of fire entered between her legs, spreading upward in a torrent of unbelievable pleasure. She withered with the unbearable intensity of it and caught at his lean body with her arms. It was like being loved by a great cat, he was all rippling muscle.

Her hips lifted to drive the full, delicious length of him into her. Each thrust of his loins a spasm of unbearable delight, again and again and again.

She heard, as from a great distance, his own moaning as her throbbing completion seemed to drain the soul from his body into an ocean of light.

When Anna came down to start the breakfast fire, Elin was standing on tiptoe peering out through the archer's slit in the hall door at the square.

Anna stopped at the foot of the stairs, folded her arms and said gruffly, "Ah, you will want to go out and see the town."

Elin jumped, tore her eyes away from the narrow opening, and turned around. "You startled me. I'm sorry, I should be . . ."

"Best get the fire built and start the porridge. It's baking day. We're nearly out of bread. You're a wife now and must think of other things than chasing around making a spectacle of yourself before the whole city. He'll be down in a few minutes and will want his meat."

Elin hurried to the wood box and began putting logs on the coals in the fireplace. She couldn't have Anna think her lazy.

"Will we need anything for the baking?" Elin asked hopefully.

"No," Anna answered sharply, "everything we need is in the cupboards or the cellar—flour, salt, yeast."

"Perhaps an egg bread," Elin suggested sweetly.

"No," Anna said. "A respectable woman keeps to her house and tends to her husband's comfort. Besides, the count's men hang about the tavern and the square. Any woman is fair game to them, respectable or not."

"I saw others," Elin began.

"Lowborn common sluts, not ladies like yourself," Anna said with an air of authority. "Get to work, girl. Your husband will be awake soon demanding something to eat. Savage as a wounded bear and twice as loud if he doesn't get it on time."

The steward, Ranulf, was coming down the stairs, and he blinked in mild surprise at this description of Owen. "Anna, I don't think . . ."

"It's a terrible life of pain and drudgery we women lead, Elin. Up before daylight, in bed by candlelight, and very little rest, even then, until we grow too old and withered by toil and childbirth to be interesting. Imprisoned by four walls all day, bending over a hot fire, breaking our poor backs, while lazy louts like this"—Anna gestured at the hapless Ranulf—"lie around expecting to be waited on hand and foot."

"I—" Ranulf said, dazed by the tirade.

"Don't stand there stammering. Get your staff!"

"My—" Ranulf said.

"Your staff!" Anna glared mordantly at Elin. "We're ser-

vants now and must do as we're told. Lady Elin wishes to
go out and look at the town. You do, don't you?"

"You said . . ." Elin began.

"I said, I said, who pays attention to what a servant says?"

Anna picked up an eight-inch knife from the sideboard
near the hearth, sheathed it, and tucked it into the belt of her
gown. It hung there, held in position by a bronze stud on the
sheath.

Ranulf came back with his mantle and a heavy stick
nearly as tall as he was, with a knob of ornamental bronze
on the end.

"Let's go now," Anna said, "and let the town look at you.
If we don't, God knows they'll all find an excuse to come
here and annoy me all day, while I try to get the baking
done.

"The count's men do frequent the tavern at all hours. Pass
any we meet with downcast eyes and don't react to anything
they say. Dung is what they are, but even they won't want
to tangle with Ranulf's staff or my knife. Now go get your
cloak and veil. It's cold in the square of a morning and only
grows warm when the sun is high in winter."

"Are you sure . . . ?" Ranulf began.

"Sure, sure, yes, I'm sure." Anna's words were rapid as
finger snaps. "Know you, boy, women are like cats and must
explore any new place until they are satisfied. If they don't
they become weak and vain, fretful and ill. You wouldn't
want your lord to think you had a hand in causing his wife's
decline, now would you?"

"Owen . . ." Elin said, gesturing toward the stairs.

Anna chuckled with salacious enjoyment. "He'll be in bed
a few hours more. The sports of a wedding night tire a man
while a woman is refreshed. I'll wager you put him through
his paces. I'd be surprised if you did not, and I'd say he came
through winningly, by the look of you—fair, sweet, and
dewy-eyed."

Elin felt a blush heat her cheeks and ears. She got her veil
and cloak and took one of Owen's knives.

"Pay attention now, Elin," Anna said as she shooed Elin
and Ranulf through the door like a couple of chickens,
"you're getting your first lesson. A woman may not be able

to fight a man, but she can often outthink him and always outtalk him."

"You can outtalk anyone in this mood," Ranulf said waspishly.

"Bah, anyone can outtalk you, Ranulf. Now keep your eyes peeled and try to look fierce. Remember the count's men."

The square was cold. Elin gathered the woolen mantle around herself and threw the white veil over her head, wrapping the ends around her neck to hold it in place as she looked around, enthralled.

The sky was clear and the yellow morning sun only lightly dusted the tops of the tall buildings. The cathedral and the bishop's house dominated the square.

The Romans who built the fortress hadn't envisioned the town that would grow up around it, but they had carefully paved the approaches to its gates with heavy cobbles and these remained as a street. The cobbles rose from the gates of the palisades below, went up through the big granite post of the Roman circuit wall, flooring the square itself, and continued past the fountain and the cathedral—with its wide porch and low pillars—then went up again, following the wall of the fortress and turning up once more out of sight.

She pointed. "The count lives there? Where are the gates?"

"They face away from the square," Anna said. "The Romans built well and put them where they could not easily be forced by an enemy. This suits the count. He does not care for our company."

From the steps of Owen's hall, the town seemed crowded, even a little cramped. Elin, having seen it from a distance, knew that this was deceptive. Each house had at least a small garden with a courtyard. But space was at a premium within the Roman wall and the tall houses were built on the street, the gardens behind them hidden by high walls. Love and care had been lavished on those facing onto the square and the bright colors and exquisitely wrought trim delighted Elin's eye.

Only a step from the porch of the cathedral stood the tavern. The bottom floor was of rather poorly dressed, dull, gray stone, but it sported windows of real glass. Inside the distorted, small panes of the windows, the shapes of several early morning patrons could be seen, all peering at Elin. Anna pointed at a small, fat, bald man standing in the doorway, wiping his hands on a towel.

"Arn, the tavern keeper."

Then she called loudly to a tall, thin woman peeping over his shoulder. "What are you staring at, Routrude? Come out and speak. His wife," Anna said out of the side of her mouth to Elin. "She is one of the worst gossips in the city and very inventive. Should you tell her that the bishop has a small cut on his finger, by sunset the whole city will hear he had lost a hand. Give her but a day more and all Paris will believe he has lost both arms and on the third day the news will reach Rome that you have murdered him, dismembered the body, and buried it in the garden. Her husband is the biggest coward in the city, afraid of his own shadow."

Routrude wiggled past Arn and was presented to Elin.

Routrude was a toucher. She touched Elin's hair, pulling it a little, apparently trying to see if it was attached to her scalp. She fingered her veil as if attempting to estimate its quality, stroked her mantle, finally prying it open, poking her sharp nose inside to get a look at Elin's figure, saying, "Eaha, she is not yet with child. If she is not yet with child, why did he bring her home?"

Anna slapped Routrude's hand away from Elin's mantle, saying grimly, "Give the man time. He probably wants the fun of getting her that way first."

Elin moved away from Routrude, who stood rubbing her reddened hands together and admitting grudgingly, "She is young and very pretty. She may have had other suitors. Did you have other suitors? Certainly you had other suitors! Who were they?" she asked eagerly.

"Routrude, for God's sake," Anna said in exasperation, "mind your manners. What a question to ask."

A look of invidious glee spread over Routrude's face. She caught Elin by the mantle, drew her head down and spoke into her ear, "Or were you abducted?" she asked in a tone of horrified delight. "Did you invite it, go willingly, or just accept the situation after it happened? What was it like? Even now, are your father and brothers hot on the bishop's heels, riding to avenge their . . . ?"

Elin jerked back, aware they now had a gallery of interested female spectators standing on the balcony of a house next to the tavern. All were young and beautifully, if a bit flamboyantly, dressed. The tall house itself was, to Elin's eye, even more magnificent than the tavern.

Curious, and desperate to break up Routrude's interrogation, she pointed and asked, "Who . . . Affah!"

Ranulf, Anna, and Routrude all elbowed her in the ribs.

"Pretend you don't notice," Anna whispered fiercely.

"You are a lady of quality!" Ranulf hissed.

"The widow's business isn't spoken of openly," Routrude snickered in an undertone. "But should we ever get the chance for a little private conversation"—she seized Elin's arm in a grip of steel—"the widow is an intimate of mine and her patrons are well-known. Some of their tastes . . . those methods that they—"

Anna broke Routrude's grip on Elin's arm, saying, "She has no need of education by you or the widow's ladies!"

"Let's get away from the tavern," Ranulf said nervously.

Elin could see no reason for his uneasiness. The count's men were nowhere in evidence, with the possible single exception of a large scarlet-faced man with a bulbous nose, sitting on a bench by the tavern door. He looked immobilized by the most vicious hangover Elin had ever seen.

Anna caught Elin by the arm and began leading her to the fountain, where two other women stood watching them. Ranulf followed. Routrude took her by the elbow. She was convinced Elin had been abducted and now was only concerned with the method.

"Did he break into your house, put the servants to flight, and seize you by force? Or was he a guest at your father's board, giving you silent glances filled with meaning. Did you in all innocence return them, until one night you found your servants bribed into silence, and he confronted you alone in your maiden bower. Did you yield because you were defenseless? No, you were not defenseless, you could have screamed. Why did you not scream?"

Routrude's brow furrowed in thought. Anna was smothering her laughter under her veil. Elin was tempted to join her but realized she had to put a stop to this. But before she could speak, Routrude continued, "Ah, I have it. You did not scream because the bold seducer overcame your scruples by the beauty of his person and the ardor of his wooing."

Elin fixed Routrude with an icy stare. "Routrude, I had no maiden bower. I slept with my three younger sisters. Now will you introduce me to these ladies?"

They had reached the fountain. Of the two women awaiting them, one was short and rather fat, but still very pretty in spite of her stoutness, with silken brown hair and long-lashed brown eyes. The other was a tall blonde, a pastel beauty with honey-colored hair and hazel eyes. She had a baby in her arms.

She held the baby out and uncovered its face. Elin admired the baby as was expected, cooing and clucking properly.

"This is Helvese," Anna said, "Osbert, the stock dealer's wife."

Helvese smiled, her lips moved, but no sound emerged.

Elin said the baby was beautiful and professed herself delighted to make Helvese's acquaintance.

Helvese continued to smile, her lips moved again.

Elin threw a look of alarmed inquiry at the grinning Anna.

The plump brunette spoke up. "Don't worry, you have not suddenly gone deaf. Helvese is very shy. Her voice goes away when she meets strangers. She was quite audible only a moment ago. She would like you to call on her."

"I would be delighted to call on her," Elin said gently.

Helvese smiled again and pressed Elin's hand in a friendly fashion. Her lips formed more words, whole sentences, then she covered the baby's face lightly against the cold, bowed, and glided away.

"What did she say?" Elin asked.

"Who knows?" Routrude said, lifting Elin's skirt to look at her stockings and leggings.

"She said she was going home and she"—Anna slapped Routrude's hand away from Elin's skirt—"hoped she would see you again soon."

"Suppose that happens when I am alone with her," Elin said, dismayed, "what will I do?"

The little brunette laughed. "You do what the rest of us

do, dear, tell her, 'Please for God's sake, Helvese, speak up,' and you may be sorry when she does, for she talks of her husband, the baby, her husband's business, the baby, the baby, and the baby. But then she's young yet. We're hoping with age she'll grow more intelligent. Since no one has seen fit to introduce me, I am Gynnor, Siefert, the tanner's wife. I, too, have babies but am used to them now, and pleased enough to leave them home in the care of my mother."

She had a basket with fresh eggs in it. She waved it at Elin. "My excuse to be out in the square this early in the morning. Every day I find a similar excuse," Gynnor added.

This side of the square had a low wooden arcade that sheltered a line of small shops just now opening for the morning business. In front of them were gathered the sellers of chickens, rabbits, eggs, and those few fresh vegetables still in season.

The women strolled along the arcade toward the Roman gate at the end of the square, Elin still casting surreptitious glances back at the widow's house where the ladies watched her from the porch. "They won't talk about it," she said in a low voice to Gynnor, indicating Anna and Routrude.

"I can't see why," Gynnor said. "Everyone knows about the widow and her ladies, who goes there, how often and for what, and—if even half of Routrude's tales are to be believed—any eccentric or peculiar behavior they display while they are doing it. Next to the tavern, she does the most business."

The widow's house had the largest balcony, a porch really, since a flight of steps led down the side of the building, but every house had at least one small one and all were occupied mostly by women taking the brisk morning air and watching the traffic below.

The houses of the shop owners above the arcade were as brightly colored, if not as ornately decorated as the widow's or the tavern. One was blue with its timbers whitewashed, another a bold red.

A shepherd came up a narrow street. He turned his flock and drove them through the doors into the big house.

"What is that?" Elin asked.

"Oh, Osbert is Helvese's husband. He does all of his business there. It is the largest house in town and the most magnificent, he thinks," Gynnor told her.

The flock of sheep and a milk cow stood near the entrance while at the back a platform supported a long table with benches and armchairs. All around the platform tapestries and other weavings glowed on the walls.

The fishmonger, arriving late to open his shop, heard about Elin. He raced down the porch of the wooden arcade, looked Elin over, then raced back to his shop. He returned with a large fish in a net bag and thrust it into Elin's hand saying, "A sample of my wares, lovely lady. I have mussels, oysters, crabs, clams, hake, skate, bream . . ." he ran out of breath, but not fish as he hastened to assure Elin, "and much, much more. Every day, fresh fish for his lordship."

Routrude grabbed at the bag but was forestalled by Anna, who seized it saying, "It was a present to my lady."

A country woman led a donkey laden with earthenware jars of honey into the square, announcing her wares to everyone in a loud voice.

She was quickly besieged by customers, including Gynnor, Ranulf, Anna, Routrude, and most of the shopkeepers, who congregated in a shouting, haggling knot around her.

Gynnor returned, having found room in her basket for honey.

"Of all the houses, I still like the widow's best," Elin said.

Gynnor nodded. "She is prosperous."

The sun was higher now, shining on the bright yellow of the widow's stucco walls. All the woodwork and the rails were fashioned into strange beasts, multihued coiled dragons, long bodies painted in red, heads in blue and fangs gilded.

The honey seller was now dealing with the widow's women on the balcony, passing jars up through the rail. They reminded Elin of a flock of brightly colored birds, in their long woolen and linen gowns. None wore a veil or headdress. Two were redheads dressed in brown and green respectively. Several were brunettes, another very dark one in tattered red, and a little blonde. She opened her jar right there and began eating greedily, licking her fingers.

Elin smiled at the little blonde occupied with the honey

jar, for Elin, having finished the apple bread, found her own fingers were dipping into Gynnor's blackberries.

To her surprise, the girl smiled back, a quick conspiratorial smile at another lover of sweet things. Then, as if abashed at her own temerity, quickly lowered her eyes. The smile vanished like a ray of sunshine put out by a dark cloud.

"It is a pity," Gynnor said, "to speak of them as some do, for none of them is there of her own will."

Elin turned away and took Gynnor's arm. They strolled on.

"Is the widow a hard woman?"

"Yes, and grasping," Gynnor answered, "but she must give them some reason to serve her will. So in the end most can earn their freedom and a good dowry. A few find generous protectors before that time."

Anna, Ranulf, and Routrude returned clutching their plunder—Anna with fish, bread, blackberries, and honey, Ranulf and Routrude with blackberries.

Anna saw Elin pop some blackberries into her mouth. "Stop that, you'll stain your gown."

"Listen to her, playing the evil, old beldame," Gynnor said. "You would never believe that it was all bluff."

"So many people," Elin said in awe to Anna.

Gynnor laughed. "No, it's not even a great market day. This is just the usual business that goes on all the time. But this is my house and I must go in and tend to my husband. He'll be awake and wanting his breakfast."

Elin turned and studied the tall house. It was only a step from the gate opposite Osbert's, but she had been too busy craning her neck at the other side of the street to see it.

Orange and black, the woodwork was decorated with long strips of carved human heads. Gargoyles protected the four corners and the roof tree.

"So," Elin said, "some things survive even the legions."

Gynnor smiled a strange smile and looked at Elin from the corner of her eye. "Yes."

"Have you a garden?" Elin asked.

"Oh, yes. I have just taken a harvest from it. All the common things and many not so common. Customers come to one for samples. I would welcome a visit from you. We could sit in the sunshine and smell the flowers. Call if I can be of any help to you."

Suddenly Gynnor's hand shot out, she pulled Elin toward her door quickly.

Three men were coming up the street from the palisade wall. People scurried to get out of their way. Even as Elin was pulled toward Gynnor's door, Ranulf and Anna planted themselves in front of her.

Routrude became the immediate recipient of two jars of honey, three baskets of blackberries, and one fish. She juggled them desperately, backing up next to Elin and Gynnor.

Elin saw the knuckles of Ranulf's right hand whiten on the staff and heard him whisper, "Bad luck. Gerlos!"

The three men were all armed and wore chain-mail byrnies. They had been hunting, and besides knives and swords they carried crossbows. Rabbits, geese, and a few wild ducks were slung from their saddles.

But the men passed, laughing together, without seeming to notice the small group standing near the gate.

Ranulf relaxed, but too soon. The leader reined in his horse and turned, his green eyes fixed on Elin insolently. He walked the horse back toward her. "There is a likely looking one. I have not seen that before."

The man next to him plucked at his sleeve and said something to Gerlos in a low voice. He jerked his sleeve away from the man's fingers with a curse, saying, "What do I care," and turned back to Elin.

Then his face changed and Elin became aware Gerlos wasn't looking at but beyond her.

"Good morning, your lordship." The voice came from behind Elin. It was heavy with mock servility.

Elin half turned. One of the biggest men she'd ever seen was standing there with a hammer in his hand.

Anna breathed a sigh of relief that seemed to rise from her toes and whispered, "Gunter."

Both men were silent, staring into each other's eyes. Gunter had a half smile on his face.

"It could happen that someday, Gunter," Gerlos said, "someone will take that hammer and make you eat it."

"At any time you feel ready, your ... worship!"

One of Gerlos's companions plucked at his sleeve again

and looked across the square at Osbert's house. Elin followed the direction of his gaze. A heavyset, powerful-looking man was standing in the doorway holding a large shaft in his hand. He was surrounded by his servants. Several held axes, the rest staves, and all carried knives similar to Anna's in their belts.

Gerlos's face tightened with rage.

Elin dropped her eyes and drew her veil over the lower part of her face with one hand while the other groped for her own knife. She would give this Gerlos no excuses.

But the moment passed. Gerlos turned his horse and set out for the fortress at a trot. His voice, intentionally loud, carried over the sound of the horse's hooves and the babble of the square. "The bishop's leman. She's too good for one who can't even grow a beard."

Elin felt her face burn.

"Well, my lady"—Gunter's voice was intentionally loud also—"you have met Gerlos, the count's bastard."

At the word "bastard" Gerlos half turned in the saddle but rode on, vanishing around the corner at the tavern.

Gunter repeated the word "bastard" and spat on the cobbles of the street.

"This is Gunter, the blacksmith," Anna said.

"Thank you, Gunter, the pleasure is mine," Elin said, extending her hand.

It vanished into the smith's big paw, but he only pressed it lightly. "Not at all," Gunter answered, "the pleasure was mine. I wish that bastard had started something. He and those dogs at his heels should stick to the widow's women and leave honest men's wives alone."

Anna was unloading Routrude, who was enraptured by the proceedings. "Well, he did pay her a compliment," she said. "Do you suppose he will try to abduct her?"

"Routrude," Anna said disdainfully, "you have abduction on the brain, and that was not a compliment."

Gunter was looking at Elin's belt, smiling. Elin realized with a shock her hand was still clutching the hilt of the knife.

"I think if he tries, he will be very sorry," Gunter said. "The lady is not one to be put upon."

"What we all should have done was to go into the house,"

Gynnor said coolly. Then as she kissed Elin good-bye, she added, "Come to see me soon."

Elin was ready to seek the security of the hall. Anna fell into step beside her. "Perhaps I should not have gone out," Elin said in a low voice.

"No," Anna said, "this trouble was here before you came."

Gunter, walking beside them, nodded. "The reason Osbert is so ready to fight is because a pack of the count's drunken scum tried to carry Helvese off as she drew water at the fountain early one morning a few months ago."

"Great God," Anna whispered, "I can't think what they intended to do with her. The poor child was seven months gone in pregnancy at the time."

"I'd rather not think what they intended to do with her," Gunter said furiously. "The girl would have died and the baby, too, most likely."

"What did the count say?" Elin asked. "Surely . . ."

Gunter stopped and glared angrily up at the fortress.

Anna explained. "Helvese screamed."

Elin raised her eyebrows.

"Oh, yes," Anna continued, "she's loud enough when she's frightened. She was able to fight them off long enough to rouse the town. The men ran away. The count said they were not his."

"But they were," Gunter said. "We convened a meeting of our"—Anna and Gunter exchanged glances as he hesitated—"prayer society. Helvese was able to identify them to us by name. It grows worse and worse. Something must be done."

They were approaching the hall, but to Elin's surprise, Anna turned away from the door toward the cathedral porch, where a group of ragged men and women were gathered. Anna walked toward them, telling Elin, "Owen feeds all who apply breakfast and supper."

"Your husband is well liked," Gunter said. "An honest man who does his duty."

Ranulf, who wanted his breakfast, gave a sigh of disgust. "Now she is meeting beggars."

Routrude cautioned, "Be careful, they have lice and fleas."

Anna stopped in front of the porch. She saluted some of those waiting there by name. Most were old. Others were maimed and blind, obviously crushed by life. A few of the women, pinched-faced and sad, carried children. Only one was an able-bodied man. He looked furtive and dangerous.

He crouched on his heels in the shadow of a pillar, head bowed. His long hair was black, with a few threads of gray in it, worn in four braids, two hanging at his cheeks and two down his back. He wore a tunic and shirt of coarse cloth, and leather leggings with crisscross binding. In his belt hung a sax—a long single-edged knife, broad across the blade. His was larger than Anna's, almost a short sword. A dirty, bloodstained bandage covered one shoulder and his tunic was stained with dried blood. His arms rested across his knees, hands clasped.

He raised his head and looked at Elin. He had a strong face, wideset eyes of gray-brown, straight nose, and a generous mouth, but with a bitter set to it. A week's stubble of beard covered his cheeks.

Something about him was familiar to Elin, but from where? The camp? But no, he aroused nothing of revulsion in her, yet the memory was tinged with something unpleasant.

As they stared at one another recognition flared in his eyes, then an immediate awareness that he'd given himself away. And she remembered a man ducking under the horse—knife out at his belly—in the forest near the monastery, and the whistling chop of Owen's sword meeting flesh.

She took an involuntary step backward and saw his body tighten as a cat's does before it springs. Elin said, "No."

"What is it?" Anna said, looking quickly from the man on the church steps to Elin and back again. "Do you know him?"

Elin stood frozen, one hand on her skirt, the other almost at the hilt of her knife, gazing into the man's eyes. She had only to speak and he was a dead man. Gunter was beside her, hammer in his hand. Ranulf with his staff and Anna and her knife were on the other side. Behind her, the square was filled with people who would enjoy the chase. Elin suspected her word alone would suffice for a hanging.

The forest brigand seemed to realize this because he unclasped his hands and turned them palms up in a gesture that was both appeal and surrender.

"Do you know him?" Anna repeated.

"No," Elin said.

The man relaxed, but still watched Elin, suspicion in his eyes.

"You're a strong fellow," she said, "and look as though you could work or fight for your bread."

The man still studied Elin, eyes glittering, mouth tight and hard, but his answer was polite. "I would do either willingly, my lady, but, for many reasons, I cannot think any would have me. And as you can see, I am wounded."

"One might wonder how you came by that wound," Anna said acidly.

"Yes," the man answered coldly, "one might."

"One might also be discreet and not ask too many questions of a stranger," Elin said.

Gunter tapped the head of the hammer lightly on the palm of his left hand. "A masterless man might fall in among those who could drive a very hard bargain," he said.

Surprised, Elin turned her head toward Gunter. She knew he was referring to the fact that many men, women, and whole families, impoverished by the constant warfare or simply the calamities of nature, sold themselves into servitude of one kind or another. He was telling her she could set the terms on which she accepted the unknown.

She looked back at the man on the steps. His eyes were those of a cornered wolf. The spirit that burned in them spoke to her own, because she shared it.

He shifted his feet and flexed his knees almost imperceptibly and she knew he could rise from that crouch as swiftly as a striking snake.

Her mouth tightened and her chin lifted. "I drive no such bargains," she said firmly, "but I have work for a strong pair of honest hands. Are you honest?"

His answer was as blunt as her question. "None I gave my word to have ever feared to turn their back on me, but not a few have been sorry to see my face." He rose to his feet. "Do you make game of me, my lady?"

Elin met his questioning look with a level stare of her own.

"No," he said, "you wouldn't."

"You're right, I wouldn't," she answered. "That's honesty enough for me. Come, eat. I'll see to your wound."

Chapter

8

*E*LIN marched the man into the hall. Anna, Ranulf, and Routrude followed. Anna directed a black look at Elin's prize. "If you are to be our guest," she said, "you might at least tell us your name."

The man dropped into a crouch again before the fire. The logs Elin placed on it earlier were blazing now, and he had obviously spent more than one night out in the cold and rain. "Enar, Fulk's son," he said.

The name meant nothing to Elin, and she hadn't expected it to. Apparently it meant nothing to Anna either. "A Saxon," she said, "but not from around here."

Elin was cutting bread on the table. The man eyed it, a look of desperate greed in his eyes. "Up north," Enar said, "from the mountains." He was still staring at the bread.

Elin brought him some, along with a cup of wine, apologizing for the bread. "I'm sorry it's rather hard. To-day's our baking day."

Routrude hovered, torn between the desire to poke around, and curiosity about the stranger. If Owen was going to kill him she wanted to watch.

Ranulf went out, bringing some of the bread to the beg-gars, now gathered at the back door of the hall, and Elfwine's brother, Ine, came in. He was barefoot despite the cold. He paused near Enar, and looked him up, then down. Enar was dipping the bread into the wine and eating cau-tiously, as befits a man whose stomach has long been empty. Ine looked at Anna and Elin, looked back at Enar, thought about the matter, and finally said, "Brigand."

Then he walked over, and stood in front of Anna expec-tantly. She pointed at the bench by the table, and said briskly, "Sit down. I'll give you something to eat."

Enar finished the bread and wine. Elin supplied him with more bread, and some of the millet porridge Anna was heating for the beggars. "A man of few words," Enar said.

Anna had finished with the porridge, and since the fish had given up the ghost during the trip home, it was necessary to cook it. Anna laid it on the sideboard and beheaded it with a chop that sank the knife into the wood an inch deep. Enar jumped. Anna glared at him. "Few words," she said, "but to the point."

Elin approached Enar to examine his back, saying, "Please take off your shirt."

He looked up from the food. "My lady, no doubt you have the best intentions in the world, but if your lord comes in to the room and finds me in a state of undress, even in the most innocent situation with all your servants about, he will draw his sword and cut my throat on the spot. As things stand, I hope to get at least a running start."

Anna picked up a stone and began sharpening the knife vigorously, saying, "Ha! I hope you are a fast runner."

Routrude, who was tasting the porridge with a little bread and butter—purely, as she said, to see if it was up to Anna's usual standard—began to giggle.

Owen came down the stairs. He didn't notice Enar at first, but made straight for his chair at the head of the table and sat down. He had eyes only for Elin. He was afraid she would embrace him, embarrassing him in front of the whole household. And, at the same time, afraid she wouldn't.

Elin didn't, and he sat down a little disappointed, but felt better when she dropped a surprise kiss on the top of his head and fetched him bread, cheese, wine, and a basket of ripe blackberries.

Ine sat the entire length of the table from him, at the foot. He was stuffing himself methodically. His blue eyes rolled toward Owen, and he began to eat faster, as though he anticipated a shouted command to stop eating, and get to work. When it didn't come, he continued to eat rapidly, eyes firmly fixed on Owen.

Owen sighed, and applied himself to his own breakfast, still feeling Ine's eyes on his face.

There was a loud bang as Anna placed a covered earthenware dish on the sideboard. Owen, startled, looked over at

Anna and Routrude and saw the filthy, ragged man crouched near the fireplace eating, like Ine, as though food were a completely new experience. Owen's eyes turned to Elin.

She faced him and met his stare boldly. "I found him begging on the cathedral steps. He says his name's Enar, Fulk's son. He has a sword cut across his back."

Owen's face remained impassive. "You could bring me better gifts."

Enar tore at the bread with his teeth. The whites of his eyes flashed; they watched Owen like a wild animal's.

"Does the length and shape of that wound match my sword?" Owen asked.

"I think it does," Enar said.

Owen was wearing his own sword. He rested his hand lightly on the hilt. "Then you're a brave man," he said, "to enter my hall."

"Yes," Enar said, "and a starving one, but not more one than the other. If death comes, it comes better fast than slow. My neck is here, and my back too sore for fighting. If I did you wrong, I have done penance for it these last two nights, and not a little by day."

Owen turned back to his breakfast. "Penance enough for a small injury. I have but cold welcome for you, but not so cold as steel. Eat your fill and be gone."

Ranulf slammed through the hall door, from the back courtyard. "It's Gerlos and his men," he gasped out.

Horses' hooves sounded on the stone of the courtyard outside.

"Bar the door and get my weapons," Owen said, standing up so quickly the chair crashed to the floor behind him.

Ranulf dropped the bar on the doors. As he did, something struck them with a thud that seemed to shake the building. Routrude screamed at the top of her lungs, but Elin and Anna didn't waste their breath. The walls of the room were studded with weapons. Anna seized a boar spear near the fireplace and tossed it to Owen, as another blow shook the doors. The heavy bar holding them closed cracked in the middle, the clean wood of its center showing yellow at the break, but it held.

Elin ran in with his byrnie. He had just enough time to drop it over his head, and draw the sword.

Another thunderous blow struck the doors. The bar splintered, and they flew open, crashing against the walls. A horse reared in front of them.

Owen leaped forward, driving the boar spear into its breast to the cross hilt. The animal screamed and blood sprayed across Owen's face and the metal of his hauberk.

The rider jerked back on the bit, and the unshod hooves of the animal slipped on the low steps in front of the door. He fell, carrying his rider down with him.

Owen lunged over the belly of the horse, driving the point of his sword at the man's unprotected groin. He felt rather than saw it enter, because another blade flared above, between him and the sky, and he had to free his blade quickly.

He jumped back, bringing his own weapon up in a ringing parry. A second horseman was between him and the sun. Then a scream rang out, and the body of the horse struck his shoulder. He recognized Elin's voice, a war cry, and knew she had somehow distracted the horseman.

God, how he loved her, he thought, ducking under the horse's belly and slashing upward at the saddle girth above him. His sword stroke cut it clean, driving across the animal's lower ribs.

The horse plunged. The saddle, held by the breast strap, stayed on but slipped sideways, throwing the rider to the ground.

Owen's shoulder struck Elin's arm as he leaped clear of the thrashing animal. He saw the gleam of the axe in her hand, and knew how she'd distracted the warrior.

He didn't see the spearman at all. He felt a blow so hard, it was humbling rather than painful and saw the stones of the courtyard wall coming toward him. He threw out his hand to break his fall, sure that the spear was in his back and he would see its tip exit his chest, and know he was a dead man. He crashed into the wall, the back of his left hand breaking the force of the impact, skinning his knuckles to the bone, twisting his body like a cat, to meet his enemy.

The spearman was above him, lance pointed at his breast, driving down.

Elin screamed, this time shrilly, a scream of terror. Between the iron of the lance point, and the stone of the courtyard wall, Owen would stand no chance. It would spit him.

A big shadow snatched the axe from Elin's hand and threw. It sheared off the side of the spearman's head.

The last spastic jerk of the man's arm pulled the rein. The horse threw his head up and back, blood and foam dripping from the jaws at the bit, and shied sideways. The spear point grated against the courtyard wall to Owen's right, the swaying horror in the saddle still clutching it.

Elin shouted again. "Look out, he's up."

The man Owen had unhorsed was on his feet and coming, but he seemed to run into a wall. Legs still pumping, he went down, a crossbow bolt through his eye, protruding from the back of his skull.

Owen looked up. Denis was sitting on the sill of the upstairs window, his good foot bracing his back against the frame, spent crossbow in his hand. While Owen watched, he snatched a freshly loaded one from behind him, and pointed it at the courtyard gate. Gerlos, still mounted, sat there, his green eyes watching Owen.

The bishop bared his teeth in a smile of rage. Every breath he drew was agony. "Not a fortunate meeting, Gerlos," Owen said, beginning to walk toward him.

Gerlos raised the axe in his hand. The scrolled silver patterns of its inlaid blade glittered in the sunlight. Gerlos shouted up at the man in the window. "Only miss once, Denis, and your master's a dead man."

The blade flashed its deadly light at Owen's eyes.

Owen, ignoring the pain clawing at him, raised his sword and continued inexorably onward.

Gerlos's axe tilted backward.

Owen screamed, "Kill him," and threw his body to one side.

The bow thrummed, the axe flashed where Owen's head had been a second before, struck sparks from the courtyard wall, and in a clatter of hooves on stone, Gerlos was gone.

Enar gave a long, low sigh that conveyed as much pleasure as relief, then he laughed. "Fine exercise for a chilly morning. Sets the blood to moving."

"I'd as soon mine stayed cold," Owen said, staggering back to lean against the courtyard wall.

Elin ran to him. He turned, showing her his back. "Am I wounded?" he asked, in a whisper.

"No, I don't think so," she answered, running her hand down his byrnie. He flinched at the pressure against his ribs. "The hauberk turned the point, but your ribs knew its force."

"God," he said softly, "I must play the man, stay away."

Enar walked over and picked up Gerlos's axe and looked at it admiringly, testing the quality of its workmanship by balancing it on one finger. Then he said, "Beautiful," and tucked it into his belt.

He fetched the other axe from where it lay across the yard, some of the spearman's hair and skin still clinging to it, and examined the blade critically. "Less good," he said, hefting it, "but serviceable."

Ranulf was standing on the step by the door, a boar spear in his hand. Enar walked over, caught him by the arm, and drew him toward Owen. "You didn't see this one, Christ Priest. He thrust at the one who was trying to spit your skull, while the lady ran at him with the axe, kept the bastard occupied while you unhorsed him."

Enar thrust the axe into Ranulf's hand, and slapped him on the back. "This I'll give to you, and teach you how to use it. Lord Christ Priest, you have enemies. Best get yourself some men. Your lady's willing, but too tender for such games."

Owen was on stage. He felt as he sometimes did standing before the high altar of the church. The courtyard gate was crowded with curious onlookers. Some had, God knows how, gotten to the top of the wall and were looking down. The fight couldn't have been more public if it had been fought in the town square.

Everything he said and did now took on tremendous importance. The report would go far and wide. His every word and gesture discussed, to be praised or criticized, from the huts of the humblest coloni, to the halls of the powerful.

The story would be told around dinner tables, by women working at their looms, by men haying and plowing fields.

There were three dead. He'd just been in a fight that would become famous. The battle took seconds, but the talk would continue for years. It was by their bearing in such matters, that the reputations of men were made or broken.

Enar knew this instinctively, hence his flamboyance.

Owen drew himself up. Now that the fury of the combat

was draining from his body, ordinary movement was becoming increasingly painful. He gritted his teeth, whispering to himself, "Play the man."

This was rendered more difficult by the fact that Enar was now playing to the gallery. "Have I earned my breakfast, Lord Christ Priest? Is my welcome warmer now?" he asked.

"Warmer by the heat of blood, at least," Owen said.

Enar knelt in front of him. "Then will you have me as your man, Lord Christ Priest?"

Owen didn't want him. He was an outlaw, and a wanderer. He might even be a stray from the Northmen's camp upriver. But on the other hand, if he rejected him, he'd look like an ingrate to all those watching.

"Very well," Owen said, "but no man of mine may steal, offer insult to any woman, and if you are not a Christian, you must accept baptism and become one. For no man may serve me, and not swear allegiance to He who is my supreme Lord."

Enar's lips twitched, and his eyes glistened with mirth. He was maneuvering Owen and Owen couldn't do anything about it. He placed his hand on his heart, and managed a sigh of purely hypocritical sadness. "Your terms are hard indeed, my Lord Christ Priest, but so great is my love for you, that I'll accept them."

"So great a love, on so short an acquaintance?" Owen murmured. Taking Enar's two big hands between his own and looking down into his face, he whispered, "You scoundrel, I think you are very lucky that there are more eyes on you than my two at this moment."

"It is but a slight misunderstanding," Enar whispered back up at him.

"Odd," Owen said, "I thought we understood each other very well. You wished to kill me, and steal all I had. I wished to prevent you."

"And you did, Lord Christ Priest. Having seen you in action this day, I can well believe I was lucky to escape with my life, if not a whole skin. But will you have me?" Enar's face was somber now, his voice remained very low, so that only Owen could hear him. "I have done much evil, and killed among my kin, but never have I lied or broken an oath once taken."

Owen felt something warm and sticky on his hand. Enar's fingers and the sleeve of his ragged tunic were soaked with fresh blood, and that blood was his own. He had opened the wound on his shoulder when he threw the axe that saved Owen's life.

Owen tightened his hand around Enar's, in a hard grip.

"On those terms, as between men, I will! Swear by any gods you wish," he whispered fiercely.

Enar swore the oath enthusiastically, and at length, on Christ's body, blood, teeth, bones, birth, death, burial, and resurrection.

"Don't try to be too convincing," Owen muttered, annoyed.

Enar then said "Amen," loudly and jumped up, asking, "Lord Christ Priest, may I have the horse of the one I beheaded?"

"That was Boso," Routrude said. "He was very given to venery. The widow's ladies will miss him, such a good customer."

The yard was full of people milling around, asking each other questions, gaping at the dead men.

Elin was at Owen's side. "You said, 'play the man,' " she told him, angrily. "Not the fool. Come in before you fall on your face. Now catch his other arm, and help him," she ordered Enar.

"Boso," Owen whispered, "and he loved venery? I didn't need to know that. I didn't want to."

"It's the truth, Lord Christ Priest. You're beginning to look like one of the dead men," Enar said cheerfully.

Between them, Elin and Enar got Owen into the hall, dumping him into his chair at the head of the table.

Elin stripped off the byrnie and his shirt. Enar returned to his breakfast. "A fine fight, Lord Christ Priest," he said, gulping the bread and porridge as though he'd never been interrupted, "with no loud brags, or empty boasts. The first hardly knew the door was open when you gave him his quittance."

Owen slumped over the head of the table, as Elin examined his ribs, and a huge, purpling bruise to the left of his spine. Her probing finger found the spot where the lance point had struck.

Owen screamed. "God in heaven above, don't do that again!"

"Not broken, I think," Elin said.

"He's young," Enar said, gulping a tankard of beer, "and all gristle."

"Nevertheless," Elin said, a hard glint in her eyes.

"No," Owen said, trying to straighten up, "the count's men may return."

"Have no fear," a voice from the other end of the room spoke, "if he returns, he will get nothing and it will be costly."

Owen looked the length of the table. At least thirty loaded crossbows lay there. More were being drawn by Ine, working methodically near Denis, who sat on one of the benches, crutches by his side.

The bar on the front door had been reinforced with an iron rod. The hall was dark, though the day outside was bright and clear. The few high windows, on the alley side of the building, that let in light were now blocked by heavy wooden shutters, closed, and bolted. Denis had, in only a few moments, strengthened the building to withstand a siege.

With the front and back doors secured, the only means of entry was through the upstairs windows, and these were fitted with strong shutters of their own, and could be quickly sealed. The attacking force would be exposed to deadly fire from loopholes cut in the doors and shutters. A few resolute men and women could hold the bishop's palace against even a small army.

Enar grinned, his teeth gleaming savagely in the firelight. "He hoped to surprise, and kill you quickly. Now that advantage is lost. The count must find another plan. Unless he is a very fast thinker, you are safe for a time." He slapped his stomach and belched. "And even if he is, you have put the fear of God into his men. God and the devil both, dispatching them all so quickly to hell."

Ranulf and Anna entered, carrying the plunder taken from the fallen mercenaries—weapons, clothing, horse tack, and armor. They dumped it on the floor.

"Hell is where they went, and all unshriven," Enar added.

Owen gave Enar a stern look, as he strove to repress a smile. "I can see that you're going to be a difficult rogue."

"Who me, Lord Christ Priest? I, who wish the best for all men? And hell seems the best, and most appropriate place to lodge that company. Three against one they thought, strip the corpse then comfort the widows."

He winked at Ranulf, who turned pale thinking of Elfwine.

"Have you a woman, little priest? It would have given them great joy to greet her, once they stepped over your dead body across the threshold of this house."

Ranulf turned away appalled, and began gathering up the weapons and armor.

Elin was working at the sideboard, chopping herbs. "Time you went to bed, and let me poultice that bruise."

"To bed?" Owen said, trying to sound surprised and firm at the same time. "But I have not long been up."

"And had a full morning already," Enar said, his nose in the tankard of beer. "If you cannot walk, Lord Christ Priest, I can carry you. It is true," Enar continued, turning to Elin, "he is long, but narrow. It would be nothing to me to get him up the stairs. Besides, it would be an entirely new thing in the world for a man to carry a mule."

This was sufficient to get Owen to his feet, and on the way to his bedroom, with Elin supporting him. "You presume a lot, upon an oath," he snapped at Enar from the steps, looking down over the rail.

Chapter

9

ELIN had no sooner gotten Owen to his room than he pinned her to the wall. It was done so quickly that she was left breathless. Within a second her skirt was up, and he entered her body with a tearing thrust.

"Mule, am I?" he whispered angrily. "That is what I am, a mule, to bear everyone's burdens."

"If it's combat you want," she hissed back, "it's combat you will have, my lord!" Her legs came up and she wrapped them around his straining body and pumping buttocks. "You'll have your pleasure of me, but I'll have mine of you first."

She was pleasure, he thought, as he moved inside her velvety softness, feeling that unspeakably sweet caress of the womb, pleasure fit for a king. "Sow," he whispered, "bitch, come, bitch, come, spend yourself on me."

He could feel her breasts straining against his chest, through the thin material of the dress. He tore it open, one handed, so his fingers could find those smooth globes.

His heart hammered, the blood behind his eyes blinded him. He was deafened by the thunder of its pulsations in his ears.

She tightened her legs then, her body on his, drawing him along with her, up, and up into the explosion of agony, of ecstasy, and release.

"To die," he moaned at the end as he was rent by passion and the pain in his body, "to die like this, in you, part of you!"

Then they lay among the wolf skins of the floor, she gasping, he nearly unconscious.

She had trouble getting him to the bed, but she did, and strapped the poultice to his ribs with a linen bandage torn from the useless dress. She stood naked looking at the rag. "You ruined it," she said.

"Never mind, when I'm dead, you can take that big Saxon as a lover. He won't care how you dress."

"When you're dead," she answered, "you won't care what I do, so don't give me any advice."

She was mixing something in a cup. She raised his body with one arm and held the cup to his lips.

He hesitated. "What is this?"

"Chamomile, black poplar, steeped in coltsfoot wine, with a little honey. All harmless, and beneficial," she said, impatiently. "Now, drink!"

He did. The taste wasn't bad, only a hint of bitterness.

She began rummaging in the clothes chest near the window, drawing out a shift and another dress, a brown one. "Elspeth's castoffs," she said, "I was lucky."

"He saw you," Owen said, "that's why he came today."

"Gerlos, yes, he saw me," she answered indifferently. "And it may have been why he came today, but he'd have come sometime, and you know it."

He was sliding into a dream, drifting away, yet he was still trembling with fear and anger, it kept jerking him awake. "He wants you," Owen said.

"No," Elin answered, "he doesn't want me." She turned. She was dressed now and he realized he must have dozed for a time.

She bent over him. He looked into those eyes, her eyes, the color of the warm summer sky, blue as the cornflowers springing up from the long green grass. "No," she repeated, "he doesn't want me, I'm not such a fool as to think that. He wants power, and to destroy you."

Then her lips were on his, soft and kind, her fingers caressed him, cooling his fevered skin. He let the river of darkness carry him away.

When he awakened and came down to supper, he found the table crowded with four new men, all young, large, and timid-looking.

Enar sat next to them, smug, and self-satisfied. He nudged the nearest in the ribs with his elbow. "Likely looking boys, eh! I wish we had time to start them younger, but we must

take what we can get. I'll teach them the axe and the sword.
Denis can instruct them in the art of the bowman.

"They're the sons of your freeholders, so they know
something of arms already," Enar said expansively. "All we
need do is put an edge on them."

Owen studied the youngsters—hulking farm boys all.
They needed more than an edge. He didn't say so, however,
only, "Welcome to my table, and my hall." Then he put himself out to be gracious, and see to it that they were comfortable.

After supper, he summoned a council of war.

Elin, Enar, Ranulf, and Denis met in his bedroom. Denis
came on his crutches, smiling. It was the first time Owen
had seen him smile since he took the wound that cost him
his leg. He had lost weight, and his normally thin face was
hollow-cheeked and pale.

Owen took his hand. Denis gripped his, returning the gesture, awkwardly standing on one leg. "Thank you for my
life," Owen said.

"I'm not finished yet. It seems I'm still some use in a
fight."

"How is the leg?" Elin asked.

Denis looked down at the stump. "I believe you worked a
miracle, my lady. The swelling is gone, it heals clean."

"We'll get you another one as soon as possible. Gunter
comes tomorrow to make the brace for one of wood. You'll
ride with the men," Enar said. "When a swordsman hacks at
this new leg, you'll laugh, and cut him down."

Denis smiled again and folded his body into a chair. "It
would help, if I had something to ride," he said. "My horse
was killed the day I lost my leg."

Elin, standing near the fire next to Enar, looked at Owen.
"We have two horses, new ones, a roan mare and a young
stallion with two white feet. You killed the third, but the
mare has only a small gash on her ribs. I treated it, and she
will soon heal. I think she is in foal."

"Denis will have both horses, then," Owen said.

"No." Denis shook his head. "Ranulf should get one. Elfwine awakened me, and her brother carried me to the window, otherwise I would have been no help to you."

Owen looked at Ranulf. He was seated on a stool in the

corner, his back against the wall, smiling, pleased with the gift, and being singled out for praise. "Your pick," Owen said to Denis.

"The stallion," Denis said, "mettlesome, but a good sound animal."

Ranulf nodded. "The mare suits me. I put her in the stable after the fight. She's gentle, that's the best quality I can think of in a horse."

"Oh, well," Enar said, "I did ask first, but then I never cared for horses anyway."

"You have the axe. It's a fine one, that's enough," Owen said, seating himself in an armchair near Elin and Enar.

"How many men has the count?" Enar asked.

"Twenty-five good ones; others that come and go, not so good or faithful. Enough that if he presses me seriously, I must yield."

"You cost him something," Enar said.

"Even so," Owen answered, "he didn't loose his full strength at me, as you so ably pointed out this morning." Owen glanced at Enar. "He knows better now. Next time he'll come in force."

Elin put another log on the fire. "Your people love you," she said. "You fed them last winter when all the count did was take. They and many of the count's people would follow you in a moment."

"Follow me where?" Owen asked.

Enar laughed. "That's the problem, how far?"

Elin's face showed the rebuff. She turned back to the fire and stood staring into the flames.

"My lady," Enar said softly, "I don't mean to disparage your words or the gratitude the citizens of this place feel for your lord, but he is young, and yet unproven. They have known his generosity, but they have yet to see his strength. Can he attract men to him, bind them, and lead them in battle against a mighty foe?"

"Speaking of men," Owen said, "those children need more than an edge. How did you get them to come?" He didn't want to ask the question, fearing the worst, but he must know.

"I didn't," Enar said, attempting a look of innocence, an impossibility in his case. "Ranulf did," he said.

Ranulf had his chin on his fist, staring into the fire, not taking much interest in the proceedings till now. He gave a gasp of astonishment. "My idea! It was yours from the first," he said accusingly to Enar.

Enar sighed.

"I'm not interested in whose fault it was," Owen said. "What did you do?"

"Offered them land," Enar said.

"What land?" Owen asked. "I have no land to offer. Most of this valley belongs to the count, the rest is freehold, and some of it is royal estate."

"But you do," Ranulf said, "good land."

"Where?" Owen asked.

"The marshes," Ranulf said.

"Very fine farms it would make," Owen said, "were it not underwater."

"It's only underwater because the river gets in," Ranulf said.

"And you have a solution to that problem?" Owen asked.

Ranulf nodded. "Build a dike," he said.

"Who will build this dike of yours?" Owen asked.

Ranulf smiled. He looked angelic, with his fair hair and blue eyes. "You will, in spring."

Owen closed his eyes, then opened them, and looked at Enar. "Blackguard," he said. "Already you've been corrupting my household."

"Blackguard!" Enar said, trying to look as though his feelings were hurt. "Blackguard? I who am the soul of honesty, and since I am the soul of honesty, let us confront a few honest facts. The man has already once tried to kill you. You had a bit of luck, and he failed. He will not fail the second time, I'll make you a wager, Lord Christ Priest. Your lands are already promised to his men. They talk of them at table, and dice for them in the courtyard of his fortress, each believing his share secure. A cripple, an outlaw, and a woman, to go against them?" Enar glanced at Denis. "No offense, you're a brave man but . . ."

Denis smiled and nodded at Enar. "None taken," he said.

"It's a wonder," Owen said, "that I being so well defended, he attacks me at all." He turned to Enar. "You think they already have my goods divided among themselves?"

Enar laughed. "Oh, you've convinced them that they might die if they try to get them. Each wants the other to do the dying, that gives you time. I and your good steward today made some fruitful use of that time."

"The count," Owen said, "is the king's man, the ruler of this valley, this city."

Enar stared narrowly at Owen. "Shall I hang myself with my own tongue?" he asked, then shrugged. "Why not? I've done it before, and often. I'll give you your precious count, Lord Christ Priest, your king's man. Do you know why I left that place where we had our first meeting?"

Owen made no sound or gesture. He simply looked at Enar.

"The count's men drove us out," Enar said, "but not because we were brigands and outlaws. That we robbed, and sometimes murdered travelers on the road, troubles the count's sleep not at all. It was because we were not sufficiently successful, and could not grease his palms with enough silver to make tolerating us worth his while. So he is now rid of us, and he has installed some of his own men in our place.

"That's your precious count, your king's man. One who compounds with outlaws and murderers. What will he do next? Eh, invite those pirates upriver to come sack the city. For a large enough bribe he would open the gates and give you and its citizens up to rapine and slaughter, while he sat safe in his fortress and laughed."

"He is treacherous to the bone," Owen said.

The room was silent.

"Well," Owen said, looking into Denis's eyes.

"I will begin training the boys in the morning," he said, rising from the chair, and getting the crutches. "If you don't ready yourself to strike back, you will be destroyed."

He nodded to Enar and Ranulf, then smiled at Elin, and limped out of the room.

Owen turned his eyes to Ranulf. The boy looked shamefaced, yet resolute. "Forgive me the lie. What I did was out of loyalty to you. I cannot be sorry for that."

"There is nothing to forgive," Owen said kindly. "In the spring, I will try to make good your promise, and it will not be a lie."

Yet Ranulf looked away and glanced at Enar. The big Saxon sighed. "Best tell him," he said.

"We talked to Routrude," Ranulf quavered.

Owen accepted this news philosophically. "You were not backward about spreading the word. She will soon have me mighty as Charlemagne, and rich as the King of Byzantium."

"How much of this marshland is there?" Enar asked Ranulf.

"A lot," Ranulf said, "it extends for miles to the sea."

"You are rich, Lord Christ Priest," Enar said.

"Rich in empty promises," Owen snapped.

"Better any kind of riches than poverty." Enar grinned wolfishly. "Only let it get us through till spring, and I'll turn the first shovelful of earth myself!"

She was too quiet, he thought, as they prepared for bed. She sat in the chair before the fire combing her long black hair.

He took off his sword, and slung it by the belt over the bedpost, where he could reach it quickly if he needed it during the night. Then he pulled off his tunic.

Was she angry? He had behaved like a goat this morning, yet she could have turned his ardor quickly into something else. A hard blow on his ribs would have sent him flying, and set him screaming also. "Are you angry?" he asked.

"No." This from her curtly.

"What then?" He walked over to the chair. It had a low back. He took her shoulders in his hands and began to massage them and her neck gently. "What then?" he repeated, feeling the stiffness in her neck muscles unknit themselves under his fingers.

"Did you mean what you said about my taking the Saxon as a lover?" she asked.

"No," he answered, his fingers continuing their gentle work. "I was angry with you about Gerlos, furious that he so much as set eyes on you. I would rather kill you"—his hands tightened on her shoulders briefly—"than see you lie in his arms."

"Is that love then?" she asked coldly. "A thing that leads to murder?"

"I don't know." His hands stopped moving and rested

gently on her shoulders. "In all honesty, I don't know.
You're mine. What's mine I keep, I rule, and give my body
over to defend. I offer you my honor, and my life. That's not
an easy thing. It's within your power to break my pride, and
take that life, insignificant though it is."

She reached back, and catching his hand, pressed it
against her cheek. "You put it very simply," she said.

"It's not," he said, stroking her soft skin with his fingers.
"Such a gift rouses strange passions, fears of treachery, and
deep distrust. I'm not immune to them."

"No one told me it would be like this," she said. "Perhaps
it won't go into words, what I feel for you. It's not desire,
yet I love your touch, the warm softness of your flesh
against mine."

He bent his head. "Come to bed," he whispered, brushing
her hair with his lips, "come to bed, and let me hold you.
It's late and the room grows cold as the fire dies down."

They slipped under the covers and lay embracing in the
darkness, breast to breast, legs twined, her head on his
shoulder.

"Your mother never told you of what happens between
men and women?" he asked.

She laughed. "Oh Lord, Wilsa didn't need to. It was our
sport to surprise couples in the barns and hayricks, peeping
at them and giggling, and sometimes burrowing into the
straw to leap out and startle some pair panting in the throes
of lust. I got the idea first, and spread it to my sisters and
brothers."

"I don't imagine the couples you surprised found it as
amusing," he said.

She giggled. "God, no! When my parents got wind of our
new game, they quickly put a stop to it. By then I'd learned
all I needed to know. That's not what I meant. Seeing is one
thing, having the experience yourself, quite another. I understand those poor lovers we tormented much better now." She
burrowed her head against his shoulder, breasts and belly
pressing against his.

"It was the same with me," he said, running his fingers
idly up and down the velvety skin of her back. "When my
father tried to tell me about marriage, I couldn't see what all
the fuss was about, and I was sure I would never want to

bother to do 'that' with a woman. But later, when what had been a worm turned into a dragon, and I found that when it stiffened, I needed to do more than pee, I understood."

"Yet they couldn't tell us of this tenderness, this kindness between two people," she said. "It may be they didn't have it."

"Perhaps they did," he whispered in her ear. "It may be that each generation of lovers must discover it again for themselves."

He was caressing her buttocks; they were firm and smooth under his fingers.

"I think," she said, "that your worm is turning into a dragon."

"Yes," he said, "and I want to do more than pee."

"Ah," she said, as their bodies joined, and she felt him moving exquisitely within her, "I have found out why men marry."

"Mmmm," he said, "why is that?"

"So that all that they yearn for will be closer at hand than the chamber pot. It is laziness."

His fingers were at her breast, the pleasure of their touch excruciating.

"I am sore wounded," he sighed, "and not fit for the effort of hot pursuit."

Then their mouths joined, and her tongue searched his gently, silencing them both for a time, as they basked in a warm delight that passed softly into completion, and then into sleep.

He woke in the night, sweating and terrified by a dream he couldn't remember, but was sure it was one of those about Bertrand, then panicked when he realized he was alone.

He sat up, reaching for the hilt of his sword with one hand, the other groping at the spot where she'd lain, and caught her wrist. "Where are you going?" he whispered.

"Not far," she answered.

"There's a pot under the bed."

"A little farther than that."

"No," he said, drawing her back, "not alone."

"I have not yet brought my kinfolk to your side."

He pulled her down beside him and embraced her again. "I don't know if I want those kin of yours at my side or at my back. Where were you going?"

"To the Lady Well."

"No, not at night, and not alone."

"It's just below the wall."

"No, no one goes there at night. I don't like it." He knew the place of which she spoke. The Romans had built the count's fortress, and the town began to grow even in their time. But before them, others had lived and worshipped here.

Who knew what hands had worked the rock into a flight of steps that started by the fortress, leading down to the river, and the well. He had seen them and had taken the path once or twice, since the stairs were almost at his back garden.

Pregnant women went there to drink the water and pray for a safe delivery. Barren women did the same, praying for a child. He hadn't interfered, being a prudent man, but when he asked about the custom, he was told the well was consecrated by a saint, and it was to the Holy Virgin that they prayed.

He had his doubts. The steps were old, older than the Romans perhaps, with deep hollows worn by the passage of many feet, and he wondered if the lady of the well was not already ancient when Christ's mother was a girl in Galilee.

"They go there at night," she said, "and they harm no one."

"They might not," he said, "but others would, should any happen to meet you on the way."

"What am I then, a harlot or a concubine, that you pay no honor to my kin?" she asked stiffly.

"You are neither harlot nor concubine, and you should know that by now," he answered. "But I will not have you straying about at night alone, a prey to anything that might be out there lurking in the darkness. Come closer, warm me."

"Are you going to get the way you got before?" she asked, disapproval in her voice.

"You didn't seem to mind me getting the way I got before."

"No, but"—she yawned—"I'm tired, and don't want to be bothered."

"Tired," he said, "yet you want to go creeping around the riverbank at the dark of the moon?"

"Oh," she said, airily, "all I need do is let them know that I'm here. They'll soon find a way to speak to me."

Nevertheless, she curled up next to him, and they lay together spoon fashion, talking.

"What did you do with Enar?" he asked.

"Put him in the stable loft."

"That's just as well," Owen said. "The horses will get a whiff of him, and he will be welcomed as one of their own."

"Oh, be kind, he's been long on the road. You were not much better when we first met, and I was worse. Ine"—she yawned again—"is sleeping downstairs, with orders to rouse the household if anyone tries to break in."

"I must find a reward for him," Owen said.

"Don't bother," she answered dryly, "he has had his reward, twelve tankards of Anna's best beer, and a very sore head and sick stomach it gave him."

"My God," Owen said, "twelve tankards of Anna's best, and he is yet alive. She puts things in that beer. She says it makes it go further and taste better."

"Things?" Elin asked, alarmed. "What things?"

"Hops, rue, henbane," he said. "I much prefer wine, and rarely drink beer. But once I saw a horse dosed with it, and he was in a very strange state for a long time."

Elin began to laugh, her whole body shaking. "Oh, heavens, a horse, what of men?"

Owen shrugged. "Most reach the puking, pass-out stage before it has its full effect, but I have spoken to a few yet on their legs after having taken a lot of it, and they told of visions, strange lights, and distant music. Why, what are those herbs?"

"Hops is nothing much, like the coltsfoot wine I gave you, it induces sleep, but rue is eaten to see ghosts, and henbane drives the soul from the body, and if enough is taken, the soul will leave the body permanently and not return. It is a poison."

"How do you know these things?" he asked.

"From my mother," Elin answered. "She taught me much, and I learned more when I traveled among her kin."

"They are your mother's kin then?" he said.

"Yes, but I honor them no less. You need have no fear of their treachery, once they accept you."

He heard her breathing begin to become even and slower, and realized she was going to sleep. He shook her lightly with the arm he had around her body. "Promise me something," he said.

"Ummm," she said fuzzily, "what?"

"That you won't try to go to that well alone."

"No."

It was a flat statement, loud in the silence of the darkened room.

Owen was tempted to play the tyrannical husband, but he sensed that might not work with Elin. Besides, he remembered Gestric deferring to Clotild on matters important to her.

"Promise me then," he said wooingly, "and I in turn will promise you that we'll go together tomorrow night. Is that fair?"

She was silent for a moment. "Yes, it's fair. I won't try to go there alone, day or night, I give you my word. Now will you let me sleep?"

"Mmmmum," he mumbled. He buried his face in her hair, holding her close against the dream, against his fear of the dark, the dark that once surrounded him like the walls of a tomb, and from which he was sure he would never escape. The wood on the hearth still smoldered, banked by a mound of white ash, a faint light in the room and reminding him of the persistence of good things even among squalor, and darkness, and he slept.

Chapter

10

MORE men arrived in the morning. The leader was his cousin, Godwin.

Owen remembered him as a man who had seemed already old at the time, patting his head and telling him he was too thin and serious for a boy so young.

When he saw Godwin sitting at the table, Owen went over to the fireplace, where Elin and the other women were busy with preparations for breakfast, took her by the hand, and drew her toward the table, seating her in a chair beside him. "My lady Elin," he said to Godwin and the men sitting near him. "I commend her to your protection."

Godwin half rose and inclined his head to Elin, the four men with him did likewise. He and his men, few though they were, were a very welcome sight.

Godwin sneezed and sniffed in a resigned fashion and asked, "How is it, Owen?"

"Not good. I need men," Owen said.

"Well," he said, glancing at those seated next to him, "I've brought you a few. I hope your luck is better than the last we served. We cut our way out when the place fell."

The men with him were still armed. They wore the chainmail byrnie, conical helmet, and sword, much the same as Owen did when he went full-armed. Their equipment proclaimed them professionals. All were big, young, and looked as though they could fight like demons. Just what he wanted.

Enar had, Owen noticed, preempted the seat on his left. Denis was beside him, and then Ranulf, and Enar's four recruits, and Ine lined the other side of the table, facing the fireplace.

They were staring at the knights with a mixture of envy, admiration, and awe, with the exception of Ranulf, whose eyes were sad, as though he looked on something infinitely desirable, yet so far out of reach as to be beyond his highest aspirations.

Elfwine and Anna began putting food on the table.

"Any news of my father?" Owen asked.

"He's hard pressed, but holds," Godwin said, "or so men say, but these days, who knows?" He sniffed again, and made a hearty attack on the food.

"This," he said, between mouthfuls, indicating the man next to him on his right, "is Edgar."

Edgar was fair-skinned with a beard that was trimmed close around his jaw, black curly hair that was cropped short, and dark intense eyes. He, like Godwin, half rose and acknowledged the introduction politely.

Godwin pointed to the one next to Edgar. "Gowen," he said.

Gowen was even bigger than the blacksmith, Gunter. A blond, long-haired giant, with a bloody rag wrapped around one forearm. The arm must not have been too badly injured, since he was using it to stuff the whole of a small loaf of bread into his mouth, while the other was similarly occupied with a venison sausage. He inclined his head to Owen and said something that sounded like, "Giniff."

Godwin turned to the two on his left. Both were over six feet, cinnamon-blond, with long hair and beards. "Wolf the Tall and Wolf the Short. Their father had many children and lacked imagination."

They both nodded to Owen simultaneously.

The Wolf seated next to Godwin, evidently Wolf the Tall, since he was an inch or so taller than his brother, braided his hair like Enar. The other's flowed freely down his back. Both had full beards, and surprisingly dark, sapphire-blue eyes. Wolf the Tall ate carefully, because he had a sword cut across his face and mouth, splitting his lips to the teeth.

Enar, next to Owen, laughed softly, and spoke in a low voice. "A beautiful sight is it not, Lord Christ Priest, killers every one. Your stock is rising."

"Tell us," Godwin said, between mouthfuls of bacon and buttered bread, "of these lands that you have to bestow."

Owen was surprised. He hadn't expected Ranulf and Enar's stories to travel so far, so fast. Owen looked at

Ranulf, whose gaze fell to his plate, then at Enar, who found something among the rafters that interested him. "Marsh land, between Chantalon and the sea," he said.

Godwin sighed. He was a tall thin-faced man, bearing a strong family resemblance to Owen. Dark, fine hair and black eyes hooded by high, arched brows, a Roman nose, and a hard mouth with deeply etched lines around it. A disquieting face—intelligent, yet with the ruthless force of will necessary to make that intelligence effective.

"A swamp?" he said.

"More or less," Owen answered truthfully.

"A swamp, more, not less," Edgar, sitting next to him, interjected, laughing.

"Still," Godwin mused, cutting another piece of bread, and wrapping it around some bacon.

"We plan," Ranulf said tremulously, "to build a dike in the spring."

"Oh, yes," Edgar said, still laughing, "in the spring."

"How much land is this then?" Godwin asked.

"About twenty miles," Ranulf said eagerly.

This was, Owen thought, about as good a guess as any about the wilderness of fens, groves, and marshes that stretched between the city and the ocean.

A predatory look entered Godwin's dark eyes. "Is this salt marsh?" he asked.

"Oh, no," Ranulf said, sensing awakening interest, "fresh water, with trees and pools, water fowl, deer; rich, good land with heavy, black soil."

"Twenty miles," Godwin said, interested.

"Maybe more," Ranulf said.

"The size of this swamp is growing," Enar said, under his breath.

"Good assorts might be cut from that much land, even without a dike," Godwin said. "That's worth a throw of the dice."

"More, if it can be shut off from the river," Owen said.

"What of the count?" Godwin asked.

"Hates me, and will kill me if he can," Owen stated baldly. "His bastard, Gerlos, has his ear, and I think Anton wants the bishopric for his cousin Bertrand."

Godwin smiled. "It may be he will learn to like you better, when he sees you have some new friends."

"I can't think so," Owen said. "He's shown his hand too plainly."

"How?" Godwin asked.

"Yesterday," Owen said, gesturing at the splintered bar of the rear door, "his bastard paid a call on me, along with three of his men."

"And," Enar said, with a grin, "received a welcome so warm, it turned the hearts of those three who accompanied him cold."

Gowen laughed. "Is there any chance that he will allow us to entertain him again?"

"It's only too likely, he has twenty men or more," Owen said.

"Well," Godwin said to his men, "have we found a home?"

"Why not?" Edgar said. "I think we may be amused here. Let us stay, and the good bishop will at least feed us through the winter. Then, in the spring, we'll see about that land."

"If you don't eat him out of house and home, and then turn on each other," Enar murmured in a low voice, but not so low the remark didn't carry.

Godwin turned a pair of very cold, dark eyes on Enar. "Taking Saxons into your service, cousin, you are indeed in difficulties," he said to Owen.

"The Lord Christ Priest is a great man," Enar said sweetly. "Only a great man finds his poor relations at the breakfast table, looking for favors."

Owen kicked Enar hard in the shins.

Wolf the Tall laughed, choking on some of the porridge, and spraying it out through the sword cut on his mouth.

Godwin's eyes narrowed. "Worse than a Saxon, a Saxon that can talk. You should not have bothered to teach him, cousin, but left him dumb like his brothers in the north, grunting and snuffing around the roots of trees."

Enar's grin broadened, and Owen knew he had thought of some reply to Godwin's sally, that could end in a brawl. They were good eaters though. Poor Elfwine, heavy with her pregnancy, was running up and down trying to keep up with their appetites. He stamped down hard on Enar's foot with his boot heel. The Saxon's face changed, and he threw a look of pained reproach at Owen.

"I was just going to say that . . ."

Owen never found out what Enar was going to say.

Elfwine gave a screech, and jumped away from the table, eyes wide and shocked, palms against her flaming cheeks.

Ranulf leaped to his feet, fists clenched. Enar grabbed him by the belt and promptly jerked him back down into a sitting position.

Just as well, Owen thought. The boy was no match for any of these men.

But Elfwine's honor was instantly avenged. Godwin turned, fisting his knife hilt, slammed fist and hilt into Wolf the Tall's crotch, then up, slamming it into the point of his jaw. He went backward off the bench, crashing to the floor. Godwin shouted down at him, "Govern yourself. This is a respectable house, these are respectable women."

Anna pushed Elfwine aside, saying, "Go sit down, girl, I'll handle this." She helped the dazed man to his feet, pinched his cheek and said, cackling with delight, "Come sit down, sweetling, you may put your hand up my skirt any time you wish."

Wolf the Tall sat down, shaking his head, and made another, more subdued assault on the food. His brother rolled his eyes at him, as if to say, "I told you so," and went on eating.

Godwin was clutching his elbow, glaring blackly at Wolf the Tall. "I have strained it again. I had the ague last month. Twice the doctors gave me up for dead," he said with relish. "But it settled in my arm. My elbow is so sore that I can hardly use it. Sometimes I have the flux still," he added gloomily.

"Perhaps," Elin said shyly, giving Godwin a beautiful blue-eyed look of sympathy and concern, "all you need is a tonic; some rose hips, chicory, a bit of mead, and . . ."

"Ah," Godwin said, "have you some knowledge of the healing arts?"

"More than a little," Denis said. "The stump of my leg mortified and wouldn't heal. She cleansed it. Now the heat is gone. My appetite's returned. I feel a whole man again."

Elin and Godwin began an animated conversation about

diseases and treatments; Godwin relating his experiences with various and sundry medicines to an apparently fascinated Elin. These included many purges and Owen, pushing his chair back from the table, decided it was just as well breakfast was over.

Chapter

11

*E*NAR didn't believe an individual needed to be started out as a child to become an effective fighting man. He was capable and deadly himself, and was able to impress his students with the basics of staying alive without too much difficulty. He found Ranulf his most promising pupil.

"They can sit on a running horse and not fall off, though I would not tax them to perform any tricks. They know the most useful thing about a lance, that being which end is pointed at the enemy, where the trigger is on a crossbow, and how to reload without shooting themselves in the foot."

"Sounds promising," Owen said.

"Indeed, I thought so too," Enar answered. "Ranulf is the best of them."

"Ranulf!" Owen's eyes widened in surprise.

Enar nodded. "I'd like your permission to give him further lessons. He has the gift of concentration, and the eye and agility to go with such a gift. There is one other problem. They need gear. Of horses and saddles we have enough, but no armor, and only a few swords of the poorest kind."

"Wait for me in the hall," Owen said. "We'll go to the smith today."

He went in search of Elin and found her in his cellar. It was a large, dry room stretching the length of the hall above. A few, very small windows, more ventilation ports than anything else, let in narrow shafts of light.

Heavy granite pillars supported arches that upheld the weight of the building above. Between them were stacked barrels of beer and wine, sacks of wheat, and jars of oil. Bins along the wall held root crops. Sausages hung from huge beams, along with sides of bacon, sacks of salt fish, strings of garlic, dried leeks, and onions.

Elin was at the back, among Anna's harvest of herbs. Myriad bundles hung from the ceiling, brushing her hair, and surrounding her with a cloud of fragrance. Shelves against the wall held jars with supplies of those, already dried and mixed into specific seasonings. Others, made into wine, kept company with them. Still more, gathered wild and for purely medicinal use, had a segregated corner of their own. Elin was examining these bundles, and was selecting a few for her own use.

He kissed her lightly on the mouth. "What are you doing?"

"Preparing a tonic to build up Godwin's blood," she said.

"Elin, I would be very careful what I put in such a tonic. I don't think there's much wrong with my cousin's blood. This morning I saw him in a fit of pique stretch a grown man out on the floor with two blows of his fist."

"There is nothing wrong with Godwin's blood," Elin said, "but a few rose hips, some red clover, a little mint, and chamomile won't hurt it either, and if it makes him feel welcome to be fussed over a bit, I don't mind. I've grown fond of him. Imagine it, Owen, he has a volume of Doscorties. He presented it to me after breakfast. I've so longed to read that particular work. All my mother owned were a few abstracts ... I have those practically by heart."

"Be good to him then, but please don't poison him."

Elin's face stiffened. She turned away, lifting a handful of dried clover blossoms, looking like tiny fox tails, into a bowl.

He put one arm around her shoulders. "I'm sorry, Elin, it's not that I doubt your skill but ..."

"Never doubt it," she said quietly, mixing an equal measure of dried rose hips with the clover. "If I poison someone, that person is going to fall down dead."

He drew back, having second thoughts. He was suddenly conscious of how little he knew her. He studied her as she went on with her task; selecting some mint leaves, she crumbled them, inhaled the scent, then discarded the bundle.

"Something sweeter," she said, selecting another mint with broad, furry leaves, then added that to the mixture. "A

little chamomile, some wine, a white I think, and it's done."
She turned to face him, bowl in her hand.

"Could you really . . . ?" he asked.

"Yes," she answered, "as easily as this." She held the
bowl up, her gaze level and open, looking into his eyes.
"Anyone who's not a mere dabbler quickly learns how. Almost
everything I know that's a strong medicine is also a
strong poison. Like that beautiful blade you carry"—she
glanced at his sword hilt—"they cut both ways."

He lifted the bowl out of her hands, placing it on one of
the shelves. He took her in his arms. "You wouldn't . . . ?"
he asked.

Her face didn't change. "If the provocation were sufficient,
I might," she said.

He kissed her lips, stroking the soft, yielding body under
the gown. He felt her passion awakening, her response to his
nearness. She tasted of the mint, and of danger. She was
dangerous. He remembered the man going down with a
knife in his throat. He pushed her away to arm's length,
hands on her shoulders, saying, "Don't even think that way.
I would have to burn you."

"Yes," she said, "I know." Her face was still calm, eyes
untroubled, clear, looking into his own. "And you would,
wouldn't you?" she asked.

"Yes," he said, drawing her body toward his again, feeling
a stab of violent desire for her. The vast dim room, the sense
of isolation, even the heady scent of herbs, were aphrodisiacs.

"Sorceress," he whispered.

"Yes," she answered between kisses, "I am."

He pushed her toward some sacks of grain in the corner.
She made no resistance, her breath coming in ragged gasps
now, as his touch roused her own desire.

"Don't tear my dress this time," she whispered. "I haven't
that many."

"Then get it up, and quickly," he commanded.

She did.

After, they lay in each other's arms amidst the dusty cloth
of the warm sacks of ripe wheat. He nuzzled her neck.

"How did we come to begin this talk of poison?" he asked.

"I'm not sure," she said, "but I wouldn't think too much of it. There are many women who could do it, but they're probably not foolish enough to tell their husbands. Anna, for instance, I can see by those stocks of herbs she keeps that she has more than a passing knowledge of medicine. Gynnor certainly."

"Why did you tell me then?" he asked. "Why were you so foolish?"

She lay in a sprawl on the brown coarse sacking, hair spread around her face, skirt still tucked above her knees, her pale skin, in the gloom, reminding him of a lily at twilight, white, soft, ethereal, yet ghostly in its crystalline assurance.

"Because I trust you," she said, kissing his neck, his jaw, then his lips. "I've never felt like this with any man before, never trusted one the way I trust you. But it's strange," she said, "I hadn't ever considered using that particular weapon, not even when I was held captive. And I can't think I would want to use it here. I'm much more direct. A knife or crossbow would be my choice. Poison is the instrument of a coward or a weakling. I'm neither one."

His hands searched her body, dropping to the beautiful bare silken thighs and easing them apart as he turned on top of her.

"Oh, heavens," she whispered, laughing, "he's ready to begin again."

A voice spoke behind them. "I might have known!"

It was Anna.

Owen jerked his trousers up and his tunic down so fast he nearly did himself an injury. Elin wiggled away from him into the bin, laughing, and covered her legs with her skirt.

But Anna was hurrying upstairs, her back turned, muttering, "Tumbling her on the sacks of seed corn, I should have known and not bothered to come looking." She called back over her shoulder, "Enar is becoming impatient."

Owen yelled after her, trying to salvage his dignity. "Tell Enar to wait, God damned! What is it," Owen said, stretching out a hand to Elin to help her up, "that's so funny about a man caught in the act?"

"It might be that expression of frozen shock on your face, when you heard her voice," Elin said. "I have seen funnier sights than that, but not many. She was as embarrassed as we were, so don't be angry."

"You saw her," he said accusingly, "and didn't warn me in time to stop."

"No," Elin said, shaking her head, laughing, as she denied it.

"I came down here," Owen said, "to get something, and show you another thing, and then we were to go to the blacksmith with Enar."

"I believe I've seen something, and felt it, too," Elin said, still laughing wickedly.

"No," he said, pulling her toward another of the bins ranged along the wall. "I'm going to give you a reason to poison me."

"Don't joke about that," Elin said, but she was smiling. "I wouldn't. Someone else possibly, but not you."

He began quickly to unload the sacks of beans, stacking them on the stone floor. The bottom was made of wood. He raised that, uncovering his strongbox. "Not harlot," he said, meeting her wondering blue stare, "not concubine, but wife. I trust you, and I'm about to trust you with my greatest secret."

The iron box lay in a hollow cut into the stone floor. He handed Elin a key.

"Behold," he said, throwing back the lid, "the last wealth remaining to the Church of Chantalon."

It lay on a cloth in the bottom of the iron box, a monstrance of pure gold, in the shape of a star, the four points encrusted with rubies.

"Everything else is gone. This and the food you see around is all that remains of my riches and the Church's glory here. As you are my wife, I give it into your charge. The count took all the rest for the bribe, but this alone might serve one more time if another is necessary."

Elin turned away with a shudder. "Is that what he covets?" she asked. "If it is, why not give it to him, and mend the quarrel between you."

"So much for greed!" Owen said. Reaching down into the box, he took something out.

Elin looked at the cellar, at the provisions piled so opulently around her. "That's not wealth to me, this is," she said, stretching out her arms in an embracing gesture. "That thing in the box is only trouble. Besides, it's a sacred vessel, not really yours. You have no right to make me heir to it."

Owen closed the box, locked it, replaced the floor of the bin, and began piling sacks in it.

"The rights of the Church won't matter to Count Anton or to those devils upriver, if either one thinks they have a chance of getting their hands on it. So far, I believe that I alone know of its existence. Everyone believes all the Church's treasures were melted down, when Anton last paid the Danegilder."

Her face was somber, and even in the shadows, he could see foreboding in her eyes.

"Why so sad?" he asked. "I thought you were the one who wanted revenge, to be part of my fight."

"It may be," she said, "that I was wrong to want that. These last few days I've been so happy. You've made me so happy. I've been able to push away the troubles of the world outside, and feel secure in your love." He walked toward her, caught her hand, and carried it to his lips. Her expression of raw vulnerability tore at his heart.

"Hush!" he said softly. "Since Godwin arrived, I've begun to hope. He and his men are the best kind of soldiers. They'll put courage and confidence into those boys Enar and Ranulf found."

But her eyes were still wide and desolate.

"Take heart," he said, "all may yet be well but"—his hand tightened on hers—"you have the key if the time comes and I am dead. Don't scruple to use that thing to buy your life, and the lives of our people. Now, promise me!"

"Very well," she answered somberly, "but then and only then. I give you my word."

The smith's house was in the lower town, near Siefert's tanner pits, close to the river. It sat on a large piece of land, with a garden and a small orchard, near the palisade.

The forge was set off by itself, beside the kitchen garden. The fire-pit and anvil were covered with a thatched roof, supported by four thick wooden posts. Gunter was leaning against one of these, a tankard of beer in his hand, when they arrived.

He nodded and smiled at Elin, bowed to Owen, and studied Enar with interest.

Owen knew very little about Gunter, except that he was a prosperous, independent artisan, who truckled to no man, not even the count or his bastard son. They, in turn, feared him, and not just because of his massive build or the assortment of hammers he wore tucked into his thick leather belt.

Gunter's family had lived in the city for longer than anyone could remember, and they had inhabited the valley before that. Some told the tale, in jest, that men of his blood forged swords for the Roman legionnaires, and it was a jest that might contain a grain of truth, because there were few in the city or the countryside around that he didn't have some claim of kinship with, by either blood or marriage.

Helvese, Osbert's wife, was his sister. Gynnor, Siefert's wife, was a first cousin, and those were only two of his many close relatives. A serious quarrel with him meant a blood feud with half the valley. A thing that might make even so powerful a man as the count tremble. Owen reminded himself to be careful and very polite.

"My Lord Bishop," Gunter said, straightening up as they approached, "you honor me. I wasn't expecting such distinguished visitors, but if you'll accept the hospitality of my house . . ."

"At any other time," Owen said, bowing in return, "we would be delighted, but today, we've come on a matter of business."

"Sit down here, then," Gunter said, ushering them into the space around the forge. "To tell the truth, it's more comfortable here than indoors, considering the unseasonably warm weather."

He turned to speak to a girl who had been standing nearby when they arrived, but she was already running toward the house. The girl came back with beer for Owen and Enar, a cup of wine for Elin. The girl handed around a platter of fresh-baked bread with butter and jam, made of honey, blackberries, and apples. She threw an almost apologetic look at Gunter as she offered the hot bread to Elin. "I had to bring some," she said. "It's such a treat when it comes from the oven, so fresh and smelling heavenly."

The girl moved away but stayed within earshot of the rest. She was big, with fiery red hair, braided into a half dozen plaits coiled like a crown on her head, and her eyes were the deep rich green of emeralds. The smith smiled and introduced her. "My daughter, Ingund. Now, what is this business?" he asked.

Owen unwrapped a chalice, and handed it to Gunter. It was silver but rimmed with fishes of gold filigree, eyes set with topaz. They leaped and danced over a delicate inlay of lapis lazuli, curved in the form of waves, edged with rock crystal.

Gunter turned it in his hands, looking at it with the appreciative eye of a craftsman.

"I need," Owen said, "gear for four men, mail shirts, swords, shields, knives, and caps of boiled leather, reinforced with steel. If the metal in the cup is not enough, there is this."

He drew his sword part way from its sheath and pointed to the rubies in the pommel. "I would never pledge the blade," he said, "but it will cut as well without as with the jewels."

Gunter returned the cup to Owen and pointed to the sword. "May I see it? I find it interesting and instructive to look at the work of other smiths," he explained.

Owen drew the sword, thinking that this was simply a tactful stratagem to get a close look at the rubies, so as to be certain they were genuine. But apparently it wasn't, because Gunter paid almost no attention to the gems, beyond giving them a quick look, to note their positioning in the hilt.

He stepped out into the sun, sword in hand, and looked carefully at the blade, studied the faint iridescent pattern of the woven steel, then whipped it through the air once or twice, testing its balance and flexibility. He placed the tip delicately against a post, and examined the workmanship just below the hilt, where it must be strongest, to take the force of a strike by another weapon. Lastly, he shaved a bit of the hair from his arm with the edge, exclaiming in pleasure at the performance of the steel, then stepped back to the forge, and placed it carefully in Owen's hands, saying, "Beautiful, I cannot fault it."

"Yes," Owen said proudly, returning the sword to its sheath, "it was a gift from my father on the occasion of the cutting of my first beard, when I came to manhood."

"No," Gunter said, seating himself, and picking up his tankard of beer, "we cannot do business on those terms."

Owen was taken aback. "It's not enough?" he asked, surprised.

Gunter shook his head. "It goes against my grain to take it. The chalice is a sacred thing, and the careful work of loving hands. The sword, why, by God, I'd almost rather desecrate a church than touch such a blade. Every part of it is perfectly imagined, the very gems themselves are important to its balance and firm the grip of the hand on the hilt."

"These are hard times," Owen said.

"Not so hard as that," Gunter answered. "I'll supply what you need, and whenever you can, you'll make it good." He grinned, took a pull on the beer, and winked at Owen over the edge of the tankard. "Remember me when you build that dike."

Enar looked uncomfortable, and shifted his feet, glancing down at the stones of the floor.

Owen flushed unhappily, saying, "That may be a vain promise; this is money in hand."

"No," Gunter said, "you're known for having a word, even"—he glanced at Enar—"when it's the word of others you must make good. Last winter you turned away no one hungry from your door, and I have no doubt that you'll feed all who come this winter. Some of those were my kin. You helped many who were hard-pressed, and saved a few who were at their wits' end, and ready to despair. You," he said forcefully, "don't know the good you did, because some are so stiff-necked that they would never admit how close they were to the bone."

Owen raised the cup. "It's no sin to take this. It's never been consecrated or used."

"Then say a blessing over it and put it in the church. My gift, that those who take the sacrament from it may delight in its beauty, and the skill of its maker. Now, let's get to the details of what you'll need for your men."

There was one other problem on Owen's mind, but he couldn't think of any way to broach it tactfully. He wanted his men to have the best possible protection, yet, in a sense, he was accepting a gift from the blacksmith. He would seem ungrateful if he complained of the quality once the arms were made. But Gunter seemed to read his mind.

"Are you perhaps thinking," Gunter said, "that since this is an offering, I might skimp a bit, cut a few corners, to save myself trouble or expense?"

"It would be only human nature to . . ." Owen began.

The big man shook his head. "No, they'll have the best, I give you my word, my personal assurance. Besides, I mean to have help with this. Siefert and Osbert owe me a few favors."

He stood up, walked over to a corner of the forge, rummaged in a box of odds and ends, and came back with some swatches of ring mail, and handed them to Owen. "Now," he said, "these are the types I commonly make. As to shields, I favor ox hide, more than one thickness, but one must also consider the weight on the arm of the bearer."

"Any stout hide, more than one thickness," Owen said, "I've found performs better . . ."

Elin stopped listening as the discussion drifted away into technicalities. Besides she noticed that an uncharacteristically silent Enar, and the smith's daughter, Ingund, were flirting, and it was obvious they were both experts.

Enar looked at Ingund boldly, but not too boldly, made eye contact over the tankard of beer at his lips, then lifted the tankard slightly to her and smiled.

Ingund lowered her eyes modestly, but within a few seconds, raised them, and met his gaze again.

Enar looked Ingund up and down, not an undressing sort of look, more a polite one of appraisal and approval.

Ingund turned her head, showing him a profile, and played with the wisps of hair at the base of her neck. The upraised arm lifted her breasts slightly, they were ample, and cleavage showed at the square-cut neck of her dress. Then she looked Enar over slowly from under her long lashes, eyes lingering at his crotch. She raised the other arm, pretending to fuss with her hair, and still more cleavage appeared rising above the cloth. Enar's eyes dwelt on it, lovingly.

She dropped her arms, turned her face toward Enar again, and looked him boldly up and down. This *was* an undressing sort of stare. He returned it, beer forgotten in his hand, eyes starting at her feet and slowly coming up, back to her face again.

Then she turned, smiling wickedly back over her shoulder, and flashing an emerald glance at Enar from under lowered eyelids, walked slowly away with a decided swaying motion of her hips that Elin hadn't noticed before.

"A fine figure of a woman," Enar said to the smith.

Owen and Gunter had been entirely absorbed by their conversation. "Eh?" Gunter said. "What?"

"I said," Enar repeated, "a fine figure of a woman."

Gunter glanced at Ingund, who was entering the house across the garden. "Ingund, yes, she is, and a better man than most."

It was true, Elin thought. Ingund was as tall as Owen, and her shape, though pleasingly feminine, was well-muscled and powerful.

"Is she wed?" Enar asked.

"No," the smith said, "and she crippled the last who asked for her hand."

"Perhaps," Enar suggested, "he pressed his suit too ardently."

"Forcefully," Gunter said, "is more the word, and he soon found out Ingund isn't a woman to be trifled with. Ingund," the smith shouted over at the house, "come here." She came, picking her way delicately among the garden beds.

The smith pointed at Enar. "This man admires you. What do you think of him?"

Enar rose to his feet.

Ingund looked him up and down again. Enar was impressive, Elin thought. A few inches taller even than Ingund, he'd managed, at some time in the last day or so, to wash, and was wearing clean clothes that Anna found for him. He'd scraped most of the stubble from his cheeks and his broad shoulders and powerful arms filled the shirt and tunic well.

Ingund, eyes alight with mischief, stepped forward, reached out one hand, pushed back Enar's lips with her thumb and looked at his teeth. Enar was so shocked, he just stood there, mouth open, allowing it to happen. Then he jerked back. "What am I," he shouted, "a horse?"

Ingund shrugged. "Horses or men," she said, "you can tell a lot by the teeth. You're strong, not drunken, but not as young as you look. What's on your mind, a tumble, or will you stand by me?"

"You're a plainspoken woman," Enar said. "Are you a scold?"

"No, I have no patience with women that do. I like a quiet life. But you need never fear you won't know where you stand with me. I'll let you know."

Enar frowned and scratched his beard. "You can't tell how the world will go, but this is my home now and, as long as it is, I'll stand by you. It gives a man a bad name to go changing women all the time. Besides, with a toothsome lass like you"—he grinned—"if I stayed gone too long I might come back and find you with another."

"That you would," Ingund said, hands on her hips. "Accept that as a certainty. A wise man looks after his wife first; what he does then is his own business. Well," she continued, "you never know how a shoe will fit till you try it."

"We're to it then," Enar said.

"Yes," Ingund said, "if you can bed me, you may wed me." She jumped back. "Now, and you are a man, do it!" She took off running for the house.

Enar gave a yell of delight, tossed off the rest of his beer, and set the tankard down. He crossed the garden with an impressive burst of speed, and was right behind her when she entered the door. A second later he came flying out, picked himself up, and single-mindedly ran right back in.

The smith raised his tankard in salute. "A brave man."

A resounding crash and the sound of splintering wood came from the house.

Gunter raised the tankard again. "I like a man willing to pay the price of his pleasures."

Owen stepped forward, hand on his sword hilt. "I don't know Enar that well," he said anxiously, "he may do her some harm."

Another resounding crash, one so loud the house shook.

"No, he won't," Gunter said darkly, "not if he knows what's good for him, he won't."

Silence. The three looked at each other apprehensively. Then a feminine cry. It was not a cry of pain. Then another, and yet another.

They all relaxed, but Owen looked uncomfortable. Elin's cheeks burned.

Gunter smiled, a pleased smile. "She seems well satisfied with her bargain," he said.

That evening Godwin and his men gave Ine and the four recruits a lesson in the art of the drinking bout. Godwin and the knights had started earlier in the day, but the four recruits were catching up fast. Ine put away beer much as though he had a suction apparatus at the end of his neck.

Godwin was singing, with Wolf the Tall harmonizing an accompaniment. Godwin did many things well, but singing wasn't one of them. His voice reminded Owen of a raven with laryngitis, and his accompanist, Wolf the Tall, emitted sounds reminiscent of a cicada serenade on a warm summer day.

Next to them, Edgar, the soberest man at the table, wore a dress, or at least a long tunic that strongly suggested a dress. It was green silk, with a silver border on the bottom. A young man slipped into the door of the hall and beckoned to him. Edgar hurried over to join him. He and the young man embraced, and kissed each other on the mouth.

Owen looked away, mildly shocked and even embarrassed. They eased out of the door together.

Gowen and Wolf the Short were trying to question Ine. "Do you never say more than one word?" Gowen asked drunkenly.

Ine emptied his tankard, and shoved it toward Gowen, who had the jug. "More," he said loudly.

"Don't give him any until he says two words in succession," Gowen said.

Ine glowered and bared his teeth at Gowen. "Beer," he roared.

Gowen grinned, raising two fingers. "Two words," he said, "strung together properly."

"Give it to him," Wolf the Short said. "You're in no shape for a fight, you can't stand up."

Gowen turned his attention to Wolf the Short. "I can stand up," Gowen insisted.

"No, you can't," Wolf the Short said. "I know," he said with a profundity of alcoholic wisdom, "because I can't stand up and when I can't, you never can either."

Ine smacked the tankard on the table top. "Beer," he bellowed.

Wolf the Short refilled his tankard.

"Thank you," Ine said quietly. No one noticed.

Wolf the Short and Gowen continued their argument about whether or not Gowen could stand up. Ine took the jug, with the remaining beer, and crawled under the table.

One of the recruits was sleeping now, with his head on the table top. Another, kneeling on the floor, was being violently sick in a chamber pot. Godwin and his companion continued singing.

Ranulf stood at Owen's elbow. "What should I do, sir?"

"Lock up your wife," Owen said.

"I've done that," Ranulf said, "though I think they're past the point of lust."

"Nearly past the point of speech, I think," Owen said. "Bar the door."

"I've done that, too," Ranulf said.

Owen nodded. "Empty all the available chamber pots."

"Anna did that before she went to bed," Ranulf said.

"Where are Enar and Ingund?"

"In the stable, tearing down the loft. Never have I seen such a combination of war and lechery. Between bouts of lovemaking, he shows her how to throw his axe."

"You've done your duty," Owen said.

"Then I'm going to bed."

"You don't want to stay and join in the fun?" Owen asked.

"No," Ranulf said. "Why would I want to be sick to my stomach tonight and have a headache in the morning? Elfwine is waiting for me." He turned and left.

Ranulf, Owen thought, had the right idea. He rose, and bade the company around the table good night. No one heard him, and he withdrew to his room. No one noticed.

Chapter

12

*E*LIN was wearing a white dress, embroidered with yellow at the sleeves and neck. A dark mantle covered her shoulders. "Isn't it lovely?" she said. "Anna made it for me. The yellow is supposed to be gold, but there is no more gold now, not even thread. I'll go to the well tonight," she said. "Remember your promise?"

He did. Elin's kin. He tried to think of what he knew of them, of the tales he'd heard. They were puzzling, and contradictory.

They were said to be immortal, yet were afraid of humans, and hid or ran away at their approach. Yet there were those they trusted, and they traded with them, sometimes making them rich, for they had all manner of nice things at their disposal: animal skins of the softest and finest fur, wild honey, amber, and sometimes even gold.

They never cheated any of those so trusted, and no one cheated them. If any cheated or injured one of them, that man or woman was followed by ill luck for a long time. At least it seemed like ill luck. Who knows why a beast strays, a horse pulls up lame before the farmer finishes plowing? Milk sours in the jar, and rats and mice do get into the grain. It takes no supernatural intervention for these things to happen.

There were stories of them stealing babies from their cradles, but he had personally never encountered a case. These were, as most ghost stories, something that happened to a friend of a friend of the teller. Owen greeted these reports with some skepticism. Many left offerings, usually of food and drink, near their trees and wells. As she had said, "It never hurts to have friends."

He armed himself, wearing byrnie and sword. Elin laughed at him, shaking her head. "They won't harm you.

They don't harm anyone, not even each other. I've never seen an adult so much as strike a child."

"How do they learn then?" he asked.

"By love and imitation," Elin said with a smile. "The way all children learn. Were your parents harsh with you?"

It was true, Owen thought. Gestric was hard to the extent that he expected his sons and daughters both to bear pain and discomfort without whining or complaining. But he seldom struck them. He sternly forbade quarrels that came to blows in his house or at his table. He was similarly well behaved with his dependents and even slaves. As a result, he was trusted and well liked by almost all the household.

"No, I don't suppose they were," he answered, as he ushered her down the stairs.

The company at the table appeared even more relaxed than they had earlier. They didn't notice as Elin and Owen left quietly by the back door.

The fortress loomed above them as Owen followed the stone stairs down to the river, its squat shape black against the star-studded sky. From inside its walls came the sound of laughter and drunken revelry.

Owen was relieved to know that the count's men were in no better shape to begin a fight than his were. The wind was rising and stung his cheeks with chill. The ancient stairs curved along the face of the virgin rock, going down and then under it. Only when he was sure that the light would be cut off from any eyes watching from above, did Owen kindle the torch he carried.

"There's a real storm coming," he whispered to Elin. "In the morning it will be very cold. Do you think they would come here on a night like this?" He was feeling his way cautiously from step to step. The wind whipped the torch, the flame hissed and sputtered—at times it nearly went out.

"We can but try," she answered. "If they don't come, I can leave some token so they can find me."

Below them the river rushed past, glinting in the faint starlight like a ribbon of obsidian. The thick growth of holly, willow, and laurel that lined the banks screened the well's grotto. The entrance was about twenty feet above the waterline.

The spring seeped from a crack in the rock and trickled

into a stone basin. He ducked under the overhang of the
opening, and examined the little room in the torchlight. It
was empty. The overflow spilled from the stone basin,
through the door, down across two limestone ledges into the
black serpent of the river.

Owen pushed his torch into a crack in the rock wall and
spread his mantle on the stone floor for Elin to sit on.

Before she did, she bent over the basin and drank from the
well, then took something from the breast of her gown and
poured it into the water; the scent of roses filled the tiny
chamber.

"What are you doing?" Owen whispered.

"I made an offering," she said, "oil of roses. It's very precious and her favorite flower."

Then she sat down beside him, casting aside her mantle.
Despite the chill of the air outside, the warmth of the day
lingered in the tiny cave.

"Who is the lady of this place?" Owen asked.

His voice was hushed. He felt compelled to whisper, the
silence was so intense. The only sound was the hiss and
crackle of the torch as the flames slowly consumed the
pitch-covered wood, and the trickle of water from the basin
to the floor.

"The lady is the lady. She has no other name," Elin said,
"not to them or to my mother."

"They worshiped her?" Owen asked.

"No," Elin said, "she cannot be worshiped because she is
always present. The rivers and wells flow from her breast,
and all life rises from her womb, and returns to it. She nour-
ishes, protects, feeds, clothes, and kills. The spirits and the
gods are her children. But it is only polite to make an offering. Who knows, she may acknowledge my greeting."

Owen knelt upright on the floor, the feeling of timelessness creeping deeper and deeper into his senses until it
seemed to permeate his very bones.

Before his people came, and even before the Romans, this
little room opened into another world, a world where there
was only the forest. Did it somehow still open to that world,
a place younger and more innocent, free of the men above in
the fortress, greedy for his possessions and his life; or those

camped upriver, with their savagery and attachment to rape and slaughter.

Might they not sleep here together, he and Elin, and waken finding town and fortress vanished into time, and around them only a vast sunlit wilderness of forest, stretching away into the misty blue distance.

She was also kneeling upright on the mantle, the way he'd first seen her naked on the wolf skins.

"Listen," she whispered, "it's the wind."

The trees and brush along the river bank sighed deeply, as if in answer to the cry of the heavens. A gust sucked at the air in the grotto, bringing in the damp, sweet smell of rain. The torch on the wall guttered, then flared.

Elin's eyes glowed in the light, blue as the sky and flowers of his lost springtime.

"Take off the dress, I want you," he whispered, his voice a rasp of desire.

"No," she whispered.

He knelt in front of her and stroked her breasts through the cloth of the dress. "Worried about what the lady will think?" he asked.

"The lady of this place would only think it a fine offering," she breathed, "fairer than the scent of roses."

Her nipples stiffened under the dress. She pulled it off and the shift under it, moaning. "Oh God, I can't resist you, you're like some fire in my blood."

He kissed her lips, her neck, her breasts.

"Fire," she whispered, "running through my veins. I burn with an agony and a pleasure."

Outside the wind sighed and the rain began, slapping and pattering among the leaves of the trees, harder and harder, becoming a downpour.

"Stand up," he said.

She did, naked, and towered over him.

He threw hauberk and clothing aside and knelt at her feet. Head thrown back, she was as faceless as the earth itself, some goddess in the dim light—milk-white breast, the dark hollow of the belly, below it the soft mound of ecstasy.

This must be the way the rain loves the earth, he thought, falling, spreading across the enameled surfaces of leaves, parting the blades of grass, running down the petals of a flower, until it enters the golden cup.

He probed gently with his tongue. She moaned softly but didn't move.

This is from whence I come, he thought, this rich softness. Here I return my fire. His rapture was a golden light in his veins.

He felt her response in his own body. Her hands were in his hair, pressing his mouth against her quivering flesh.

Then he *was* her and his tongue a lance of delight echoing in his own loins. He drank her body as the earth soaks up the rain. And like the rain, he wanted to enter that warm darkness, and rise among the meadow flowers into the light.

He stood and, catching her in his arms, lowered her to the floor beneath him. She throbbed with desire, blue eyes open, lips parted, breasts rising and falling with each panting breath. He closed his eyes and entered her slowly, feeling at once the voluptuous pleasure of filling and being filled. An absolute totality of ecstasy, as he became her and himself both, lover and beloved, as one.

He was afraid, afraid so much delight would burn his life away in one flaming instant. And then it no longer mattered, nothing did, because it was upon him like a breaking sea, shaking his body with an anguished delight, consuming them both at the flash point of pleasure and pain. He looked down into her eyes, and back into his own at the same second, just before everything burned away, and the world itself vanished.

He opened his eyes, he hadn't known they were closed, and was himself again.

She sat against the basin, pulling on her dress, fear and some awe in her expression. "I'm not sure we should have made love in this place," she said.

"If you do, you can learn many things, some you may not wish."

Owen leaped to his feet. The voice came from the shadows near the entrance. A man crouched there. Owen didn't reach for his weapons, there was no threat at all in the man's voice or attitude.

He dressed quickly, but left the mail shirt and sword lying near the wall.

The unknown man sat easily on his heels, waiting. Most of the people Owen knew were to some extent weatherbeaten. But this man's skin was tanned to the color and consistency of old leather. His eyes were so dark that they appeared black in the torchlight. His hair was brown, but shot with gray.

His clothing was as simple as any peasant's: soft leather shoes, leather leggings tied with crisscross bindings, and a homespun shirt. But no peasant ever owned a tunic such as he wore. The softest and supplest of deerskin, decorated with a pattern of triangles in red, black, and white, with a border of spirals and meanders, worked in dyed leather, at the hem and neck. It was simply cut, having no sleeves but only a hole for the neck. It hung nearly to the knees in front and back, and from the shoulders, as far down as the forearms.

Around his neck he wore the skull of a stoat, set with a jewel of amber. It was one of that kind with an insect trapped in the glutinous stone. This one was the biggest Owen had ever seen. A beetle and the shimmer of the iridescent wing cases faintly visible even in the dim torchlight.

He stroked the skull and the jewel idly with one hand as he studied them both, eyes bright with interest. Elin spoke to him in his own tongue. He answered at length in the same way.

"What did you tell him?" Owen asked.

"My name, my mother's name. He's heard of me and that I was believed dead. He's happy that I survived, and he's trying to figure out how we are related."

"Suppose you're not?" Owen asked.

Elin looked surprised that Owen would even ask such a question. "We are all kin, somewhere, somehow. When he can trace the connection, then we will talk."

The man remained crouching, seeming deep in thought, using his fingers to tally something. Then he said, "Ah," smiled and spoke rapidly to Elin.

She returned the smile. "We are close kin through my mother's sister. Her daughter married one of his brother's sons."

Another man slipped past the first and crouched along the wall, then a second, and a third. The next two were women.

Their dress was much the same as the men, as were their adornments.

Three children followed the adults in, bringing the number of people in the grotto to eleven. Owen backed up against the basin to allow room for them.

"What is it that you wish?" the man asked.

"How do you know I want anything?" Owen replied, surprised.

A soft ripple of laughter swept the group. The man with the stoat skull around his neck grinned.

To Owen's surprise a woman wearing a necklace of gold and rock crystal beads spoke up. "We are nothing to you, less than animals. From them you at least derive some benefit. Us, you would not even take as slaves. When one of your kind so much as sees us, you try to kill us or run away."

She looked around at the others for confirmation of her statement. There were murmurs of assent from the rest.

Owen, feeling foolish because he couldn't deny the truth of the woman's words, spoke. "Help me against the band of Vikings camped upriver."

"Why?" the man with the stoat skull asked. "They're not our enemies. They don't even know we're here."

Elin stepped forward and began to speak in their language. First she exhorted, pointing at Owen. Then she pleaded, her hands spread wide, her voice soft. Then she drew herself up, looking like a young queen, chin lifted, eyes flashing, voice commanding, pointed at her breasts, and ceased speaking. They began to talk rapidly, excitedly among themselves.

"Now we must wait," Elin told Owen. "It takes some time to decide things, for each must agree."

"The women also?" he asked.

"Yes," Elin said, "they are especially powerful, for the wells and springs that mark each band's boundaries belong to them. But Alshan, the one who first spoke to us, I think I won him. If I have, the rest will follow."

The rain outside was slowing down but the grotto, even with the heat of so many bodies crouched into it, was growing colder.

Alshan said one sharp word. The talk stopped abruptly. "The wind is from the sea and it drives the storm before it.

Everything, man and beast will seek shelter tonight, and so must we." He turned to Owen. "I will see you again in the morning."

Then as quietly as they had come, they were gone.

Owen stepped out into sleet and bitter wind-driven rain. He wrapped Elin tightly in both cloaks and led her as quickly as possible up the stairs.

In spite of his haste, it took a long time. The stone was slick with water and a thin coating of ice, and the torch hissed, sizzled, sputtered, and finally was extinguished halfway up. He made the rest of the climb in darkness, body pressed against the rock, wind battering him and rain blinding his eyes. Elin, behind him, clung to his belt as he felt for each step with his foot, slowly, one at a time.

They were both numbed and grateful when they opened the back door of the hall and entered.

"God," Elin said, "it was a dreadful battle and they lost."

The hall did look as though a massacre had taken place. But the bodies strewn on the floor were living still. The loud snores rending the air all around testified to that fact.

"The fruit of malt and wheat is ever triumphant," Godwin said.

He alone was still sitting upright. True, he swayed a bit, but upright he was.

"I'm old," he murmured. "And the old have heavy res . . . res . . . ah, burdens. While my comrades sleep, I keep watch. Besides, as the commander, I must prove myself the strongest and I have," he said, listing steeply to one side, then pulling himself upright, he began to take inventory.

Edgar lay stretched out the length of the table. He still wore the green tunic.

Godwin sniffed him. "Honeysuckle," he said. "This month the honeysuckle is in bloom."

The four recruits lay in a jumble of arms and legs near the head of the table. They'd gone down still fighting heroically; several pools of liquid, all evil smelling, attested to this fact.

Godwin stuck his head under the table. "By God, I see only six, I should see eight. By this time I always see eight, two are missing."

He rubbed his eyes and looked again. "No, by God! it's twelve, but it should be sixteen, I think it's sixteen.

"Help me," he appealed desperately to Owen, "they multiply so when I drink. Two or one or possibly more of them is missing."

Owen looked. The two Wolves slumbered peacefully in each other's arms under the table. Ine slumped against one of the trestles, a smile on his face, embracing a jug of beer. "No sign of Gowen," he said.

Elin's eyes searched the hall anxiously. It was sparsely furnished; nothing big enough to conceal an object as large as Gowen.

"We'll find him somewhere. He can't have gotten far," Owen assured Godwin.

"Ah, woe, woe is me," Godwin howled. "My comrade, my comrade in arms is lost." He lowered his forehead to the table, tears streaming down his cheeks. "Till he be found, and his bones given sanctuary in Christian ground, so will I mourn, cry out, and never be consoled."

"I doubt," Elin said sympathetically, "that it stands so ill with him that he needs burying."

"Or even the last rites," Owen said bitingly. "He'll live to swill more of my beer."

"It's true," Godwin said, lifting his head and refilling his cup, "he'd be more likely to die of the lack of it. But where can he be?"

Elin glanced around again. This time she gave a stifled scream and caught Owen by the sleeve.

"Look." She pointed up.

The walls were supported by heavy oak beams. There was a space between them and those that upheld the floor above.

Gowen was lying on one of them, stretched out lengthwise, arms dangling. It was a good twenty-foot drop to the stone-flagged floor below.

Godwin stared up at him, eyes wide, mouth open in surprise. "How came he there?" he gasped.

"What does it matter?" Elin said. "He'll stir before he wakes and fall."

"Do something!" Godwin appealed to Owen. "I'm not brained as I should be. Help him."

"I'll watch and see he doesn't fall," Elin volunteered. "Call Enar, he'll think of something."

Owen got a tight grip on her arm. "No, he'd make three of you and two of me. I want nothing that I need or love under Gowen if he falls. There are many things I'll sacrifice for those of my household but I draw the line at my wife. You'll come with me."

Owen woke Enar, sleeping beside Ingund in the stable loft, with a vicious kick in the ribs he'd like to have given Gowen.

Enar came awake with a howl of fury. "As Christ is God, had I not sworn a mighty oath that I'd obey you, I'd . . ."

"It will keep," Owen said. "Come with me and bring a ladder."

"A ladder?" Enar gibbered, staring through the open door of the stable at the sleet and blowing rain. "A ladder?"

"A ladder," Owen snapped, "and follow me, quickly."

"Yes," Elin said, "Gowen has . . . well, you'll see."

Enar saw, sat down on the floor, and laughed till he cried.

"Get him down," Owen commanded.

Enar sobered. "My lord, he weighs nearly as much as the horse he rides and eats more. With respect!" Enar's eyes rolled slowly, ominously toward Owen.

Elin shook her head. "No, tie him to the beam and leave the ladder nearby. When he's awake enough to untie the knots, he'll have the sense to climb down."

"You credit him with more wit than I do," Enar said.

But that was what they did, and Godwin staggered off to bed, singing happily to himself.

"My father kept his men in better order," Owen said once they were upstairs. Elin started changing into a thick woolen bed gown. In spite of the roaring fire on the hearth of their chamber, the air was icy. Outside the wind slammed at the heavy shutters and the whisper of rain changed to the rattle of sleet.

Owen sat by the fire, staring into the flames. Elin scrambled under the covers and pulled the thick wolf-skin blanket over herself, shivering. "I think I won them. Alshan is a great man and his words will carry weight. Some will follow him; others won't care, and if any have a strong objection, they'll probably leave the band for a time and join others that roam the forest. You'll know by nightfall tomorrow. They give sureties and so will I."

Something in Owen's mind came to full alertness. "What sureties?" he asked. "What did you promise them?"

She lay quietly in the darkness of the bed for a few seconds, not certain she should tell him. But he would have to know sooner or later.

Would he beat her? Would he kill her? She considered the prospect cold-bloodedly. If he didn't kill her, how much would he hurt her? Enough to keep her from running away if she had to?

No tie on earth or heaven bound her to him, except the ones, yet fragile, they had forged between themselves. If they weren't strong enough to hold, well, better they be broken now.

"I am with child," she said. "I will give it to them."

"You will what!" he roared.

He was out of the chair with a bound and standing over her.

"It's not yours," she said.

His eyes were flat black holes in the dim room, his face white, skin drawn tight over the bones. "You let me call you wife and you knew this!" he shouted.

Elin had seen the God-madness before and she saw it now in Owen's eyes. In a split second she was on her knees in the bed. His sword was slung at the bedpost. She snatched it from the sheath and swung it at him.

He leaped clear of her clumsy slice easily. He was the trained fighting man, not she.

Oh, God, Elin thought, the sword was so heavy. Owen handled it casually like a twig in his grip. But it took both of her hands to hold its quivering point at his throat. She moved from the bed to the floor and tried to back away toward the door. He blocked her easily.

"Stay away from me," she hissed between her teeth. But he kept coming. His face was emptied of all humanity. The dead dark eyes were black holes leading away into nothingness.

Owen danced away from the sword's tip, staring at Elin with a detachment born of absolute rage. He realized she was lunging for the door. No, he thought, she won't shame me by running screaming into the bosom of the household. No. I won't allow it.

She backed toward the fire, the sword's tip high, only inches from his throat. Her eyes, the length of the blade away, were blue stones.

In a second he knew her back would be against the wall. Cornered, she'll try to kill me, he thought. She won't succeed, but she'll try.

He ducked under the sword and wrenched the hilt from her hand. His fingers peeled hers back easily and he jerked her off her feet. As if in slow motion, he saw her going down—hair flying, eyes wide with primal terror.

Owen's rage ebbed. He snatched at her wrist with his free hand trying to break her fall. He missed. He saw her head strike the hearthstone, heard the terrible crunching give of flesh and bone, saw the hideous distortion of her features as she crashed against the rock. Her whole body jerked once and she lay still.

His body felt numb. He remembered her as she'd come to him at Reynald's, to his bedroom, so proud and beautiful, in her borrowed finery, refusing to be cowered or intimidated by his anger and despair. So easily can we destroy those things we love. Had his moment of wounded pride, his stupid frenzy, snuffed out that fragile courage? Would the strong spirit that survived so much anguish be ended as easily as this?

She was bleeding terribly, it seemed, her face the ashen color of death, mouth slack, blood pouring from it, down her chin and spreading across the bodice of her gown, staining it with its evil brilliant scarlet.

He knelt, closed his eyes, and held her against his shaking body. He felt a heartbeat, but couldn't be sure it wasn't his.

Owen knew a lot about death. A heartbeat, even some breath meant nothing. Many a man he'd seen die had lived for a little time after the killing stroke. Human flesh clings to life and doesn't relinquish it easily.

So he knelt, and prayed, "Let her live, please God, let her live, even if she hates me and leaves me."

What would he do if that heartbeat faltered and stopped, if slowly as the night dragged on, she turned to clay in his arms? He could see the pommel of his sword from where he knelt, the dark ember glow of the rubies, reflecting the fire-light. "That beautiful blade you wear," she'd said, "it cuts both ways."

He might want to test that rather than face his household and the town tomorrow with a dead woman in his arms. But for now, he could do nothing except kneel there cradling her, until she either awakened or grew cold.

"You hurt me," she said finally. Her tongue was thick. "I didn't think you could hurt me this much."

She sounded dazed.

"No, no. Don't you remember, you fell." He set her kneeling upright, on the skin rug. His hands shook so badly he could hardly hold her.

She swallowed.

"Don't do that," he said, "it will make you sick."

"Then give me something to spit in. It's staining my gown," she said.

A clean chamber pot was under the bed. He set it in front of her, then he searched her cheek and eye with his fingers gently. Some swelling, but the bones under the flesh felt sound.

The blood from her nose was a trickle. She spat a few more times into the chamber pot. Then that, too, ebbed. "I bit my cheek and tongue," she explained thickly.

Owen closed his eyes. "Whose child is it?"

"I don't know, one of theirs. A lot of them had me. What difference does it make?"

"So I could find and kill him," he said bleakly.

"And that would make no difference either. The seed is planted. I thought to kill it myself, but then I knew I could use it to bargain."

Owen's rage was dead in him, succeeded by a sickness in his soul. "Oh, God, forgive me, I've given my love, and put my soul in peril for a witch. Why would you destroy it?"

Tears were running down her face, mixing with the blood on her mouth and chin.

He was glad he was bigger and stronger than she was, be-cause the eyes that stared at him from the broken face were filled with as implacable a hatred as he'd ever seen.

"To save your honor," she said. "I know of no one here

who cannot count to nine, and I'm two months gone. So for *you*, I'd make the potion, and then drink it."

"Some die of drinking such things," he protested, agonized at the thought of such a risk.

"Some do, most don't," she said.

"But to give it to them," he said, unconsciously echoing the woman in the cave, "they are less than animals."

"Less than animals?"

She put her hand to her jaw. The first numbness wrought by the force of the blow was receding and she began to be aware of how badly she was hurt. A pounding headache, and sharp claws of pain dug at her cheek and tongue. But she mastered it and spoke in wonder and fury.

"Less than animals? I've learned all I need to know of animals from *them*, those animals who raped me not once, but again and again, until I pretended to be mad and rolled in the dirt with the pigs. I babbled and growled and covered myself with filth to escape them."

Her head was bowed, the room hazed away as hated tears poured down her cheeks. "And from you," she whispered, "you who would have killed me."

"I believe . . ." Owen whispered, wretchedly, "I believe just for a moment I would have."

"Yes." Her voice was weary. "Why didn't you draw your sword? Why don't you draw it now, and finish the work you've begun?"

Her head throbbed and wave after wave of dizziness swept over her, along with gut-wrenching nausea. She hated him, and wanted to flail out at him, but she could do nothing but crouch over the chamber pot, retching violently.

When the nausea faded, she realized he was holding her up, supporting her head over the basin. She tried to pull away, but found she had no strength at all.

"Sorceress, witch." His voice was very soft, his lips close to her ear. "Whatever you are, I don't want you to die. I can't understand you, but I love you." There was anguish and bitterness in his voice.

She was utterly spent, drained by nausea and pain, her body relaxed against his. She began to shiver and Owen realized that the room was frigid. Even near the fire, now burning low, the cold was intense.

Outside the window the sound of sleet was fading away and was succeeded by the faint, airy tinkle of falling snow. A first snow, its big flakes sounding like tiny, distant bells.

He had wronged her. The mention of the sword brought that home to him. If he wanted to avenge his honor, he should have drawn that sword and killed her with one clean stroke.

He carried her to the bed. She curled up, exhausted by pain and sorrow. He stripped off his clothing and climbed in, covering them both, and wrapped his body around hers to warm her.

The nausea seemed to have passed, but her body was cold. He clasped her hands in his and rested his feet against her legs. Her shivering passed and the trapped heat under the heavy skins created a gentle lassitude. The last hour had been as an hour on the rack for both of them.

And they slept.

They woke in the morning into a whiter world.

There was blood on the bed cover, the skins of the hearth, and Elin's gown.

A purple bruise extended from Elin's jaw to her hair on one side of her face. One eye was nearly swollen shut, the white shot with red; the other was rimmed with black.

He rose silently and dressed, leaving her lying in the bed.

"You've shamed me," she said, "and they will all know it."

He wasn't any longer in a rage, but he was still angry, a cold bitter anger that seemed to eat like acid into his vitals. "I've shamed you, and what have you done to me? I called you my wife, put you in charge of my household. Had you any kin here, I'd have gone to them and asked their permission to take you, as an honorable man does. And all this time you knew you carried the bastard of one of those . . ." His voice broke with the tears in it. "The shame is mine, for leading you to my bed, for loving you."

"I was a virgin when I was captured. Neither I nor the child had any choice in the matter."

"How could you be virgin living among such a people?" he said contemptuously.

"You still don't understand them," she shouted, "and yet you mouth your stupidities at me. They were my brothers, sisters, friends, and companions. I'll leave you and return to them. I'll find she who was my mother among them, and together we can return to the great forests of the north. I'll be free and the child will grow up free also."

She writhed in the bed. The part of her face not blue took on a greenish-white pallor and sweat broke out all over her body. He ran toward her, thinking she must be having some sort of seizure. But she sat up, gagging. "The pot," she gasped.

He got it under her face just in time.

The spasm of retching seemed to last for an eternally long time. Then she lay back and spoke in the incredulous voice of a sick child. "I'm hurt. The room is spinning around me, I can't even run away. Every time I try to sit up, my gorge rises."

He sat on the bed beside her, clasping her two hands in his and looking down at her face. "Do you hate me so much?" he asked.

She shook her head but quickly stopped because that movement brought a wave of dizziness also. "No, I can't hate you. I wish I could, but I can't," she said helplessly, tears in her eyes.

"Nor I you," he admitted. "Do you still wish to give the child to them?"

"Yes. They are powerful allies; you don't yet understand how powerful. They live in the forest as the fish do in the sea, coming and going at will. By night, they own the world, even slipping in and out of the dwellings of men. It is their art, stealth. The child will seal you to them with a blood tie. It's the only thing that would make them believe in you."

"Elin, think, what kind of a life would it have?"

"What kind of life would it have here? They can all count to nine," she said miserably.

"Elin, it may die!"

"So do many here die."

That was true enough. A vision of the infant he'd found in the marsh floated before his mind's eye.

"With them," she continued, "it will be honored, protected, and loved."

He stood up. "Elin, I beg you, lie quiet now, and let me call Anna. Don't do anything till your anger has a chance to cool. If we go on gouging at each other, you may do yourself an injury. I would . . ." He paused, as if it were a struggle to put the thought into words. "If I lost you, it would be as though a part of my body were torn away. As to the shame, that belongs to both of us."

Elin closed her eyes. "I'll lie," she said. "Say we had some wine together before we went to bed. I got up to make water in the night, tripped, and fell. Not wanting to rouse the household during such a storm, you assisted me."

"They won't believe it," he said. "Elin, when a man and wife have a shouting match and the wife appears the next day with bruises on her face, no one believes she fell."

"Some will, some won't. They need you and would rather think good than evil of you."

She lifted her arm and covered her eyes against the gray light that was seeping into the room around the shutters. "My head aches. Go call Anna, she'll tend me and clean up the mess."

He fetched Anna. She and, surprisingly, Godwin were building up the fire, trying to warm the hall. Gowen was down, the knights and men at arms sat around the table clutching sore heads, looking hollow eyed.

All he said was, "Assist my lady, she needs you." But the look on his face sent Anna up the stairs in a hurry.

She entered the room slowly, and approached the bed. Elin's arm was still covering her eyes. She raised it. Anna sat down beside her and very carefully touched the bruise, the bruise that almost entirely covered one side of her face.

"I fell," Elin said, "and struck my head on the stones of the hearth, in the night."

Anna's old eyes looked down into hers, filled with an ageless compassion, for pride that must be defended, and dignity that had to be preserved. "Yes, my sweet, my pretty," she said gently, brushing Elin's hair back from the still spreading ugly purple and violet marks. "Yes," she said, "of course you fell."

And Elin at last gave herself up to grief, sobbing without restraint in Anna's arms.

Chapter

13

O WEN went into the church. He was still sick with anger and guilt. He couldn't pray, but he wanted to be alone.

Standing in the cold gloom before the altar, he felt darkness all around him, and in his own soul. How could he blame Elin? What she said was true; she had no choice, and the child was utterly innocent.

He lifted his head and looked up at the Christ on the cross. The small, high, clerestory windows were catching the first light, and the crucifix stood out clearly—not an image of sacrifice but a reminder of the darkness that surrounded him.

It was a figure of death, and the painted wood showed the contorted body of a man whose death throes had been agonizing. The flesh was livid, and the wounds of scourge, thorns, and nails gaped open, raw, yet no longer ran with the blood of life. The lips were parted, showing the teeth all painted with the scarlet froth of death's finality.

He dropped his eyes. There was the penalty for failure in his world, hanging within the sight of everyone. Would he not look as that Christ did—lying in a ditch, his armor stripped away, body twisted, blood in his mouth, naked, feeding the crows.

The count was the king's man, but that kingdom was a failure. Its rulers squabbling fools, its minions corrupt as Count Anton was, ready at the slightest hint of danger to ride away or crawl behind his strong gates, safe, while the Vikings murdered and pillaged at will. No, nothing was left of the kingdom of the great Charlemagne but ashes, pounded by the hammer of grim necessity on the anvil of despair.

"He hangs upon the tree," a voice behind him said.

The small brown man, the one whom Elin called Alshan, stood in the shadows near the altar.

Owen's skin crawled. "How did you get in?"

"This place is old," Alshan said, "and has many secrets. The Romans killed the bull where the man hangs on the tree. The bull's blood fell on those below and made them strong. Before the Romans, fingers of stone picked out the seasons, allowing those who could read them to call the months and days by name, telling them when to plant and harvest. The grating, where they killed the bull, is still in the crypt, and one of the stone fingers is worked into the altar where you make magic to your God." He stepped into the light. "We came to an agreement more quickly than I thought. The bargain is made. You will be our lord also."

"The child isn't mine," Owen said bitterly.

Alshan fingered the stoat skull that hung on his breast. He shrugged. "I forget such things are important to you. But it doesn't matter; I saw you in the grotto together."

"What was that, a man's lust, a woman's acquiescence?" Owen said.

"No," Alshan said, "that wasn't what it was. It was an act of worship. You worshipped, in her flesh, the power that gives you life and she in yours. The woman belongs to you, and what pertains to her is yours also."

Alshan spoke the truth, and Owen knew it. The sense of possession that made him lead her to his bed also made him father to the child in her womb. No matter that it was conceived in the darkness of rape and slavery. No man, of all those devils who had her, could lay claim to it. But he, by virtue of the fact that he had taken her by force of arms and offered her his loving protection, could.

And if she had told him the truth from the beginning, he would have done nothing differently. Her pleasure belonged to him, her pain and any child she bore were his also.

"It's agreed then," Owen said, "but there's no going back. Hunt them, and they will hunt you."

The brown man's laughter was soft as the rustling of dry leaves. "Many have hunted us, and we are still here. Now they come seeking you this hour, by those paths along the river."

"This hour," Owen said, astonished. "So soon?"

Alshan nodded. "Along the river, near the farthest settlement from the city."

It was a test of strength. If he allowed them to raid the villages that surrounded Chantalon unchallenged, they would return again and again, until everything up to the walls was destroyed. The citizens, burdened with starving refugees of the countryside, would be easy prey then.

A few minutes later he was mounted on the bay, Godwin and his men following, Enar and the recruits bringing up the rear.

The hall doors were barred, and Ranulf and Ine posted at the loopholes with crossbows.

The city was a half-circle with its back to the river. The farms and villages stretched out farther into the forest along the river. It was the logical place to strike first.

They went through the city gates, steel-shod hooves of the war-horses echoing on the stone. Owen set the pace, a fast trot. He didn't want to use up the horses. It was a long ride.

The world around was covered with snow, blue in the first light of day. The sun, only just beginning to rise above the low clouds on the horizon, brushed them with a dazzling, golden shimmer of light.

The first village they passed through lay in deep purple shadow. Sleepy people stood in their doorways, women clutching children against their skirts, and gaping at the party of armed men thundering through their village at dawn. The new sun glinted on the pennons streaming from the lances of Godwin's men. The snorting breath of the war-horses smoked in the icy air, their steel-shod hooves churning the snow to mud.

Halfway to the next village the sound of the tocsin rent the air. It was being rung from the belfry of the church ahead.

Owen kicked the bay into a gallop. God! he thought, I might die this day, but I've never felt more alive. All the frustrations of the last few years fell away, those years of waiting, watching in the count's shadow.

The freezing air was clean and sweet in his nostrils, and though the shadows were still dark blue, the rising sun was laying an overleaf of gold on the purity of the snow. He felt the extension and return of the muscles of the powerful horse under him, and even the steady beating of the giant heart.

Godwin shouted, joy in his voice, "We're for a fight, boys! Faster! Don't let your lord outpace you!"

The village was closer, the hysterical clangor of the tocsin was a yammering in Owen's ears. It stopped and the priest from the village church was running toward him. "The new town," he shouted, "damn them to hell. The people were caught in their beds."

Then he leaped aside as Owen and his men dashed past.

Through this village, smoke ahead was a black stain against the blue of the sky. The new town near the river had only a dozen or so farms. Houses were in a cluster surrounded by freshly cleared fields, stumps still standing in them. The road curved, following the river. Then dead ahead he saw it—the houses were burning. They were still at their looting, black figures scurrying against the white snow of the street.

One looked up, pointed, and shouted. Owen heard the shout, faintly carried by the wind to his ears. They dropped their plunder and ran for the woods.

Owen and his men were on them like an avalanche. The burning houses flashed by, giving Owen a glimpse of the carnage in the stricken town.

A child lay in the street, its head a mass of bloody scraps. A man's body lay fallen across a doorway, a pool of blood near his neck; a woman crouched over him. Owen saw the pale oval of her face against the background of fire, looking up as he passed at a hard gallop.

Then his eyes were on the black knot of raiders running in the open just beyond the village. Owen knew a moment's doubt. Twenty men, twice his force, and more. Doubts or not, he lowered his lance and couched it, spurring the bay to full speed.

The men ahead turned quickly and formed a ragged line, shields overlapping, swords and axes raised. From the corner of his eye, Owen saw Godwin and his men spread out on either side—Godwin riding knee to knee with him on the right, the enormous Gowen on the left.

Then there was only the thunder of hooves and the scream of wind in his ears. The shield wall loomed before him.

The lance in his hand snapped with a ringing crack, numbing his arm to the elbow for a second. The shock of contact threw the bay back on his haunches. But the shield wall broke with screams of agony and the sound of splintering wood. The bay staggered across the line, crushing something under its hooves, and the remaining pirates were running ahead of them toward the forest again.

Owen pulled the bay to a stop and turned around. At least ten men were lying in the red and trampled snow, some dead, others still struggling.

Enar and the recruits moved in for the kill. Enar's axe flashed and one of the men fighting to rise lay still. The recruits leaped from their horses and took aim with their crossbows at the rest, finishing them in seconds.

Godwin and his men caught up with the cluster of running men. Owen was puzzled for a second. What was he doing?

The knights split into two groups, herding the fugitives together, then they were between them and the safety of the trees.

Two bolted, one throwing away his weapons, the other carrying his sword and shield. Gowen galloped after them, almost lazily it seemed. He drove his sword through the unarmed man, lifting him spitted, kicking and screaming on it. Then he threw his flailing victim on the still-armed other, running just behind. He went down. Gowen beheaded him in a spume of blood, even as he fell, with craftsmanlike precision.

The remaining raiders bunched themselves together tightly, clinging to their weapons, shields up. For a few seconds it was a frozen tableau—the knights on their horses, lances lowered, chivying the knot of men across the snow-covered stubble of the fields.

Then the wind changed, bringing the smoke of the flaming town to Owen's nostrils, and with it, the stench of burning flesh. He threw down the stump of his broken lance and drew his sword. "Let's make an end."

The men with Enar howled.

"Kill them all," Owen screamed.

Enar and the crossbowmen dashed forward.

More men ran past him, and Owen realized that the priest from the neighboring village, the one who'd sounded the alarm, had mustered all the able-bodied men of that town and sent them to help. They carried a fearsome array of improvised weapons—clubs, flails, knives, and axes.

Owen rode back into the town. The big priest was there trying to gather up the women.

He struggled with one in the center of the snowy street. "The baby," she screamed despairingly, "the baby."

The priest held her, arms around her body. "My sweet sister, there's nothing alive in that house," he said.

Nothing alive in any of them, Owen thought. They were all blazing. The furnacelike heat poured from the doorways, melting the thin covering of snow in the muddy street.

Owen dismounted. Another woman, near the one he'd seen from the horse as he rode past, was still trying to drag a body into the street. It was a futile effort. The man's throat was cut. But repeatedly she challenged the heat of the fire, trying to catch him by the arm and pull him away from the flames.

Owen grabbed her by the shift, bunching the fabric in his hand, and thrust her at the priest. A few of the other surviving women, clearer-headed, joined him in helping to herd the others away from the town and into the open. The houses were falling now, throwing timbers, sparks, and flaming brands everywhere. A spray of embers stung the haunches of the bay, and it reared.

Owen seized the bridle, and pulled its head down, and saw his final vision of destruction. He thought the big priest had gotten all the women out. Not this one.

She was a slender blonde, skin white with the bloodless pallor of the snow itself. She wore only a shift. It was ripped open at the neck, baring one breast. Clearly, on the blue-veined skin of that breast was the mark of human teeth, a circle of oozing red splotches. More blood ran down her legs, staining the snow at her feet.

Her eyes were wide, gazing into the open door of one of the flaming houses. It was an incandescent pyre, and should no longer have even been standing. She stepped past Owen, eyes wide, stare fixed ahead of her.

Realizing what she meant to do, Owen made an ineffectual grab at her arm. But it was too late, and she was past the threshold. In a second, she was wreathed in flame.

He saw her eyes clearly through the veil of transparent fire as she turned facing him and reached both hands up to catch the white-hot central beam of the roof. It resisted her for an unbelievable second, but then fell, bringing the blazing timber down on top of her.

The raiders fought to the death, which wasn't long in coming, caught as they were between the kinfolk of the people they'd massacred and Godwin's knights.

It was left mostly to Owen to try to comfort the survivors. He helped the big priest, whose name he learned was Martin, dig a grave for the dead. All the men had been killed, and most of the children, with the exception of a few girls the raiders had considered old enough to travel. The only reason the women still lived was because they were preserved as the spoils of war, to be sold to the slave traders.

Owen left the women with Martin. Most had families in his town, and the rest elsewhere. Just to be sure they'd be welcomed with open arms by their kin, he gave each a horse. The raiders had come mounted, and the horses were found concealed near the edge of the forest.

He gave two horses to Martin in return for his help, letting him, in spite of a few glares from Godwin's men, take his pick from among them. The priest took a young stallion and a fine mare. It was plain he considered them a magnificent gift, and was almost embarrassingly effusive in his thanks. Then Owen started back for Chantalon, the bodies of the dead raiders in a cart at the rear, drawn by four oxen.

Owen was weary, the exhilaration of the battle gone. The despair of the women he'd left at the church and the eyes of the one who'd immolated herself in the burning house haunted him. Then there was Elin, too. Would she still be there when he returned? She'd said she would leave him and, considering the matter, he didn't doubt that she could if she wanted to.

Behind him Enar was talking to Gowen. "Doesn't your head hurt?" he asked the big knight.

"No," Gowen said, "my head never hurts."

"Never! Not even after a night like last night?" Enar said.

"I wish I could pass all nights as well and happily as I did that one. It's a fine house the Lord Bishop keeps," Gowen said.

Enar trotted up beside Owen. "He's dead from the neck up," Enar said, "but the rest of him, oh, God! Remind me never to annoy that man, Lord Christ Priest! Did you see what he did to the pair that tried to run away?"

Owen nodded.

"A warhorse," Enar said, "dim, but very dangerous. The only way I'd fight him is with an army at my back, and then I might want to hide behind them."

Enar's cheerfulness was offensive to Owen now. He pushed the bay faster, wanting to be alone.

"Lord Christ Priest," Enar said, "if you will forgive me . . . ?"

"I probably won't," Owen said.

"Yes, you will, Lord Christ Priest," Enar said, keeping pace, "you're a forgiving man. But your demeanor is not that of one who has just had a very easy victory in battle."

"I wish we had come sooner," Owen said.

"You came as quickly as you could. The count would not have bothered to come at all," Enar pointed out. When Owen didn't respond, he added, "Lord Christ Priest, you listen too much to the wailing of women. Listen to something pleasant, such as this."

He shook a sack near Owen's ear. It clinked.

"What is it?" Owen asked.

"Your share of the loot. They were fat with it, those love-lies." He gestured at the naked corpses in the cart at the rear. "You are the lion and got the lion's share. We took a fortune from their bodies, and there was more in the woods. Every man here is rich."

Owen looked around. It was true. Now there was no need for the blacksmith's gift. All the recruits wore mail shirts, steel helmets, and carried good swords, and most led additional horses. Every man had some piece of jewelry. Rings and armlets gleamed on their bodies and brooches were pinned to their cloaks.

Enar himself had a helmet of silver inlaid with gold, and a brooch with the blue glitter of sapphires. Owen looked into the sack Enar handed him; a miscellany of coins, jewelry, gold, and silver met his eye.

Godwin, riding on the right, gave Enar a hard stare.

"Oh!" Enar said, slapping his forehead, "I almost forgot."

"Ha!" Godwin said.

Enar presented Owen with a sword. The hilt was worked in the shape of gold acanthus leaves supporting a sphere of rock crystal at the pommel. "It's very old, but a fine one," Enar said, partially drawing it from the sheath. It was, the steel had the luminous glow of woven metal.

"I personally counted every piece in the bag," Godwin said. "Show them to me when we reach the hall. If any are missing, the world will be the better for one less Saxon, and Enar knows which thieving Saxon I have in mind."

With this parting word, he cantered off ahead to join Edgar and Wolf the Tall.

Enar sighed. "I'd hate to be a martyr to an old man's failing memory."

"I'm sure," Owen said, "that my cousin has an excellent memory." He shook the sack gently. "Anything you wish to add?"

"No, Lord Christ Priest. I'm a reasonably honest man, especially when I'm reasonably certain I'd be caught. It's all there."

Owen looked down at the sword belt slung from his saddle. It was a pity. The sword would go into his strong box, possibly never to be used again. It was of an old-fashioned shape, broad near the tang, and such blades were passing out of fashion in favor of the narrow one such as he wore. He lifted it by the scabbard and placed it in Enar's hands.

"Take the sword for yourself, seeing you have none," Owen said.

Enar, to Owen's surprise, turned scarlet and looked ashamed. "My lord, I took my fair share and more." He pulled a cloth-wrapped bundle out of his shirt and opened it. A ruby necklace blazed in the sunlight.

"A treasure," Owen said. "How did Godwin miss that?"

"It was sewn into the hem of the chief's shirt," Enar said, "and the shirt fell to me. I felt he might have something or other concealed here or there about his person. A thief has a nose for such things."

Each link was of gold filigree, set with a ruby in the center, and at the end, a pendant ruby, large as Owen's thumb, glowed like a drop of blood.

"If the shirt was given to you," Owen said, "in all fairness, it's your good fortune."

"No," Enar said, "take it for your lady. I can't say I thought of that when I found it, but I do now. She might forgive you for her face."

"Does everyone know?" Owen asked unhappily.

"No one knows anything." Enar spoke in an undertone. "Ingund said she lied boldly and looked Anna in the eye. That's a woman for a man. Throw the bauble around her neck in the hall before everyone, and put gold rings on her fingers. The talk will die out, and all will believe she must have missed her footing in the dark."

"A gift to Elin through me?" Owen asked.

"Why not?" Enar said. "In my own land I'd have served her with a right good will. Here it's different. Wives and husbands are more one person, but I first loved you for her sake."

Then, as if ashamed to have spoken so bluntly, he reined in his horse, dropped back, and said no more.

Owen looked down again at what Enar called a bauble. He'd never seen anything so beautiful. He held a fortune in his hand. His father had been accounted a rich man but he'd never owned anything as fine as this. He slipped it carefully around his own neck under his shirt. If Elin waited for him at the hall, she would receive it immediately. If not, he would return it to Enar.

He shook the bag. Enar was right—it was a pleasant sound. Owen stared out over the countryside, and began to lay his plans.

Chapter

14

*I*T was dusk when they reached the city. Except for giving orders to sling the bodies of the raiders by their heels from the palisades, Owen spoke to no one and rode directly to the hall.

Elin sat by the fire in an armchair. She wore a white linen dress with flowing sleeves over her shift and a blue woolen mantle against the cold. The swelling on the side of her face was down. Her eyes were clear, though there were black rims around both.

Before he spoke to anyone else, he went to her, bent down, and very gently kissed her on the lips.

"You had a victory?" she whispered.

"Yes," he answered softly, "and I know who gave it to me."

Her face was cold, mouth set, eyes glittering with anger.

He pulled out the necklace and dropped it over her head.

There were gasps from behind him, exclamations of awe and astonishment at the magnificence of the gift. But nothing in Elin's face changed.

She looked down at it, at the ruby lying between the soft curves of her breasts, then lifted it with her fingers and raised her eyes to his face. "Am I supposed to be impressed by this, bought by this? Get your collar from around my neck." Her voice was low, but not a whisper—a sibilant hiss.

His own answer was equally soft but equally angry. "The gift is not mine but Enar's. He placed it in my hands for you."

Elin rose slowly to her feet. Owen half turned. The big doors to the square were open. It looked as though the whole town was trying to crowd through them into the hall. Every eye was fixed on them. No one spoke a word or made a sound.

Godwin and the knights stood around the table, the old man's gaze focused narrowly on him. He realized they all waited to see what he would do. He turned back to Elin. She held a silver wine cup in her hand. She extended it to him slowly, a smile on her lips, but her eyes were ice.

He took it from her and raised it. His eyes locked with hers over the rim of the cup. He could read nothing in her face. If he spilled the wine or put it aside, they would all know he feared her. No one would dare say so, but everyone would know.

His fingers tightened around the stem of the silver vessel. He was tempted to toss its contents into the blazing fire.

The room was cold, but he was aware that he was sweating. He could feel it dampening his armpits, breaking out on his forehead. Christ! what a trap she'd prepared for him. If he drank, he might die, and if he didn't, he'd look a suspicious fool.

Even as he wavered, she spoke. "Come my love," she whispered and smiled; the smile showed her teeth. "Why do you hesitate? It's a vintage I prepared especially for you, my sweet, to quench your thirst."

He closed his eyes. He could no longer stand the hurt and fury of those blue ones, so ready to meet his own, even while she perhaps held murder in her heart.

"What," he whispered to her, over the rim of the cup, "is life worth without courage and love?"

He drained it to the lees. The wine was a red—dark, strong with a smoky flavor. An autumn vintage of those grapes that must have rested longest on the vine. He had no way of telling if he drank death or not. The taste of such a wine would mask even the bitterest of poisons.

He placed the empty cup in her hand. Elin looked down into the black dregs that lay like clotted blood at the bottom of the cup's luminous silver bowl. When she lifted her head, the hurt and anger were gone from her face and tears stood in her eyes.

She refilled the cup, using the same jug from which she'd taken the last draught. She raised the cup to him. "To my love," she said loudly, "in thanksgiving for his victory today and in honor of the splendor of his gift to me." Then she, too, emptied the cup.

All at once some spell seemed to be broken; the room filled with the babble of talk and laughter.

Elin seated herself in the chair before the fire. Owen set the sack of treasure at her feet and turned to the people crowded around the doors to the hall. "Let's feast now, and thank God for our safety," he said.

He was answered by cheers when he gave orders to slaughter the oxen that drew the death cart of the raiders. Even louder cheers rang out when Elin contributed some gold coins she found among the rest of the loot to buy beer for the citizens.

Owen turned back to Elin. The traces of tears were still on her cheeks. She gazed into the knot of coals on the hearth. He shook with both rage and reaction. "For a moment," he whispered, "I thought you meant to kill me."

"Yes," Elin said softly, furiously, "you thought what I wanted you to think. That's one of the powers my people taught me. This morning you sounded as if you despised them. We are not fools, and though we don't fight, we are not powerless."

"Is that what power means to you?" Owen asked. "Deception?"

"One of the powers, yes!" Elin answered. "I could have killed you if I wanted to."

"And paid the forfeit," Owen snapped. "Godwin and the men at the table would have seen to it."

"No!" Elin said. "I pay no forfeits but those I choose. Before you fell in your death throes, I could have been part of the shadows and gone. The night is my home. And the eternal night of death is my ally.

"I know," she rasped, her voice still low but hoarse with anger, "that by now you're beginning to feel very brave from having looked death in the eye, or so you thought, and stared it down. My people don't fear death; we embrace it."

"Do you?" Owen shot back at her. "You struggled hard enough for life in the Viking camp. You seem to have a bottomless ability to endure humiliation and degradation. I know this to my cost. You visited the fruits of their depravity on me."

"Oh, then," she said softly, "was the courage all yours, the sacrifice? The first morning after we met I could have left you. Fled away like mist before the sunrise. I didn't! I came here with you to a place where I might die fighting beside you!"

She reached out and caught him by the wrist. "Take my hand," she commanded.

Owen clenched his fist and almost jerked away.

"What?" she asked, still very softly, "are you afraid?" Slowly she guided his hand upward until it touched her breast. "Feel my life," she whispered.

He opened his fingers slowly and his palm pressed against the two soft mounds. At the center he felt the throb, the gentle continuous come and go that beats out the term of existence. He could see the echo of its pulsations in the soft white column of her neck, see it glow in her lips—the color of a returning sunrise—and face its steady power in her unflinching stare.

"How like a footstep it is," she said. "Like the feet of one striking the earth on a long journey. Now"—her fingers tightened on his wrist—"feel it slow."

Staring into her eyes in unbelieving horror he felt the speed of the soft pulsations change under his hand. Her lips grew pale, her skin became clammy to the touch.

"Feel it falter," she said.

It seemed to Owen that a dying bird fluttered beneath his fingers. Her sapphire eyes misted and Owen saw a darkness terrible as a killing storm engulf their blueness.

Owen snatched his hand away as quickly as though he'd inadvertently touched a serpent.

Elin's eyes cleared, the flush of life returned to her lips and cheeks. "That was not deception," she said, "but certainty, for nothing is more certain than death."

Owen stood perfectly still for a moment feeling the rush of air in his lungs and the steady hammer of blood in his ears. His chest heaved with the storm of emotion raging within him.

He spat at her in fury and repulsion. "This morning I was afraid you might leave me. Afraid because I love you. But now ... After you've faced me with this horror, I almost wish you had gone, never to return. I'm not sure I can love you. I'm not sure I know how."

Elin flinched slightly at the cruelty of his words, but her blue gaze still challenged his. "Go to the table, man. Go sit with your friends. They'll despise you if you're too doting. After all, I'm only a woman."

Then she turned and took her seat in the chair. The light of her eyes reflected the ever-changing flames.

The feast was for everyone. In spite of the cold, the doors of the hall were thrown open. Bonfires to cook the oxen sprang up in the city square. A little gold bought a lot of beer and the first casks were broached even as the oxen were being led to slaughter. Flutes, drums, and handbells appeared, and the dancing began as the beer started to circulate among those gathered around the cooking fires.

Inside, the knights settled down at the table to drink and boast of their exploits to the rest of the household.

Anna brought cheeses, hot bread, roasted nuts, and a whole haunch of venison to the table. Wine, white and red, flowed freely. Cold air, the yells of the merrymaking crowd, and the smell of roasting meat drifted in through the doors of the hall.

Godwin now had the seat on his right, but Enar had taken the one on his left. Owen felt hemmed in. They both tried to fill his cup at once, but Enar's hand won the race. Godwin drew back with a smile at Enar, who similarly bared his teeth at Godwin.

Godwin studied Elin, seated in her chair by the hearth, alone. "I wouldn't like to meet that woman in battle," Godwin said. "If ever I saw a man out-generaled, cousin, it was you."

Enar grinned again and said, "We all thought you might have some doubts about what was in the cup."

"I had no doubts," Owen said.

"No?" Godwin's eyebrows rose. He looked amused. "There she sits, the price of at least twelve manors around her neck, a dowerless girl, an unknown."

"It may be," Enar said, "that she has more to offer than appears on the surface, eh, Lord Christ Priest?"

Owen didn't answer. He lifted the cup, drank, and helped

himself to some bread and cheese. He found himself very hungry.

"She was not," Gowen shouted at Wolf the Short, near the end of the table.

Godwin rapped hard with the hilt of his knife on the boards. "What's going on?" he asked loudly.

Wolf the Short retorted, "You were just lucky to cut him down."

"Stupid," Gowen roared, reaching for him.

"That's the pot calling the kettle black," Enar said.

Godwin slammed the hilt of his knife down with a crash on the table. "Start a brawl in your lord's hall, and I'll shave both your beards with the edge of my sword. I mean it," he shouted.

The prospect didn't sound attractive. The fair-skinned Gowen was very stubbly and Wolf the Short's beard reached his chest. Both men fingered their chins thoughtfully and sat down.

"As for you," Godwin said, addressing Enar. The point of Godwin's knife was suddenly under Enar's chin. "One more word and it will be you I'll be shaving, Saxon.

"I think a visit to the whorehouse might be propitious," Godwin said. "Stick to honest whores, no married women. Start a blood feud for me to settle and I'll do more than shave, I'll flay the three of you."

Gowen and the two Wolves stood up and ambled through the open door of the square to join the revelry outside.

Godwin removed his knife from under Enar's chin.

"Did you ever really do that?" Enar asked Godwin, wide-eyed.

"What?" Godwin snapped.

"Shave a man with the edge of your sword," Enar said.

"Yes," Godwin said, "not one, two. Both men lost a lot of skin and screamed pitifully. It served them right, starting a fight in the master's hall. I thought of hanging them, but a dead man's no use in battle. The shaving seemed more amusing and preserved their lives, so they could be of at least some use in the world."

Enar scratched the stubble on his cheek vigorously.

"It becomes particularly unpleasant when I reach the upper lip," Godwin said with relish. "If they don't hold their heads perfectly still, it can be cut off. It's very difficult to eat or even talk without an upper lip. And the general effect of its loss, on even the handsomest features, renders them quite repulsive to most women. Not to mention the fact that, pleasant activities such as kissing . . ."

"Say no more," Enar said.

Edgar rose and touched Enar lightly on the shoulder. "He really did shave those men. I saw it. They were scum, but much better-behaved scum when Godwin was finished with them." Then he drifted through the door to find entertainment of his own choice.

The party outside was in full swing. Arn, the tavern keeper, had taken over cooking the oxen. He trotted from fire to fire basting them with a concoction of his own devising.

The oxen weren't done, but Routrude and Helvese had contributed kettles of soup and these steamed over the fires. Everyone in the crowd walking around the square carried a cup and bowl filled with something. The beer was being handed out in front of the tavern by Routrude. Everybody was returning for refills, and Owen noticed that no one seemed troubled any longer by the cold.

The table was nearly empty, the recruits having long ago gone home to impress their families with their new finery.

Owen looked around. "Ine?" he asked.

Enar rapped on the table.

Ine came out from under it. "Gone?" he said hopefully.

"Yes." Enar explained, "The knights torment him, trying to get him to say more than one word."

Enar draped his arm over Ine's shoulder. "We meet with persecution everywhere," he said.

"How much of Anna's beer have you had?" Ingund asked Enar. "Come, let's sweat some of it out of your skin." And she dragged the protesting Enar away to join the dancing outside.

Godwin dozed over his wine.

Outside in the square, a woman screamed—a terrible cry—one of horror and fear, then came the sound of steel on steel.

"Damn them!" Godwin roared, jerking into wakefulness, "I'll shave those fools yet. I told them no married women."

Elin rose from her chair and started toward the door, but Owen, on his feet and running, got there before she did.

The four cooking fires lit the sky with a bloody light. A dozen of the count's men were driving the crowd back, flogging them away from the roasting meat with whips and spear shafts. As Owen watched, one of them split a keg of beer with a blow of his sword. It emptied, foaming on the cobbles under the horse's hooves.

Gerlos reined his horse in and guided it up the steps to Owen's door. "We were overlooked when you gave the feast," he shouted, "so we invited ourselves. Come, Owen, womanslayer, and join us."

Gerlos's eyes glittered under the helmet. He was fully armed: sword, shield, spear, and leather greaves on his shins. He drove the pointed spurs into the horse's flanks, lunging it up toward Owen, striking at him viciously with the spear.

Owen leaped to one side, drawing his own sword as he did, and chopped the shaft in two, even as the head flashed past, burying itself in the door post.

Gerlos had drawn his own blade. It flashed before Owen's eyes, and he parried upward.

At the last second, Gerlos twisted his blade, catching Owen's sword at the hilt behind the hand guard, sending it spinning away into the darkness.

Owen heard it land with a ringing clatter on the stones of the square.

Gerlos chopped down at Owen's head. Owen leaped back and fell, even as the tip of Gerlos's blade drew a line of agony across his chest through the mail he wore.

He rolled down the steps and out onto the stones of the square. Then Owen was on his feet. He lunged toward the darkness near the shops, where he believed his sword had landed.

But Gerlos brought his horse down the steps with a clattering rush on its haunches, eyes rolling, foam dripping from the bit, between Owen and the weapon, aiming another down slash that just missed his face.

Owen ran into the open space between the cooking fires, putting them between himself and Gerlos.

"What's wrong, womanslayer?" Gerlos screamed, twisting the horse's head around. "Is it that I'm not your wife?" he shouted, as he drove the horse forward at a gallop between two of the fires right toward him.

All that was left in Owen's brain was a red madness. Half blinded by the fires, he saw the head of Gerlos's horse plunging toward him. He reached into the flames, lifted the heaviest branch, and swung it upward, toward the silver flash that was Gerlos's descending sword blade.

Both men and horse seemed to vanish in a cloud of fire as the wood exploded into a cascade of embers and burning fragments.

Gerlos raised his shield to protect his horse's face.

Owen had had a second's fear that it wouldn't be enough. He felt the slowing blade skid, agonizing even under his hauberk, over the curve of his shoulder and down his left arm. He reached up, his fingers closed around Gerlos's arm, at the extreme point of the down stroke, and jerked backward, throwing his whole body into the pull.

Gerlos smashed the edge of his shield into the side of Owen's head, but the forehoof of the already frightened horse dropped into the fire. The animal screamed, shied, and reared.

Gerlos came down across the scalding meat and into the flames. He rolled, tearing his arm free of Owen's grip, scattering fire and kicking the meat and spit to the cobbles.

Owen reached down into the heart of the blaze and came up, his hands seeming to drip burning coals, and threw them at Gerlos's face, trying to blind him.

He nearly succeeded. Gerlos, who hadn't made a sound when he fell, cried out, and raised his shield to protect his eyes.

Owen looked around wildly for a weapon of some kind. Gerlos's men were packed in front of his house; Godwin was overmatched.

He heard a loud shout and saw his blade arching through the air, the steel red in the firelight. He fielded it, not caring where it came from. His hand snapped shut around the hilt.

Gerlos was up. Owen went for him like a wolf going for the throat of its kill. He held the sword two-handed, and slammed it into Gerlos's shield, across the scarlet dragon painted on it. The first layer of leather split.

Owen screamed like an animal balked of its prey and

swung again, driving the edge of his sword against the wooden edge of Gerlos's shield. The wood and leather cracked, and Gerlos felt the bite of Owen's blade across his knuckles through his leather glove.

Owen screamed again. He was incapable of speech now. He'd forgotten it existed. He wanted not to kill Gerlos, but to annihilate him, make the creature in front of him cease to exist, wipe it out entirely.

Gerlos turned sideways, driving the edge of his broken shield upward for Owen's teeth. Owen leaped back and swung his own sword down, two-handed again, on the leather rushing toward his face. The shield splintered and fell away from Gerlos's arm.

Gerlos chopped at Owen's neck. Owen parried, driving Gerlos's arm back, shoving him toward the fire behind him.

Gerlos backed away, his blade flashing under Owen's guard, driving a murderous two-handed slash at his ribs.

Owen gave a whistling grunt. The hauberk turned the edge, but still the air was driven out of that lung.

But it was like hitting a dead man. Owen didn't seem to feel it. His lips were drawn back from his teeth in a skull's grin, and his eyes were pools of blackness. His sword came whistling back, catching Gerlos's left arm above the elbow. As with Owen, the mail turned the edge, but a flare of agony paralyzed Gerlos's arm to the wrist.

Gerlos felt the heat of the fire behind him through his byrnie, and for the first time knew the fear of death. The man in front of him was not human.

All Owen saw was a black shape outlined against the fire.

Gerlos screamed for his men. "Kill him," he screamed. "Hell's curse on you, kill him!"

Owen staked all on one throw. He dived at Gerlos, slamming his head into Gerlos's midsection, sending him backward, down into the flames.

For one eternal instant Gerlos saw death. Owen, with his skull's grin, hair on fire, coming down on his chest, one hand pinning the wrist of Gerlos's sword arm to the coals, the other raised, fire dancing on the metal of his blade, descending to brain him. He withered in agony. Owen's blade missed, chopping away part of his cheek and ear.

Gerlos's arm was charred, his hair burned away. The hot

breath of the fire was in his lungs. Gerlos screamed like a
woman—a high, shrill, unbearably piercing shriek. "Jesus,
Jesus, save me."

His sword fell from his hand, and the flaming wood under
him was scattered by his wildly thrashing body. He threw
Owen back, broke free, and ran, still screaming.

Owen was up and out of the fire, holding both swords,
one in either hand.

A half dozen at least of the count's men were rushing him,
lances down. Owen leaped back into the open, toward the
center of the square, raising the swords to meet the charge.

Suddenly, the man closest to Owen stood in the saddle
clutching at the axe buried almost to the hilt in his forehead.

The mob howled. The sound chilled Owen to the bone. It
was the most horrible thing he'd ever heard: the voices of a
hundred throats screaming for blood. They streamed into the
square from around the shops, where they'd been pushed by
the count's men. A dozen hands caught the warrior with the
axe in his head, and dragged him down.

The others pulled their horses to a rearing halt. Above the
heads of the mob, even in the ruddy light, Owen saw their
faces go pale with fear. But Owen saw more men riding
from the street to the count's fortress, to reinforce them.

Somewhere Gerlos still shrieked demonically.

"Dogs!" The voice was a bull's bellow, audible above the
yells of rage around Owen, the women's screams, and even
Gerlos's wild keening.

"Dogs!"

Owen saw Gowen standing on the porch of the widow's
house, next to a blond girl. He was stark naked and in a state
of complete erection. He leaped to the top of the rail. "Are
you dogs," he roared, "to hang back, while your lord fights
alone?"

Gowen seemed more than human, standing there a giant,
one of the gods or heroes of old, with his long blond hair
and the firelight dancing on his naked skin.

One of the count's men hurled a lance at him. A bad mistake.

Gowen, with a speed belying his huge bulk, dropped like
a cat to the stones below. The beer was stacked next to him.
He seized one barrel and hurled it, emptying a saddle. The

mob pounced with a scream of rage, surging forward at the count's men. The fallen man was dead in seconds. Another one of them went down, the tines of a pitchfork thrown from somewhere in the darkness buried in his throat.

Someone scooped up the still-gibbering Gerlos and they fled, followed by a swelling roar of anger and hatred, jeering and curses ringing in their ears.

People swirled around Owen; none touched him. He stood alone, a dazed expression on his face. Women were screaming and tearing their hair, some were praying, others stood still, heaping curses on the count and Gerlos.

After a slight detour to retrieve his axe, Enar fought his way to Owen's side.

Routrude fell to her knees in front of Owen, seized his hand, and pressed it against her face. Suddenly she screamed.

The sound cut through Owen's head like a knife, it was so like Gerlos's final howling. "Look, look," she shouted, holding up his blackened hands, each still holding a sword.

The people around Owen fell silent, peering at his hands, but now Routrude was touching his face and hair.

"He is unmarked," Routrude shouted. "He went through the fire and did not burn. It's a miracle," she screamed. "A miracle of God." She threw up her arms, spun like a dervish and fell, twitching and thrashing, into the arms of her husband, Arn.

Another woman touched Owen and did the same, and then one of the men.

Owen knew he was marked, the breath in one of his lungs felt like fire, his shoulder was sore and swelling. But it was true, the hands he'd scooped up the coals with were blackened but unburned. His knees were turning to water and his bowels threatened to do the same. "No," he whispered in shock, "no."

Enar pulled the swords from his hands. He was terrified of the crowd around Owen. It was impossible to count the number of people writhing and twisting now on the ground at Owen's feet. And more were pressing in on all sides, trying to touch his clothing, his limbs, pulling at his hair.

Godwin pushed through to Owen's side. Ingund was with Enar now, trying to fend off the hands clutching at Owen. Enar grabbed Godwin by the shirt and pulled his head down, shouting into his ear, "Get these people under control. They'll tear him apart for holy relics."

Godwin pushed those nearest back, raised his arms and eyes to heaven and roared, "It's a miracle of God. Now, down on your knees and pray. Do you hear me?" He put his hands on the closest man's shoulders and forced him to his knees, yelling, "Down on your knees, pray."

All at once Osbert and Gunter were at his side, pushing people to their knees, shouting, "Pray, pray."

But still the voice of the mob deafened them, screaming, shoving, clutching. People were falling everywhere, falling at Owen's feet, moaning, foaming at the mouth.

"Pray something," Enar shrieked at Godwin. "I don't know any prayers."

Gunter backed a man away from Owen with a hard push that sent him flying into that sea of faces and outstretched, reaching hands that seemed to writhe around them in the flickering yellow glow of the fires. A low growl of anger rose from those the man crashed into.

"No, no!" Ingund screamed, throwing her arms around her father. "In this mood, they may do anything."

It was true. Godwin knew it: violence would be met with violence. He raised his arms and shouted again, trying to be heard over the swelling cry of the mob. "Our Father who art in heaven, repeat after me. Do you hear me?"

"Our Father who art in heaven . . ." a voice near the tavern bellowed. "Our Father who art in heaven . . ."

The mob quieted as more voices took up the words.

"Hallowed be Thy name . . ."

The voice near the tavern echoed Godwin's words and then the rest in unison.

"Thy kingdom come . . ."

Godwin began pushing Owen toward the hall.

"Thy will be done . . ." Godwin shouted at the top of his lungs.

And the response was nearly as loud as the screaming had been earlier.

Godwin felt a sweat of terror break out all over his body as he realized that he couldn't remember any more prayers. He was sure he knew some but they seemed to have flown clear out of his head. He pushed Owen forward as fast as he could, running a winding gauntlet of outstretched hands and pale uplifted faces.

He saw Gowen over the heads of the kneeling people, standing by the tavern, still stark naked, quenching his bottomless thirst between responses, with sips from the bung hole of a beer barrel he held in his hands.

Godwin was nearly at the steps of the hall when, as he feared, the Lord's prayer ran out. But by that time, Ranulf was at his side, and he knew a lot more prayers. The boy had a clear, carrying, pleasant tenor voice, and was well launched into the Magnificat when the rest shepherded Owen into the hall.

Gowen was still standing by the beer. He wasn't surprised that Owen had come through the fire unscathed. Owen was a holy man of God, and a bishop. Besides, he had seen the good bishop attacked by a fully armed, mounted man, and Owen had successively deprived his attacker of horse, shield, sword, and finally, humiliated him.

All this merited Gowen's unqualified approval. Such a man was worth following. Still, he was sorry the count's soldiers had run away so quickly. He was planning to feed a few more to the mob. He'd already picked his targets. But no one could have everything.

He looked up. The girl was still standing on the porch, looking down at the people praying in the square with Ranulf leading the responses. She was pretty, more slender than he liked them, but still a succulent morsel, with the curling blond hair flowing over the soft cones of her breasts. She crooked her finger and beckoned.

Gowen smiled, wiped his mouth, corked the barrel, and tucked it under his arm. She'd complained when he tried to get on top of her. Women were a nuisance that way. They couldn't bear his weight. But they'd done well enough when he set her on top of him—very well, in fact.

He began climbing the outside stairs to the porch, thinking that if Owen were a saint, his blessing might be worth something. But then he really felt blameless, and had no particular sins on his conscience. True, there were a few married women in his past, but their husbands had been amply compensated by Godwin. None of them ever wanted to fight him. Still, just to be safe, he'd call on Owen and ask for his blessing but, he thought—as he followed the girl's attractive backside into the widow's house—in the morning.

Chapter
15

WHEN they got into the hall, Owen fell into Elin's open arms. She led him to the table.

Godwin and Enar collapsed on the benches opposite. Enar grabbed a wine jug and filled a cup for himself and Godwin both.

"What happened?" Owen asked.

"A lot," Enar said.

"A riot," Godwin said, drinking deeply.

Enar immediately refilled both cups, and they drank again.

"Stop it," Ingund told them, "you'll both be drunk as hogs."

"No," Enar said, "no hog could ever get as drunk as I'm going to get."

Elin felt Owen's hands, his face, then his forehead. "You're freezing," she said.

He just sat staring at his hands, shivering.

Anna took something from a cupboard near the fireplace, poured a cup, and handed it to Elin. "Tell him to sip it slowly."

Owen had no choice. His hands trembled so badly that it threatened to spill and the cup rattled against his teeth. She laid her hands over his to steady them. He looked up at her, his eyes dark pools of misery. "I don't want to be a saint."

"Never fear," she reassured him, "my oath on it. You're only a man."

"I don't know," Godwin said. "When I touched him I did feel something strange, the stiffness left my joints, and . . ."

Enar made a sound of disgust. "You were afraid of the mob, and by Christ and the devil both, they were a thing to fear. Two men butchered in less time than it takes to draw one good breath. They'd have downed the rest if they hadn't fled."

Godwin nodded and tossed off another cup of wine. "For once, Saxon, you're right. How did anyone get the idea he was a saint?"

"At some point in the proceedings," Enar said, "Routrude . . ."

"Oh heavens," Elin sighed, "say no more. Routrude is . . ." Words failed her and she shook her head.

Owen set the cup on the table. It burned his throat but the warmth spread from his belly up, out, and over his skin.

Enar reached out, picked up his hands, and began examining them. "He may not be a saint, but he's a Berserk. By the ghosts of the gods, he belongs to the one-eyed. A fire walker. I've seen them fight, take a half dozen mortal wounds, and still cut men down." He nudged Godwin. "Speak, haven't you seen it yourself?"

"Now who's talking nonsense?" Godwin said. "They train for years, devote their bodies to the gods, practice magic, and work themselves into a frenzy. He hasn't, I knew him as a boy. A good Christian all his life." Godwin's eyebrows rose. "I always thought rather ordinary."

"Undistinguished." Owen laughed, then buried his face in his hands whispering, "Oh, God, oh, God, why was I not burned?"

Elin pulled off her mantle and wrapped it around Owen's shoulders, glaring at Enar and Godwin all the while.

"But to be one," Enar said, "the talent must . . ." He caught Elin's eye and closed his mouth.

Elin turned to Ine, who was standing near the fireplace, staring at Owen as though the bishop had just grown a complete set of antlers sprouting from above each ear. She said, "Bath."

He pointed at Owen and said, "Bath," and padded out.

Enar sniggered, and he elbowed Godwin. "She's beginning to sound like him."

Godwin elbowed him back. "Just so she doesn't get to look like him."

Then they began laughing hysterically at their own humor. Ingund and Anna, sitting by the fireplace, started to giggle.

They were drinking the same thing Anna had used to warm Owen.

"This is wonderful," Ingund said to Anna. "What is it? Soon I'll be as drunk as Enar."

"Pure essence of the grape," Anna said. "Freeze the wine, pour off what remains from the ice crystals."

Elin could see they were rapidly catching up with Enar and Godwin. Owen, who had finally polished off the cup she'd set before him, sat quietly but with a faraway look in his eyes.

Ranulf came into the hall, closed the door behind him, and walked toward the stairs, head bowed.

"Come here," Owen commanded.

He did, sitting down next to Owen.

"Here's the one you should thank," Ingund shouted.

Owen looked at her inquiringly. "Why?"

"Who do you think put the sword in your hand, and just when you were in desperate need?"

Ranulf looked down at his feet, and Owen knew he must be blushing. He hated to be seen doing it. "They didn't notice me," he said.

"Yes," Godwin said slowly, "I had four spears at my breast and they were watching Lady Elin too."

"I slipped through the back door," said Ranulf. "Ingund saw where it landed and passed it to me in the darkness."

"By rights, he should have Gerlos's blade," Godwin said, "in return for such a deed."

Ranulf raised his head and Owen saw his cheeks were scarlet. "What use have I for a sword?" he said. There was a strange look in his eyes.

"None at all," Owen said shortly, throwing a look of dislike at Godwin. "I'll find some more fitting way to reward you," he promised Ranulf gently. "How is it with the town?"

"Listen," Ranulf said.

Distantly, through the heavy doors of the hall, came the sound of flute and drum.

"The dancing has begun again." Enar laughed.

"Now that the evening's entertainment is over," Godwin added mockingly.

"I wasn't greatly entertained by it," Owen snarled at both of them, then turned to Ranulf. "Tomorrow call all the parish priests together. I want preparations made to gather all those in the countryside into the fortress, in the event of an attack. They will be my agents in the matter. When you speak to the priests, make it clear from the outset that they are to be here tomorrow. I'll sing a Mass of Thanksgiving, and then, after the Mass, they are to come to the hall for a dinner. After dinner, I plan to open my mind to them. We'll discuss our present danger, and what is to be done about it. So that all may attend the Mass, we'll begin at sunset. Elin, drag out every light we have, candles, lamps, whatever is necessary. Put the best cloths on the altar."

Ranulf's shoulders slumped wearily. "I'll have to start at dawn."

Owen reached out and took his hand. "Don't think that I undervalue what you did today."

Ranulf lifted Owen's hand, soot-blackened and swollen from the force of the sword strokes he'd used to break Gerlos's shield, and carried it to his lips.

Owen put one arm around Ranulf's shoulder and hugged him. "My friend, my . . ." Owen paused. "My most loyal one. Now go to bed. I know I lay a heavy charge on you but that's because I trust your courtesy and tact, your ability to see that my message is delivered and understood."

Ranulf rose and went up the stairs. When he was out of sight, past the top, Godwin said, "You should have given him the sword. I think you do undervalue what he did. He's no fighter, and had any of the count's men seen him, they'd have chopped him down without mercy."

"I don't know if they'd have found it that easy," Enar said. Godwin gave him a look of inquiry. "The boy's intelligent and very fast on his feet," Enar said slowly.

"How would Ranulf look strutting around with a sword," Owen said, "and a sword he doesn't even know how to use? He'd only make a fool of himself. Besides, he has no rank."

"Ah, yes," Enar said, "that's true, unlike those sprigs of the nobility that follow Godwin—Lady Edgar, Count Lout, and the two Dukes of Boredom."

Godwin's face turned puce and then a rich, deep violet, as he unleashed a spray of beer and laughter at the same time. "Oh," he moaned, hunching with mirth, "it's true, it's only too true."

"Not to mention," Enar continued, "Frankish gentry, flashing Saxon names." All the humor vanished from Godwin's face. "Who are you trying to fool, Godwin?" Enar asked.

Godwin looked at Enar. There was no laughter in his expression now. The flat dark eyes held a deadly warning.

"Saxon," Godwin said, very, very softly, "don't go too far. Drink does have an unfortunate effect on my vision, but I might pick out one or two of the three or four of you I see, and just on the off chance I'd be right, kill him."

"I can't think," Enar said owlishly, "that it would do you any good. There'd still be at least one of us left."

Godwin was very far gone in his cups and it took him a few seconds to penetrate the logic of that statement. When he did, everything Enar did or said afterward was funny.

With Ine's help, Elin put Owen into the tub. Owen gave a yell when he went into the hot water. "What!" he shouted. "Am I to be poached like a fish?" All he felt for a few seconds was several yards of cold skin heating up, but when the process was completed, he felt refreshed and alert. Slowly, with a shudder, he sank his shoulders below the water. "Dear God, it's hot," he whispered.

"Stop whining," Elin said. "Cold water would have you stiff as a board by morning. If you will go brawling in the street . . ."

"Brawling in the street!" Owen exclaimed indignantly. "I was not—" He broke off because Elin, sponge in hand, was advancing on him. "What are you going to do?" he asked.

"Wash the soot and blood off your face," she said.

Mindful of the cut on his cheek, Owen said, "No."

"Yes," Elin said, "and stop thrashing. You're getting water all over the floor."

When she was finished, Owen sat quietly, watching little curls of steam drifting on the surface of the water. Elin walked over to the fireplace to dry the skirts of her gown. In the distance, beyond the bolted shutters of his bedroom, Owen heard sounds of revelry drifting from the square. "What are they doing?" he asked anxiously.

"Getting drunk," Elin said.

"How wonderfully sensible," Owen said. "Make it easy

for the count's men to come down and slaughter them in their beds."

"They won't," Elin said. "If the sounds coming from the fortress are any indication of what's going on up there, the count's men are just as drunk. One side celebrating victory, the other consoling themselves in defeat. It's all the same. Probably none of them will remember what they fought over by daybreak."

The rough treatment by Elin's sponge had opened the cut on Owen's face. A trickle of blood ran down his cheek and dripped into the tub—a spreading red stain in the warm water. "I will remember," he said.

Elin nodded. "Yes, but you broke Gerlos. I don't think he'll face you again."

"No," Owen said, closing his eyes and leaning his head back against the rim of the tub. "No. I think you're right, he won't. Gerlos woke something in me tonight. Something neither he nor I knew existed. Something you saw in me when we quarreled. Something that made you take the risk of threatening me with my own sword."

Owen opened his eyes and raised his head. "What is it? What happened in the square tonight? It destroyed Gerlos and very nearly destroyed me. Elin, you know more of such things than I do. I've never seen anyone who could . . ." He hesitated, then continued. "Elin, you nearly stopped your own heart."

"The remedy, the power, and the freedom," she said.

"What?" Owen asked, bewildered.

"The remedy when all other remedies fail, the power when all other power is lost, the freedom when all other freedoms are taken away. And sometimes, the final revenge."

Owen knew there were many arguments he could throw against Elin's conviction that in death the human spirit finds its final freedom, but for the life of him, he couldn't even think of one. The Church's teaching on self-murder? Did he himself really believe in it? The Church's laws to him were only little black letters that crawled like insects across the pages of books—books he had once read in a monastery, now ashes.

The debates of scholars far removed from life paled into

insignificance before the grim realities of torture and slavery. It was as though she had bypassed the churchman and even the husband in him and had spoken directly to the warrior, and the warrior understood. There were depths of suffering and degradation he, too, would rather die than face again.

So he was silent, his fists slowly opening and closing on the sides of the tub, studying Elin. Between fire and darkness, her shadow loomed large on the wall. "They say a man must rule his wife," Owen remarked.

"I cannot be ruled, Owen, by anyone. I stay or go at my own pleasure." Her voice was sad, lifeless.

"My dark counselor," Owen said. "I'd love to say I didn't understand you, but I do. Oh, God help me, I do. Elin, what happened in the square tonight?"

"You called on the powers and they answered."

"Why?" Owen asked.

She laughed, but there was a tormented quality about her laughter and a grim tightness around her eyes and mouth. "How like a man," she jeered, "and a churchman at that to wonder about such a thing."

Owen sat up straight in the tub and reached for a length of coarse linen. "Churchman am I," he said despairingly. "A bishop in a see bought and paid for by my father's money. Sometimes I feel as if the only religion I have comes in those occasional moments when I doubt my unbelief. Bertrand tore away whatever faith I had in his penitential cell. Elin, when they attacked the town today, they killed the children first."

She laughed again, jagged laughter edged like a knife. "Of course," she said. "They're the weakest and can't fight back."

Owen stood up, climbed out of the tub, and threw the linen cloth over his shoulders. "It's unbearable," he said. "I can't face it without God. I didn't arrive in time to prevent the slaughter. I only avenged it. That was all He allowed me."

She was very near and suddenly he was aware of her womanhood in the jolting overpowering way he'd been aware of it at the Lady Well. The white linen gown flowed over her body, clinging to breast, hips, and belly softly as a caress.

"I can smell death," he said, "and still I want you."

"The innocents died and the world didn't end," Elin mocked. "Fool! It never does."

"I want to possess you," Owen said.

"Me or any woman?" Elin asked.

"What difference does it make," Owen whispered. "There is no one else here, only we two."

She stood only a few feet away and swayed toward him. Her lips parted slightly and he knew how they would taste on his own. "I thought," she taunted, "you'd forgotten how to love me."

"What I feel right now has nothing to do with love," Owen answered. "I'm not sure what love is, just as I'm not sure what God is, but desire for you is rooted in every fiber of my being."

Her sigh was his answer. A sound of profound surrender. "Oh, how you arouse me," she whispered. "Standing there naked, your skin still wet and warmed by the bath. I can feel your heat and see it strongly rising at your loins." She seemed to float toward him, lips moist, the flush of love's first pleasure burning in her amber skin.

"As you see me, so let me see you," Owen said.

She let the gown fall to the floor and stood naked before him, head thrown back, her hair a black waterfall at her shoulders.

Slowly he reached out and touched her gently between the legs, feeling the warm, wet softness. Her back arched slightly and she gave a hoarse, soft cry. He drew his hand away, saying, "Shameless, shameless witch."

She caught his face between her palms, one hand over the bloody gash on his cheekbone. The pressure was just short of pain, her thumb traced the curve of his lips. "Shame," she said. "If you want shame, take some mewing virgin, some simpering little bitch who has never looked beyond the confines of her bower. She will turn her eyes away, not look at you as I do now. Look at you and desire you, too."

"Oh, be quiet," he said with a wolfish smile. "Don't you know women argue best with what's between their legs?"

She kissed him fiercely, driving her tongue into his

mouth, and then drew back. "Better than men," she said. "Men think with what's between theirs."

Owen picked her up, carried her to the wolf skins and threw her on her back.

He stayed perfectly still after he entered her, feeling as though if he moved the storm of the flesh would overwhelm him.

She didn't move either, but stared up at him, a dark triumph in her eyes. She stroked him with her body and Owen felt wave after wave of pleasure flow through him.

"Succubus," he whispered. "Witch. Pagan bitch, your body is a temple of Venus."

She scored his face with her nails and a few drops of blood fell and glowed like rubies on her naked breast. "Then worship me, you bastard," she whispered. "Worship me," she moaned.

Their bodies moved together, both of them thrusting, seeking. "God damn you," she said. "One day you will have your mewing virgin . . . remember me to her."

Owen heard the words clearly though he was lost in an ocean of light.

Chapter

16

"YOU have dyspepsia," Anna told Godwin.

She was poaching two eggs in wine with a little chervil and thyme, using a shallow, long-handled pan held over the fire.

He sat staring grimly into a cup with some watered wine in it. "I drank too much," he said.

"It happens when you don't drink, doesn't it?" she asked.

"Yes," he said.

"Did your parents quarrel at the table?"

"On those rare occasions when they were speaking to each other, yes, they did," Godwin said.

Anna nodded. "I'm convinced that's the root cause of a nervous stomach. Did drink cause them to quarrel?"

"He was a mean drunk," Godwin said, "she a melancholy one."

"Christ!" Anna said. "He raged, she wept."

"Exactly," Godwin said.

Anna shook her head in commiseration. "Do you like the yolks soft?" she asked.

"Runny," Godwin said.

Anna nodded and dumped the two poached eggs into a bowl, then toasted and buttered some bread, and served eggs and toast to Godwin, saying, "Here, eat, it'll settle your stomach," and began to prepare the same breakfast for herself.

"My husband," Anna said, "was an amorous drunk. Of course he was the same sober. We were married several years before I shared his favors with no less than three other women. But all the same, we were happy. My only regret is that none of our children lived."

Godwin sat hunched over the table eating the eggs, dipping the toast in the yolks. "Ahh," he sighed, "just what I needed."

Anna sat in the big armchair by the fire; she ate hers with a spoon, taking bites of toast on the side. "It does make a good breakfast," she said contentedly.

Three screams rang out, each in a different voice, from the second floor.

Godwin's body jerked. "Oh no," he moaned, "what now?"

"Nothing," Anna said, "those were mouse screams. Ingund is cleaning upstairs, and one probably ran out and startled her. Elfwine!" Anna shouted. "What's wrong?"

Elfwine came to the end of the stairs, poked her head over the railing, and answered. "Oh, Anna," she said, in a tone of horrified delight, "Ingund found a woman in the knights' room."

"Is that any reason to go screaming the house down? Besides," Anna groused, "what do you expect of a group of young men besides filth, stink, and bugs, I mean? Must I come up and tend to her?"

"No," Elfwine said, "Lady Elin is doing that."

"Then why in heaven's name did you scream?" Anna asked irritably.

"I don't know," Elfwine said. "The girl screamed because Ingund uncovered her and she was naked. Ingund screamed because she was surprised to find her. She thought the bed empty. And I screamed because Ingund did."

"See," Anna told Godwin, "it's nothing. Eat your eggs, don't let it upset you."

"Nothing" stood on the floor of the knights' room shivering, while Elin wrapped her in a blanket.

She was the tiny blond Elin had seen eating honey on the porch of the widow's house, and the girl who had been with Gowen when he came out to confront the count's men the night before.

The entire household was gathered in the doorway staring at her, with the exception of Owen, who was still asleep, and Gowen, who was in bed, trying to sleep.

"I told you," he said, turning over and punching his pillow, "you should have stayed with me. She was afraid I'd roll on her and crush her ribs," he explained to the assembled company, then stared at the girl with one open eye. "I want my rest. Scream again and I'll beat you," he threatened.

"Nothing," who had only looked frightened before, now seemed to be terrified. Elin put one arm protectively around her and led her quickly to the door. The mere thought of something as big as Gowen striking something as small as this girl was dreadful. "She must go back to where she came from," Elin said.

"She can't," Gowen said, "she's bought and paid for. I gave the widow a brooch."

He was beginning to look annoyed and annoyance was, in Gowen's case, a thing to be treated with caution.

"I see," Elin said, backing out the door, leading the girl.

He raised his head and raked the household with a glance that reminded Elin of the stare of an abruptly awakened lion. He was conscious, didn't want to be, and not pleased with those who'd interrupted his nap. And they'd best let him return to his blissful coma or they'd suffer the consequences.

"Don't take her too far, she's mine," Gowen ordered, rolling over and punching the pillow again.

Elin brought the girl to an unoccupied room, followed by Ingund and Enar, and sat her on a bench against the wall. She had two enormous blue eyes and a tangle of spun-gold hair that hung around her face in elflocks.

Enar twitched one corner of the blanket aside. "Gowen got his money's worth," he said. "When the ladies rise from the foam of the sea or the clear water of their rivers and fountains, to call the springtime, carrying flowers in their hands, they must look much as she does." His large gray eyes were clear and kind.

Ingund smiled at him. "You're a man of experience," she said, "too much experience."

"I haven't heard you complain," he said.

"She needs a dress and some shoes," Elin said, and sent the two of them off to find something for the girl to wear.

Then she sat next to the frightened child on the bench and settled an arm around her shoulders.

"Now," she asked, "tell me how you come to be here."

"I don't know," was the hesitant answer. "No one told me I was sold. The widow was in the hall. She and the two, the one with braided hair and the other with the red beard."

The two Wolves, Elin thought.

"She likes them very much," the girl said.

Birds of a feather, Elin thought.

"They drank together nearly all night," the girl said. "Gowen opened the door of my room. I was tired but he awakened me and said, 'Come.' When he tells you to do a thing . . ." The girl paused.

"Yes," Elin answered, tightening her arm slightly, "I understand. It's safer to do it."

"Yes, it is," she said. "He brought me downstairs where they were drinking. The widow laughed and told him to pull off my shift since I might belong to him, but my clothes belonged to her. I began to cry. The widow's house is the only place I know. I was thinking another might be worse. But Gowen began to pull off my shift. The red-bearded one lent me his mantle, saying I shouldn't go out into the cold naked. And Gowen brought me here."

Ingund returned with a dress and some shoes. The blue eyes stared at Elin in mute appeal.

Elin kissed her cheek. "It won't be worse for you here, I promise. Now, let Ingund dress you."

She went downstairs to talk to Godwin. As she approached, he turned two red-rimmed, bloodshot eyes on her. "My Lord Godwin," she began gently.

"My Lady Elin," Godwin said, "don't manage me, I'm not in a mood to be managed. Tell me what Gowen's done now."

"How did you know it was Gowen?" Elin asked.

"Because it's always Gowen," Godwin said venomously, "unless it's the brother Wolves. Edgar's debaucheries are invariably carried out discreetly."

"He bought a woman from the widow."

"Deo Gratia," Godwin said, "at least I won't find a husband at my door waving an axe. Send her back. I'll get his money from the widow, and we'll say no more about it."

Ingund came down the stairs leading the girl by the hand. She was wearing a simple white dress, her hair braided into a single plait hanging down her back.

"Christ," Godwin said, "I thought you told me he bought a woman. At that size, he should get two for the price of one."

The girl tried to hide behind Ingund, and succeeded fairly well.

"I have no objection to her staying," Elin said. "It might have a quieting effect on Gowen. But," she said softly, sitting down next to him, "I don't want slaves in my house. They have no incentive to behave well, to be honest. You see that, don't you?" She gently laid a hand on his arm.

"At the moment, I see very little except that obviously you want me to deal with Gowen." Godwin sighed.

"Ah, yes," Elin said, "he's a most formidable . . ."

"He's afraid of me," Godwin said. "Of course I'm not sure just why, and the worry that he'll get over such a foolish notion is a source of some disquiet to me from time to time. Still, presently he fears me, and will do as he's told. Free the girl," he said impatiently, "but only on the condition that she shares Gowen's bed, and keeps him from prowling around after more settled ladies."

Elfwine leaned over the railing and called down. "I have a backache. You told me to call you when I got a backache."

"Is it a bad one?" Elin asked dulcetly.

"No," Elfwine said, "but it comes and goes."

Anna poured something into a cup and set it by Godwin's hand. "A little of your tonic and a bit of what we had last night."

"Do you think," Godwin asked hopefully, "that it will prove fatal to whatever is growing on my tongue?"

"I guarantee it," Anna said. "And it will fortify you for the coming ordeal."

"What ordeal?" Godwin asked apprehensively, raising the cup to his lips.

"Elfwine is going into labor," Anna said mordantly. Then Anna shouted up the stairs, "Get to your room, Elfwine. I'll bring you something to eat. Start walking up and down."

A thunder of hammer blows shook the hall; they came from the back.

Godwin leaped to his feet, hand on the hilt of his sword.

"It's the carpenters starting on the dovecote," Elin said.

Godwin let out a hissing breath between his teeth and tottered back toward the bench and his drink. Before he reached it, another flurry of blows shook the front door.

"Should I entertain everyone with another violent start or is there some innocent explanation for that?"

"No," Elin gasped, then ran for a crossbow.

Ingund did the same, pushing the blond under the table.

Godwin helped himself to one also, staying well away from the archer's slit. One could, after all, fire in as well as out. He approached the door cautiously.

Chapter

17

OWEN woke to the sound of saws and hammers. Elin stood at his bedside, a look of anxiety on her face. He realized he'd slept late. The air in the room was warm and the sun was shining through the window into his eyes.

He rolled over and yelped loudly. His muscles had stiffened during the night. He tried to raise his arms and the shaft of pain that struck his left shoulder brought tears to his eyes.

"Oh, my God," he shouted, then took a deep breath, and his ribs informed him forcefully of their condition.

This time he whispered, moving carefully, "Oh—my—God."

Elin said, "Get dressed."

Owen said, "Christ! Dressed? I can't move."

"Stop moaning!" Elin told him. "You were in two battles yesterday. A little soreness is natural."

"A little!" Owen gasped.

"Hurry," Elin exhorted, "something important is happening."

Owen glared up at her. "There's nothing more important than my ribs."

"No?" Elin said, folding her arms. "Count Anton, Reynald, and Bertrand are here."

Owen sat up, then writhed when his body reminded him he shouldn't be doing anything suddenly. "Call Godwin," he whispered through clenched teeth, his hand groping for his sword hilt.

Godwin entered the room. "They haven't come to fight," he said.

"You're sure?" Owen asked. "Did they bring an escort?"

"Yes," Godwin said, "but only a few men, five in all. Enar has them in the stable, and at the rate he's pouring beer down their throats, they may depart across their saddles, not in them."

"Where are your men?" Owen asked.

"Here," Godwin said. "Not too steady on their legs, but able enough should the need arise. I don't think it will."

Owen climbed out of bed. His calves and thighs commented briefly on their condition, but not with any unbearable degree of poignancy. Elin began helping him to dress.

A flurry of rapid hammer blows shook the window casement. Owen gritted his teeth. The blows seemed to resonate in his skull. "What the hell is that?"

"I'm investing your money," she said.

"God-in-heaven-above!" Owen screamed. "My elbow doesn't bend that way!"

"Strange," Elin said, "it did just now."

"What are you investing my money in?"

"A dovecote, and a sweat bath," she said, turning him around to get his tunic on.

"Pigeon shit all over my walls," Owen said. "What's a sweat bath?"

"Something the Saxons do. Enar said you'd like it," she said.

"Anything Enar's Saxons do," Godwin said darkly, "is probably an unnatural perversion, and a mortal sin, requiring papal absolution."

"Sounds interesting," Owen said.

"Hold still!" Elin commanded.

Owen held still, afraid she'd bend something else the wrong way.

A small blond girl in a white dress brought in Owen's shaving water and set it on the table.

Recognition tugged at one corner of his memory. "Who's that?" he asked suspiciously.

The girl drifted out as quietly as a wraith.

"Oh," Elin said, "that's just Rosamund," as though the matter were unimportant.

"Is that her name?" Godwin said, with raised eyebrows.

"Well, it's the one she chose," Elin said.

"She's . . ." Owen stopped. "You brought a"—he stopped again, swallowing the word—"into my house?"

"No," Elin said, "the poor thing had no choice. Gowen bought her for a brooch."

"Is that what he paid," Godwin asked, "for that little bit of fluff? He was cheated. Also, he should have been more discreet. Owen is a bishop."

"She'll behave well enough, given the opportunity," Elin said. "Women are what men make them. She's only a child."

Owen was stopped by the flattery implicit in the statement, but Godwin's eyes rolled slowly toward Elin. "Oh?" he asked. Owen was only half listening. "What will I say to Count Anton and Reynald?"

Elin was working on his hair with scissors, evening it out. It hadn't the invulnerability to fire that the rest of his body apparently possessed; some of it had burned off.

Elin didn't answer his question, only looked at Godwin.

"My lady has no advice to offer?"

"You first," Elin said.

"Very well," he answered, "don't say anything and above all don't promise anything. Listen! Let them do the talking and make the promises if any."

"That sounds like the best possible advice to me," Elin said.

They were waiting in the hall. The sounds of saws and hammers stopped when Owen started downstairs. He knew ears were positioning themselves all over the house.

Reynald was on his feet, staring into the bed of coals in the fireplace. Bertrand and another monk were seated at the table with the count.

Anton sat at the head of the table, slumped over a silver decanter with a cup in front of him. He looked even more dissipated than Owen remembered. His paunch was bigger and the harsh daylight pouring through the high windows brought out the scarlet spiders of broken veins in his cheeks. He looked old—no, more than old, despairing. Owen pitied Count Anton, remembering him from days gone by, a guest in his father's hall.

He had been a bluff, hearty man, full of life, and devoted to all its pleasures: gaming, drinking, and wenching, with an almost animal vitality. Now he'd forgotten all but the wine cup. It was said he kept that filled. Beginning in the morning, unsteady on his legs by noon, sodden and stuporous before sunset.

Well, as far as Owen was concerned, if the pleasures of the grape were all that were left to him, he should be allowed to enjoy them in peace.

Anton's brother, Reynald, was a different matter. Owen looked on him as an ally, rooted as he was here among these people. He might be won over.

It was unfortunate they had seen fit to bring Bertrand with them. Everyone knew how much Owen hated Bertrand and why.

Owen reached the foot of the stairs and bowed. "My lords," he said, approaching the table, "I'm sorry I wasn't up to greet you, but your visit comes as a surprise."

The count waved his hand at Owen. "No more pretty words, please. You know why we're here." He slammed his fist on the table. "I want compensation paid for the injuries to my son. And the leaders of that riot delivered to me at the fortress, bound and at my mercy."

Owen took a deep breath. In the fury that filled him, he no longer felt the pain in his body. "No! There was no riot until your son and your men began it. Any attempt to arrest the people will start another riot and a bigger one this time. The food and drink were given to the citizens by me. Your men tried to take it from them, and paid the price. Gerlos attacked me at my own door. I defended myself, as any man has a right to do. He's lucky he escaped with his life."

The count drew himself up. The small red eyes, in the puffy flesh of his face, glared at Owen with the stupid blind ferocity of a wild boar's. "Gerlos is my captain. He came here to collect what is my due as the commander of the garrison."

"I've given you your due," Owen said furiously. "It was turned over at harvest time. I have kept careful accounts. What remains is but provisions for my household, and the city poor."

"And the small army you're collecting around you?" Reynald said, speaking for the first time. He studied Owen, a slight frown on his face, his eyes opaque. But his expression might almost have been one of admiration.

"Not an army," Owen said, "only an escort for my protection, which it seems is necessary."

"Your 'escort,' " the count shouted, "will bring them all down on us. If they see what's hanging on the city wall, they won't spare one living soul inside it." Anton lifted the wine cup and drained it. He set the cup down, hands trembling. "What's possessed you, are you insane?" The fury was gone from his eyes. There was a trace of a whimper in his voice.

"That's the crux of the matter, isn't it?" Owen said. "Someone must arrange a defense for the city. If you won't I will. I won't desert my people. Pride and manhood both forbid it. Nor am I willing to die a martyr, slaughtered, as some have been, on the altars of their churches."

"I bought them off," Anton insisted, "they will not return."

"Oh?" Owen said. "If you could question the children of that town burned yesterday, they might differ from your opinion. I would call them as witnesses, but most are quite beyond the reach of my voice."

"A raiding party," Reynald said, and shrugged. "This city has a strong wall, and stands safely."

Owen stretched out his hands to Reynald, in a gesture of appeal. "A city is like a tree, its roots are in the countryside. Cut off a sufficient number of them, and it dies as surely as if an invader battered down its gates and put its people to the sword. They came once, and will come again and again. Taking each time a little more until nothing is left, leaving us to sit starving behind your 'strong walls,' waiting for the end."

"Speak to him." The count appealed to Reynald. "He listens to you. He is dragging us over a precipice."

Reynald shook his head. "Owen," Reynald said quietly, "they are too strong. We cannot fight them."

"I don't speak of fighting, only defense, so that the people of the countryside can gather themselves inside the walls with sufficient food and other provisions to withstand a siege, if we must," Owen said.

"That does sound reasonable," Reynald said slowly. "But if you have some idea of raising an army . . ."

"I have no such ideas," Owen said firmly.

"Good," Reynald said, "take down the bodies of the dead, return them or see that they're decently buried."

The count looked away, almost shamefaced. "I'll take them and see to their disposition."

"They've spoken to you already?" Reynald said.

"I received an emissary from the camp this morning," the count said. Then he turned savagely to Owen. "They want the price of those men's blood. It is up to you to pay it."

"No," Owen said, "I pay no more danegeld. When next those devils lay hands on what is mine, it will be when my breath is stilled and death stiffens my arm so it can no longer strike."

"Fine words, my brave young cockerel," Reynald said. "Take care. That may happen."

"Even so," Owen answered, "the words come from my heart."

Reynald sighed, reached out and put his hand on Owen's shoulder. He gave it a slight squeeze of affection, and looked him sadly in the eyes. "Ah, that we had a thousand with your resolution, but we haven't. Am I an old fool or are you a young one?" He looked away from Owen for a second, his eyes turned inward. "But, no matter." He faced Owen again. "I'll pay the blood price that there may be peace."

He stretched out his hand to Owen and Owen took it in a strong grip, and smiled.

Reynald was about to continue, but he was interrupted by Bertrand. "And I will take steps to see that you are removed by the archbishop, so that you may do no more harm."

Owen turned from Reynald, to the count and Bertrand sitting at the table. "Why?" Owen said, surprised. "On what charge?"

"My son's strength was broken by more than human means," the count said. "How else could a proven warrior be overthrown by an inexperienced boy?"

"A what?" Owen shouted.

The count rose from his chair, pointing a quivering finger at Owen. "He was overthrown by witchcraft."

Owen's left hand dropped instinctively to the scabbard of his sword, his right crept toward the hilt.

Reynald stretched out his arm quickly, saying, "I think this discussion would be best left—"

He was interrupted again by Bertrand. "You've been observed hatching your vileness."

Owen's first thought was that he and Elin had been spied on at the Lady Well. He controlled the fury in his voice carefully. "What vileness?" he asked.

"You were seen in the church in conversation with a demon," Bertrand said. "The imp appeared beside you in a cloud of smoke. You did not dismiss it, but spoke words of welcome and listened to its temptings. Listened, nay"— Bertrand's voice was filled with malevolence—"seemed much pleased with them.

"When its business with you was done, its aspect became like unto a dog. It fell on all fours, red-eyed, with a muzzle filled with many long sharp teeth. Its mouth breathed fire. It fawned about your feet, as if owning a master, then it vanished away."

Owen steadied himself. This was dangerous. The accusation was not directed at him, he knew, but at all those who must be listening. Every word of this conversation would travel through the city and into the countryside. His name would be on everyone's lips and in such a way as this!

"No, I have no truck with demons, Bertrand. If anyone saw something like a dog fawning at my feet, it was because it was a dog, and nothing more. None of my hounds, to the best of my knowledge, breathes fire."

Bertrand paid no attention but continued, his voice growing louder and louder. "He told you secret things, this messenger from hell, things you could not know by any means proper to a Christian. Then, before all the town, you held fire in your hands, bathed in flame, and was not burned."

Bertrand's voice was a scream now, spittle flying from between his lips as he spoke. "Your spirit is intractable, contentious, and perverse. Steeped in pride and anger, even as a boy lodged in a holy place, you welcomed the night walkers to your bed; so that by morning, the very sheets you lay on were wet with the discharges of your most foul and secret lusts. Your body flowed with a plethora of unnatural seed . . ."

Owen stood gaping at Bertrand and then realized with as-

tonishment, he believes this! And then his astonishment became fury. "Damn you," he roared, "but that you stand
under my roof as a guest, you'd answer such filthy lies with
your life."

"Bertrand," Reynald said, interposing his body between
Owen and the table where Bertrand sat, "Bertrand, you go
too far."

"I go too far?" Bertrand screamed. "This false priest bargains with the devil and cools his hungers in a witch's
womb! This house," he screeched, "is host to a spirit summoned from an unconsecrated forest pool, to serve his filthy,
unending lechery. The heat of his desire would sear earthly
flesh . . . and drive—"

Owen's face was the color of clay, his beard stood out like
a dark stain against his skin. "Get out," he whispered, "all
of you get out of my house."

"Be silent," Reynald shouted at Bertrand, then turned to
Owen. "Think, my lord, think before you drive us away!
Many will believe these accusations are true."

Owen walked to the table, snatched the cup of wine from
in front of the count, and drained it, then set it down slowly.
The wine on an empty stomach acted quickly and calmed
him.

"We shouldn't have these quarrels between us," Reynald
pleaded. "Our enemies are many and we are few."

"Answer these charges, then," the count said to Owen.

Owen's rage had cooled and his mind was working furiously. "Answer what? Were they not mortal insults directed
at my lady and myself, I would laugh. My wife is but a
woman, unfortunate in that her family were murdered by the
Northmen. Seeing that she was well born and gently bred, I
offered her an honorable match.

"As to the first, he who saw me trafficking with the devil;
the man should change taverns, or better yet, you, Bertrand,
lay a penance of six months abstinence from strong drink
upon him. It may be that his encounters with demons will
cease."

"My son . . ." the count began.

"Your son was bested in single combat," Owen shouted,
banging the heel of his hand down on the table. "Moreover,
in single combat where he had all the advantage. It's not un-

known for a beaten man to find such excuses as he may to account for his failure."

"He said you never felt his blows," the count shouted.

Owen pulled up his shirt and showed them his ribs. A huge violet bruise covered his left side. "Does this look like something a man would not feel? I am the son of a noble house. My father began my training in arms at seven years. Pain is part of the learning and the practice. In the heat of battle a man takes blows. He fights on. Any soldier, even the meanest, masters the fear of suffering and death. I can yet hear my father's voice, his derision when I ran whimpering from pain as a child. I don't do so now!"

"You dare," Bertrand screamed, "you dare boast of your rank." The dark eyes under his tonsure bored holes into Owen. "The serfs who plough my fields are better born than you are. Your grandsire, what was he but a successful freebooter? And his son, your father, the same pirate breed. He got you on a spiritless drab. Her kin were too weak or greedy to defend. I tried to flog the sin out of you, the more fool I. You are all evilness, and know no Godliness. Immune to all good counsel and correction, lecherous, cowardly, foolish, and given over to every kind of vice!"

Reynald shouted, "Bertrand, enough!"

Owen was beyond anger. The room blurred away before his eyes, leaving only Bertrand's fanatic, hate-filled face before him. His sword cleared the sheath before he knew what he was doing.

Suddenly Godwin's lean form was between him and Bertrand. His captain's powerful arms around him, pinning his sword arm to his body, voice in his ear. "Think what you do!" Godwin hissed. "He's a churchman, a guest, and unarmed!"

Unarmed did it.

Owen stepped back out of Godwin's embrace and sheathed the sword so quickly that the hand guard whacked against the metal rim of the scabbard.

Godwin turned and stood beside him. "End this now," Godwin said. "Otherwise, I cannot answer for my cousin or," he added quietly, "myself."

Reynald backed slowly away from Godwin toward the table, saying, "I think it might be well if we did." Then he ap-

proached Owen with open, empty hands. "I had no part in
that," he said to Owen, "and am not in agreement with Bertrand. But I believe these storms will end. No wise man,
and you are wise, my friend, starts a fight he stands no
chance of winning. They could," he warned, "this day,
strike downriver at you, sailing their longships to the city.
More provocation, and they may.

"Give me your hand"—he stretched his out to Owen—
"that the friendship between us be unbroken, for we may
have great need of each other before this winter ends."

Godwin stood to one side, his hooded eyes studying
Reynald's face.

Reynald seemed uneasy and shivered slightly. "Owen," he
appealed, "have I ever been anything but a friend to you?
Please promise me no more rashness." His back turned to
Bertrand and the count, Reynald winked at Owen. "A wise
man waits till winter to rob a bee tree. This harvest is not yet
ripe for our reaping. Let us delay a bit. Our opportunity may
come yet."

"Very well," Owen said reluctantly. He took Reynald's
hand again in a firm clasp.

Then Reynald turned away and shepherded Count Anton
and Bertrand out.

Owen swung around abruptly, looking into the fire. He
didn't want Godwin to see the tears of pain and humiliation
in his eyes. "I played the fool," he said.

"No," Godwin said, "you let your temper get the better of
you, that's all."

Elin was by his side. "Sit down," she said, "break your
fast."

"Leave me alone," Owen said bitterly, "I am unmanned."

"By what?" a voice spoke up from the direction of the table. "That performance?"

Owen turned. The monk who'd accompanied Bertrand
was still sitting at the table. He'd appropriated the count's
wine cup and was helping himself to the jug.

"My name is Alfric," he said to Owen. "That pitiful performance," Alfric repeated, "was an expression of intense
fear. You are the only one not blinded by it. You and perhaps
Reynald. They are as men who stare into the eyes of a serpent, not daring to look away or stir a hand or foot, lest they

be eaten. Forgetting all the while the serpent is master and will take its prey regardless of what they do."

Owen and Godwin both looked at the little monk with interest. He was a small man with gray hair bristling around his tonsure and bushy gray eyebrows. His eyes were dark, with deep crow's feet at the corners. He had a round cheerful face and a mouth that looked as though it smiled often.

"As for Bertrand," the little man said, "such ranting and raving. But give him clogs and mask, set him on stage, and in days of old he'd have had the crowds in Athens at his feet. And the count, what more could you expect? I hear tell that his son ran pissing and screaming away, did he not?"

"He did," Godwin said, "so fast we could not see between his legs. But I'll warrant he rusted his hauberk."

"So he makes you out a sorcerer," Alfric said.

"An untried boy," Owen murmured, still angry.

"You might have told him," Alfric said with a beautifully ingenuous smile, "that you'd now been tried and not found wanting."

"I wish I'd thought of that while he was here," Owen said.

"Alas," the monk said, "we always think of these brilliant retorts when the occasion for their use is past. They are the product of a cool head and a clear, reasoning intellect. All of those are destroyed by passion."

"And what man would not be riven by passion?" Elin said, "having such insults heaped on him."

"It may be that was what the count wanted," Alfric said thoughtfully, softly, looking away at the door. "But"—he turned back to Owen—"for myself, I seek employment. I'm a scribe, returning to my home in Wessex. But to my sorrow, the small store of silver ran out, and the coldhearted ship's captain would give me no credit, and abandoned me here on the dock. I and my few books. I could get no farther."

Owen felt like embracing the little man. He would like nothing better than to put his chaotic account books and the diocesan records into someone else's hands. But the man was unknown to him, and the very fact that he'd come with Bertrand roused Owen's suspicions. "I don't know," he asked sarcastically, "are you apt to see demons?"

Alfric chuckled, smiled, but then his face sobered. "Do

you know, my lord, that's a very interesting question," he said, raising one finger and pressing it to his lips while he studied the proposition. "I can't say. I've never seen one. And having no experience of the breed, I'm not sure, if I did see one, that I would recognize it. Who knows what a demon looks like but the black archangel himself? And he is the father of lies."

"Are you then my partisan?" Owen asked.

"Frankly, yes, my lord, because I lodged with Bertrand for a time. The man is mad, most unpleasantly mad, and he hates you. And I thought, I must meet this man whom the late Lord Abbot hates with such bitterness, and I haven't been disappointed."

Owen walked to the head of the table, saying, "Come join me, we'll have some breakfast." He took Elin's hand and said, "You also, my lady, I want your company."

The hall was filling up now, and Anna, with the small girl Elin had called Rosamund, was putting food on the table. Gowen was already attacking it with much the same vigor he'd shown against the raiders the day before.

Edgar slipped in and sat down on the bench at the foot of the table away from the rest. There were traces of paint on his face, and a strong smell of jasmine hung about his clothing. Owen decided he wouldn't ask any questions about what he'd been doing.

The two Wolves arrived and sat down gloomily, eyes bloodshot, and partook of the rather ample breakfast cautiously.

A large gray cat appeared and climbed into Godwin's lap. Owen looked at it. "How did that get in?"

"I can't say," Godwin answered, "but she seems to come and go at will. One of your humbler, but more useful servants. She keeps the stable free of vermin." He fed the cat from his plate. It was definitely a she, body heavy with cat progeny.

"A messenger of the evil one," Gowen said. "She knows her own kind."

Alfric extended his hand to the cat. She hissed, but without fluffing her fur or giving any other sign of warning. Alfric left his hand where it was, in front of her nose. She sniffed it cautiously, then allowed her back to be carefully stroked and her ears scratched.

"One of God's creatures," Alfric said, eyeing Gowen's formidable bulk, "and rather harmless, in comparison to some of the others."

Gowen paid no attention. He was watching Rosamund moving around in front of the fire with Anna.

"The girl is free," Godwin said.

Gowen sat up straight on the bench, resting his big hands on a pair of thighs the size of tree trunks. He and Godwin stared at each other.

Godwin continued to feed the cat, a slight smile on his lips, as he met the full impact of Gowen's stare.

Finally, Gowen looked away, back at Rosamund. He scratched his stomach and said thoughtfully, "Very well, so long as she doesn't run away. I've had them do that you know, run away."

"How strange," Godwin said softly.

"Not at all," Gowen said, "I frighten people. I've never met a man whose bones I couldn't break"—He glanced at Godwin again slowly—"if I tried."

"There's always a first time," Godwin said. "One never knows."

"See that she stays until I'm tired of her," Gowen said, rising from the bench.

"I'll do my best," Godwin promised the knight's back as he walked toward the stairs, and then went on eating calmly, from time to time making an offering to the cat.

When Gowen had disappeared past the top of the stairs, Elin turned to Godwin. "Thank you." It was almost a sigh of relief.

"Oh, not at all," Godwin said, "I always find it very reassuring to know that Gowen still thinks I can kill him."

"Alfric," Owen asked, "why did you say the count wanted me to fly into a rage at Bertrand?"

Alfric smiled and shrugged. "What better way to ruin you? It's true, Bertrand is not . . . well liked. But he is a churchman and, moreover, was unarmed and a guest. Had you cut him down, many who now trust you would have turned away."

"No," Owen said, "it's too farfetched. Bertrand is Reynald's brother-in-law. Reynald wouldn't lend himself to such treachery. I can't believe it."

"Amazing," Godwin said, "I can believe it so easily. Reynald need not have known what the count had in mind."

"You acquitted yourself well against them," Elin said.

Owen turned toward her, mildly astonished. "How so?"

"She's right," Godwin said. "They got nothing they came for. You gave them direct answers and made no commitments. As for Bertrand's driveling about witchcraft . . ."

Alfric laughed. "It's only too plain how much he hates you." He smiled again that beautiful smile. "And will a man be the less respected if those who follow him believe that, if God rides before him, the devil rides behind?"

Owen's mouth dropped open as Godwin began to laugh.

Elin sent Alfric to the scriptorium and then showed Owen the dovecote under construction.

The economics of the dovecote didn't appeal to him. But he examined the sweat bath and decided he liked the idea. Just the place to relax and get clean after a hunt or a long day in the fields. He was pleased to see that it was big enough for two. Elin could join him, and he spent an enjoyable few minutes anticipating that pleasure, imagining how she'd look and feel, her soft skin glowing and bejeweled with moisture.

She'd also procured some rabbits, a rooster, and half a dozen hens, placing the rabbit hutches along the courtyard wall, and the hens in a corner of the stable.

Ingund was settling the hens in their roost. She'd already taken an egg to hatch between her ample breasts.

"I can't do that," Elin said enviously.

"Just as well," Ingund replied, "it's not natural, a woman being built like me. I was lucky you brought Enar that day. I sent a dozen packing before he came. Do you think Anna needs any help with Elfwine yet?"

"No," Elin said, "she had some food and now must walk for a while. Her water's not broken yet. She tells me that in her family, when it does, things go much faster."

"She's in labor?" Owen asked. "I shouldn't have sent Ranulf away, he should be here."

Ingund laughed. "Why? His work's done, was done these

many months. That's the way of it. Men have the joy, women the pain."

"Maybe I should send a rider . . ." Owen said, alarmed.

"No," Elin said, "he's best off where he is. Men are a nuisance at that time, fainting and puking."

"Underfoot every minute," Ingund said, "pestering the midwife, asking silly questions."

Anna stuck her head out of the upstairs window. "It has happened," she shouted laconically.

Owen jumped. "What's happened?" he asked quickly, fearfully.

Ingund and Elin looked at each other as if to say, "See what I mean."

"Her water's broken, that's all," Elin said, patting his shoulder as she would reassure a nervous horse. "I asked Anna to call me when it did."

"I'll go fetch the herbs you wanted from Gynnor," Ingund said.

"A midwife," Owen said anxiously, "what of a midwife?"

Elin fixed him with a stern glance. "I can see that you will be as bad as Ranulf. I'm a midwife."

"Elin, it's not that," Owen began fearfully, "but . . ."

"I saw my first when I was eight and assisted my mother when I was but twelve," Elin said firmly. "Ride out and visit your tenants. I don't want you underfoot either."

As Elfwine began to cry out, Owen rode away, thankful he had errands elsewhere. He was pleasantly surprised at the reception he got that afternoon on his manors. Tales of the disaster at Newtown were on everyone's lips. Serfs and freeholders alike were more than willing to listen to his plans for the defense of the city and make promises of cooperation. The rest depended on him. None would surrender their hardwon surplus for nothing. He must guarantee them some means of subsistence should the winter crop fail. Thanks to his victory, he was able to promise payment in cash to those who sent him supplies.

The count's people were more difficult—some were all but ruined by Gerlos and his men, having little to give, even if they would.

But they listened, though they hid their women when he and Enar arrived, and had the look of men who'd heard promises before. A few yielded so far as to say they would load and send whatever they could spare tomorrow. And Owen was sure he could win them as soon as the rest saw how they profited by their dealings with him.

When he entered the hall, Elin was coming down the stairs carrying a bundle of bloody linen in her arms. She looked exhausted and pale, wisps of her pinned-up hair were stuck to her forehead with perspiration.

Owen went up to her as she handed the sheets to Ingund, saying, "Best get these in cold water at once."

Owen put his arms around her and asked after Elfwine.

"Fine," Elin said, "and the child is a boy. Perfect in every way and healthy. This was my first alone, though Anna was a help, and thanks to Gynnor's medicine, Elfwine had only a little pain at the end, and I doubt if she'll remember it. But I was so nervous, and I didn't dare let show."

"What's wrong then?" he said, lifting her chin with his hand, and looking down into her face.

"Gynnor came," Elin said. "She told me Bertrand's accusations have spread and the gossip about us is terrible."

"I expected that," Owen said, "didn't you?"

She nodded, but still looked hurt and defeated.

"Elin, you must come to the church tonight," Owen insisted. "All the household must be there. Sit near the altar through the Mass. Everyone knows no unholy thing can abide the sanctuary once the real presence of Christ is on the altar. Then I'll speak, and try as best I can to counteract Bertrand's accusations. For it's only by our actions that we can defend ourselves. It's only through our actions that others understand us. So let all see clearly what you are."

Ingund returned and touched Owen's arm gently. "The church is ready. It will be as day in there. The whole city and the countryside are gathered to hear you speak."

Chapter

18

WHEN Owen reached the church he found Ingund had spoken the truth. Crossing the altar to reach his seat, he looked out over a sea of faces. The crowd packed the cathedral and spilled out into the square. Every inch of the space was filled by people, standing so close together, there was not even sufficient space for them to kneel down.

Ranulf sang the mass, served by Alfric.

Owen sat motionless in his chair, except when the responses were called for. The chair he sat in was old, so old few remembered its origins. It was all of one piece, carved from the heart of an ancient sacred oak—a tree felled by some of the first Christian missionaries to come to the town when it was little more than a Roman castrum set on the riverbank.

Owen thought about Bertrand's accusations, that he didn't belong to these people. That was a lie. It might have been true of his grandfather, a hard, womanizing old man whom he could only dimly remember, whose house was full of quarrels because he remained pagan and had three wives.

Gestric was a different kind of man. He had himself baptized and had taken one wife after the Frankish custom, bestowing much property on her. She was treated with great honor by all his father's kin, and he reaped the reward of this, since she brought many of her own relatives to his side, to the advancement of his power. His father's and mother's blood mixed well. She had borne him eleven children. Owen was the last.

No, he was as much her blood as his father's. Finally, he was sealed to the Lord Christ by his own anointing.

He had been a poor priest and an even worse bishop. He

promised his Lord, humbly, to do better. Then was ashamed because it seemed a kind of bargaining. No, what he was about to do was his duty, he'd been brought to see that.

But I didn't ask for this, he thought for one rebellious, angry moment.

Then Ranulf raised his hands in consecration, lifting the host high. *Ecce Homo,* "behold the man."

Owen went to his knees. *Yes,* Owen thought, *behold the man whining about his fate before his God. I did not ask, but neither did Elin.* He could see her face near the altar, head bowed in prayer in the soft glow of the many candles. She didn't ask for rape and slavery, the murder of her kin. Then it was borne on him, in sudden revelation as he looked at the Christ on the cross above the altar, neither did He, but was offered by His father, even as Owen had been. The one, the gift of a heavenly father. He, the gift of an earthly one.

Owen bowed his head and placed himself in the hands of that other victim and if he had before offered his fidelity, he now gave unstintingly of his love.

So deep was he in wordless prayer and in peace of soul, that he was surprised when Ranulf ended the mass and went to the side of the altar. Everyone waited for him to speak.

He rose and felt carried forward by a strength and sureness infinitely greater than his own. He had set the golden monstrance to one side, covered and hidden out of fear. Now those fears seemed childish. He would carry it before him, a symbol of his love and trust. His love for the hand that seemed to guide him, his trust in all those who stood so silent, his people to whom he belonged.

He barely felt Ranulf place the cope on his shoulders. He carried the monstrance, still covered, to the center of the altar, and placed the consecrated body of Christ in it. Then wrapping his hands in the cope, he turned and lifted it, and traced slowly and deliberately the sign of the cross.

He heard the gasp of astonishment that went through the crowd as a wave rolls through the ocean or the sigh of wind in the forest.

Then there was utter silence, the very air was still. The flames of the candles burned straight up, each tiny fire seeming to gather unto itself something of that infinite light before which even the sun is only a candle.

Owen set the monstrance on the altar. It blazed in the candlelight, a golden star, encrusted with the undying fire of the rubies. Then he turned and spoke. "You know we stand in deadly peril. Only places defended by a great lord are safe. But"—Owen paused and pointed at the monstrance—"I say to you, this city is defended by the greatest Lord of all."

His voice rang out like a trumpet, filled with a strength and assurance he didn't know it could possess. Then slowly he walked down the steps to the foot of the altar and stood at the rail.

"For, if the arms of a cross can stretch to the ends of the universe, they are also the beginning of an embrace."

He raised his arms in the form of a cross. And staring out at all the watching eyes, as though he wished to look into and touch the mind behind every one, began to speak.

"All of you know that I was given great help in my quarrel with Gerlos. I have given this much thought and prayer. Why should I, all unworthy and a sinner, be shown such favor? My prayers were answered and I understood. The message was not for me, but for you, that your cause is just."

Owen's arms dropped slowly to his sides. The word "just" echoed in the living silence, echoed under the roof as the breath in his lungs. A whisper.

He closed his eyes and clenched his fists, looking inside himself for strength. Then his eyes opened and his voice rang out again with the same bell-like clarity. "Many lords, yes, even bishops, have deserted their people. I will not. I will stay here, stand with you, and if it comes, die with you."

He raised his right hand. "That is my oath and if I be forsworn, then may my soul be cast down to burn forever in the uttermost pit of hell."

Then he turned, walked up the steps, lifted the mass book, and carried it down to the rail. "I am but a man. A man can die. A man will die." He extended his hand to Elin. "My lady, come here."

Elin walked toward him, chin lifted. He saw the love for him, the pride, burning as brightly as the candles, in her eyes.

He took her by the shoulder and turned her to face the people. "This is my wife; she carries my child." He felt the start she gave through his hand on her shoulder, but she said nothing.

"Godwin, come here," Owen commanded. Godwin stepped forward. He frowned slightly, but his hooded eyes burned with a courage that once faced down the eagles of Rome.

"They will each vow themselves to you with the same oath that I have sworn," Owen said.

Elin placed her hand on the book and her voice was a silver trumpet, a challenge to the heavens, as she took the oath to hold the city until death.

"Now you, Godwin," Owen said.

Godwin looked up into Owen's eyes and placed his hand over Elin's. The silence awaited his words. It was almost as though they were dragged from him, and they were as harsh as the clamor of steel on steel, but they came.

"I lay this charge on you both," Owen said, "do not fail it at the very peril of your immortal souls!"

He walked up the altar steps and set the book beside the monstrance, and stood to one side. "Now I ask an oath of you!"

His voice ran away from him, echoing under the roof. He had meant to vow them to himself. But all he had ever dreamed or wished now seemed a distant memory. All selfishness and fear burned away, transmuted, as the wicks of the candles, into clear light.

The hand of that same God Who once struck him down now guided and swept him on. The words he spoke were carried with marvelous clarity to the ears of all. Those standing near the doors to the square heard him as clearly as the people standing at the sanctuary.

"I ask that you bind yourselves in brotherhood to one another and that, in this time of great trouble, there be great love between you, that you be one in Christ our Lord. And if any of you finds his courage fails or he falters, that one may turn to his brother and find strength waiting in his heart, his hands, and on his lips."

Again he stretched out his arms to them. "That you be one as God is one and never divided, swear this not to me." He turned to the monstrance. "But to the Lord who holds this city."

The cope, encrusted with lace and brocade, seemed a yoke on his shoulders, pushing him down. "Now, kneel," he said gently, "and help each other, for the press is very great." And he was on his knees, bowed down before the Lord.

He didn't see the people in the church follow his example, going down in one long rippling wave as the high grass does under the breath of the summer wind.

He didn't afterward remember how his feet found their way to the altar rail, but there he stood with the mass book in his hands.

They came up, rank on rank, some wanting only to touch the book, token of their vow. Others kissed his hands, his robes, his face. He knew overwhelmingly that he was nothing; no more than the marble of a statue, or the earth, whose clay makes up the tints of a painting, are anything. The homage and the love were bestowed far higher. For a moment he, a vessel of time, had been filled with the light of eternity. They had seen it shine in and through him and the poor vessel that had borne the fire must now bear the honor, both penance and absolution for having been lifted so high.

Each had a turn and he suffered all. He greeted those he knew with an embrace and gave his hand to strangers. Women lifted children up to touch his face. It was done in amity, no pushing or shoving. Those behind cleared a way for the ones leaving the rail, and then came up themselves.

When it was over and the church nearly empty, he still stood quietly at the rail, filled with the love he felt, and a great peace.

The candles were burning out, guttering in their sockets on the altar and in the huge wheel of a lamp hanging from its chain high above. The darkness was creeping in, bringing sadness with it.

For a few moments, he had been part of something greater than himself. Now he would be carried along with it, as a drop of water is swept by a mighty river to the sea.

He had made his gift and it had been accepted. Just what form that acceptance would take, he had no idea. But he was emptied. His self returned to its self and he stood alone.

A shadow stirred near one of the pillars that supported the roof. It was Reynald and Elspeth. They drew closer to where Owen stood.

"It was a wonderful and terrible thing you did here this night," Reynald said. "I've never seen the like."

"I," Owen said, "I did nothing. I had no part in that."

Reynald stepped into the dwindling circle of light before the altar. He looked up at Owen, admiration and fear mixed perfectly in his eyes.

"It doesn't matter," Reynald said. "You could not have chosen a better way to seal them to you. They will follow you now even over that precipice the count spoke of."

"If that's to be the end of it," Owen said, "better a fall, and a quick death dashed against the stony ground, than to see all I love destroyed before my eyes."

Reynald stretched out his hand and Owen felt something pressed into his palm. He closed his fingers around it as Reynald and his lady slipped away.

The priests were waiting in the hall. Only when everyone had eaten their fill, and wine was served, and the chairs were pushed back from the table, did Owen speak his mind on the defense of the city.

They listened in silence. At first none of them said a word. Owen felt fear and guilt building in his heart.

He hadn't tried to make friends of them. Except for the most minimal administrative functions, he'd ignored them, intervening only in cases of gross misbehavior or when a quarrel threatened to become a blood feud.

Finally, one of them, Huda, a handsome old man with a head of white hair, spoke. "I'm pleased that you have at last awakened to our necessity. I feared you would while away your time amidst your horses and hounds, staying always in the count's shadow."

Owen sensed a leader. He knew Huda chiefly because he'd been the target of Bertrand's most venomous attacks. Huda had, after ancient custom, when his first wife proved barren, married another.

Despite Bertrand's nagging and prodding, Owen had refused to intervene, seeing that both women and their families were more than satisfied with the arrangement. To tell the truth, Owen had been afraid to interfere. The match had been made some years before Owen became bishop.

Huda was a power of sorts. He came from an enormous

family. Between his blood kin and those of the women he
married, he was related, like Gunter, to half the people in the
town and countryside. Such an individual could do much for
him.

"Before"—Huda's eyes swept the priests assembled at the
table—"we ever came here, all were in agreement with your
intent. The only thing that needs to be settled now is the
means."

Owen heaved a sigh of relief, sat up straighter at the head
of the table, and responded, "I will pay in coin for each load
of produce brought to my storehouse. Every man who comes
will walk away with silver in his hands."

Huda nodded and Owen continued. "When the weather
grows colder, I'll organize hunts to put meat on the tables of
my households."

One of the priests seated farthest away from Owen, in a
humble seat at the foot of the table, spoke up. "Will you
have warning if they attack, as you did this time?"

He leaned forward as he spoke, and Owen recognized
Martin, the priest who had come to his aid during the battle
at the new town. He was a big man, black bearded, with
arms as hairy as a bear's. Above the beard, a pair of gray
eyes burned with anger.

"Yes," Owen said quietly, "I'll know."

"Then can we not do more?" Martin's fist struck the
boards of the table with a crash. "My sister lived in that
town. Now she sits in my house and her tears never cease.
Her husband fought for her, little enough, he did what he
could, just awakening from sleep. She saw him killed, and
the child at her breast ripped away, its brains dashed out
against the hearthstone. They don't deserve the name of
men. I was pleased you hung them from the walls. It would
have pleased me better if they had been yet living when it
was done."

Another of the priests spoke up. "I think he speaks for all
of us. My question is the same as Martin's. Can we not do
more?"

Owen, sitting at the head of the table, realized that he had
what he'd openly repudiated to Reynald, the makings of an
army. They'd already granted all he wished, even before being asked, and now he saw, looking at the faces of Martin

and the others turned eagerly to him, that they would gladly offer more.

But he didn't want to frighten the count too badly. The man still had power and could make more trouble for him.

Huda, watching his face, seemed to realize the origin of his reluctance, and turned to his fellow priests. "The Lord Bishop is a mighty fighter," he said gently. "I think we've all seen the proof of that. But the first order of business is to provision the city so that it may be a refuge if we are attacked."

He reached up, smiled, and deliberately pulled at his earlobe.

There were smiles in return from the rest, and knowing looks, even from Martin, who had been so passionate in his anger. They all reached for their wine cups, and the talk at the table turned away from war to diocesan matters.

Eventually, Owen saw them to the door. Most had far to go, but some would be guests at the houses of kinfolk in the town.

Huda hung back, saying to Owen, "I have a favor to ask of you also."

"Ask then," Owen said. "If it's within my power to grant it, I will."

"I have three sons," Huda said. "Two are well content to be farmers but the third"—Huda paused—"well, Alan has larger ideas. It may be that he's a fool. If so, send him back home properly chastened."

"If he's your son," Owen said, "I'll wager he's not a fool."

Huda smiled a gentle half smile filled with fatherly affection. "I have a good opinion of him myself," he said.

Owen returned to the hall, making a mental note to tell Godwin to welcome the young man and make a knight of him. Even if the boy didn't know one end of a sword from the other.

Chapter
19

WHEN Owen returned to his room after seeing the priests, he found Elin waiting for him. She stood beside one of his chairs near the fire, her hand resting lightly on the tall back, gazing pensively into the flames.

He paused for a moment just to look at her, and breathed a short prayer of thanksgiving that she hadn't died or suffered serious injury from her fall the night of their quarrel. Even with the fading bruises on her face, only yellow marks now, she was so beautiful—slender and graceful as the long rushes that grew by the river, with midnight hair and summer sky eyes.

Her every movement reminded him of a tall, ripe wheat stalk, bending and bowing before the love of an autumn breeze.

Perhaps she felt his eyes on her, because after a moment she turned and said, "Owen?"

He stepped out of the shadows in the hall and into the room.

"Did you get what you wanted from the priests?" she asked.

"Everything I wanted and more," he answered. "Why do you ask? Weren't you listening?"

She shook her head. "No, I was with Alshan and my people. He had a message for you."

"What?" he asked.

"Hurry," she said, her face full of grave concern. "Hakon the raider chief has called in his men. They travel about, you know, stealing from the weak and trading with the strong. Now, no more. They are at the fortress refitting their ships and readying themselves for . . . an attack."

"How many ships?" he asked.

"Alshan said as many as the fingers on one hand. Big ships. War ships."

He entered then and knelt at her feet on the wolf skins. He raised his hands to warm them at the blaze. "Between four and five hundred men."

She nodded. "I think so. Alshan thinks so, too, but he can't count that high."

"Very well," Owen said. "I'm making ready to meet him. The main thing is to have sufficient food in the city so it may be a refuge for everyone. We can think about armies later on. Now we just have to survive."

She nodded again in unspoken agreement.

"Thank you," he said, looking up at her.

Her brow furrowed slightly. "For talking to Alshan?"

"No," he said, "for not calling me a liar in church tonight."

"They know you're a liar," Elin said. "I have the marks of ... what I was ... on my body, the weals on my back, the scars of fetters on my wrists and ankles. After our quarrel, after I fell, Gynnor and Anna tended me. They saw and I could tell they knew."

"It doesn't matter," Owen said. "I spoke under oath on the altar of a church with half the town as witnesses. No one will ever be able to dispute your claim, or mine."

"No," Elin said, "it's not that easy. Both the child and I belong not to you or even the city, but to my people. I bartered it for their friendship."

"It's not a claim," Owen said harshly, "but a payment."

"A what?" Elin said, astonished.

Owen rose to his feet facing her. "Elin, because of you and your friends I first tasted wealth and power. What I gave you in the church was only your due. Alshan told me they were coming and now the looted gold of those scum I killed swells my coffers. Their mail shirts are on my men's backs, their swords in my men's hands. Besides, if I fall, you will need the name of wife to continue the fight. If you do continue it."

Elin turned away from him and walked toward the bed. "I will," she said. "You had my oath on that long before tonight. Yes, I will go on alone if I must. I wouldn't want to, but I would. When I said you were all your people had, I spoke better than I knew. The count is a sot. Bertrand is mad."

"Oh, yes." Owen laughed mirthlessly. "Quite mad. And worse than mad, useless in a fight. I don't think he'd care if the Vikings took the town and put its people to the sword so long as I perished along with them."

Elin walked back toward the fire and sat down in one of the chairs near the hearth. Owen relaxed, sinking down on the wolf skins, and rested his head against her knees, his eyes closed as he tried to recapture the peace he'd left in the church, the sense of love.

She stroked his face gently with her fingers and played with the soft, fine curls at the base of his neck.

"Elin," he said, "you said we both had defied the gray sisters. I can understand this for myself, but what did you do?"

She drew her hands away from him and folded them in her lap. He opened his eyes and looked up at her. She stared away into the distance, into the shadows in the corners of the room.

"We are fine midwives," she said.

"Yes," Owen answered. "Gynnor praises your skill at healing. Anna and Denis half believe you can work miracles."

"We are summoned to the bedside of many a woman in labor," she said, "but this time I came too late. They were waiting for her to die. The priest had come and gone, her lips were blue, and candles burned at her head and feet. She lay on her bier ready to be carried to her grave. They were only waiting for her to take her last breath.

"Yet," she continued, "when I felt her belly, the child still kicked in the womb. Feebly, to be sure, but still it lived and hungered for the light. I mixed a potion double strength, stronger than I ever had before, and forced it down her throat."

Elin paused for a moment. He could hear her harsh breathing and the loud crackle of the flames in front of him.

"What happened?" he asked.

"She screamed," Elin said, her voice toneless and dull, "screamed and fought me as if she hated me for bringing back the pain she'd escaped. Her husband cursed me for giving her more useless suffering. And the child came into the world in a rush of blood and water as its mother died. Her husband cursed me again, saying the child would starve because there was no one there to put it to the breast. But I knew of a kinswoman of the dead mother who had a living child. I knew she would accept it as her own. So I swaddled the child and bound it to my breast. I took off running . . ."

"Was she very far away?" Owen asked.

"A little matter of thirty miles or more," Elin said, "with a weakened infant to protect, through the winter rain. A bitter and difficult journey. But I brought the child to safety . . . or so I thought."

"I haven't heard anything so terrible," Owen said quietly.

"I have a mother among my people, Owen. She who taught me my arts. She said the child should have died. The spirit, she said, would have flown to the womb of another woman. She told me I was always the rebel and I'd defied the gray sisters and must stand by what I'd done. I'd fought off death with my two hands and there would be an accounting."

Elin rose from the chair and began to pace back and forth, her gown rustling softly as she passed.

"The accounting came. The woman would not sleep quiet in her grave, but walked in her husband's dreams, stretching out her arms to him and calling for her child. I was sent to sing her spirit to sleep. It was my duty to go. I went, but first I journeyed to the stronghold where I left the child so I could assure its dead mother of its safety. But I found . . ."

"You found," Owen said, resting his forehead on his knees, his eyes closed, "what I found so often along the river—a few charred timbers, weed-grown fields, and desolation."

Elin clasped her hands tightly in front of her, fists against her stomach. "Yes," she said. "There were charcoal burners in the forest. They know our people. I stopped and asked after the woman, the family, the child.

" 'Lady of the forest,' they said. 'We buried them, but we cannot say what we buried for the beasts of the fields and the birds of the air had gotten there before us.'

"So I went to the mother's grave outside the churchyard, near the wood," said Elin. "But at moonrise when she came toward me with pale hands and empty eyes, my heart failed me and I fled. As I ran, I knew I could no longer live among my people. I hurried away to warn my uncle. He didn't listen to me, didn't mount a guard at his villa, and I was taken in the Vikings' nets."

Owen rose and put his arm around Elin's shoulders. Two cups and a jug of wine rested on his shaving stand in the corner. He poured a cup and held it to Elin's lips. Her skin was cold and he made her drink until he felt it warm. The wine was a coarse, musky red, almost salty with a hint of tears or blood.

Elin drew back, wrinkling her nose at the taste. "Bitter," she said.

"But these are sweet," Owen said as he slid her gown down over her shoulders, baring her breasts.

"Oh, no!" she exclaimed, half laughing.

"Oh, yes!" Owen said. He held her tightly to him with one arm while his other hand delightfully explored. A few seconds later it wasn't necessary for him to hold her and both hands wandered.

"We argue," she said, her breath coming in rapid, shallow gasps. "I always lose."

"One day you won't," he said.

"I know," she breathed, her head resting on his shoulder, her eyes closed. "And our happiness will be ended."

"So soft," he murmured, "like a chicken breast or a horse's nose."

"A what?" Elin cried and her eyes flew open. She whirled away, and her dress slithered to the floor, leaving her naked. He clung to her wrist as she pulled back from him at arm's length.

He stayed where he was, lost in the simple pleasure of looking at her. Her fire-painted skin was the color of old ivory, except that ivory never showed under its surface that faint luster of rose. Her hair swirled around her face, dark as a storm cloud echoing the shadowy gray of her eyes in the dim light.

"What?" she asked in mock horror. "Now I'm a chicken breast or a horse's nose. You need teaching."

"Do I?" he asked in return. "I'll tell you something, Elin, the only thing I ever learned from Bertrand." Owen saw her face sober at his somber tone and the mention of Bertrand.

"Pain is a necessity in this world, but happiness is an accident. I don't know or care what brought you to my bed—
chance, fate, my God or your goddess—and I don't care. I
only know a brutal universe blundered and sent you to me.
I'll never willingly let you go."

"Please," she said, trying to pull free, "don't."

"Besides," he said, his sadness fading like a shadow in
bright sunlight, "they are soft."

She frowned. "What?"

"Chicken breasts," he said ingeniously. "You know how
they feel, all those feathers when you reach under them to
get the eggs."

"Oh, stop," she gasped, struggling with mirth. "One minute you make me want to laugh. The next . . . cry!"

"Laugh," he said as he pulled her toward him. "Laughter
is always better than tears."

"It's not fair," she said as his arms closed around her.
"I'm naked and you're fully clothed."

"Promise not to run away from me again," he said, "and
in a minute I won't be." True to his word, a few seconds
later he wasn't.

"So lusty," she said darkly as they embraced in the
warmth of the bed. "You meant what you said about the fes-
tival at planting time. When the bonfires glow in the fields,
you'll slip out of the house and take anything that comes
by."

"No, I won't," he said, as he entered her body and felt her
spasms of delight caress him. "I'll put you in the cart and really give them something to worship. But I, and only I, will
have the privilege of carrying you off into the darkness. I'll
have you among the furrows. You make me feel a god, fit to
spill my seed into the womb of the earth herself."

Their final outcries came together as the fiery pleasure
bore them both away.

Owen lay beside the sleeping Elin and was almost asleep
himself when he thought of the packet Reynald had thrust
into his hand. It was in his belt. He'd concealed it there, realizing at the time Reynald had given it to him that he
wanted it to be a secret.

The packet was a note. Owen carried it over to the fire and unfolded it carefully.

Owen, I feared to speak my mind in the hall. That we may have communication in private, meet me tomorrow at sunset near the scene of your battle at the new town. The ruins will be shunned by all and deserted till spring. No one will see or hear us.

I am much more inclined than you know to fall in with your plans, but I fear my words will reach Count Anton's ears before I wish it. It's important that our talk be private, away from the prying eyes and the ever-present gossips of the town. Don't fail me. I am steadfast in my affection for you. Reynald.

Owen knelt before the fire, clutching the small piece of parchment in his hand, thinking furiously.

Hurry, Alshan had said. That meant he had to be ready to meet an attack on the city walls within a short time. Reynald would have every reason to help him. If the Viking chief struck downriver at Owen and the city fell, Reynald's smaller stronghold wouldn't last long.

Reynald could, without stripping his walls of defenders, easily put fifty more able-bodied men at Owen's disposal. True, they weren't the sort of elite professionals Godwin commanded, but they had seen a few fights, and could swing a sword. They would help immeasurably in stiffening his defenses at the walls. In time, when his troops were used to battle, he might even begin to think of launching an attack on this Hakon.

"Come alone." Owen didn't like that, even from Reynald. His first thought was of some kind of treachery, but for the life of him he couldn't think of any way that would profit Reynald. The count, though a close relative, was a broken reed. He couldn't be relied on, and Reynald seemed to regard Bertrand as more of a nuisance than anything else.

He looked over at Elin in the bed and wondered if he should awaken her, show her the note, and ask her advice. But at length and with some reluctance, he decided not to.

He didn't doubt that she could keep a secret. However, she already was a close friend of Gynnor's and well acquainted with many of the other women in the city. If she dropped one unguarded word in the wrong place, this golden opportunity for a fruitful alliance with Reynald might slip through his fingers. He didn't dare risk that.

So, Owen crumpled the parchment in his fist and threw it into the fire. He watched it curl into black ash and vanish in the flames.

Chapter

20

*E*VERYONE worked in the yard. The arriving foodstuffs had to be sorted, inventoried, and stored, and the men who brought them paid. This was Owen's job, and by noon, he was running short of silver coin. He stood over the box, fingering a heavy gold armlet molded in the form of a stag being pulled down by a wolf pack, thinking it would be a shame to cut it up, when Alfric came over, pen behind his ear.

"I have no more silver," Owen said, "some of this must be melted down."

Alfric looked up at him. "You are an innocent," Alfric said. "What are your feelings, my lord, about Jews?"

"Why," Owen said, surprised, "I have none. I've never met a Jew."

"Then," Alfric said, "wait. Pay no one until I return, and prepare yourself for a new experience."

A few more carts straggled up the alley into the courtyard. The noon sun blazed down from the sky. The short cold snap that brought the snow was past and the usual mild autumn weather had reestablished itself. It was hot now, and everyone was thirsty.

The farmers, with the ingrained patience of those who till the soil, seemed in no hurry for payment, but were content to rest in the shade of their wagons, gossiping with each other and some few of the townspeople who dropped by to pass the time of day.

Elin hospitably broke out a few kegs of beer; someone cut a wheel of cheese.

Owen began to get nervous. It looked as though the whole town might drop in for a visit, and his provisions be consumed on the spot.

He noticed Rosamund standing apart, bantering with Wolf the Tall. The big knight smiled, reached out, patted her behind affectionately, and put something into her hand. She returned the smile demurely, and tucked away what he'd given her in her belt pouch. Morgengabe, the morning gift between two who might be nothing more than casual lovers, Owen thought. His protection might only be an excuse for Rosamund to collect a lot of Morgengabe. Well, he thought, she said she wouldn't be sold, she hadn't promised not to sell herself. He disapproved for a second, then thought, well, what of it? The girl, newly freed, with no kin to look to for protection must consider her future. So long as she confined her attentions to the unmarried men of his household, he'd look the other way. He made a mental note to tell Elin to drop a word in Rosamund's ear, "No married men."

Alfric arrived, followed by the most beautiful or the ugliest woman Owen had ever seen. She was tall, but full breasted and full hipped. Her face was long with the prominent nose always ascribed to her people, but it suited her sinuously curving lips. Her eyes were nothing short of magnificent, large, dark brown, with lids that lifted smoothly to high, arched brows.

She wore a gown of white linen with flowing sleeves, scalloped and richly embroidered with golden roses and a mantle of blue and gold brocade. She held the hem of her skirt up, as much to show off the wide band of jeweled embroidery that bordered it as to preserve it from the dust.

She was followed, in keeping with her queenly appearance, by an entourage: three maids and five armed men. Two carried a strongbox, chained and padlocked, three served as guards, one walking on either side and the other ahead with a large mace in his hand.

The woman waved a hand and the mace carrier beckoned one of the three maids. She came running, carrying a folding chair and fat red cushion. She set the chair on the broad top step of the hall and plopped the cushion on the seat.

The chair was as much a visible symbol of the lady's wealth as was everything else about her. It was one of those kinds that opened around a central pivot, X-shaped, the bottom of the X forming legs, the top two crossbars the arms, supporting a cloth seat and back. Owen had many of the same kind in his house, but they were ordinary serviceable furniture, whereas this might be rated a modest throne. It was wood, old black oak, oiled and polished to a satiny sheen. The cloth of the seat and back were of heavy red-silk velvet.

The noise level in the yard dropped abruptly. Though there were murmurs of appreciation for the magnificence of the spectacle and general comment on the beauty and artistry of the chair, a thrill of anticipation ran through the crowd. Entertainment was in the offing. More people came scurrying up the alley to watch.

Alfric's impressive guest didn't take her seat immediately, but walked over to Owen's still-open strongbox and peered in. The inclusiveness of the brief glance suggested she'd taken inventory, weighed the value of everything in it, and arrived at an accurate estimate of his net worth. Then she raised her head, looked Owen in the eye, brushed at both sleeves in a rolling-up gesture, and said, "We can do business."

Only then did she walk over to the chair and take her seat.

The crowd moved back, though there was some pushing and jostling as everyone tried to find a good spot to view the action.

Alfric stepped forward, saying, "This is Judith, daughter of—"

"He knows," Judith said, with a wave of one glittering hand.

Owen did know; he'd never met the man, but he was locally famous for his wealth and the success of his various voyages. He was called Lullus, the Usurer. Owen felt a brief pang of pity for Holofernes of the Bible. This Judith looked quite as beautiful, capable, and ruthless as her famous ancestress. She turned to Owen, saying, "Now, what have you to offer me?"

Owen cleared his throat nervously. He had no experience with borrowing against his possessions, and he knew miserably that to salvage his dignity he'd probably accept the first offer this imposing woman made him.

But Alfric stepped in. "My Lord Bishop is a nobleman and a right ready man of his hands, but this business is beneath him."

He lifted Elin's necklace from the strongbox and handed it up to Judith.

She rotated it slowly, studying each link closely.

Owen drew himself up, trying to maintain the composure proper to the solemnity of the occasion and succeeded, in spite of his old linen shirt and leather leggings, better than he knew. Then silence fell as everyone waited for Judith's verdict.

"It is old," she admitted.

"A genuine antique," Alfric said.

"No link is exactly like any other. Poor workmanship," she said flatly.

"My lady," Alfric gasped, "each is a separate and individual work of art. Each a perfect setting for the rubies."

"Garnets," Judith said.

"Garnets!" Alfric cried. "Why, you yourself said it is of great age, and look, not one stone is worn or dimmed by so much as a scratch. Rubies," he said, drawing himself up and folding his arms, "rubies, my lady."

"I will allow," she said, holding the necklace up to the light of the sun to examine the stones, "they are hard. They may be rubies. How much?"

"Fifteen thousand dinars," Alfric said.

"Fifteen thousand! What!" Judith shrieked. "My heart!"

She pressed one glittering hand to her breast and stretched out another to one of the maids standing around her. "Take my pulse, fetch my physician, my heart is palpitating," she moaned.

Then she snatched back the arm she held out to the girl and pointed at Alfric. "Two thousand and not a penny more."

Alfric turned to one side, then threw his arms out. With a look of disdain he said, "You insult me and my lord, the bishop. Twelve!"

"Insult?" Judith shouted, outraged. "He speaks of insults, he who seeks to take advantage of a poor, weak, helpless, defenseless woman. Five thousand, and I will creep home to my father's house and hide my head in shame, waiting in fear and trembling for his return, lest he beat me for allowing myself to be so foully abused." She pressed both hands to her breast and bowed her head.

Alfric fell to his knees, threw up his arms, and raised his eyes to heaven. "I was mistaken and deceived, oh, Lord. I believed the house of Lullus to be an honest one, famed far and wide for fair dealing and righteousness." He leaped to his feet, fists clenched. "Nine thousand and not one penny less. It's worth twice that and you know it."

Judith now looked skyward and raised her arms. "Oh you heavens look down on this greedy thief." She dropped her arms and glared at Alfric. "A man who, when my father found him, was sitting penniless on the quay, the salt of his tears mingling with the cold rain. A destitute outcast, begging the bread he ate, with hardly a shirt to cover his back. Is this how you requite my charity, my hospitality, with such ingratitude? I think I could go seven, though." She pressed the fingers of one beringed hand to her forehead. "I know not how I will feed my children," she said disconsolately.

This was a little thin. Everyone knew Judith's children were grown, well established, and prosperous in their father's business.

"Eight," Alfric said, and looked at Owen.

"Eight," Judith echoed Alfric's words and also turned to Owen.

"Will you sell it outright or use it as security for a loan?" she asked.

Owen started slightly. He as all the rest had been mesmerized by the histrionics.

"It belongs to Elin," he said, with a bow to where she stood among the women near the cellar door.

She stepped forward with a smile. "I'm guided by my lord in all things," she said sweetly, with only the merest tinge of irony. "I'm part of this. Sell it if you must."

"I'll pledge it till spring," Owen said.

"Seven then," Judith said.

"Done for seven," Owen replied.

"In May, repay eight," Judith said and handed the necklace back to Alfric, who returned it to Owen's strongbox.

Judith then leaned over and beckoned to one of her maids and one of her men. She spoke to them in an undertone. They both left quickly.

Alfric accepted the coins from Judith's strongbox and placed them in Owen's.

Owen drew closer to Judith. "Thank you," he said, "but you haven't taken the necklace."

"No thanks are required," Judith said. "It's a profitable accommodation between friends, I hope. I hope we are to be friends?" she added.

"But the necklace," Owen said.

Judith and Alfric looked at each other.

"He's not aware," Alfric said, "of how these things are arranged."

The strongbox was beside Judith on the top step of the hall. She beckoned again to one of her maids. The girl brought over a fat yellow cushion and set it on top of the strongbox. Judith invited Owen to sit down and survey his yard.

He did gingerly, saying, "I've been working and . . ."

"Not at all," Judith said, waving a hand negligently. "Now, as to the necklace, that is simply a surety. I'm satisfied that it exists and is of at least the stated value, if not more."

"It's worth fifteen," Alfric said.

Judith pursed her lips. "No, but ten at least, if I could find a buyer. That's the difficulty, everyone is poor. I'll grant you, Alfric, it is a work of art. Each link, as you said, frames the individual gems perfectly. There's no need to deprive your lady of its possession and use."

Judith looked narrowly at the carts that crowded the yard, laden with sacks of wheat, rye, oats, sprinkled with bacon, ham, and other salted meats; one was piled high with dried fish. "All that will double in value long before spring," she said.

"It may be eaten by spring, if the Northmen come," Owen answered.

"But if they do not, you will sell it and repay the loan."

"I see," Owen said. "It doesn't matter how the debt is repaid as long as it's paid."

"Exactly," Judith said. "In fact, I would rather not have the gems. It would break my heart to destroy a thing of such beauty. Yet I'm sure I couldn't sell it."

Owen realized she spoke the truth. "You don't always think of money then."

"No," Judith said with a laugh. "Of course not. I heard

you speak in the cathedral. Oh, but that was incomparable," she breathed. "A leader, I thought, an idealist, ready to lay down his life for the city and its people, but so unworldly and naive. He needs my help, I thought. So," she said commandingly, "I've come to help you."

"How?" Owen asked, bewildered and a little overpowered by Judith's strong presence.

Judith reached forward and tapped his forehead with one finger. "Think, man," she said, "no one will hate you if you make an honest dinar because of your own forethought. Put"—she pointed to the food carts—"that on the market in spring. It will hold down prices. The people will love you, and the good silver will flow into your coffers. Now," she continued, "the rest of the gold in your strongbox, the beautiful monstrance. Will you let that lie idle? Would you buy a live horse and never ride it? Take a hawk of majestic beauty and never fly her? Why man, you have wealth and its power, only put it to proper use."

Enar had drawn closer and asked, "What should he do with it?"

"Why," Judith said, "let me make a loan against it and invest in my father's next voyage and—"

"No," Owen said, "thank you for the offer, but no." He started to rise, saying, "I have no right to risk church—"

"But there is no risk," Judith said, astonished, "or I should say there's a way to minimize the risk. Donatus, the cloth merchant, for a small fixed sum, will undertake to return all your loss should my father's next voyage, God prevent it, be a disaster financially, heaven protect him, or in any other way."

Enar began backing away. "Can this be possible?" he asked. "Something must be wrong somewhere."

Judith skewered him with one glance of her dark eyes. "That's a fine sword you wear."

Enar immediately gripped it tightly with both hands.

"Gold included," Judith said, "worth about one hundred and forty dinars. But pledge it to me for that sum, and leave the money in my hands to set out at loan. I will return the sword in one year and fifty dinars less my commission, of course."

Enar backed away, still holding the sword very tightly.

Elin drew closer in a sort of controlled drift. She was fascinated by Judith's clothes and jewels, but a little envious and afraid of making a fool of herself. Wilsa, Elin's mother, had sternly drilled her in all the complex womanly arts needed to run the difficult, extended households, but Wilsa had the convert's enthusiasm for Christianity. She had forbidden her daughters what she considered merely vanities, paint, perfume, or silken gowns.

Judith was obviously well acquainted with all three. There were no flowers blooming in the garden, but their scent was in the wind and the color in Judith's lips and cheeks was a little too rich to be quite natural.

Judith observed her approach, while talking with Owen, out of the corner of her eye. When Elin was a few yards away, Judith rose from her chair and was down the three low steps in a moment. "You are the Lady Elin," she said, enfolding her in a quick, irresistible, perfumed embrace. "All speak of you in praise of your beauty, charm, and distinction."

"Thank you," Elin said, "but . . ." She touched the yellowing bruise on the side of her face, embarrassed.

Judith ignored her embarrassment completely. "But you're even more lovely than I was led to believe. Ah, those eyes, the purest lapis, and honey skin. I've taken the liberty of bringing a gift for you."

She looked around impatiently for the two servants she'd sent out earlier. They'd returned with two linen-wrapped bundles. Judith opened one and pulled out a bolt of blue and white brocade. She held it up to Elin's cheek, covering the bruise. "Ah," she said, "it is as I thought, the blue matches the color of your eyes."

Elin's fingers caressed the rich stuff gently. "Why, it's so soft," she said.

"This for a mantle," Judith said as she returned it to its linen wrap, "but this," she said, opening the other bundle, "is for quite another purpose." The smile on her lips was filled with feminine wickedness. Salmite of a very thin weave, a gauze, almost transparent. She passed it gently over Elin's hand.

"How beautiful," Elin said, "for a veil. But it's so large . . ."

"Oh dear," Judith sighed, "no, no, no." She punctuated each "no," lifting her hands, palms up, higher and higher, until they were at the level of Elin's shoulders, then she placed them there, leaned over, and spoke into Elin's ear.

Elin's eyes widened and her lips parted. She looked pleasantly shocked. "Oh, I couldn't," she gasped.

"And why not?" Judith said. "They are fascinated by what is seen, and yet not seen. Veiled charms, each movement revealing some new beauty to the eye. Mine becomes quite wild. Be careful," she cautioned, "it tears easily."

"But such rich gifts. I couldn't accept . . ."

"Of course you can," Judith said, "I desire your friendship and your lord's. I need not have come here, had I not wished to meet you both. Alfric could have served as go-between.

"Now, promise," she said to Elin, "come and visit me and bring that cookbook of Alfric's with you."

Judith kissed the tips of her fingers. "The priests haven't stopped smacking their lips and boasting of your dinner, and will not for weeks yet."

She embraced Elin again, repeated her invitation, then swept out, leaving the scent of her perfume in the air.

"She paints her face," Owen said.

"And so well," Elin said, "that it seems as if the color came from nature. I wish I knew how to do it."

Owen lifted the fine gauze and imagined Elin wearing it. "She had some very interesting ideas."

Elin stroked the silken material gently. "It's so fragile," she said.

"No matter," Owen answered, "I'll have you out of it in no time at all."

Chapter

21

*T*HE sun was westering when Owen rode out to meet
Reynald. He brought Enar with him, even though
Reynald had said come alone.

He'd debated with himself all afternoon about accepting
the invitation, but finally decided it was too good an opportunity to consolidate his position to be missed. For the life
of him, he could see no harm or danger in a quiet talk with
Reynald near the forest. The countryside was open. Any
large party of men approaching would be visible and he
would not allow himself to be drawn in among the trees.

Besides, he trusted Reynald. They had often hunted alone
together; had he wished to harm him, it would have been
easy to accomplish then, and things hadn't changed that
much. Reynald had no great loyalty to the count, and he
seemed to regard Bertrand as more of a nuisance than anything else.

Owen looked up at the sky. It would storm sometime tonight. He smiled, anticipating the pleasure of lying in the
darkness of his bed, Elin in his arms, hearing rain drumming
down on the roof. All around him the countryside basked
quietly in the beautiful, golden light of the late afternoon.

He stood in the stirrups and urged his horse into a gallop,
but Enar stopped him, grumbling, "I don't like horses, Lord
Christ Priest, and this pace hurts my backside."

So Owen slowed to a leisurely walk and asked, "Is that
better?"

"Yes," Enar said, still sounding disgruntled. "Where are
we going?"

"Nowhere in particular," Owen answered.

"Wherever nowhere in particular is, I hope it's not too

far," Enar said. "I'll want my supper soon. I've put in a hard day's work in your cellar—"

"Doing as little as possible, and getting your ears boxed by Ingund when you tried to throw her down behind the oil jars," Owen said.

"Oh, God, that woman has an arm," Enar answered. "My ears are ringing yet."

"So," Owen said, "I ask myself how a warrior of proven valor and fidelity can bring himself to play the buffoon?"

Enar threw back his head and laughed, his white teeth gleaming in the dark stubble of his wind-burned face, laughed until tears started from the gray eyes. When he'd conquered his mirth, he answered, "Why, Lord Christ Priest, consider me an antidote."

"An antidote?" Owen said, surprised.

"Against the Lady Fortune. She sits on your table now and blesses your bed. But I distrust her, for she's at best an inconsistent mistress. I'm here to see that you don't forget trouble. What else are friends for? What is life after all but a series of disasters?"

"You're a better talker than the serpent that whispered to Eve," Owen said.

"I but speak the truth," Enar protested. "The first of man's disasters is birth. Do the young of other animals come into the world wailing and lamenting? No, Lord Christ Priest, they do not. But the spirit of a man cries out because it knows it is born human and heir to all the misfortunes of the breed. The last disaster that overtakes us is death. In between, we must be prepared. I'm sent to you as a rod to see that you remain ready and staunch of heart."

"The spirit of man," Owen said, "is sacred and immortal."

"Have it your own way, Lord Christ Priest; for as men do, you will. But in my book, the spirit of man is unfortunate and too knowing."

"And what book have you ever read?" Owen asked.

"The book of life, Lord Christ Priest," Enar answered darkly, "and you may think as I do ere you turn a few more of its pages."

"You could outtalk the devil himself," Owen said, grinning.

They had been going along together talking so compan-

ionably that Enar hadn't noticed that he and Owen were on
the road along the river that led to the ruins of Newtown.

"Why are we riding here, Lord Christ Priest? The sun is
going down. It will soon touch the rim of the hills," Enar
said, pulling his horse to a stop. "I want nothing to do with
this place. The ghosts of those slaughtered there will wander
among the ashes calling."

Owen snorted in derision. "You reject Christ and joke
about the devil, yet you believe in ghosts."

"I've never met Christ or the devil," Enar said, his eyes
turning hard, as the shadowed sunset light brought out the
grim lines around his mouth, "but I have met ghosts in that
place where we had our first, unfriendly meeting."

He was speaking of the monastery ruins on the road to
Chantalon. "The church was the worst, Lord Christ Priest.
All night, weeping and cries of pain. A great dark hole. Not
even the bravest would approach it after sunset."

"The wind," Owen suggested, reining in his own horse,
stopping beside Enar.

"No, Lord Christ Priest. No, I know the wind well, and
the sounds it makes. Bertrand ran away, taking his favorites
among the monks, but he left many there to face the fury of
the sons of Odin, and it was terrible indeed. They butchered
all they found there. All except those few they kept alive for
a time, until they died, screaming over slow fires or strung
up from the beams of the church, their bodies torn asunder
by weights tied to their feet. For they didn't believe Bertrand
took all the wealth of the place with him, but thought it must
be hidden nearby. Oh, God, such pain, and no way to make
your tormentors kill you. Think of it, Lord Christ Priest."

Owen did, closing his eyes and signing himself with the
cross. "Don't speak of it! You sound as though you'd seen
it."

"No, Lord Christ Priest. Had I prevailed when I attacked
you, I'd have killed you clean and taken your lady gladly.
But I have no stomach for torture and the murder of women
and children.

"No," he said, starting his horse again, but in a path that
led around the village through the abandoned fields, "I came
there not long after. The bodies had been left to rot, still
hanging or lying in the ashes of the fires wherein they died.

The monks sheltered in the church at the last. It stank of the abattoir. The roof beams were open to the sky and flocks of carrion birds nested among them. We, brigands and outlaws that we were, gathered the bones and buried them out of pity and fear."

The town did look sinister in the light of the setting sun. The blackened stumps of the house beams cast long shadows. The dead had been buried in a common pit, a scar of newly turned earth near the charred timbers of their fallen homes. Perhaps they did still keep watch or wander about in the dark, crying for their lost loved ones.

Owen kicked his horse into a gallop and rode over to the grave, leaving the astonished Enar alone. When he reached its edge, he dismounted and knelt.

His memories of the place were of horror. The bodies of dead men and children, stretched out where they had been left by the hands of their murderers, still grotesquely contorted by their death struggles. He didn't know if he could pray. He bowed his head. The earth dampened and cooled his knees.

Prayer came to him like a friendly hand outstretched to take his own. Quickly and surprisingly, he felt at one with his God.

"Let them sleep," he prayed, "and not wander in the night, crying for their wives and mothers. And may they be comforted by Your love and life. Both the living and the dead."

He felt again that wordless assurance of final mercy and compassion.

He opened his eyes and looked away at the river in the distance, flowing blue beneath the wide and empty sky. Peace descended on his soul. He raised his hand and blessed the grave and then the burned-out town. Give them rest, he prayed, and take into account when judging their souls that they died suddenly and were innocent. Then he mounted his horse and rode back to Enar.

Enar was as nervous as he had been before. "Lord Christ Priest, I want my supper."

They moved away from the town toward the forest. It began abruptly because the brush and trees had been cut by the settlers.

Enar peered into the black ranks of its leafless trunks stretching away into the distance. "My Lord Christ Priest, I don't like this place any better than the village. Only God, and possibly the devil, knows what lurks waiting in that world, waiting for darkness, to strike at us. Have you some reason for riding here? We are not well armed, and there are no other people about."

"Reynald," Owen said. "He asked that I meet him here."

"He has not come," Enar said. "Let's return home."

Reynald rode out of the forest toward them. He pulled his horse to a stop beside Owen and threw his arms around him in a quick, friendly embrace.

"It's good to see you," he told him, smiling. "I must apologize for the outrageous behavior of my brother-in-law. Since his abbey was destroyed, he's been very bitter. Sometimes I think his mind is unhinged."

Enar gathered his horse's reins into his hands. Reynald's presence didn't reassure him as it did Owen. The countryside slumbered around them. The sun was touching the hills now, the silhouettes of the highest trees were outlined against the fiery orb. The light was bloody.

"My lord," Enar said loudly, "I do not like this place. Let us go home."

Reynald shot him the cold look he would have given any too forward servant, then dismissed him as not worthy of anger. "Don't," Reynald continued, "let our sweet friendship be spoiled by Bertrand's rantings."

"No," Owen said, "I value your friendship and wise counsel."

"Good," Reynald said with a laugh. "It may be that together we can do much to keep the city safe. Besides, I would miss our hunts. We'll have a fine one this winter."

He pointed to a stump very near the forest. It was a tall stump, what remained of a huge oak, still standing higher than a man's head. "A bee tree," Reynald said. "I found bear signs on it. The people of the village must have left it standing, thinking to harvest the honey this winter."

"Bear," Owen said excitedly. "I've never hunted one. What a trophy that would be."

"Come see for yourself," Reynald said, and trotted his horse toward the tree.

Owen followed quickly. Enar moved slowly, looking around. He was deeply disturbed and not sure by what.

Reynald was leading them toward the forest, and the long shadow of the bee tree lay on the golden earth like a black finger pointed at the burned-out village. Reynald stopped beside the stump and pointed high up on the bark.

Owen pulled his horse to a stop and peered at the giant claw marks. "I had heard of it, but never seen it. It is a bear, and a big one." He was delighted. "This would be a wonderful quarry."

As he turned toward Reynald, something hit the side of his head hard. His arms and legs went numb. He saw Reynald's arm upraised to strike him again, and Enar staring stupidly down at an arrow in his chest. There was time for sorrow, pain drenched and despairing.

"No, my friend," he whispered, already beyond resistance. "No!"

Then the second blow fell, and he didn't know that his body slid from the saddle or feel it hit the ground.

Chapter

22

E NAR felt something strike his chest. Simultaneously he lost both the reins and stirrups of his horse. The second arrow buried itself in the mare's chest. She bolted, carrying Enar toward the black woods. He saw the trees coming toward him as though they were flying and not he. In seconds the mare was among them, a wild runaway.

His big hands locked themselves desperately under the pommel of the saddle. He barely felt the low branches lashing his face and body. She ran toward the river, gaining speed with every bound. If she plunged into it, he would die. This was no safe ford, nothing could swim it here.

The broad water looked deceptively tranquil, flowing smoothly toward the sea. But the current was terrific, and a sucking undertow lay waiting to drown man and horse in seconds.

Faster and faster, branches tore at his clothing, trees flashed past in the twilight dimness of the oncoming night. Then he felt the horse slow as she hit the soft turf of the riverbank, throwing big clods of mud from her hooves.

Enar knew it was his last chance. Willows grew at the edge. Beyond them the river spread, a shimmer of golden death in the setting sun. Enar let go of the saddle and reached up blindly.

His fingers tore at leaves and twigs, then slapped, stinging, against a branch. He clutched it, fingers closing like the talons of a bird of prey.

The mare leaped clear of the shore, her head a black shape against the gold-coin glitter of the water.

Enar felt the branch bend, green, flexible as a wand.

The mare's four hooves touched the water.

"Oh God," Enar groaned inwardly, "it will break." The

branch whipped back, jerking him from the saddle. The muscles of his shoulders and arms felt like they were being torn away from the bones. Then he was hanging by his hands, for the moment, safe.

His mare was in the water, swimming strongly, her head lifted against the dull molten gold of the last sunset light. The current took hold and she was spun around, thrashing. It looked as if she would be swept back to the shore and safety. But suddenly she threw up her head. The powerful current eddied around her body and, with an almost human scream, she vanished, sucked down. Enar heard shouts behind him. Ignoring the pain in his hands and arms, he pulled himself onto the branch and went up the tree, moving as he did inward to better footing at the trunk.

When he heard sounds directly below him in the forest he froze, legs over two branches, embracing the tree with both arms. The light was blue, the sun-gold gone from the water. He looked down and saw the smoky haze of torches in the gloom.

Reynald and three of his men stood beside the trunk of the willow Enar sat in, examining his horse's tracks closely.

"He went into the river, my lord," one of them said to Reynald. "I heard the man scream as he died."

"Too bad," Reynald answered. "I thought to have him take the blame."

A fifth man entered the circle of torchlight. He led the gray, Owen's horse. Owen was slung over the saddle like a sack, face down, arms and legs tied under the horse's belly.

Dead or alive? Enar wondered. Probably alive or they would have thrown the corpse into the river. That was what any sensible man would do with a corpse.

The torches were following his track among the trees. "He didn't jump off. I see only hoofprints," a voice called.

"One way or another he's a dead man," Reynald said. "Godwin will kill him if he returns alone, and he has at least one arrow in his body. Let's ride. They will be waiting."

Enar's eyes followed the torches as they departed along the narrow track paralleling the river away from the city. Only when the lights winked out in the distance did he drop from the tree to the ground. He reached up and felt for the arrow embedded in the big muscles of his upper chest, thinking only, *Not deep.* He'd taken many worse wounds.

He pulled it out without flinching, feeling the warm gush of blood flowing down his chest and stomach. In a moment it slowed, then stopped. He moved his shoulders experimentally, forcing only a little more blood from the wound as it closed and looked at the arrow head in the dim starlight long enough to see that it was intact, then threw it aside. Not iron, only sharpened bone. Reynald squeezed even his fighting men.

He began to follow Reynald along the path by the river at a fast walk that soon turned into a jogging run. The night was moonless. Above the river, the flowing curve of the Milky Way dusted a black velvet sky. Faster and faster Enar ran, as his eyes fully adjusted to the darkness. The wind cooled him, whispering softly among the leaves of the willows and poplars above him.

Enar had told Owen once that he was a hard man; that was true. That he'd killed among his kin, that was true also. Few men would take in an outlaw such as he was, and honor him with a seat at his table and a gold-hilted sword. Owen had. It was Enar's duty to rescue him, if living. To take revenge, if he were dead. Besides, it was an abomination that a man should outlive his lord when they faced battle together.

Enar felt for the axe in his belt. The sickle curve of the blade rested comfortably against his belly muscles. The only reason Reynald still lived was because Enar was sure Owen lived also. Had Reynald's men made as if to throw Owen's body into the river, Reynald would have died on the spot, Enar's axe in his skull. But with Owen yet living, it was Enar's duty not to spend his life foolishly.

The faint sparks of torchlight came to his sight far ahead, traveling along the river. Enar adjusted his pace to keep them in sight without drawing so close that Reynald would discover him.

The sound of his footfalls were lost in the murmur of the forest that surrounded him. He was hard on the track, till the chase should reach its end, in rescue or death.

Chapter

23

WHEN the sun touched the rim of the hills, Elin began expecting Owen back momentarily. Few stayed away from their homes after nightfall.

Ingund was at the fireplace, cooking supper. The knights and men of the household began gathering at the hall's long table.

Elin went upstairs to check on Elfwine and found the girl in a chair, nursing the baby. Ranulf watched them both adoringly.

"Is he not beautiful?" Elfwine said, reverently looking at the child. "I can't believe something so wonderful came from me. See, Elin, he has his father's eyes."

Elin did her duty and admired the baby's eyes.

The baby, indifferent to the wondering gazes of both parents, sucked avidly at one of Elfwine's big pink nipples.

"Owen promises he will be a knight," Ranulf said happily.

"Where did Owen go?" Elin asked.

Ranulf, roused from blissful contemplation of his offspring, raised his eyes and shook his head. "He didn't tell me, just saddled his horse, took Enar, and left. He had only his sword and brought no food. I thought he meant to ride into the marshes and check the snares he set for rabbits. He didn't tell you?"

"No," Elin said, trying to throw off a sudden feeling of apprehension, "but he'll probably return shortly."

Ingund came in with a tray. Elfwine handed her the baby. She burped him vigorously, and set him in Ranulf's waiting arms. He cradled him proudly. The baby screwed up its little mouth in something that almost might have been a smile, gave a soft gurgle of contentment and repletion, then went to sleep.

Elin walked to the window. The setting sun was only a red glow on the horizon, and the indigo blue vault of the heavens sparkled with stars. She closed the shutters, bolted them, and lit another lamp for Elfwine. "He can't have remained in the marshes with night coming on."

"Oh, he didn't go that way," Elfwine said, looking up from her supper.

"No?" Elin asked, beginning to be increasingly fearful. "Where then?"

"I was walking with the baby near the front windows. I saw him ride out with Enar. He turned at the city gates and went upriver. I thought he was going to visit Huda."

Ingund and Elin went downstairs to serve supper to the men.

In spite of the day's hard work, Elin was restless. The later it grew, the more uneasy she became. She made her rounds of the house, shutting and bolting the shutters by lamplight.

Outside, the stars were blotted out by an increasingly heavy overcast. The wind picked up and the big house, half wood, half stone, always noisy at night, now seemed filled with whispered conversations, soft footsteps crossing empty rooms. The stair treads snapped and popped as though invisible feet climbed them.

Twice, walking through the darkness on the upper floor, she thought she saw figures standing just beyond the circle of lamplight, but when she turned to confront them, they were gone.

She woke Ranulf, who was sleeping with Elfwine, the baby in the big bed between them. As she touched Ranulf's shoulder, he opened his eyes, sat up on the side of the bed, and covered himself with the counterpane.

"My lady?" he asked sleepily.

"He is still not returned," she said. "Does he often do this?"

Ranulf frowned, puzzled, still not fully awake. "No, my lady, never," he said.

Lightning flashed, a sudden blue glow beyond the heavy shutters of the window, followed in a few seconds by the low, deep drum roll of thunder. Then hissing whips of wind-driven rain battered the sides of the house, setting the shutters to clattering in the blast.

Elfwine stirred, moving in the bed. She didn't awaken, but cuddled the baby closer with one arm.

"It may be," Ranulf whispered back to Elin, "that finding himself caught out, with night coming on, he might have stopped with one of the priests. Come to think of it, he has done that a few times."

Elin sighed with relief. "Likely that's what happened," she said softly.

The hammer of the rain outside became louder and louder.

"Don't be afraid, my lady," Ranulf said, troubled by her obvious anxiety, "he'll return safe and sound at dawn."

Elin tiptoed out, so as not to wake Elfwine and the baby. The upper hall was so drafty now, with the storm wind crying and moaning around the eaves, that her lamp guttered, its flame turning blue. In sudden terror of the darkness that gathered so quickly around her, she almost ran to the stairs that led to the light and company of the hall.

Elin woke before dawn and dressed quickly in the cold room. The rain had passed over during the night, leaving the sky clear, and a biting chill in the air.

Ine still slept downstairs in front of the fireplace, crossbow nearby. No Owen. Elin awakened Ine and started breakfast.

Godwin was down first and joined her. "I don't like this," he said.

"I didn't know you noticed."

"I did, but said nothing." Godwin settled himself into a chair by the fire. "He has too many enemies hereabouts to play such a game, if a game it is. Elin, speak the truth, this is no time for delicacy. Has he another woman?" Godwin's eagle face looked at her with its cold, dark raptor's eyes.

Fear was a hollow in Elin's stomach, a pain in her throat. She pressed a hand against her body. "The bread that I ate when I came down feels like stones in my stomach. As the light grows outside, so does my fear. Don't make it any greater, I beg you. What can I do? Raise an alarm? Go in search of him? I can't do any of those things."

She stood up suddenly, pulling at her dress in nervous irritation, as though she hated it.

"No," Godwin said, realizing he was taking out his anger at Owen on Elin. He spoke gently and took her hand. "No," he repeated, "you can't. Don't frighten anyone, but keep your people close to the house today. If he doesn't return soon, I'll begin to search quietly for him. Now tell me, Elin, is there another woman—"

"No, there isn't."

The voice that spoke came from behind Godwin's chair. It was Edgar. Godwin looked up at him. "You know I have friends in the town already, and my friends are terrible gossips, but even they consider him a paragon of chastity." Edgar smiled only a small smile but a complimentary one and bowed in Elin's direction. "That is, until recently."

Godwin seemed satisfied by this and turned again to Elin. "Did he tell anyone where he was going?"

Elin gave a negative shake of her head, then said, "But Elfwine saw both he and Enar turn on the road along the river toward the forest."

Edgar said, "I'll go now, see what I can find out."

"Ranulf said he might have stopped with Huda or one of the other priests," Elin said, returning to her cooking.

"Indeed, that may be so," Godwin said, sitting back in the chair. "Two poached eggs, please, and I like my bread lightly toasted, with only a little butter. Perhaps he sat up late drinking?"

"He's usually temperate," Elin snapped, irritated by the two poached eggs, on top of everything else.

"Usually," Godwin said, "but any man's foot slips now and then. Wine and a little chervil and thyme with the eggs, please."

Denis clumped down the stairs on his new wooden leg, carrying a big crossbow he'd just finished and was eager to try out. He was followed by Rosamund, a self-satisfied smile on her face, wearing a new ring and a bracelet of twisted silver wire on her wrist. She scurried over to the fire to help Elin, who gave her the job of poaching Godwin's eggs. The self-satisfied smile disappeared as he fixed her with a cold eye and gave the same explicit instructions he'd given Elin.

The table filled up, the men at arms following Denis.

Anna and the two Wolfs and Ingund came in, yawning. Elin
was suddenly too busy to worry about Owen.

Edgar returned with Alfric, followed by Ine. Edgar turned
to Godwin. "There's a crowd of armed men gathering in the
square."

Elin froze, one hand at her throat, her face white. Godwin
leaped to his feet and caught Elin by the arm. "Armed men,"
Elin whispered. "Godwin, they have made away with him
somehow and now are coming for me."

Godwin turned to the men at the table. "Up! Arm yourselves! Now! Rosamund! Anna! See that all the doors and
windows are bolted shut."

Rosamund stood white-faced before the fire, knuckles
pressed against her mouth.

Godwin's fingers snapped. "Jump, girl!"

Rosamund jumped.

"My lady," he turned to Elin, "upstairs, put on your best
dress. Ingund, attend her! You, Alfric, Ranulf, collect the
processional crosses, relics, all the religious tokens that you
have about, now!"

No one questioned him. In seconds the food lay forgotten
on the table, the hall a hive of frantic activity.

"They will try to blame this one on Enar," Ingund said to
Elin, as they rushed up the stairs.

"Hush," Elin said, "say nothing. They're not thinking of
Enar, but of the gold Owen has in his strongbox, and the
stores in his cellar."

Elin returned dressed in the white linen with the heavy
blue mantle. The household gathered at the door. Denis had
his men all armed and carrying crossbows.

"My lady will lead us out," Godwin said. "You"—he
directed this to Denis and the men at arms—"will fan out
around her, your bows cocked and ready to fire, but, on your
lives, do so only at my command. Gowen, you and Wolf the
Tall on one side, Edgar, you and Wolf the Short on the
other."

"The women . . ."

Elfwine was lacing up her dress. "I'll stand with my
lady."

"You can hardly stand at all," Ranulf said.

"Do you think when something like this is happening I would be left out of it? No, I must see and hear all."

"She will lean on me," Ingund said, taking her arm.

Anna positioned herself on Elin's right, Godwin on her left.

In a few moments he'd transformed himself from a crotchety, middle-aged nuisance into a warrior. He wore his mail, the long sword, sax in his belt, and a gold-inlaid helmet that marked him a commander. He carried the big kite-shaped shield of a horseman. It was painted with a golden dragon on a field of blood red.

He plucked the baby from Elfwine's arms and handed it to Rosamund, saying, "Here, take this and stay out of sight. Some of these men know your face only too well and will be hard put to defend the women without worrying about a baby in arms."

Rosamund's cheeks went scarlet with anger and mortification, but she stepped back, holding the infant.

"You, Ine!" Ine was standing at the fireplace, stuffing oat porridge into his mouth with one hand. He held a crossbow in the other. "To the back door, and let nothing pass in or out!"

Alfric stepped in front of Elin, holding the tall iron processional cross. "I'll walk before the Lady Elin," he said calmly. "Not many will shoot down a man of God."

Elin stood, hands clasped, so that no one would see how they were shaking.

Godwin rested his shield against the loophole in the door and peered out past it. Then he turned and spoke to Elin and the rest. "We must play out this comedy or the world will think we have something to hide. If they attack, I'll cover the Lady Elin with my shield, the rest of you women get into the house. If we put a bold face on it, I don't think they'll attack. They're dogs and cowards who think they've come to terrify one woman. Let's show them she's not alone!"

He turned back to the doors, lifted the bar, threw them open, and they all stepped forward together.

The square was filled. The count was there with his men and Gerlos, bearing still the half-healed burns on his face and arms. But it was Reynald who commanded the strongest force, fully thirty men.

To Elin, blinking in the morning light, it seemed an army indeed. But to Godwin's more practiced eye, they appeared a motley bunch. Their weapons were a miscellany: leather armor; here and there an old-fashioned cuirass set with metal plates; many wooden spears with fire-hardened tips; longbows; and axes. Few swords, no crossbows, no chain mail.

Many had uncertain expressions on their faces. This was a representative of the Holy Church they were threatening. The cathedral rose on their left, the squat stone pillars of its porch frowned on them.

Alfric stood before them in his sober brown and gray. On the blue and red of the enamel cross he carried hung not the sacrificial figure of the altar, but Christ the King in silver— stern-faced, crowned, and robed in a lord's dalmatic, ablaze with blue citrines.

Alfric set the tall post of the cross on the lowest step of the hall and looked out at them, his calm brown eyes seeming to say, "I remind you where you are."

Elin's household took their positions behind and beside her.

Anna, standing next to Elin, spoke up first. "Why do you disturb the quiet of this house before we have even broken our fast? I was but rising from my prayers when I heard of an army gathering before my door." The fingers of her hand tightened on Elin's arm.

Elin looked up and met Reynald's eyes. She knew at once he was the dangerous one. He sat slouching to the side in his saddle, as if to rest his backside. But his eyes met Elin's with a cold masculine assurance of power and contempt for her weakness, as if he knew she was now only a woman alone.

Involuntarily Elin lowered her eyes from his face to the people. Since this promised to be the event of the year, beginning with some windy speeches by all participants, and possibly culminating in a bloody showdown between the count's men and the bishop's, everyone in town was gathering around the square with unseemly haste.

Absolute silence fell as Anna spoke again. "Answer me, why do you disturb this house?"

The count rode out into the clear space before the half dozen shallow steps that led up to Owen's door. He raised his hand as if to command the silence that had already fallen.

"Where is the Lord Bishop?" the count asked in a loud voice.

Elin looked into the count's face. The heavy-lidded eyes were empty and indifferent, the mouth had a faint set of cruel satisfaction.

They have killed him, she thought, turning her eyes to Reynald's face and finding that same sensual mockery.

She said, "I ..."

The sun glinted on the weapons and armor. There was enough steel there to throw the light back into her eyes, blinding her.

She whispered, "I ..." again and found her tightening throat couldn't force the breath past her lips. She had no answer and they knew it.

It was Alfric who answered. "Why," he said loudly, "he rode to visit you, Lord Reynald."

Reynald's whole body jerked; he sat up straight in the saddle. "He told you this?" Reynald said, surprised.

"Yes," Alfric said with an expression of such perfect limpid innocence that it was impossible to disbelieve him. "Just in passing, as though it were a matter understood between your lordships. Oh, heaven have mercy, has he met with some mischance?" Alfric continued, beginning to sound alarmed. "I beg you, Lord Reynald, tell us what happened."

"Bitch!" Gerlos shouted. "I tell you the bitch will never yield unless we force the issue. The old fool lies in his teeth; the bishop has run away in spite of his oath."

He drew his sword and rode up beside his father in front of the steps. The count's men began to press forward.

Elin felt Godwin jerk her toward his side, saw his shield rise. In the crowd a woman screamed.

The crossbow bolt struck with the whack of a meat cleaver.

At first Elin couldn't see where it landed, then she did. It protruded, embedded to the fletching of the shaft, in the forehead of the count's horse.

The horse simply died. It never made a sound or gave any

sign of distress. But a second after the bolt landed, its legs folded, it sprawled on the cobbles, neck extended, blew once from its nostrils, and died. The count lay, still in the saddle, pinned by one leg to the ground, under the horse's body, an expression of utter astonishment on his face.

Denis dropped the spent bow, snatched another from one of his men, and pointed it at the count, where he lay pinned under the dead horse. "Move, Gerlos," Denis screamed, "and the next is through your father's heart."

The three-flanged bolt glittered wickedly in the sunlight, the edges of each blade razor sharp.

Count Anton looked up at it, mouth slack with terror, then raised his shield and cowered under it.

Denis laughed. "The last," he shouted savagely, "went through the skull of a horse. It will make nothing of shield and byrnie. Through them and you it will go, to the stone of the street and strike you dead!"

"No," the count moaned, "no."

Gerlos, on his horse, sword in hand, hesitated, irresolute.

"Gerlos!" It was Ranulf's voice that shouted. He, too, held a bow and stood near Denis. "I've chosen you, Gerlos," Ranulf said, in a voice edged like a knife.

The boy's face was a study of hatred, teeth buried in his lower lip, the whites of his eyes showing around the irises. Ranulf looked as if he wanted to pull the trigger. His bolt was pointed at Gerlos's heart; he held it without wavering for an instant, eyes fixed on Gerlos's face.

"Don't stir another hand or foot toward us, Gerlos"— Ranulf's voice was a low guttural snarl of fury—"back away!"

Gerlos did, easing his horse very carefully and slowly toward the middle of the square.

There was a minor, silent commotion among Reynald's men as some in the first rank tried unsuccessfully to hide behind those in the second.

Elin heard a hissing breath behind her. Ingund, too, had a bow, and it was pointed at Reynald. Ingund's face was a Valkyrie's, her hair gleaming copper gold in the sunlight, eyes burning green in a perfectly white face.

Denis still stood over Count Anton, teeth bared, crossbow

in position. "My lady would speak. Be silent and listen," he shouted.

Elin pulled herself free of both Godwin's and Anna's hands and stepped down beside Denis. They had seized the initiative and she meant to keep it. "He lies," she said, pointing up at Gerlos, backing away on his horse. "My lord would never be forsworn. He would not be false to his people and his friends."

She stood in the sun beside Denis, still staring with concentrated hatred down at Count Anton. The white gown clung to her body and lay in lily purity around her feet.

She raised her arms, a lone figure, pale against the background of dark warriors, the crossbows raised in their hands, bolts gleaming in the sun. The flowing sleeves of the gown slipped back from her raised arms and bared them. Her fingers softly curved against the sky.

"I will prove it," she said, reaching down into her belt for the keys Owen had given her to his treasures. "Get the monstrance," she said to Ranulf.

He resigned his crossbow to one of the men at arms gathered around Denis.

Then Elin pointed to Reynald. "False traitor, what have you done with my love, and my lord?"

Reynald pulled at the bridle; the animal stamped its feet and threw its head up. "I protest," he shouted, looking around at the crowd and his own men, who were giving him strange glances.

"Protest," he shouted again. "I came here only to see justice done."

"Justice?" Godwin roared. "Damn you, what kind of justice brings forty armed men to threaten one woman?" He raised his shield; the golden dragon flashed in the sunlight.

"What right have you to bear that shield?" Gerlos shouted, pointing at the shield.

"Every right, bastard!" Godwin said. "My blood is noble and I am of the race of kings." His voice was of iron and brooked no contradiction. He stepped forward and stood beside Elin. Everyone believed him instantly and drew away.

Ranulf returned, the monstrance covered in his arms. He uncovered it and raised it slowly in his two hands. If it blazed in the candlelight, it was fire in the sun of morning.

Ranulf stood, holding it raised, and turned it slowly so that every eye in the square could look upon its perfection.

"Hear me," Elin shrieked, pointing up at the monstrance in Ranulf's hands. "What man running away, as these dogs say"—she gestured at Gerlos, the count's men, and Reynald— "would leave such riches behind?"

Godwin alone heard Elin make the sound; he'd heard the same grunting moan from men who took a mortal blow.

Her hands flew up into her hair, tearing it down around her face. Her nails ripped at her cheeks. "My love is dead, my dear companion taken from me forever!" She fell to her knees at the foot of the steps.

"Restrain her," Godwin shouted at Elfwine and Anna, "she'll do herself harm."

Elin looked up from her knees, cheeks bleeding, the gown spread around her on the cobbles, and pointed at Reynald. "I'll have your life! Murderer!" she screamed.

It seemed to Reynald for a second that there were only in the world those two blue eyes glaring into his own.

"Murderer," Elin screamed again. Then, in a lower voice, she whispered, "I'll have your life in payment. I demand it. It is my right. It is my due!"

Reynald turned his horse; his men fell in behind him. They thundered across the square, down the narrow street at a gallop and away.

Elfwine and Anna reached Elin, catching her clawed hands; Ingund put one arm around her waist. They carried her, struggling, into the hall. The rest retreated behind her, at Godwin's signal. Denis still held the crossbow pointed at the count lying in the street. When they were inside, Godwin took Elin from the women and led her to one of the benches beside the table. She had stopped struggling when they entered the door, but she had a fixed stare that he didn't like at all. "They have killed him," she said.

"Get me some of your strongest drink," Godwin said to Anna. "It's very possible that they have," he said to Elin.

Anna returned with a cup. The entire household gathered around the table. Godwin eyed them with approval; he was a man who loved courage. "You acquitted yourselves well, better than I had hoped."

Denis was still watching through the loophole in the door.

"Are they going to attack?" Godwin asked.

"No," Denis said, "the count is drawing his men together and retiring to the fortress." He left the door and returned to the table with the rest.

"They say," Godwin said, reaching for the big crossbow in Denis's hand, "that no man ever grows too old to learn. I believe it now. Never have I seen the like of that weapon."

Denis shrugged modestly. "Many are in use for hunting."

"Not like this one," Godwin said.

"No," Denis said proudly, "it's my latest and best. As you can see, the prod, that part of the bow that draws the bolt forward, is of wood and horn; the string is sinew. It takes a mighty pull to draw it, but once drawn and cocked, well . . . you saw how the count's horse died. I was afraid to kill the man, I feared the rest would attack. And besides, Alfric had already placed the blame for my lord's disappearance where it belonged. Everyone had but to see the proof that he didn't leave of his own will in that great golden vessel."

Ranulf stood near the table, still holding the monstrance.

"Lock that thing away," Godwin told him, and turned to Alfric. "How did you know that Owen rode to Reynald?"

"I didn't," Alfric said with one of his beautiful smiles, and a self-deprecating shrug, "it was but a guess. I chanced to hit upon the truth."

"A guess!" Elin looked up, shocked. "But I accused him."

Alfric lowered his eyes and folded his hands, a look of pain on his face. "Reynald's guilt is, to my mind at least, apparent, Elin. The Lord Bishop believed Reynald was a friend and trusted him. He wouldn't have turned his back on Count Anton or Gerlos. But Reynald . . ." Alfric paused, leaving the rest unsaid. "And there was the small matter of his presence here today in the company of Count Anton, clear enough proof in the eyes of anyone with wit to see it that he was part of some plot."

"A fine and active nest of vipers," Godwin said with a sigh, "Count Anton, Gerlos, and Reynald."

He twisted a large gold ring from his finger and put it in Alfric's hand. "In token of my esteem for your great and timely wit. We must prepare to leave this city now."

"No," Elin said, rising from the bench and turning to face Godwin. "No, I swore an oath, so did you, to hold this city until death. I mean to keep it." She walked toward the fireplace, brushing back her hair with her hand; it flowed in ebony waves down over the shoulders of the white gown. She faced the household as they stood around the table.

"Elin," Godwin said, "be reasonable. I'm your friend. As you were my kinsman's wife, I love you, but Owen was a man of the Church. This belongs to the Church. Our claim on it dies with him."

"What of the rest?" Elin asked. "Will you leave them behind to face the vengeance of the count and his son?"

The baby, still cradled in Rosamund's arms, began to cry. She handed him back to Elfwine, who put him quickly to her breast.

"No question," Godwin said, "the men can ride with us. That presents no difficulty. The women . . . I'll find a cart, or damnation, steal one, but we must leave quickly; whether you will it or not, Elin, I'll have you on a horse within the hour and we'll be gone."

"No," Elin said.

"I stand with Lady Elin," Ranulf said. "My wife can barely walk, much less ride. And as for the baby, such a journey would be his death. Besides, my lady is due something; much of the property my lord owned was his and not part of the Church's lands. I trust her, for I've seen enough of her doing to know she's no common woman!"

"I'm your lord's captain," Godwin said, facing Ranulf. "You dare to defy me?"

Ranulf backed quickly out of Godwin's reach, but didn't turn away. "I'm a free man," he told Godwin, "though, I admit, not much more than that. My knees are trembling even as I speak, but yes, I do! My wife and her kin will help us."

"I can't ride," Rosamund said, walking toward Elin to stand beside her, "but I can fend for myself. I have before. I'll stay here with Lady Elin."

Elin draped her arm over the girl's shoulders.

"Denis?" Godwin asked.

The thin young man turned quietly to his men, the four archers Enar had recruited. They were no longer green boys, but wore proudly the weapons and mail they'd won in battle and carried the heavy, powerful crossbows Denis had given them with the familiarity of use.

"Godwin, these lads all have families here and other kin. This is their home. As for me, well, I have no home, but where I lay my head. I came to Gestric's hall an orphan, with only a good name to recommend me. I ate at his table, an honored guest, until I was old enough to fight. Since then I've served Gestric's son, the Lord Bishop. He used me kindly, always, even when I was sick and wounded, only another useless mouth to feed. I won't desert his lady in her hour of need! Besides, Ranulf's right, much that's here belongs to Owen and should, in justice, pass to her and the child." Denis spoke mildly but deep feeling was in his voice; this was a long speech for him.

Elin hugged Rosamund, then unpinned the brooch that held her mantle. The brooch was a simple silver one adorned with the blue-water purity of aquamarines. She put it into Rosamund's hands. "My gift to you, most loyal one," she whispered, kissing a soft cheek.

She went to Ranulf and took his hand. "As a brother my lord loves you. Be my brother also and I your sister in tender concern."

Ranulf blushed an absolutely unbelievable shade of scarlet, mumbled inaudibly, and kissed her hand.

Then she passed to Denis and took his hand. "Never call yourself orphan while you stand under my roof, but friend and trusted kinsman. This is your home. I'll strive always to make it a happy and comfortable one. And never call yourself useless; without your great skill we would have this day perished. That bow is a miracle of power and stands strongly between us and our enemies."

Then she stood before Godwin; she went gracefully to her knees. "My lord, I beseech you, be my champion. It's true, as Ranulf says, I'm no common woman, but woman I am and weak."

She stretched out a pair of white arms to him in a gesture of supplication. "Noble, you said, and one of the race of kings. Don't abandon me, my lord, to the fury of my foes." Then she bowed her head and knelt silent before him.

Godwin was balanced halfway between fury and admiration. He understood the grand manner and appreciated an expert practitioner when he met one, but he wasn't fooled for one minute. He reached down, caught one of Elin's arms, and lifted her to her feet with undignified speed; she stumbled and nearly fell. "Don't kneel to me and don't try to outmaneuver me; I'm not Owen. Owen is dead. Use your good sense, woman. Why wouldn't they kill him, if they had him in their hands?"

"Use yours," Elin flashed back at him, eyes blazing. "They'd produce his dead body and blame it on Enar."

"Then what can have happened, I ask you?" Godwin said, helping himself to some of the wine on the table.

"I don't know," Elin said, "but I will know tonight. I have friends who will tell me." She turned again to the household. "I can give to you, Godwin, the same advantages I'd have given Owen had he been willing to use me. Christ, if only he'd told me he was going to meet Reynald, I'd have had the man watched and his treachery found out. Even now, I will have that whoreson's life; I swear it!"

Godwin scratched his chin thoughtfully. "Can you do this?"

Elin spoke to Alfric. "Does Reynald still sacrifice to the old gods?"

"With more fervor than to Christ, my lady," Alfric said.

Elin stretched out her hand to Godwin and slowly closed the fingers into a fist, saying, "Then he is mine!"

"Don't do it, my lady," Alfric cried, "it often ends in the death of both."

"Speak," Elin said, her hand still outstretched to Godwin. The hooded dark eyes studied her. She was no longer the supplicant, but a young queen, her unbound hair streaming down around her white face, her eyes blue flames. "I am no common woman, Godwin. You say you will take me away, but already I could be gone, as a cloud driven before the wind or the white cold mist that rises from the water, borne aloft and flying, light as sun or moonbeams, on the wings of the storm. I came here of my own will, not begging for my love's protection. Of my own will I stay to help stand between the city and its fate. I'll give you Reynald's life, crush it like a dead leaf, and drop it at your feet. Now say, will you be my champion?"

Behind him, Godwin heard Gowen mutter, "Before God! Bertrand was right, she *is* one of them."

"Never," Godwin said, "have I had such a challenge. I

will!" He reached out his hand and caught her wrist with his own metal-studded leather glove. Her slim white fingers closed around his gauntlet at the wrist. "As one man to another," he said, "you are still my cousin's wife until death— his or mine."

Elin answered, "I will be true."

She let go of Godwin's arm, and spent by the intensity of her struggle to win him, almost staggered away.

The women surrounded her. "A linen dress," she said to Ingund, "undyed and never worn. A clean bowl and a stone knife."

Anna embraced her. "You risk the child," she said.

Elin seemed not even to hear her. "Prepare the sweat bath; I must fast and purify myself."

Godwin sat at the table watching her, intrigued.

"Stop her," Alfric pleaded with him.

"I've heard of it," Godwin said, "but never seen it done."

Elin moved away toward the stairs, surrounded by the women. Elfwine, carrying the baby, accompanied them.

Rosamund was standing with the knights. Gowen reached out from behind her, caressing her breasts. She turned, wrapped her arms around his neck, kissed him fiercely on the mouth, scratched his cheek with her nails, and drew blood. "She'll kill him; I feel it," Rosamund said.

Wolf the Tall had her by her tiny waist. He was nuzzling her neck with his lips. All three men were running their hands over her body. She undulated sinuously as a slender, blond snake under their fingers.

"I'm first," Gowen said. No one disputed him as they climbed up the stairs together.

"It's loose among us," Alfric said in despair, sitting down on the bench beside Godwin.

Godwin began to unarm himself, setting his sword on the table. He pulled the mail shirt over his head, and began, deliberately, to remove his gloves.

Alfric said, "Stop her, Godwin; as you are a man and a Christian, stop her. You can't imagine what she intends. Stop her."

Godwin smiled a strangely resigned and ironic smile. "How will I do that, Alfric? I'm not sure even the knights would follow me now. Besides, if she breaks Reynald, I may be able to deal with the count and his son. I'll stay and see if she can."

"The count is the lawful lord here," Alfric said.

Sudden fury shook Godwin's whole body. He drew his sword.

Alfric sat perfectly still, hands on his knees, gazing at Godwin, clear-eyed and unafraid.

Godwin held the sword up between them like a cross. "This is all that's left of law and lordship in this realm."

He spoke to Alfric past the gleaming blade. "I know, Alfric, because I have seen, in my lifetime, law and lordship die. I stood with Odo at Paris and saw the Viking ships sail past. The brave citizens of that town were betrayed by a fat, vile old king. I was beside Arnulf on the dyke; we won, but at what a cost. The countryside a blackened husk. The people, famine-stricken skeletons wandering over it, eating their own dead.

"No, little monk. I'm tired of kings and lords and law, and even religion. The count is a weak, cowardly old fool; Reynald, a strong, treacherous one. If Elin can kill the strong fool, I'll deal with the weak one."

He sheathed the sword with a crash, laid it gently on the table, and leaned back beside Alfric on the bench. "Now, poach me some of those eggs. I'm starving. I'll even settle for dark toast."

Chapter
24

OWEN awakened, looking at a fire and a pile of gold. Still stunned by the two hard whacks his head had taken, he felt only his eyes and ears. The voices were faraway and unimportant. They were bargaining.

"Give us the town," one said.

Owen's vision cleared. The illuminating fire burned under a huge oak. The trunk was black and squat, big branches stretched out on all sides bending low to the ground, gnarled and twisted as the fingers of an old man, their contorted shapes clearly visible by the light of the leaping flames.

Reynald knelt before a heap of gold and caressed it. Rings, armlets, loose coins, the hilts of jeweled weapons, necklaces, bracelets, silver and gold. And riding the crest of the pile, half sunken in it, was a great mass chalice of the pure, soft, red metal, bent, but richly ornamented with silver and pearls.

"Not enough," Reynald said.

"Not enough?" another voice answered indignantly. "A king's ransom, the dowry of a princess. How much more would you have?"

"The merchants of Chantalon are fat," Reynald said, "their coffers studded with silver and gold. Compared with the wealth of the city, this is a pittance. The women are beautiful, and will command the highest prices in the slave markets.

"I saw him," he said, pointing to Owen, "hold more than this in his two hands. Have you not heard of the magnificent treasure he owns? The monstrance lit with rubies, set in pure gold, the weight of a man's head."

"The count lied to us," another voice said, "telling us we had gotten all the wealth of the citizens."

"Not a tithe of it," Reynald answered.

"Very well," the other voice said, "open the gates and you will have two more like this by weight."

Reynald stared at the gold, eyes fixed on it in burning fascination, as though he saw in the scraps of shining metal all the hopes and dreams of his life fulfilled, as though greed were the central passion of his heart. "Two more like this?" he whispered.

"Yes," the voice coaxed, "and more, much more, when we're finished."

Reynald's hand closed around the mass chalice, the soft gold bending under his fingers. "It will be too much trouble to kill them all and many will not be worth selling as slaves."

"Then they will need a strong hand to keep order, to rule. That strong hand could be yours." The voice was now oiled with flattery. "Had you been weak, we'd never have come to you."

"Done," Reynald said.

"You drive a harder bargain than Judas," Owen said.

Reynald jumped to his feet, looking down at Owen, revulsion on his face. Owen was jerked to his knees by a hand in his hair. He cried out in pain. "I had thought him still unconscious, perhaps nearly dead," Reynald said, his voice shaking. "Kill him! It sickens my soul to look at him. Get a rope and give him to the one-eyed."

"Kill what I can sell? Not I." The speaker was the one holding Owen by the hair. He spoke to the man who'd been bargaining with Reynald. He shook Owen's body violently. "Look at him, Hakon, this is what you were afraid of. Faugh! He's all bone and has hair like a woman's. I'll wager he can't even grow a beard." He shook Owen's body again, then dropped him.

The other, the one called Hakon, stared down at Owen's limp form in dispassionate appraisal. He was a big man with a heavy thatch of black hair, one gray streak through it. At some time in the past, he'd taken a sword cut across the face and skull. The scar silvered his hair, then ran diagonally in a white line down his forehead, across the bridge of his nose, and ended on one clean-shaven cheek. Obviously a powerful warrior, and a wealthy one. His upper body and massive shoulders were covered with a fish-scale cuirass of golden overlapping plates. Both the pommel and sheath of the sword he wore flashed with the fire of gold and jewels, as did his belt and baldric.

"I agree with Reynald," he said, mouth set grimly, "kill him."

"No," the other said, "half at least of all that treasure I have taken in this raid went to buy this"—he kicked Owen in the ribs—"skinny bag of bones. His father will pay good money for what's left when I'm finished."

Owen looked up at Reynald, who avoided his eyes. "I believed you were my friend."

Reynald did look down at him then, the leaping flames casting strange shadows on his face. "I was your friend," Reynald said. "In a way I still am. That's why I'm trying to get him to kill you." Reynald looked away and shook his head. "You wouldn't see reason in the matter of the town or anything else. We could have come to an agreement had you only been more reasonable."

Owen twisted on the ground. He couldn't do much more than that since he was bound hand and foot. "You fool," he shouted up at Reynald, half mad with frustration and despair, "when they are done with me and Chantalon, they will turn and rend you."

Reynald turned his back on him and began gathering the gold into a sack, but he continued speaking. "Always one for fine words. We will see how fair your speech is when Osric is finished with you. Kill him," he exhorted Hakon again. "He was a brave man, that at least. Don't make him suffer too much."

Hakon stood still, one thumb hooked into his golden belt, watching the three of them, Osric, Owen, and Reynald. Hakon's eyes were gray—a strange gray, clear, pale, and empty as two pools of water standing on ice.

He needed Reynald. Owen could see that, because he smiled, though the smile never came close to thawing those eyes. "I'll see to it that he dies," he promised.

Reynald seemed to take that as some sort of reassurance, because he looked down again into Owen's face, then quickly away, as if what he found there was unbearable, and mounted his horse. "The men will remain with you. I'll ride home alone so none will know of this night's work," he told Hakon.

"Ever cautious," Osric mocked, standing beside Owen's body.

"I have found in secret dealings caution pays," Hakon answered smoothly, unperturbed, then turned to Reynald. "Good-bye, my friend." He smiled again. "We'll meet soon and talk."

"The city?" Reynald asked.

"Caution pays," Hakon answered.

Reynald nodded and rode into the darkness.

Osric stepped away from Owen toward Hakon beside the fire, and Owen saw him clearly for the first time. He was handsome, possibly the most handsome man Owen had ever seen. He was blond, even featured, with soft fair skin. Even in the night chill he went bare armed, in a black tunic that set off his blond good looks to perfection. His body was well muscled and perfectly proportioned, not too massive as Gowen was or with the hint of boyish uncertainty that marred Ranulf's face. Osric was self-confident and totally assured. He seemed to preen himself as he walked.

"My friend," he mimicked, staring at Hakon with contempt.

"I think you know," Hakon said impassively, "how good of friends we are."

"You and I or you and Reynald?" Osric asked.

"Both," Hakon said.

Osric laughed. "You'll see that he dies. Did I hear you make that promise after you talked me into putting up half the money to buy him?"

"I did promise that, but I didn't say when," Hakon answered. "We all die sometime."

Osric's face twisted into an almost petulant scowl. "He must stay alive at least until his father pays for him. I still think it was a bad bargain."

"Bad or good," Hakon said quietly, "it's made. I see no point in thinking of it." He glanced at Owen again, bringing those frozen eyes to bear on him. "I will speak again and then say no more. Give him to his God, the one-eyed. Use a rope or throw him into the river bound as he is to drown. The merit of the sacrifice will come to us."

"No," Osric shouted angrily, jerking Owen to his knees by the hair again.

Owen found himself kneeling, facing the fire's white heart—a pair of branches discarded by the giant oak above—now blazing, the points of the flames nearly reaching the low limbs of the tree. He shifted his knees on the tightly packed, brittle dead leaves of the clearing's floor.

With two blows by Reynald, in one second he'd been stripped of everything: honor, position, family, and finally, life. He stared into the fire and hoped for the courage to die well. He had no one to blame for his situation but himself, and carried the added burden of Enar's death in his heart. He'd seen, before he fell, an arrow lodged in the Saxon's chest.

And the city. Oh, God, he thought in agony, *Reynald will give them the city, my people. He's made his own words true. I've led them over a precipice as he foretold.*

"Look well on the fire, Christian lord. Look well, it's the last sight you'll ever see," Osric taunted him. He held Owen's sword. He drew it and thrust the tip into the glowing coals at the root of the flame.

Owen laughed, praying, *Let me die well. Reynald puts his trust in fools.* Aloud he said, "Only a fool would ruin the temper of a good blade to blind one man."

Hakon gave a shout of rage and caught Osric's wrist, spinning him around and jerking the sword from the flames. Osric howled in fury and beat at Hakon's cuirass with his free hand. Hakon ignored him, his hand still gripping Osric's wrist. He slid it up slowly until his fingers closed around Osric's on the sword hilt. He squeezed.

Owen saw blood spurt from under Osric's fingernails. With a screech, Osric released his grip on the sword. Hakon pulled it from his hand and examined the tip closely.

"Barely warm," he said. "You are a fool. This," he brandished the blade, "will sell for its weight in gold and twice its weight in silver."

Osric stood back, glaring at Hakon in fury, clutching his hand. Osric wore a sword, Owen noticed, but he didn't try to draw it. Few men, Owen thought, probably ever drew on Hakon willingly.

Instead he reached for a slender burning branch and

snatched it from the fire. Owen's sickened eyes were fixed on the glowing red end. *Oh, God,* he thought, *let me die well.*

Hakon laid the flat of the sword blade against the sleeve of Osric's tunic. He spoke carefully, as one speaks to a slow child or possibly a demented one. "Osric, do one of two things—kill him now or leave him be." He paused and looked down at Owen. "When I go to sell him to his kin, I want to present something still recognizable. Cutting pieces off him makes the price go down."

Osric chewed at his lip. "That's true," he said and nodded. "I want my money back. More than anything, I want my money back. You're sure they'll pay?"

Hakon shrugged. "They or the slavers, either one, but"—he pressed the cold steel against Osric's arm to emphasize his point—"make sure he's never fit to meet me in battle. Promise me that or I cut his throat, now!"

"No," Osric said, stamping his foot. "I want my money. I promise," he said sulkily.

Osric at once set about keeping his promise. For the ride to the camp Owen's legs were fastened under the belly of the horse, hands tied behind him. There was no way for him to brace his body against the animal's movement. He was rubbed raw by the saddle and every hoofbeat reverberated in his skull, still aching from Reynald's blows.

They reached the camp at dawn. Owen was stripped of shirt and tunic and flogged. At some time during the flogging, Owen passed out from pain so all encompassing that it made nothing of his mind or will.

He must have borne it well enough, since, as he lay on the ground staring up at the sky through gummed eyelashes, he heard Hakon trying to buy him from Osric.

Osric only laughed and had him dragged to the cage. "This is better than blinding," he told Hakon. "In time his limbs will twist, then lock. He'll never meet anyone in battle again. And he's still worth money and can work."

The cage looked a little like a gallows. It was what remained of a tall pine, with the branches lopped off, and a crossbeam nailed to the top, where the cage was suspended by rope and pulley, so that it could be raised and lowered. A man penned in it couldn't stand up, only kneel or crouch.

The cage was raised, and Owen was left to endure the torment of sun, thirst, and the flies that swarmed around his raw back. By noon, he began to scream. Osric lowered the cage at once, and Owen, groveling in the dirt at Osric's feet, wolfed down the food and water he was given and understood what was being done to him.

He knelt quietly, eyes on the ground. The food, and especially the water, revived him. There must be a way to escape this, if only into death.

Osric meant to sell him back to his father. He didn't know if his father would pay Osric's price, but his mother would. What would their gold buy? he wondered, as he was pushed back into the cage and it was raised again. Nothing worth having, he was sure.

The cage jerked to a stop at the top of its rise up the pole. Owen looked out over the camp. The island was a long oval shaped by the flow of the river. The Northmen had done their best to render it both impregnable and comfortable, in the midst of its guardian water. Surrounding it, except for the shallow beach at the edges, was a high palisade of sharpened stakes.

In the center they had built a hall. It faced a clearing filled with hearths, where the cooking was done. Longhouses, for the men and the women they had taken, surrounded this open space. On either end of the island were pens. In one were kept horses and other livestock. The one at the other was nearly empty. But from the few wretched figures he could see moving in it, he knew it must be for the slaves captured in raids. When Osric was finished breaking him, he would join them, to wait for the shame of being sold to his father or the hold of one of the merchantmen who plied the rivers, buying up the human plunder of the countryside.

He shifted his knees on the bars at the bottom of the cage and made a little strangled sound of pain as the release of pressure brought life back into the flesh of his kneecaps. The cage itself was of willow lashed together with strips of plaited hide and animal sinew, as nearly unbreakable a prison as the hand of man could create. The pain was beginning, seeming worse now that he was revived by food and water than it had been before. It clawed at his neck and back, and the calves of his legs cramped savagely.

Soon, he thought in despair, I will begin screaming again. He found himself trembling with fear that perhaps Osric wouldn't lower the cage when he did. He knew that when this became his greatest fear, Osric's work would be done.

He shifted his position, ignoring the growing numbness in his legs and feet. This allowed him to straighten his shoulders and rest his body against one side of the cage, thus relieving the worst of the pain. He closed his eyes, and without really knowing it, drifted into sleep.

It was spring. He was walking in a meadow with Elin. The grass was lush and green. It bent beneath their feet, only to leap up again as they passed, brushing his legs and the trailing skirts of Elin's gown. She turned to him. The sky above was blue and reflected in her eyes. In her hand, she held a branch covered with white apple blossoms. She reached out and caressed his cheek with the soft petals.

He took her hand and pressed her fingers, warm and perfumed by the flowers, to his lips. But she pulled back and pointed away, and Owen realized that the sunlit meadow was surrounded by the darkness of the forest. At its edge, just under the trees, an old man stood. He wore a black cloak, a broad hat, and carried a staff. One eye was covered by a patch.

Owen returned to consciousness slowly, outside of his body, looking at the wretched thing crouching in the cage, beaten, with tears on its cheeks. Then abruptly he was one with it again.

He thought of Elin, of freedom, and the spring. They were the same to him. And the pain in his soul was worse than the suffering of his body. "Oh, my love," he whispered, "forgive me. I would come to you if I could, but I cannot. God be good to you and may He care for you as I do. And may He have mercy on me, for my only springtime is in dreams." The tears poured down his cheeks and were salt, a bloody taste in his mouth.

He thought of the one-eyed man. Forsake him, we have forsaken him, yet he still walks the forest. They had met before. The memory was buried in the mist of youth and time. No, not the old man of the forest, only a recollection of someone seen while he hunted in the mountain fastness near his father's lands. A face that haunted him strangely. Not the dream of a god of long ago.

Owen spoke aloud to himself. "Now I must find a way to die." He levered his body forward so that he could look down. He must have slept longer than he realized, since the better part of the afternoon was over. Women were working around the cooking fires and the smells rising to the cage were another source of suffering. He was ravenously hungry. The little bit of bread he'd been given at noon was long gone, and his stomach tormented him with its futile demands.

Beyond the palisade, the sun hung low over the leafless branches of the distant forest.

How to die? Owen began to search the cage itself. If he could find a way to break one of the bars, he could use it to pierce his heart, or throat, and so cheat Osric forever. He tried the lashings with his fingers, seeking a weak spot, and found one.

His heart lifted. The maker of the cage had, when he placed the last few bars, run out of the tanned and plaited leather he used for securing them and substituted strips of green hide. Green hide wasn't weatherproof, and it rotted more quickly than the finished product.

Owen clawed at it. The hide flaked under the scratching of his nails. It was true that, beneath the hide, animal sinew secured the wood, but sinew stretched when it got wet and, if he could moisten them enough, the lashing would give.

Methodically he began scraping at the hide with his thumbnail near the knot, eating through the stiffened leather bit by bit. He closed his eyes, concentrated, and the strand of leather became the only thing in the world.

Voices from below jolted him back to awareness.

"He has not begun to scream again." It was Osric's voice.

"Maybe he's dead." This from Hakon.

The cage began its jolting descent. Owen dropped his hand. The thumb was bloody at the tip, the nail worn away. He hadn't felt it.

When he was down, he looked up through the bars at Osric and Hakon. "I was sleeping," he said. "You awakened me."

Hakon began laughing at Osric's nonplussed expression.

"Haul him back up," Osric yelled.

"No," Hakon said, "not yet. You are hungry?" he asked Owen.

"I don't feel it," Owen replied.

"Thirsty?" Hakon inquired.

"Not so much," Owen said.

Hakon stepped back from the cage and looked at Osric. "He sounds like something the poets sing about. On the next slaver that weighs anchor here, out he goes. This man is dangerous."

"His body will bend and twist to fit the cage," Osric vowed. "I'll cut off his thumbs so he can never hold a sword in his hand again. Haul him up."

"No," Hakon commanded, and Owen noticed it was Hakon's voice that was obeyed.

He passed a clay bottle of water in to Owen through the bars and some bread. "On the next slave ship, Osric," Hakon ordered, "and in chains!" Then he turned on his heel and walked away.

"Haul him up," Osric yelled. This time he was obeyed.

Owen, kneeling in the cage, methodically ate the bread, using only enough water to wash it down, saving the rest for the knots. He looked calmly out at the stars appearing in the sky one by one, as the light died, and the blue above became violet, then black. He had mastered his pain; he didn't know how he'd done it, but he had. If he thought strongly enough about something it replaced all else. He closed his eyes and this time sought the dream.

It was summer, and the forest was lush, hot, and the vines and branches drooped with the thick growth, leaves cut and polished by the hand of God. Owen walked in a narrow ravine between two big boulders. He rested his hand against the trunk of an oak weighted with a burden of lichen, moss, and mistletoe. The stars of moss on the trunk were pearled with lenses of dew each catching and magnifying the chartreuse of the living carpet. It was soft under his fingers. He caressed it.

The earth, he thought, my earth. Power ran up into his body through his legs buried in the rich drifts of loam beneath his feet, piled, not rotting, but returning, moving downward then up into the sun-burnished, sun-loved canopy above. The one-eyed stood before him.

Owen raised his hand in salute. "I had forgotten you, father of fathers, father of kings."

The one-eyed turned and led him through the humid green tunnel of life's absolute abundance, then turned and faced him.

They met as equals. Eye to eye, Owen's two staring into the lone gray one, darkness on the other side.

"I have not forgotten you," a voice spoke in Owen's mind. "Behold," the one-eyed said, raising his staff.

It was carved in the shape of a woman, faceless as Elin had been in the cave, but with breasts and vulva.

Owen felt as if his whole life drained into his loins. His manhood was as stone. He concentrated with all his power on the staff, and was outside the cage, looking at himself kneeling face upturned, to the uncaring stars.

He could do this at will. He knew he could control it simply by thinking of the staff. As I am a man, Osric can never take my manhood, he thought triumphantly. He could watch that dirty, beaten rag of flesh suffer and die, indifferent.

Then what? But he turned his mind from that problem. He could be killed, but not broken, he was sure of it now. Willing himself back into his body and its attendant pains, he returned to his struggle with the knots.

Chapter

25

*E*LIN sat in the sweat bath. The steam clouding the air was warm, but she was cold, her hands icy. She put them under her arms, then rested them between her thighs, trying to bring life back to her chilled fingers.

Vengeance, not the luxury of passion, but a duty. A law.

She remembered her father's face as he explained to her mother, Wilsa, why he had just hanged a man.

"It's the law," he said to Wilsa.

"Not the law of Christ," Wilsa had said.

"No," he'd answered grimly, "but it is still a law. The woman's kin came to me. Had I not done it, they would have. Now her people are acquitted of the guilt of his blood, and his people can't come seeking theirs. He was duly outlawed and I shed no blood."

"And yet," Wilsa had said quietly, "you killed him."

Her father buried his face in his hands and when he raised it and looked again at her mother, she'd seen something almost like hatred in his reddened eyes. "Rather say, wife," he'd answered, "his own actions killed him. You are dearer to me than my own life, but if you ever say such a thing to me again, I'll send you away and deny you.

"These people look to me for justice, but as they are the law, it is in their hands. Her kin had a right to his life and claimed that right. Had I not hanged him, the killing would never have ended. The facts were clear, secret murder done for gain. The woman's people brought their case to me so that there might be no blood feud. And there will be none. Now, say no more, the matter is ended."

Wilsa had stared at his face, horrified by her husband's cold words. Elin had seen her mother's lips part slightly as though she wanted to speak, but then those lips closed and her eyes dropped. She never mentioned the hanging again. Wilsa adored her husband and unquestioningly accepted the Christian dictum that his word was law.

Vengeance. She'd seen the hanging. Elin was a bold girl, her mother's child. Ever since she could remember, her strong swift legs had served Wilsa's crippled ones. Her arms had been the first to receive and cradle her younger brothers and sisters.

Wilsa expected independence, responsibility, and industry from her eldest daughter, and Elin tried never to disappoint her adored mother. But perhaps without realizing it, Wilsa was creating in Elin a strong-willed, self-reliant woman. Elin was only twelve at the time, but beginning to move away from her mother's tutelage and do her own thinking.

So when she stood with the other children watching the man driven, sobbing, pleading for his life, from her father's hall, Elin followed, through the gates out into the fields.

There, the man fell to his knees, clinging to her father's legs. Elin's father backed away, tearing free of his grasp, and the prisoner was dragged, shrieking, into the forest.

Elin followed, moving quietly, as her mother's people had taught her, staying always in the shadows, until the party of men reached their destination: a clearing darkened by ancient trees. It was a sinister place, and the children were never allowed to play there.

Faces looked into the clearing, faces cut deeply into the wood of the tree trunks long ago. Faces whose names were never spoken aloud by day, in the presences of Elin's father or the priest. But faces whose names every child living in the village knew by heart, and Elin could call every one.

She crouched, almost hidden, behind the heavy, twisted roots of an oak, whose trunk was so thick not even the outstretched arms of two men could span it. She hugged her body and tried to make herself invisible, knowing she was going to see something terrible.

Vengeance. The prisoner was forced to his knees, facing Elin. His features a blank mask of horror, fear concentrated in his eyes. The sounds coming from his mouth not even human, until a man Elin recognized as his brother stepped forward and kicked him, saying, "Carry yourself like a man, at least in this."

At the kick, the prisoner doubled over, retching, but when he was set upright again, his face was drained of everything but despair.

"He's had a priest and time for shriving. That's more than he gave my sister and her little ones," another said. "Have done. His death ends it."

So deep was the gloom under the old trees that Elin didn't realize what her father meant to do until he did it. He swung the club from behind the kneeling man, striking him on the side of the head once. The club cracked against his skull. The man still knelt, but his eyes emptied. Elin's father lifted the club and swung again, this time harder. The man fell facedown on the moss and dead leaves.

Then, so quickly she was shocked into paralysis by the speed of his action, a noose was around the man's neck, the rope thrown over a limb, the body dragged, jerking, into the air. Elin's father's hands placed the noose and pulled the rope.

Elin had never seen her father's hands raised in anger against anyone. Vengeance.

Elin was still cold. She knelt on the floor of the sweat bath and poured more water on the rocks. A gush of steam rose, nearly blinding her, filling the tiny room with moisture.

When the thing at the end of the rope dangled limp at last, her father lowered it to the ground, saying, "Let the guilt be on this rope and the witnesses receive his soul."

The witnesses! Elin knew he hadn't meant the half dozen or so of the men who stood with him, but the faces carved so deeply into the trunks of the trees.

The stench of human excrement filled the heavy air of the tiny clearing.

"A wolf he was," the man's brother said, "and like a wolf he died. Let him be buried like a wolf in the wilderness, that his spirit may never return to the houses of righteous men."

Vengeance, Elin thought, tears running down her face. Tears of grief for Owen. If he was dead, let his spirit hear her. If he yet lived, she prayed to preserve him alive.

Vengeance. Was this her fault? Were the powers punishing her for forgetting it? She had smeared her face with Dominola's blood, and in Owen's arms she had so quickly forgotten Dominola's death.

Women were weak, easily swayed by passion, driven by desire, lust. Owen lit a fire in her body, a fire that still burned, even in his absence.

Elin still knelt on the matting, eyes closed, the radiant heat of the rocks before her seeming to sear her flesh. Her fingers clasped between her thighs, warmed now, pressed against the soft curly mound covering her sex. Locks of her long hair brushed against the sensitive tips of her breasts, rousing her to an absolute fury of desire.

She had only to move the fingers clasped between her thighs inward, to caress, and she would collapse shuddering, drained of strength and will by the pleasure, by the orgiastic fire. To think of Owen was to desire him.

"Oh, my love," she whispered, and more tears came. Desire faded.

Dominola's blood.

When Elin came to her uncle's villa, she had come openly, without excuse or apology, to warn Agelf and Dominola that the Northmen were overrunning the countryside.

"They have taken an island in the river," she told him, "and captured many weapons and horses. They travel like the wind when on a raid. Warn my father, send a rider at once."

She stood before him in the hall wearing the leather leggings and short tunic of her mother's people, her hair braided and covered by a leather cap.

Agelf hadn't recognized her at first, and when he did, he was furious. "Look at you," he shouted. "I told that fool brother of mine he spared his hand too much. Spoilt is what you are."

The back of his hand cracked against Elin's cheek, knocking her to the floor. Elin had gone down without a cry and lay looking up at him steadily, blue eyes fixed on his face.

"See," Agelf shouted at Dominola, "she has no shame."

"Can't you hear what I'm saying, Agelf?" Elin had said, even while realizing that he couldn't. "You and your whole family are in mortal danger. If you don't care for yourself, at least warn my father," Elin had pleaded. "Send a rider, warn my father!"

He made as if to take off his belt and beat Elin where she lay, but Dominola stopped him. "No, whatever she's made

of herself, she's a grown woman," she said, clutching at
Agelf's sleeve, "and not ours."

"Lock her up, then," he shouted, dragging Elin to her feet
by the ear and twisting it painfully. "Four years she's been
away. Four years and her mother and father frantic with
worry over her. Now I must send a rider at once!"

"Warn him," Elin had repeated, hopelessly, "please,
please, Agelf. Oh, God, I've seen what they leave behind
them . . . the horrors."

Agelf had slapped her then, shouting, "What decent
woman would even look at such things?"

"Come, dear," Dominola had said, wrapping her arms
around Elin. She whispered in her ear, "You're just making
him more angry. I'll speak to him later. He'll listen, I promise."

Dominola and one of Elin's young cousins did lock her
up. The cousin was one she didn't know, a rather stiff, self-
righteous young man, proud of his new sword, but beginning
to show a strong resemblance to her Uncle Agelf. He took
her by the arm while Dominola fluttered nervously along behind them. Elin was placed in a storeroom where the spices
and seed grain were kept locked up. It was a tight, dry room
with a heavy bar on the door. Dominola brought her some
women's clothing.

At her aunt's insistence, Elin had donned it, still pleading
with Dominola to send a rider to her father and set at least
a watch on their own walls.

Her words beat like rain on the rock of Dominola's self-
complacency. Her aunt's reply to everything she said was,
"I'm sure Agelf knows best," or "Such stories are always
exaggerated. Tales grow in the telling."

When Elin told her stormily that her warning wasn't
based on stories she'd heard but things she'd seen,
Dominola's face closed. Elin realized that the woman before
her couldn't imagine the familiar patterns of her world ever
being totally changed or even seriously disrupted by any
outside force. No, nothing could be that strong.

Elin had appealed to her young cousin. He looked mor-
tally offended that anyone would presume to criticize Agelf,
even by implication, and said stiffly, "I'm sure my father
knows what he's doing," and turned his back.

Their self-assurance was so great, that in the end, Elin began to doubt herself. Perhaps they were right. Her uncle's villa was a strong point perched on a hill, surrounded by a bank and ditch, topped by a palisade fence. Perhaps these marauders would hesitate to attack such a forbidding defense, Elin thought as she lay down to sleep on a pile of sacking in the storeroom.

Her mother's people had warned her that Agelf might not listen. But Elin had paid no attention. She left them and set out running, following the long stretches of forest that invaded the open plain, traveling all of the night and part of the day at top speed to reach her uncle's home.

Now it was night again, and as she drifted into a sleep of exhaustion, she thought ruefully that all her good will had gotten her was captivity. She was caged and would be sent back to her father in disgrace. And it might be that they didn't even need her warning.

Dominola awakened her at dawn to bring her food and washing water. She left the door to the storeroom open, and Elin, sponging her face at the basin, could look out through it at the sun. The red arc was just beginning to rise above the thick white mist covering the gently rolling countryside.

Her aunt patted Elin and consoled her. "Today, you'll see, we'll send for your father. He'll be angry at first, just as Agelf was, but he'll be so happy to have you back again, it won't last, his anger, I mean. But that marriage. That was a fine marriage and a good boy. He waited for a year, hoping you'd come to your senses, then took another. It was a terrible disappointment. He'd have made you a good husband."

Elin listened in stony silence to her aunt's chatter, smelling the sweet clean air of morning and eating the wine-soaked bread her aunt brought with her.

"Now, put on a dress and try to look respectable. And don't run to Agelf demanding he listen to you. He's a grown man. You're only a young girl and know very little of the world . . ."

They came, out of the mist, seemingly almost out of the ground, moving swiftly and silently, with the skill and speed of practiced warriors. Elin saw them first, yet so quick and surprising was the attack that her brain hardly understood what her eyes were telling it.

A dozen were over the gate before she could scream a warning. Her uncle's men were cut down and the gate was opened. A mass of men, mounted and on foot, streamed into the yard.

Elin did scream then, and pointed.

Dominola turned, her body blocking the door, staring frozen with uncomprehending eyes at the carnage. Carnage it was. The raiders killed every man and many of the women without mercy. Most were weaponless and many were caught in their beds. Even those few able to seize their arms fell quickly, clumsy amateurs fighting seasoned professionals. It was all over in seconds.

Throwing down the bread in her hand, Elin tried to pull Dominola from the door to close it. She had no clear idea why, thinking only it might buy them both a little time. But it was useless. The terrified woman was impossible to budge. The first of the raiders to reach Dominola killed her. He used the terrible one-handed swordsman's slash—the cut that kills with one blow. Dominola never knew what hit her. The cut begins at the shoulder, carving through the ribs and spine, ending at the hip. Dominola fell, her body almost in two pieces, a spurting corpse, the look of blank astonishment still frozen on her features.

The man turned to Elin. He caught her by the arm and slammed her back into the wall while he scanned the room quickly. Then he turned, shouting to his men to come gather the valuable spices and seed corn. Flames were already leaping from the roof of the hall, the thatch blazing fiercely. The first of the men to rush into the storeroom kicked Dominola's body out of the way. Elin, feeling the grip on her arm slacken as he shouted instructions to his men, tore free but only to run to her aunt's body and smear her cheeks with Dominola's blood.

The raider caught Elin again, slapped her, not hard since women Elin's age were valuable and sold for excellent prices, but only hard enough to put a stop to any resistance, and he dragged her away toward the barn.

The yard was a kaleidoscope of horror. The few living wounded lay screaming among the dead.

Elin saw Agelf between the gate and the hall. The flies

were already settling an iridescent black coating on the sword cut that clove his skull to the teeth.

Elin could spare no pity for him. Had they manned the walls, that tall palisade, the attack might have been turned. The self-righteous boy lay near him, still, to Elin's horror, moving a little in a pool of blood silvered with the twisting coils of his guts.

They reached the barn. Elin was slapped again, sent spinning by an expert blow that she understood was not intended to kill or even cripple her, only render her helpless for what must inevitably come. She lay quietly in the straw while the screams outside died away, becoming moans and then silence, broken only by the roar of fire and the sound of the wind.

When the raiders began to enter the barn, some of the women began screaming again. A few fought, needing to be quelled by blows. Elin heard and seemed to feel them in her own flesh.

Elin lay quiet. It was the way of her people. One who forced another was beneath contempt. One who needed to was despised. But she was pinned. One man lying across her chest while the warrior who had so quickly murdered Dominola knelt between her legs.

Elin wondered, sitting in the sweat bath, what that had to do with passion or desire, and decided—nothing.

It was justification. They had murdered the men and must prove, on the helpless bodies of the women, that they were truly stronger. Prove it to exhaustion, Elin had thought, looking at the grunting, straining bodies all around her, crouched over the women in the straw. Not even pleasure was in it for them.

Eyes watched her from the corner of the barn. A small group of children, those that had been allowed to live by the raiders, huddled there watching their mothers and sisters being raped.

That was all Elin could remember, and she was thankful. After that her memory slid in and out of nightmare.

Osric got her. Her almost animal stoicism piqued his curiosity.

All day the surviving captives were driven along, chained by the neck to one another. Elin simply walked with the rest

and walked easily, helping the others when they stumbled
and fell down in despair and refused to rise. A few had the
courage to rage and scream at the killers of their menfolk.
Often, Elin learned chillingly that when Osric found a baby
one of the younger women had managed to conceal, he
killed it. Their children were laughed at or ignored. Others
wept unceasingly. These went almost unnoticed. Elin simply
walked and thought.

Many things about her would endear her to her captors. She
was beautiful, and more, skilled in all the domestic arts.
She was a healer of great ability. But as she walked, and
stunned shock gave way to cold visceral hatred, she knew that
she would never willingly give them anything. They would
get only what superior strength could compel.

In this she had some luck. Later during the day, the party
split and those captives who knew her were driven off in another direction.

She was on her own. That night when they camped, she
was dragged away by Osric. He threw her down and pushed
up her shift.

As he hammered at her soft insides, the pain was bad, but
not intolerable, Elin thought, and turned her face away.

There were violets growing in the grass, the flowers deep
blue washed with the gold of the sunset. She concentrated
and tried to forget the man, Osric, was alive.

This angered him and he slapped her across the face with
his open hand, screaming, "Frankish bitch, you will try to
give me more pleasure so as to avoid pain yourself."

Elin went for his eyes with her thumbs and was knocked
unconscious. It was her last act of defiance.

When she awakened, Osric beat her again, this time with
a whip.

It was a duel and Elin's people were excellent tricksters.
She spoke only her mother's language, feeling safe in the as-
sumption that none of the raiders or even their slaves would
understand it. They didn't.

She greeted words addressed to her in any other tongue
with dim blue-eyed incomprehension. She reduced Osric to
pointing and pantomime, but was careful never to let it get
too far. She performed with diligence any task she could be

persuaded to understand. It was just that she couldn't be persuaded to understand many.

Osric loved good food. The food Elin cooked was inedible. Osric was clean, fastidious about his person. Elin never washed unless threatened with a flogging, so she oscillated between occasional cleanliness and filth. Osric was sure he was irresistible to women, and after the first beating, he was much gentler with Elin when he tried to make love to her. The very sight of Osric nauseated Elin but, just to be safe, nightly she exhausted every ounce of desire in her body, and she lay like a corpse when he took her.

Elin risked death by doing this. Once he very nearly did kill her when she was punished in the manner she described to Owen—beaten and laid in the sun with salt in her mouth. But Elin was beautiful and Osric greedy. In the end he abandoned her, selling her to Ragnar.

She was living in the camp by then. Most of the raiders were convinced she was mad. She babbled to herself in a strange tongue no one understood, rolled in and sometimes ate filth.

But she had been beautiful when captured and Ragnar hoped she might recover and become a salable commodity again.

He ordered his men to leave her alone, but put her to the heaviest and dirtiest work he could find, that of cleaning up after the horses and other livestock kept in the pens at the end of the island.

Elin worked so well that Ragnar was pleased. She was good for something after all. In truth, Elin preferred the company of animals to humans now. Strong as she was, the work wasn't difficult, and she had begun to have hope of escape.

One hope was the river. It was high now, swollen with the spring flood, but in time it would drop. When it did, driftwood would be left stranded in the shallows. She might climb the palisade, push off on a log, and ride it downriver to freedom. Another hope was that now that Ragnar had seen she was so good with the horses, sometimes she was taken along when foraging parties went out, to do the heavy work of caring for the animals.

True, they had never come close enough to the deep

woods for her to make a break for freedom. A horseman could run her down too easily in the open, but there was always a chance that they might not. Once among the trees, she would be gone.

So Elin was quiet and didn't try to frustrate Ragnar as she had Osric, at least not until the day he frightened her.

He sent some of his other women to wash Elin. They performed this task brutally, but efficiently, and ended by burning her clothes and dressing her in a clean shift. Elin boiled again with fury and terror, certain he meant to sell her to one of the slavers docked at the island. But she found that all he wished was to take her to his bed. Her relief was so great that when he began to caress her body, she was afraid she might feel pleasure with someone gentler than Osric, and whom she hated less.

Elin quickly found this fear laughable. He was so clumsy that she began to regret his efforts to rouse her. She had to use all her self-discipline to keep from crying out in pain when he squeezed her breasts roughly and rubbed her sex. Then he mounted her and she lay like a corpse of a woman and let him have his will as she always did.

He grew angry, didn't or couldn't complete the act, and pushed her out of the bed to the floor. As she knelt, he caught her by the ear and jerked her head toward his mouth. "Listen, fool woman, give up this pretense."

He loosened his grip on her ear and caressed her hair. "You are very pretty. Give over a little and some man will take you. Move your hips a bit when he comes to you, whisper nice things, and he'll love you, give you pretty clothes, get slaves to do your bidding. It takes only a little work for a woman to make a man happy. Easier than the work you're put to now."

He buried one hand in her hair, thinking that, if she became a bit more cooperative, he wouldn't mind keeping her for himself. A woman who could take the abuse she'd taken and still remain beautiful was a remarkable creature.

"Come now," he put his lips to her ear again, near the smooth cheek. His breath stank of beer and rotten teeth. "Come now, get into bed, make me happy, make yourself happy." He squeezed her breast with his other hand.

Elin looked through the door of the longhouse into a patch of sun.

Was this the bargain women made, their souls and bodies for food and protection? Should she make this bargain? Betray the dead at the farm? Act as if she welcomed his caresses? In time, clumsy as he was, she might. She was a passionate woman. The way she'd had to drain her body to keep it from responding to Osric had taught her that.

Why not? It was life of a sort. She would survive, maybe even grow content. And part of her would die.

She'd become afraid of this man's displeasure and crawl cringing at his feet, afraid of losing the things she had, the good food, the safety of his protection.

She couldn't make a pretense of yielding. She knew herself better than that. Such a pretense would in the end lead to the real thing.

Two paths opened before her. One led at least to temporary safety and comfort; the other into only the desperate hope of freedom and the unknown. Something in Elin's mind said, *choose.* She turned and looked into Ragnar's face. She saw an aging man, weak hair beginning to gray, nose red and swollen from too much drink, cheeks thick with stubble, and broken veins.

He saw—an animal.

There was no mercy in Elin's face, but no hatred either. The look said as clearly as if she had spoken it, I can't kill you, so I must endure you, but don't ask for my love.

Ragnar had seen the same look once long ago in the eyes of a captured bitch wolf. The people on the farmstead had hoped to breed her and get puppies. But she killed the dog sent to her. And one night she slipped her collar, tearing off one ear in the process, ripping the other, and escaped, leaving a trail of blood, scarlet drops on the white snow. But the lop-eared wolf ran free under the moon.

Elin held Ragnar's eyes for a long moment while a chill lifted the hair on the back of his neck and ran down his spine. Then Elin looked away, turning those awful eyes toward the door again.

Her bladder was full. She emptied it on the boards of the floor, smiling and dabbling her fingers in the warm yellow stream.

Ragnar dressed and left hurriedly.

Elin was sure she would be punished, perhaps killed.

He didn't do either one. A lifetime of degrading other human beings takes something out of a man, and it had taken its toll on Ragnar. There were powers stronger than he and he had seen them look at him out of Elin's eyes.

As for Elin, she knew she'd passed some sort of test. There were only two things left for her now, freedom or death. Her strength grew instead of failing, even when she realized she was pregnant and must escape soon.

She had steeled herself to try the river when Ragnar led out the foraging party and encountered Owen.

It may be that what Ragnar saw in Elin's eyes was his own fate. Because a few seconds after Elin's screams, Owen's sword went through his throat.

Elin slept for a time, facedown, nude, on the bench of the sweat bath. Strange shapes walked in her mind. The hanged man, jerking in the gloom of the grove; Ragnar's face. He had been the only one in the camp to behave toward her with any kindness or humanity. His actions were highly self-interested; he hoped to sell her for a good price. Yet she couldn't find the same hatred in her heart for him as she had the rest. He was the only one who hadn't treated her with either cruelty or contempt, and her scream had killed him. He had never understood her heart.

The end of freedom was death to her people. But most women were never free, and understood nothing about it, living as they did, under some man's heel from birth to death. Elin was Abreka's daughter also.

Where was she, that foster mother who had accepted Elin into the covenant of her mother's people, crowning her with roses, the sweet, wild, pink rose of the hedgerows. Then pressing the thorns into her scalp and forehead until the blood trickled down her face, saying, "This is our life, the flower and the thorn."

Elin bore the pain without flinching, understanding that it was expected. She still heard Abreka's voice in her ears.

"I love your mother, how could I not, for she is my sister, yet she is not one of us. She has chosen to be the bondmaid of a stoneman.

"The rose is the freedom of our lives, the thorn the price you pay for freedom. Only you can judge if the rose is worth the cruelty of the thorn."

Death and the fear of pain—weapons the strong used against the weak.

Her people had mastered the weapons of their adversaries. Elin could control pain when she needed to do so, and she could choose her death and go willingly into darkness.

She had the strength of the powerless, her own brain and hands.

Reynald would not escape her.

As her father had said, "It is the law."

Chapter
26

*E*LIN completed her preparations by dark. She walked down the stairs into the hall alone. The fire was the only light. None of the women had bothered to set the customary torches.

Her skin felt clean and fragrant, still glowing from the sweat bath. She was dizzy from the fast and everything around her stood out with unnatural clarity. She wore the plain linen gown and was barefoot. A chaplet of rue was around her brow. Her hair hung unconfined down her back. From the knights' quarters came the sound of Rosamund squealing and rough masculine laughter.

In one hand Elin held a bowl with the potion she'd prepared, in the other the stone knife. The floor was cold under her feet.

Alfric and Godwin sat at the table.

"Elin," Alfric said.

"Be still, priest," Godwin said. "She does what she must."

"Come with me, Godwin, for I am filled with fear," Elin said. "See there is no iron about you, though."

"I understand this," he said.

Elin went into the church. Godwin and Alfric followed. The horn-shaped lamp burned alone in the silence. She fell to her knees, joined her hands, and bowed her head.

The shadows cast by that one flickering lamp were, Godwin thought, almost worse than darkness. They hung about the place, fluttering around the walls and roof like the armies of hell. The faces of the men and women in the wall paintings peered at them out of the gloom as the faces of ghosts might.

"God," Elin prayed aloud, "have mercy on my child and

Owen, if you can have none on me. Preserve their lives. My own I willingly lay down."

"Elin," Alfric cried, "think of your youth, your child. The world is before you. These things will pass. While you live, love will come again." He raised his hand to bless her.

"No! Alfric, stay back," she ordered, "your goodness is such that it would drive away those spirits I wish to attend me. It would melt the iron in my soul to ash."

She rose and took the stairs to the crypt. Godwin kindled a torch and followed. Elin passed among the stone tombs of the bishops and priests of Chantalon, pale and quiet enough to join them, to the back of the crypt under the nave. An iron grating was set in the floor of the living rock on which the cathedral and fortress rested.

"Lift it," she told Godwin.

The grating was crusted with the rust and mold of centuries, but it came up easily in his hand. Stairs led down into the blackness below. They curved around the wall, cut from the stone, only wide enough for a single pair of feet stepping one before the other.

Elin descended, eyes unseeing, as though her feet knew the way. Godwin tightened his hand on the torch and followed. The cavern below was huge. Godwin's torch lighted only a small part of it. In the area under the grating there was a bench and a pile of faggots on the floor. The stone under the grating was black, stained deeply. Godwin looked up at the grating and then back at the stone floor. To create a stain that deep, blood must have poured down through it again and again. "What is this place, Elin?" he asked softly.

She started slightly, as though awakened from sleep. "I know not." Her voice echoed in the darkness of the cavern. "Many have come here. Worshiped. The Romans before them, others. One thing I do know, it is not Christ's."

She seated herself on the bench and spoke loudly into the darkness. "Where is my lord? Where is my husband? Answer me!"

Godwin's skin crawled. "We are in the bowels of the earth, Elin. To whom do you speak?"

"To my people," she said, "and I am a queen among them."

"And now?" he questioned.

"We wait," she said.

They waited. Godwin sat, elbows resting on his knees, hands clasped, wondering if she were not deceiving herself. He had known people's minds to snap under the pressure of pain and grief. Was this happening to her?

She stood, lifting the torch from its bracket on the wall, walked to the center of the room and raised it. A stalactite hung from the ceiling. Water running down its surface had formed a small blue pool on the floor. Elin paused at the edge, holding the torch high. Its light was reflected in the water.

Godwin saw the room clearly for the first time. Dear God, he thought, the rock the cathedral and the fortress rested on must be hollow. The walls were shot with holes. Little ones, big ones, holes filled with blackness; anything might crawl out of one and answer Elin's cries.

"Where are you?" she said in a voice of command. "Answer me!"

Something did, only a single word, and that one Godwin didn't understand. He found himself crouching, fumbling for the hilt of his sword, and bitterly regretting he'd left his weapon behind.

"Where is he?" she asked again.

This time the voice answered in a tongue he understood. "They have taken him. He is a prisoner within their camp in the river, held fast, caged high up."

"Osric," she whispered in horror. "No!" she screamed, her voice echoing in the stony room. "No! Why did you not warn him? Why did you not prevent this," she raged.

"We didn't know. The man, Reynald, sold him." The voice was plaintive, sad.

"So," Elin said, the sound of command returning to her voice, "where is the Saxon, Enar?"

"He follows, but what can he do?"

"Find him. Send the women. Help him," she commanded. Then she walked back to Godwin and thrust the torch into his hand. "Hold it high," she ordered.

He did. It illuminated Elin and the pool. She pulled the dress off, dropped it to the floor and stood naked. Then she picked up the knife and bowl and walked to the pool.

"I make"—she hesitated for a second and closed her

eyes—"a death curse for Reynald. And if you do not help the Saxon rescue him, a death curse for you, too. For witch queen am I, and the daughter of one, and she the daughter of another, to the very beginning of time."

She drank the contents of the bowl and threw it to the floor, where it shattered. "Never used but once. May he be broken as it is broken." Then she struck herself in the left breast with the knife. "Wounded as I am wounded."

The blood poured from the gash in a stream that ran down between her breasts and thighs to the floor and into the pool, staining the water black in the torchlight.

Then she walked back to Godwin and took the torch from his hand. Her eyes were brilliant in its light, glittering like broken glass, the pupils drawn to pinpricks within them, flat and blue as ice. "The faggots, arrange them in a circle. The drink is working in me. In a few moments my soul will fly from my body and I will think no more."

He did as she told him. She stepped quickly into the center and set them alight with the torch. They burst into flames with a roar. Elin cried out.

Godwin reached for her, but was driven back by the heat. The cavern filled with smoke drawn away by drafts into the surrounding tunnels.

Elin stood within a circle of flame. She raised her arms. Her lips parted, but the voice that spoke was not her own. It was guttural, deep, and laden with such a freight of malevolence that Godwin's heart turned to stone in his breast.

"May his flesh burn with my fury. May his bones freeze with my hate. May he not speak, or hear, or feel, or see. And, imprisoned in his rotting body, may he die." She gave a long keening wail.

The flames burned out, leaving the wood smoldering and stinking. The darkness was as abrupt as the light had been and Elin fell, twisting in a convulsive twitching and thrashing.

Enough! Godwin thought.

The torch was almost burned out. It cast only a small circle of light into the utter primordial blackness that returned to the room. Godwin picked Elin up, and using the last faint light of the torch, scooped up the dress and carried her up the narrow stairs to the crypt.

Another torch was burning at the foot of the stone stairs that led up to the church. It was dark, but compared with the hole he just escaped, the crypt seemed a place of light and comfort. He looked down, Elin limp in his arms.

The torch below was out. He stared into darkness. Something moved. In seconds he had the grating back in place. He half carried, half dragged Elin up the stairs through the church. Alfric was waiting there. They stood just outside the hall in the scriptorium, at Alfric's insistence, to pull on her dress.

"This is folly. I think something is following us," Godwin snarled, glancing back into the shadows of the church they'd just quitted.

"What?" Alfric asked.

"I don't know," Godwin muttered between his teeth, shoving Elin's arms into the sleeves, "and don't wish to find out."

"They won't harm you," Elin whispered, "they harm no one."

Godwin didn't answer. He opened the door, shoved Elin and Alfric through, then slammed and barred it behind him.

The fire was burning bright and high on the hearth. Ingund knelt before the flames, pushing more fuel into it.

"Welcome back, Godwin." Edgar spoke from the table. "We had our own entertainment while you were gone."

Ingund took Elin from the men and seated her in the arm chair by the fire.

There were two dark objects on the table. Alfric took a step closer, saw what they were, and turned away, retching. Gowen, sitting at the end of the table in darkness, a half-naked Rosamund in his lap, laughed. "He has a weak stomach."

"Faugh! Christ, so have I. We eat here," Godwin said.

The dark objects were the heads of two men.

"They followed Rosamund and we followed them," Gowen said.

"You used her as a lure?" Alfric said.

"Yes," Edgar said quietly. "I wanted to know the count's plans. He intends to strike at us tomorrow, and kill us all.

His pretext will be that we've done away with the Lord
Bishop in order to steal the golden monstrance."

"How many men has the count?" Godwin asked.

"Too many for us to defeat with Reynald helping him,"
Edgar answered.

Godwin ignored the heads and sat down on the long bench
by the table. "Reynald may not be the ally he hopes,"
Godwin said, chewing one knuckle thoughtfully. He pointed
to Elin in the chair. "What she has done this night may touch
him. I think it will."

"Suppose it doesn't?" Edgar asked.

"We can't run, the time for that is past. We'd never get
through the gates," Godwin said, shaking his head. "I'd
rather defend the church. It's stone and won't burn. We've
thinned the ranks of the count's men and given them something to think about. Reynald's men are a mixed lot, family
men, not soldiers, most of them. Kill a few and the rest may
draw back."

"It will touch him," Elin moaned.

Ingund saw the blood on her dress and looked down inside it with an exclamation of horror. She got some cloth and
began to stanch the blood as best she could while shielding
Elin's bared breasts from the men.

Suddenly Elin started upright in the chair and screamed,
"A serpent in the fire!"

Ingund leaped back. Elin's eyes were dilated with terror as
she looked into the flames.

"Elin," Alfric said, his voice troubled and heavy with
compassion, "there is nothing there." He pulled off his own
woolen mantle and wrapped it around her.

"I saw it," she said, squeezing her eyes shut and shaking
all over with a chill. "I still do, coiled, head lifted to strike,
fangs dripping poison. Fear not, Godwin, he will feel it. And
so, dear God, will I."

Chapter
27

WHEN Enar saw Owen being put on a horse by the two Northmen, he knew Owen was still alive. He couldn't think of anything to do except follow blindly. Had it been only Osric and Hakon who led Owen away, he might have considered some stratagem. But they had six handpicked warriors with them, too many to challenge.

So he followed. The woods thinned out, but the trees were still thick near the water. The night was black, as the clouds rolled in from the sea. Darkness ruled the earth. The few human dwellings he came close to lay in silence and ruin.

It was close to dawn when he saw the lights of the Viking camp. He chose a copse of birch trees, thickly overgrown with blackberry bushes. The heavy vines formed a hollow under the trees where the heavy growth had killed those branches nearest to the ground. He crawled into it and slept.

He woke at noon, ravenously hungry. There was a loaf of bread and a big piece of cheese near his hand. He didn't give their presence a single thought until he was half finished eating, then realization smote him.

He tried to stand up. The blackberry bushes caught him so viciously across the back and buttocks that he dropped flat again and bit his hand to keep from screaming.

Then he reconnoitered more cautiously, crawling among the dead leaves below the tangle of thorns. There was nothing to indicate he'd been discovered. No sound or sign of human presence, nothing, not even a footprint.

Food was food, no matter where it came from. Enar shrugged and finished it off. He was lying on his stomach under the vines, trying to figure it out when he fell asleep.

When he woke up, it was dark. Something very soft was

under him. Deep in his mind a small voice warned dryly that it had no business being there. He ignored the voice, giving it the excuse that he was having a particularly pleasant dream.

Two soft hands wandered over his body, caressing gently. Enar made a sound reminiscent of the purr of a large tomcat. Yet another pair of hands was undoing the laces of his breeches. He lifted his body slightly to give them more room to maneuver.

"He is very big," another voice commented. This voice was not in his mind.

The scratching hands found their goal and got a tolerably firm grip on his balls. "And growing bigger," it observed with a feminine giggle.

Enar came fully awake and remembered where he was. This time he had the good sense not to try to jump up. Of course, that pair of hands holding a most intimate and precious part of his anatomy had something to do with his decision.

"Christ," he whispered.

A number of voices laughed. He was most firmly pinned, hands on his arms and legs. He was kissed on the mouth. A tongue searched his.

"Oh, he has gone limp." This from the owner of the pair of hands between his legs. It sounded disappointed.

"No matter, he will soon rise again," another remarked.

"Please let me go," he pleaded. "It is true that I have done much that is sinful."

"And thinking of doing more." The voice attached to the hands in his breeches chuckled. She was getting the expected response in spite of his protest.

Who were they? All the stories he'd heard of wood sprites or those more chilling ones of the ghosts of women betrayed or dead in childbirth ran through his mind.

He was kissed again, this time by one who had much experience with kissing.

"In the name of Christ," Enar said, rather half-heartedly, "be gone. I repent of my many sins." Then trying to put more conviction into his tone, he added, "Most truly I do."

A volley of giggles broke out in the darkness all around.

He was kissed again. This time he was sure by a different, but equally competent pair of lips.

"Why are you afraid, Saxon? We are fair and many of us are here. It's a long time till dawn," a voice near his cheek purred seductively, then gently bit his earlobe.

Enar counted the hands on his body. "I am only one man," he said, dismayed. "My wife won't like it," he said desperately. "I'm not strong. In two days I've had only a loaf of bread and a piece of cheese."

There was general hilarity all around. Velvet lips brushed his cheek. "Oh, fear not, we don't starve our captives," the voice breathed. "We'll give you food."

"And make you earn it," another said ominously. This coming from the general direction of the hands clutching his nether anatomy.

Enar tested his strength against them cautiously. There must be several on his back, another across his kidneys, and something pinned the backs of his knees. He couldn't move.

The Christians were right, his sins had found him out. He was in a panic. Oh, God, to meet his fate among too many women, even for him. He decided on cajolery. "Sweet ladies, it were a pity that your charms should be wasted on one man alone, when in the world there are so many who would delight in encountering them, and still others who stand in dire need. If you let me go, I'm sure that I could find eight"—but he decided this might be too few and increased the number—"ten, or even twenty strong, young men who . . ."

The voice of the one who'd been nibbling his earlobe spoke up. "He's fair-spoken and free with honeyed compliments. It's plain he's a practiced liar. What think you, Sybilla, is he worth keeping?"

This evidently addressed to the one with the intimate grip, because she began exploring with the fingers of one hand while she maintained her hold with the other. Enar moaned, but not with pain. "Ummm," she said at length, "he's better than a mouse, but not by much."

"Mouse!" Enar cried, outraged, and succeeded in shifting his weight.

"You're making him angry." This time the voice was masculine.

"I'm not angry," Enar said hurriedly, "no, no, not at all."

"Good!" the masculine voice continued. "If you promise not to run away or do any other foolish thing, I'll tell the women to let you go."

"I'll do no running, I swear it," Enar said fervently.

"Don't lie," the voice cautioned sternly, "or next time I'll send the men, and they are not so gentle."

If the women did such things, Enar thought, what might the men do? He didn't want to find out. "I promise, I swear," Enar repeated.

A fire sprang to life near where he was lying even as all the hands released him. He rolled over cautiously, lacing himself up, and sat.

The blackberry vines had been propped higher with a stick. The thick layer of thorny branches above formed a small dry cave floored with autumn leaves. They sat around him in a circle, the women still giggling and whispering together.

Were they human, these small people? What had he fallen into? Their brown dress and leather leggings seemed part of the tree trunks and dark coils of vine. In a moment they might melt into the drift of brittle dead leaves he sat on and vanish.

Then one of them, a girl with rosy lips and green eyes that reminded him of Ingund's, spoke and mimicked his voice. " 'My wife won't like it. I'm weak and hungry.' "

Everyone in the circle laughed uproariously at his humiliation.

"I am bigger than a mouse," Enar said, sounding even to his own ears disgruntled.

This caused near prostration.

When she could speak, the girl with the green eyes lifted her hand and held her forefinger and thumb about a quarter of an inch apart. "Only by this much," she said. Her eyes laughed into his, and he was sure that they were human.

He shook his head and pulled a mournful face. "And you called me a liar."

More laughter all around.

After that he felt completely at ease. They fed him again. Bread, cheese, and some meat that he was suspicious of until he ate some and realized it was only pork.

He got to know them quickly. Some of them had names similar to the Frankish or Saxon ones he was used to. But others had sounds in them he'd never heard before: Akella, Ilo, and Sybilla, the girl with the green eyes. Alshan introduced himself. He was the same who'd concluded the bargain with Owen.

He told Enar simply, "I am a man of the tree. The lady sent me to help you."

"The Lady Elin?" Enar asked.

Alshan fingered the stoat skull with the amber jewel and smiled. "In a way," he said, "yes. She would rescue the bishop."

Enar swallowed some pork and wiped his mouth. "I would like very much to do that also. But I've seen the camp. There are more than one or two men in it."

"As many as six or eight or twenty." The girl Sybilla grinned.

"Yes," Enar said, "as many as that or more."

"You are a mighty warrior. You could fight them," she teased.

Enar didn't feel like being teased. If Owen was alive, his situation must be desperate. "Yes," he answered grimly. "I could, but however mighty a warrior I am, I would not win."

The laughter of Sybilla's remark died away.

"That's true," Alshan said very simply, "but he must be rescued. We need him and so does the city."

Enar took another bite of pork and studied Alshan and the rest narrowly. "Why?" he asked. "What does his fate matter to you?"

The old man paused and looked into the fire. "The old gods and the new are met in him. While he lives, he will not fail his trust. We need a father among the horsemen. He will be that father. Now, when you have finished eating your fill, you will come upriver with us tonight. Sybilla and I will guide you."

Enar tore at some bread with his teeth and stuffed some of the cheese into his mouth, wishing for some wine or beer. He was not happy. He didn't see what these strange people could do to help Owen, and a botched escape attempt might mean both of their deaths. He glanced skeptically at the circle of faces around him. All were unarmed and most were women. "With respect," he said to Alshan, "I cannot see how—"

"Saxon," Alshan said, "today I made my way close to the Northmen's camp. This took much courage, Saxon, for their warriors were all about. They had him in a cage, suspended high up, hung from the trunk of a tall pine. The man, Osric, who calls himself cruel and boasts of it, is trying to break his heart."

Enar knew more of the camp and its inhabitants than he'd admitted to Owen. He knew of Osric. He knew he'd directed the slaughter at the monastery. The man was an evil legend.

"You agree, I think," Alshan said, "now, that he, the Lord Owen, has not much time."

Enar stopped stuffing himself, saying, "I travel best if not too full of food. When do we start?"

"As soon as possible," Alshan said.

Enar had to admire their speed and organization. Some hands put out the fire, while others packed the food. He was surprised to see that both Sybilla and Alshan reversed the fine deerskin dalmatics that they wore. The undersides were dark and undecorated. He jumped back with an exclamation of surprise when Sybilla took soot from the fire and smeared it quickly all over his face and hands.

"Stand still," she ordered. "Would you have a tarnkapen?"

"The cloak of invisibility?" Enar asked.

"Yes. If you would be guided by me."

He acquiesced, saying, "That's clever. Something black against black, one sees nothing."

"We are very clever. You'll soon see that, too," she told him, with an air of superiority. "Now come!"

They left the rest and took off running, following the trees, Enar keeping up as best he could. They set a stiff pace. Enar had been brought up to have fear of darkness, but the knockabout, catch-as-catch-can life he'd led cured him of some of his fear. Yet, these people were astonishing. They moved as easily through the shadows as the wind itself and might almost have been part of the night.

After a brief burst of speed, during which Enar decided they must have been testing his wind, his companions dropped back into an easy loping run that was child's play for his powerful legs and lungs.

Alshan ran ahead. Sybilla followed behind him.

"How is it with you, Saxon," she asked after the first mile or so.

"Very well," Enar said. It was, he ran easily. "Sometimes I fear for my footing in the dark," he said.

Sybilla giggled. "Watch Alshan more closely, and glance down quickly and often as you run."

Enar studied Alshan's movements. He went around bushes that caught on Enar's clothing, stepped over dead branches that cracked under Enar's feet, and avoided piles of dried leaves that whirled up, rustling loudly, as Enar ran through them.

He took her advice and soon the run became even easier. These people knew many strange and useful things, and Enar became determined to pick Sybilla's brains. "How do you know where you're going?"

"We follow the river."

They were in the deep forest now. Enar could barely see his hand in front of his face. The night was moonless and it was a chore to keep his eyes on the moving darkness that was Alshan ahead of him. "What river?"

"The forest is also a river," she said.

And it was borne in on Enar, as they continued on, that it was. The open land and the dwellings of men were islands in it. Sometimes the forest thinned to a trickle, only a double line of trees, but then it broadened into a flood, covering them with its rich darkness, and deep, yet somehow alert, quiet. It was to Enar as though he'd encountered a strong, kind friend he'd never known existed before.

Twice they skirted the outlying overgrown fields of abandoned villages. The timbers of their ruined halls and shattered palisade fences standing—stark, black shapes against a star-filled sky.

"We avoid these places," Sybilla told Enar. "If any of the inhabitants survived the raids, they'd keep fierce dogs and sleep in fear behind barred doors, not even daring to show a light, for the Northmen have tried to exterminate all human life near their camp, that they may be more secure."

They left the village behind them, plunging again into the embracing safety of the darkness under the trees. What they ran through now was more parkland. Though it was still al-

most always possible to stay among the trees, it was sometimes necessary to dash through a clearing. Enar noticed
Alshan always put on a burst of speed when he did so.

Enar became aware they were being followed by something. Three shapes that moved as secretively as they did.
They met on the riverbank.

Sybilla put a wineskin in his hand. "Here, drink up,
Saxon," she said in a low voice.

Enar sat down on a fallen tree and squirted the wine into
his mouth. "You have a boat?" he asked Sybilla hopefully.

"No," she said, "when we want to ford a river, we don't
usually use a boat."

"I thought not," Enar said. "I should have known." He
squirted more wine into his mouth, watching as they freed a
big log stranded in the shallows.

They mounted Enar on it. The wood was wet, slimy with
its long soaking. Enar threw the wineskin over his shoulder,
gripped the log tightly with his knees, and locked his fingers
around the stubs of two branches.

Sybilla, and the three they had met at the river, each took
a branch, two on each side. They left Alshan on the shore.
"He will make magic and call on the spirits to help us,"
Sybilla explained to Enar as they, guiding with their hands
and paddling with their feet, drove the log in the direction of
the powerful current in the middle of the river.

"I hope his spirits love him," Enar whispered between his
teeth. "I cannot swim."

"Good," Sybilla said, "that means whatever happens, you
won't be so foolish as to let go."

At that moment the current caught the giant snag. It
swayed, wobbled for a few heart-stopping seconds, then
steadied and went straight forward swiftly.

The snag shook under him, threatening to dunk or possibly drown him. Enar's slippery perch on it was by no means
secure either. His buttocks tended to try to slither from one
side to the other instead of staying safely in the middle, each
oscillation nearly throwing him into the millrace of the black
water. Enar looked at the silhouettes of the dark trees on the
bank, stars caught in their branches, as they rushed past him.

Knowing he was committed, Enar stared forward at the island fortress far ahead and entered into a brief, savage de-

bate with himself concerning which God he ought to honor with his prayers. He decided ultimately on Christ, since he was Owen's God and would have more than a passing interest in rescuing him.

He considered what he could offer Owen's God. His soul? Did Christ really want the company of a slightly drunken, more than slightly lecherous brigand in paradise? An individual, if the truth be known, whose chief accomplishment was the ability to split the skull of a man with a well-thrown war axe at thirty paces.

Enar finally concluded an open contract would be best. If he got out of this alive he'd ask Owen or Alfric what sort of sacrifice he should make. He was laying this before the Almighty when the log grounded in the shallows near the tip of the island, without any warning at all, throwing him into the water with a belly flop he was sure could be heard for miles and would bring at least a hundred murderous warriors down on him instantly.

He lay struggling for breath and composure in about a foot of water, thrashing like a grounded turtle, and staring up in terror at the row of stakes that formed the outer palisade wall of the fortress.

No one came. The sounds of laughter and drunken voices drifted on the night wind. Enar's panic disappeared and Sybilla helped him wade ashore.

In order to set the stakes of the palisade, the Northmen had dug a deep ditch, placing stakes above that, sharpened ends pointing outward. A rather pointless effort, Enar thought, since the defenses would have been chiefly useful against cavalry, which couldn't get across the river in any case. What they had succeeded in doing was to create a blind spot under the palisade.

Enar and the rest crawled into the ditch. After he recovered from his shock at emerging alive from his ride downriver, Enar began to feel cold. He was soaking wet, his teeth chattered, but his companions seemed content to sit patiently in the deep, muddy hole, staring into the night.

Every time Enar opened his mouth to say something, he was told to "hush, be quiet." So he ground his chattering teeth, remembered the wineskin, and comforted himself with a drink, while he thought raging tirades of curses until he wore out his bad temper and fell asleep.

They woke him, laughing softly like children about to play a trick on grownups. The rest were in the process of building a fire in the ditch.

Enar felt a thrill of pure terror. He could think of no better way of attracting attention to themselves than this. Then he realized that the ditch was deep enough and the outward projecting row of stakes was thick enough to shield anything but a bonfire from the eyes of those inside.

The morning mist was rising from the water of the river, drifting over the island. They had not built one fire but many. Each had wet driftwood from the shore piled over it. The wood was smoldering, smoke mingling with the river mist, spreading a choking cloud. It drifted through the close-set stakes of the palisade into the camp. One of the men slipped away from the rest, came, and whispered in his ear, "Be ready."

Enar nodded. He saw their intent and was wolfishly pleased. Even when the fires were abandoned, the prevailing wind would continue to carry their smoke into the camp. They hoped to create enough confusion and disorder for Enar to slip in, rescue Owen, and escape.

Enar climbed through the ditch to the wooden wall and put his eye to one of the chinks between the posts. The camp lay before him, dark and silent. At the door of the great hall, in the center, burned the last torch of the night.

Owen's cage hung suspended to one side of the hall, the top in darkness, high above.

The smoke was already drifting, carried by the rising mist, between the longhouses. At the far end of the camp, a horse neighed and stamped its feet. The animals, more alert than the sodden human sleepers, could sense danger first.

He must be over the wall before their cries of alarm roused the men. Enar took a deep breath, checked the position of the axe in his belt, then reached up and caught the sharpened tops of two of the posts. He felt a quick, hard boost from behind, then he was up and inside.

The earth was packed by the coming and going of many feet. Enar crouched and oriented himself by the great torch burning in front of the hall. It was ahead, down the narrow aisle between two of the longhouses.

He brushed his hand before his eyes because they seemed veiled by something, and only then did he fully realize how thick the smoke was.

At the far end of the camp, the horses were making more noise. Enar began to hurry. He was puzzled. The light from the hall was growing. It was not yet dawn but the wall and thatched roof of the longhouse he was running along next to were clearly silhouetted against the sky.

The light was bloody. Fire, and not in the ditch outside. The roof of the great hall was burning.

One horse screamed, then another. The loud crack of picket ropes breaking rent the air.

Enar was at a dead run. A dozen horses were screaming and there was a thunder of hooves on the earth. Enar reached the end of the longhouse and stood before the hall. The roof was a pyre, flames roaring up into the sky. Owen, he thought, and looked up.

The cage hung above him, clearly visible in the light from the burning roof, swaying slightly in the hot updraft of the fire. Empty! Owen was gone.

Chapter
28

OWEN was alone, high up with the stars. Even if he got out of the cage, he realized that he had no hope of escape. The island was big and there must be easily five hundred men on it. More than enough to blanket the countryside and hunt him down.

The pain in his body now was terrible and would only grow worse in the days that would follow this one. Were it not for the periods of detachment that he managed working the knots with his fingers, he would be screaming for mercy even if only the mercy of death.

His calves and thighs cramped. His shoulders burned, pain knifing up his neck into the back of his skull. The pressure of the bars at the bottom against his knees numbed them unless he moved them. Each release of that pressure was raw agony. He couldn't feel his feet and toes at all. He might have found some other position, equally painful, in time, but at least a temporary relief, had he not refused to give up on the stubborn little piece of hide he clawed so assiduously.

He was sure the thong was wearing through. Then his arm cramped, the muscles jerking violently. The pain was so terrible that he nearly did scream. He grabbed at the jerking arm with his left hand. As his fingers closed around the wrist, the back of the hand brushed the bar. It moved.

He pressed the cramping limb against his chest and slammed the bar with the heel of his good left hand, in fury and frustration. The weakened thong snapped with a soft pop. The moistened sinew stretched, not far but enough. Owen reached up and, with fingers that shook with terror and joy, pushed the loop up carefully over the top of the willow branch. The stick, still tied at the bottom, hung out at right angles to the cage.

Owen's whole body shook so violently that it moved the cage. He clutched at the still cramping arm, trying to control the shuddering joy that wracked his whole body.

Dear God, oh, dear God, had he been seen?

Still trembling, he reached out and eased the bar back into position, then looked down. A torch stood burning brightly in front of the great hall just below him, a huge oak knot held in place by an iron bracket.

The cooking fires smoldered dark red, abandoned now in the darkness before its door. Inside, a woman was singing a sad, sweet song, slow and measured. A lament. The tongue was Frankish, his own. But there were no hands fumbling with the ropes of the cage. No sounds of alarm.

The cramping in his right arm eased. He opened and closed his fingers cautiously, then clutched the loosened bar with both hands and closed his eyes. His whole body was still quivering.

The song rose above the sounds of talk and laughter from the hall, its melody a clear bright thread in the darkness. Then the sound of a blow, a woman's cry of pain, and the song ceased.

Owen thought, "They do not even leave us our sorrow."

Here Elin had suffered as he did. The face of the one-eyed was before him. The remaining eye was as gray as a sky on a winter morning or the storm-driven sea sluicing a wind-swept beach. His voice spoke in Owen's mind.

"I yielded the other for wisdom, for wisdom is a thing born of pain and the bearing of it. Oh, man, if you would be more than you are, reach for it bravely and pay the price."

Owen's eyes opened slowly. He felt as if they had been closed for a long time. He had the means of dying now. If death was what he wished. But if he could loosen one bar, might he not loosen another, if he were willing to bear the pain?

They had destroyed his life, taken everything from him. His fingers tightened on the bar until he felt the stubs of the twigs trimmed from the willow branch bite into his palms and fingers, drawing blood.

"Father of fathers. Father of kings. Help me make them pay," he whispered into the darkness.

Then mastering his rage, Owen began on the second

branch. This one took longer. It was better tied than the first. He had to use his left hand since the nails of the right were worn to the quick. He hadn't managed to scrape through the green hide. His blow had broken it and the water he'd used to moisten the hide had loosened the sinew. He adopted the same approach with the second, moistening, clawing, then pounding, until his knuckles and the heels of his hands were raw.

For a long time it seemed as if he got nowhere. He cursed the builder of the cage for binding the bars so tightly. Finally, after how long a time he couldn't tell, exhaustion overwhelmed him. He stopped and realized the camp was asleep.

The only light was the big oak branch in its iron holder before the door of the hall, flickering and hissing in the wind from the river. It was late—even the night birds had ceased to call, and the only sounds were the whisper of insect voices and the faint rush of the river flowing past in the darkness.

He tested the bar and realized that in the short time he'd rested the leather had dried and tightened again. The wave of despair that washed over him was as black as any moment he'd ever endured in his whole lifetime.

He had no more water, and then he remembered another source of moisture in his own body. He used the empty water bottle to collect it.

The first strip of hide on the cage lashing parted but he found its builder had used an additional one for reinforcement. All his urine was gone. He couldn't squeeze out another drop.

He was as wildly frantic as an animal gnawing its own leg to escape from a trap. But there was also blood. Most of his thumb nail was worn away, but a tough ragged edge remained. He searched his left hand for the ridges of the big veins on its back then tore and tore again and again with the ragged nail, until he felt the hot trickle between his fingers. He had to escape now. With the coming of dawn they would certainly notice the damage to the cage, and he would be penned and perhaps chained. It was now or never. He moistened the last remaining leather and the loops of the sinew under it with the blood. Tearing and tearing with the broken nail until the hole in his vein was a ragged pouring gash.

He smeared the leather and the loops of sinew, soaking them with the blood, then began to pound with his fists on the bar. When his knuckles became too bruised and raw to pound any longer, he used the heel of his hand. The uncured leather didn't break but it stretched, not far, but enough. He was breathing like a spent runner when slowly he worked the lashing out over the top of the bar, then snaked his body from the cage to the top. The twig stubs on the remaining bars slashed at the raw skin on his back. He loved that pain. It was the agony of freedom. Rowels going into his flesh to spur him on.

He was free. He lay prone on top of the cage high above the camp, sucking air into his heaving chest. His legs were numb to the hips. And when he stood up, he would be in agony. But the empty cage swayed dangerously under his weight and he feared it might tilt and throw him down if he remained lying where he was for very long.

He reached out and caught the short chain that held it to the pulley on the crossbar and lifted himself to his feet. He very nearly fainted and did vomit as the blood returned to his feet with a savage rush. But when it was over, he was standing in command of himself again. Free.

Oh, God, what luxury. His cramped muscles and tendons unknotted themselves.

It was very quiet, that breathless hush just before first light. He stood, knees still trembling from the pain he'd just endured, and looked around. He hadn't considered what he would do once he was free of the cage. To his left was the tall pine that served as support for the cage. He couldn't see it clearly, in the faint light of the torch, but he had noticed that the trunk had a few stubs where the branches had been cut away.

It would take him time to negotiate the crossbar, then more time climbing down the pole, and he was by no means sure that there were enough projections left by the lopped-off branches to take him all the way to the ground. The rope? Hopeless. It was tied at the bottom to the pole and, given the condition of his battered hands, he couldn't even grasp it, much less undertake the difficult and complicated task of going down hand over hand. That, too, would take time. And time was something he was now rapidly running out of.

He still had no thought of saving his own life, only adamant determination not to be taken alive. Never would he allow himself to fall into Osric's hands again. Never. He refused even to think of it.

On his left was the roof of the hall, high thatched and steeply pitched. It ended only eight or so feet above the ground. That was the only way.

He relaxed and looked up at the stars. A slight breeze was beginning to blow. The air was cold and it chilled the sweat on his body. He was sure that he saw on the eastern horizon that faint blush of brightening that signals the dawn. The stars still hung in their full splendor above him, a reigning light.

He thought of Christ. What had Christ to do with what he was about to do? Yet he prayed, trying to forget that in the cage he'd addressed his prayers to another god, then realized he couldn't forget and must ask for what forgiveness he could. He prayed for himself, the ancient prayer for the dead, *Libera me domine de mortua eterna.*

Deliver me, oh Lord, from eternal death. Forgive your not-so-faithful servant. Give me the lowest place in heaven, but forgive me, for I am now about to die in your service.

Then without giving himself time to think, he turned and launched his body into space. It was like landing in a hay-rick, surprisingly soft, then the stars spun terrifyingly above him. He felt the ridge pole of the eaves slide under his back and he hit the ground.

His arms and legs went numb for a moment, but he was already moving. In a second he was on his feet. He stood motionless for perhaps a moment, not believing he'd really done it, listening to the rush of breath in and out of his lungs, smelling the sweet, damp air of morning.

How easily we fall in love with life, he thought. Even now it would be easier to run away. And how far would I get?

He seized the still-burning torch from its iron bracket. The roof of the hall was one big source of tinder. He threw the torch. It arced against the stars like a comet, landed, rolled, scattering sparks, then caught. Within seconds a column of fire leaped toward the sky, as the dry grass of the thatch exploded into flame.

The doors of the hall were open. A double row of tables with benches were set around the two side walls and back, leaving a clear open space in the center. He nearly stumbled over a step up and realized it had a wooden floor. The light of the torch he'd just used had dazzled his eyes. He paused for a second to let them adjust to the darkness, and found himself facing a raised dais at the back where the chiefs sat. Here and there on the benches lay the dark shapes of men sleeping off the drunken revelry of the night before.

Wake in hell, bastards, Owen wished them fervently, and looked around for a weapon, any weapon. He started toward the benches, sure that one of the sleeping men must have a sword or an axe.

Just then the thatch burned through and a bundle of flaming grass fell past the rafters to the floor in front of the high table.

By the yellow light of the flames, Owen saw Osric sleeping, head on the table, and by his hand, the ruby pommel of Owen's sword.

He sprinted for it and his fingers closed around the hilt just as Osric awakened and blinked, bewildered at the sudden light.

The scabbard fell away as Owen vaulted the high table and landed on his feet at Osric's side. He caught Osric by the hair and, twisting his head around, screamed, "Look, look at my face and see who kills you!"

Owen saw the comprehension in Osric's eyes and his shoulder lift as he reached to draw his own weapon. The tip of his sword found its way into Osric's belly just above the groin and he sliced upward.

Hakon awakened just in time to hear Osric's long, bubbling scream as he doubled over, scrabbling for his guts on the floor, and Owen's face, set in the death mask of the battle frenzy, staring into his.

Hakon had not lived so long by being slow. He leaped back, drawing his own sword as he did. As he fell back, he looked up and behind him. The woolen wall hangings above the chief's table were a tapestry of fire and big patches of the roof were ablaze.

Owen lunged at him over Osric's still-writhing body, nearly sending him back into the fire. Hakon stood still in a paralysis of terror.

Owen felt rather than heard the one at his back. He turned swinging. The sword chopped through the arm of a man holding an axe, his second swing decapitated him. Owen vaulted over the chief's table and ran toward the center of the hall. He had them trapped now. He must kill them. The spray of blood from the headless trunk of the fallen axeman splattered across Hakon's face and body, jerking him out of his paralysis of shock.

He knew the look on Owen's face. Men with that look in their eyes seldom failed in their intent.

Osric had stopped screaming, but all around the roar of the fire was in Hakon's ears.

Owen, standing in the center of the hall, looked at the dripping sword in his hand, raised it and yelled exultantly, "I owed Osric a debt. As you see, I have paid it. I owe you another for keeping this sharp. Come, Hakon, and I will pay that." The men on the benches, minds still fogged with sleep and drunkenness, moved away from him and crowded toward Hakon.

The entire roof was now a seething mass of fire and the rafters were catching. Owen blocked the only exit. He was a magnificent sight and a deadly one, half naked, the flames gleaming on his sweat-covered skin, the death light in his eyes. It was plain to Hakon he meant to hold them here until the roof collapsed. Hakon didn't want to die yet. "No, I am not Osric," he shouted back at Owen. "He did you wrong! You are avenged! Surrender to me and I promise you honorable treatment and I will send you to your kin without ransom."

The flames from the wall behind him were scorching his back.

Hakon meant the offer and Owen knew that he would try to keep his promise. He raised the sword to him in salute. "No. I stand between you and my city. I'll atone for my stupidity in trusting a false friend with my life."

The blazing wall hangings began to fall. Hakon, and the men with him, scrambled over the table. One, on fire already, rushed Owen, sword swinging. At the last second,

Owen crouched, and with a vicious chop of his blade, amputated both of the man's legs below the knees, then, leaping aside, cut off his head and threw it at Hakon and the knot of terrified men crouching around him in front of the dais.

Burning grass from the thatch was now raining down on all of them, stinging, a thousand fiery darts.

"No one will sing a paean for you, fool," Hakon screamed at Owen. "No one will know."

"I will know," Owen shouted back in ultimate defiance. "And you are a man, Hakon, try me to the last."

The hall was filled with smoke now and they could barely see each other. Hakon threw one quick glance at the roof above. The rafters, outlined in fire, were sagging. They, one way or another, had no time left. He charged, shouting, "It's both our deaths, fool."

He nearly reached Owen. They were about to cross swords when he was knocked flying. Owen jumped aside. A horse stood between them, a stallion, beautiful and proud as a king's palfrey.

The horse was red, his scarlet coat gleaming like watered silk in the firelight, slender of leg and hoof, with a small head, almost a barb. The horse turned toward Owen and whickered. The white showed around his eye and his nostrils flared with alarm. The long mane curled in waves over the arched neck, the tail lifted, carried high, a banner behind him.

The stallion blew, snorting, as if impatient with the slow human at his side, stamped twice, a thunder booming on the planks of the floor. Owen reached out, twined the fingers of one hand in the fiery mane, and vaulted onto its back. The horse leaped forward at a gallop, taking Owen on a drumming, triumphant circuit of the hall. Horse and rider both flew through a rain of fire from the falling thatch, then out through the door of the hall into the morning beyond.

Hakon, on his feet, again found himself carried along by the press of terrified men to safety behind Owen.

Chapter

29

*E*NAR stood uncertain before the burning hall while the camp leaped into panicked wakefulness around him. A horse ran past, followed by a man screaming curses and trying to catch the trailing lead rope. Three horses followed at a gallop. Enar had to jump aside to avoid being trampled.

A woman in the longhouse beside him began screaming and throwing clothing, pots, pans, and other paraphernalia out through the door. Others followed her lead, and Enar found himself ducking to avoid flying chairs, stools, and bedding.

The fire from the hall had leaped to the two nearest longhouse roofs and ribbons of flame were fanning out over the thatch. Smoke was a thick, choking blanket everywhere around him. A man dashed out of the haze, naked but for a sword in his hand, careened into another equally bare-assed but for an axe. They aimed wild blows at each other, both missed, stopped, stared, each realizing simultaneously that the other was not an attacking enemy, then turned and ran off in opposite directions.

No one paid the slightest attention to Enar. True, he was a big, roughly dressed, fierce-looking individual, but the camp had an ample supply of these, all racing in and out of the smoke, trying to catch escaping horses and slaves, or trying to find an enemy to fight. They were too busy to realize he was a stranger.

A broad grin spread across his face, but the grin vanished as he wondered how he was going to find Owen in this confusion.

A naked woman ran past, carrying her baby in her arms.

Her husband followed, hot on her heels, waving her dress like a banner and shrieking at her to put it on.

Enar had been too busy dodging furniture to notice the horse run into the hall. But he saw it gallop out, followed by Hakon and the rest, because just at that moment the roof of the hall collapsed. The walls followed, folding almost gracefully inward at first, then vanishing into the inferno of the fallen roof. The crowd around Enar scattered with a one-throated scream as an enormous whirlwind of flame rushed upward toward the brightening sky of morning.

Hakon staggered into Enar's arms, staring in consternation at the reigning chaos around him.

Enar had eyes only for Owen on the stallion in front of the hall. As the roof fell, the horse reared, head outlined against the fire, so high Enar was afraid he might tumble over backward, but he didn't. Instead, the forehooves dropped forward, and he began a dance of uncertainty, terrified by the sound and smell of the human hysteria surrounding him.

Hakon grabbed Enar by the shoulder, spun him around, pointed at Owen, and shouted, "Stop him!"

Enar flashed his grin at Hakon, saying, "Oh, yes, my lord, right away," and ran toward the stallion.

It seemed to Owen he had ridden from death into hell. In the twilight of daybreak, at least a dozen fires were burning on the thatched roofs of the longhouses. Half-naked men and women ran everywhere, screaming and howling around him. The stallion tried to rear again and Enar grabbed the forelock, shouting, "Lord Christ Priest, come!"

Owen was sure he was dead, and wherever he'd gone, Enar had been sent to accompany him. It was a comforting thought. It shouldn't have been a comforting thought, but it was.

The stallion seemed about to balk. Enar looked quickly back at Hakon. The man was still staring around astonished, but he would get his wits back quickly. Enar pulled hard on the horse's forelock. Just then, two mares ran by. The stallion obeyed stallion and horse nature. He followed, heading for the gate, Enar running along beside him. The gate was gigantic. It opened outward and was held closed by a bar usually lifted by three strong men.

Enar still clung to the stallion's mane, not trying to guide him now, but for support. A terrified mass of humans and animals were pushing and clawing at the great bar, trying to open it. Enar knew that to lose his footing in this whirlpool of terror meant death.

Enar screamed up at Owen, "Lord Christ Priest, help me!"

Owen shouted, roaring out, "Back! back!" as he somehow persuaded, with heels and hands, the stallion to rear again, and laid about among the press with the flat of his sword. Enar forced his way through the tightly packed mass of humanity to the bar. He was nearly crushed as the mob surged back all around him, pinning his body to the wood.

The big shoulder of a roan horse squeezed the breath from his lungs. Enar slapped savagely, desperately, at the roan, catching it on the tender nose. The roan threw his head up and kicked out with his heels, scattering the mob for a moment. Enar got his back under the bar and heaved upward with all his strength. It lifted and fell away.

Enar caught the swinging gate and rode it out over the river, to avoid being trampled by the mob behind him. He flew over the water, clinging for dear life to the top while his feet scrambled for purchase on the bottom cross bar, as the gate carried him back to the beach and palisade wall.

Enar dropped clear, landing on the shallow beach, watching as it seemed the entire fort tried to empty itself through the gate at once. Men, women, horses, cattle, and even chickens, sheep and, here and there, the odd pig, shot through, all plunging into the river, struggling in the shallows or scattering along the narrow strand. Owen trotted out on the stallion.

At the very tip of the island, the forest people stood near the boats half beached, half moored on the shore. Enar shouted something incoherent at Owen, waved his arm, and beckoned. Owen managed to turn the stallion with his knees. Enar began running toward the boats. Owen passed him, stallion at a trot.

The forest people jumped into one of the smaller of the river craft. Enar, running behind the horse, turned and looked back. As he did, he saw Hakon. No mistaking the man's huge frame, the white streak in his hair.

Hakon shouted and pointed at them. The men with him

began running toward them. The stallion had come to a stop near the boat occupied by the forest people. Owen, on its back, tried vainly to urge it in.

Enar caught up and slapped the stallion hard on the rump. The horse gathered itself calmly, floated over the gunwales, hooves landing with a thump on the curved planks of the bottom. Enar caught the prow post in his arms. The high-carved dragon reared above him, painted red and green.

More men had mustered from those crowded along the shore. They were less than fifty yards away and coming fast.

Enar closed his eyes and threw his whole weight against the ship. The bottom ground against the gravel and mud of the shore, then floated free. Owen's sword slashed the mooring rope and the current caught it broadside, swinging the prow around, Enar still clinging to it with both arms and legs.

Then they were in the middle of the river, the island behind them. Flames could still be seen leaping beyond the palisade, the whole fortress wreathed in smoke. Slowly at first, then as the swift current carried the ship faster and faster, it vanished behind them, a dusky shadow in the rising mist of morning.

Chapter
30

*I*NGUND rose early. She had spent a night of horror and hadn't slept. She dressed Elin and left her, gray-faced and quiet, in a chair beside the fire in the hall, putting Elfwine on watch, with strict instructions not to let Elin out of her sight.

Then she went out in search of news of Reynald. She was sure Elin had succeeded and was convinced that whatever Elin was, she was no ordinary woman. But such things as curses had their limitations, and it might be that Reynald had found a way to turn the worst of Elin's wrath. She must know.

She was stiff and sore from a night spent dozing in the chair and her eyes were gritty with the dry feeling long watches bring. Elin would not sleep but walked, eyes staring, speaking to and describing horrors only she could see.

Ingund had put her to bed a dozen times. Each time she tossed and turned, moaning and sobbing, until at last she got up and began to wander around the room again, holding whispered conversations with the shadows cast by the candlelight, or telling Ingund to hush so that she could hear what the voices in the fire were telling her.

Once while Ingund dozed, Elin wandered away. Ingund woke terrified to find the bedroom empty and Elin gone. Ingund ran to the bedroom door and threw it open. But the darkness of the corridor outside was like a malignant presence, the mouth of an open grave waiting to engulf her. So she lifted a burning stick from the fireplace, using it as a torch, followed Elin downstairs, and found her kneeling before the banked coals of the fire, arms raised in supplication, muttering in a language Ingund had never heard before. She held a knife in one hand and her arm had a deep gash in it.

Ingund was a strong woman, but when she tried to move Elin, force her to rise and return to the bedroom, she found she couldn't shift her weight. It was as though the girl's body had turned to a mass of lead. Touching Elin's skin was like touching a corpse, she was so cold.

Alfric stepped out of the darkness. Ingund shrieked, then gasping with relief that it was only Alfric, shouted, "Lord, don't frighten me that way. Help me."

Elin had ceased speaking and was as still as a statue.

"She'll freeze," Ingund said to Alfric.

"No," Alfric said quietly, "she won't. She knows what she's doing. You don't, I don't, but she does. There is some mighty struggle here and she's winning." The little man's eyes were sad and the lines in his face were deeply etched and weary.

Just then the fire on the hearth made a *wumph* sound and olazed up, filling the fireplace, flames leaping into the chimney, lighting Elin's face and body, frozen, head thrown back, arms lifted, straining in invocation.

Ingund recoiled.

"How cruelly she uses herself," Alfric said sadly. "How much she loves him. I wonder if he'll ever know. It's the darkest, coldest hour of the night, yet she keeps her watch. We must watch with her until it is ended," he said, sitting down on the bench.

Far away Owen struggled with his own darkness in the cage.

Ingund pointed to the cut on Elin's arm. The skin was split by the knife, the red meat of muscle and even the white rope of a tendon showed in the gash. "She doesn't bleed," Ingund said.

"No," Alfric answered, "she can't bleed or cry now."

"Why did she do it," Ingund asked, "cut her arm?"

Alfric shrugged. "Only to test her power, to see if she would bleed. When she didn't, she was sure of herself, and undertook her task."

It was true. The lines of strain were taut in Elin's body; it was as though she were among forces that held her rigid where she was, locked in unceasing struggle.

"You're a Christian priest," Ingund said to Alfric. "Is this evil? Will she come to harm? Is she somehow with him?"

"Would you care if it were evil?" Alfric asked.

Ingund's face hardened. For a moment, the beautiful girl looked old. "No," she said, "she is my lady. We're in a battle. We win by whatever means we can."

Alfric nodded, watching Elin closely. The fire blazed up, sucked by the draft in the chimney, then began to sink down as the half-consumed logs fell to white ash. "That's good," he said, "because I have no answer to your questions. But I do nothing because I believe it would be dangerous to interfere with her. This is her art, not mine, and it leads her."

Ingund looked away from the bright blaze of the fire at the hall, which lay in darkness all around them. She and Alfric were half in shadow. Only Elin could be seen clearly by the light of the flames. "Oh God, the darkness," Ingund whispered fearfully.

"The darkness is always present," Alfric answered. "Say rather that light is the exception."

"Yet few dare to look into it," Ingund said.

"And fewer still dare to contend with it as she does," Alfric said.

"I have," Ingund said bitterly, "and given my own dead into that everlasting night." Wrapping her mantle around her body against the cold, she walked to the wood box and tended the fire, saying defiantly, "I can keep her warm if nothing else." After that, she waited.

It was close to dawn when Elin's arms fell to her sides and her eyes opened. Ingund didn't ask any questions, only led her away to bed. Elin dozed fitfully for a few hours, then, when she awakened, she was calm and coherent. Ingund judged it was safe to leave her alone. The heavy wooden door of the hall closed behind her with a bang.

Routrude was fast. She spotted Ingund as she stepped through the door and, before her foot touched the cobbles of the street, Routrude was in front of her, finger outstretched in accusation. "She is! She is!" Routrude crowed in triumph. "You needn't deny it! She has cursed him. She has!"

Ingund looked mulish. "Since you know so well, why don't you tell me?" she snapped at Routrude.

Routrude fastened a grip on her sleeve. "They say," she whispered, "that he was taken with it last night at supper when he sat down to eat. He hasn't eaten since, and will not till he dies. Is it so? How was it done?"

Ingund tried to pull herself free of Routrude's grip as Gynnor approached. "How was what done? What is this silly talk of curses? My lady is a respectable woman." Feeling very guilty, she said defensively, "I can't think it was a secret, she spoke openly before all the household, to Godwin, and—" She caught Routrude by the wrist and pulled her hand free of the folds of her sleeve. "Routrude, let go of me."

But Routrude persisted. "No! No! No! She spoke to Godwin? Is it true he has given her a book? Come to think of it, no one knows anything about him either. And the knights say that he's in league with the horned—"

"Routrude," Gynnor broke in, exasperated, "many women can read. I can, and I see nothing strange in Elin's kinsman giving her a present."

"Reading, that reading is a very dangerous habit. Look where it got the bishop. Saddled with a fairy wife. I've often told your husband, Siefert, that he shouldn't allow you to indulge yourself too often or too long. It withers up a woman's pelvic organs, they get all tight and knotted." Routrude clenched her fists over her belly, presumably illustrating the potential condition of Gynnor's pelvic organs. "Learning is very bad for a woman and as I've often told Siefert—"

"You told my husband what!" Gynnor shouted at Routrude, her cheeks scarlet with fury.

The expression on Gynnor's face awakened Routrude's instinct for self-preservation. Elin wasn't the only woman in town who sometimes did strange things and dipped from time to time into books for instruction or amusement. Routrude backed up quickly.

Ingund took this opportunity to escape. She seized Gynnor by the elbow, towing her into the crowd near the stalls of the jewelry sellers.

"I'll kill her," Gynnor shouted, outraged at Routrude's effrontery. "I'll kill her. Talking about me to Siefert behind my back."

"He led her on, and well you know it," Ingund said. "She amuses him."

A loud voice hailed her. She turned and saw her father

standing at the door of Osbert's house, near the old Roman wall at the end of the square. She pushed her way through the crowd to join him. He was drinking beer among the men of Siefert and Osbert's households. Usually she was greeted boisterously, enthusiastically, with broad jokes and rough compliments, as they invited her to share in their enjoyment. Not today. They looked more like a group of conspirators standing together, mantles pulled around them against the cold wind.

Gunter reached out, folded her in his big arms, and kissed her on the forehead. Ingund found tears were running down her cheeks. Gunter pushed her out to arm's length. "What's wrong?"

Ingund shook her head. "I passed a bad night, the Lady Elin was . . . ill."

Siefert, standing near her father, laughed shortly. "Yes, and I'll wager Reynald is iller. I hear she's laid such a curse on Reynald that he wiggles on it like a bug on the end of a pin."

Ingund rounded on him, fists clenched, eyes blazing. "My lady is a good woman. You've been listening to that addle-brained Routrude. She—"

"Don't play the innocent with me, Ingund. I've known you since you were in swaddling bands. You well know what's going on in the bishop's hall. She's gathered the household around her, persuaded Godwin to stay, and now defies the count to do his worst. Do you think I mourn Reynald, liar that he is? I only hope she's strong enough to fry the bastard in his own juices. Without her curse, he'd be here now and the bloodletting begun in earnest."

She had known most of these men all her life, yet now they seemed like strangers, dangerous strangers. Muffled as she was against the cold air, she saw now that, under the thick cloaks, all were armed. One had a mail shirt under his tunic; another, a leather cuirass studded with metal plates. All carried knives and axes. Her father had a sword and three of his biggest hammers tucked into his heavy belt. Conspirators they had looked, conspirators they were, and ready for a fight. Like Routrude, they wanted information, and Ingund was prepared to give it to them.

"My lady is a mortal woman, but I think . . . a mighty sorceress. Yes, she has cursed Reynald, but I don't know if she can kill him. She is ..." Ingund hesitated, not knowing if she should go on.

Her father spoke up. "This is the end. We can bear the count no longer. Those bribes he collects and says he pays to the Northmen, while he puts half into his own coffers. And that madman, Bertrand, who would pry into the business of every family and even tell us when we may lie with our wives."

"I wouldn't put it past that sot," Osbert said, "to open the gates to the Northmen and drink himself into a stupor while we perish at their hands."

Ingund didn't dispute this. She, like they, was sure it was true. "She, the Lady Elin"—Ingund licked her dry lips, then continued—"she is one of the Old Ones."

All the men looked at each other. No more needed to be said. The Old Ones were a legend, they and their priestesses. So were the things they could do.

Siefert frowned. "Gynnor says the bishop isn't dead."

"If he lives, they'll stand together," Ingund said. Then she related all that had happened in the hall after Elin's facing down of Reynald in the town square, and that night, finishing with, "So, Edgar and Godwin believe the count means somehow to strike at us today."

"I don't doubt it," Gunter said. "You should leave that place, my girl."

Ingund's chin lifted and she looked her father in the eye. "You know me better than that."

"Yes, I do," Gunter said gravely, "too brave for your own good." His face was somber. "Too brave now, I think."

Ingund paled under her coronet of shining hair. "Would you have me less?" she said defiantly, as the faces before her were blurred away by her tears.

Gunter seized her in his arms, almost fiercely. "Stop it. Stop it, now," he whispered, stroking her hair and back as he had when she was a child. "I'm sorry. No, I wouldn't have you less. Hush now, hush, my girl."

Ingund pulled away from Gunter, trying to compose herself. "I can't leave Elin. She has no one but me. Elfwine is but an empty-headed girl, Rosamund ..." The men glanced at each other, a certain type of smile on their faces. "She is, well ... no better than what you would expect, seeing the place she came from. Anna is sweet, but old ..."

Gunter put his arm around her. "Never fear, my girl, you won't be left to stand alone." He looked at Osbert, Siefert, and the rest.

Osbert shrugged. "We could do worse than Godwin. Remember the dragon on his shield. He said he had a right to bear it."

"His men say he does, and the name Godwin is the one given him by the West Saxon king, Alfred," Ingund said. "And so ..." she said, looking around at the faces of the men, "what now?"

"That depends on others," Gunter said. "Elspeth wavers, not knowing if it were worse to send men to the count or stay out of the quarrel and not provoke Elin further—" He broke off because Judith was approaching.

"Oh, Lord," Siefert whispered, "no. That woman's tongue wags at both ends, she's worse than Routrude."

"And a lot more intelligent and better informed," Gunter said.

"She has twelve good men in her house," Osbert added quietly, "and their captain obeys her orders."

"Yes," Gunter said slowly, speculatively, "yes. I hadn't thought of that, I hadn't thought of that at all."

"Ingund, just the person I want to speak with. Come," Judith said, throwing her arm over Ingund's shoulder and trying to draw her aside.

Ingund shook herself free of Judith's arm angrily. "Not you, too!"

"I told you," Siefert laughed, "she's worse than Routrude."

"Routrude!" Judith exclaimed. "You dare compare me! Me!" she said, pointing to her breast. "To that!" she sputtered out and turned to sweep away.

But Ingund, perhaps remembering the twelve good men or possibly in genuine contrition, for Judith was celebrated for her kindness to Christians and Jews alike, reached out and took her hand, saying, "Oh, Judith, no, I'm sorry. It's just that I passed a very bad night, and when I stepped into the square, Routrude caught me and began filling my ears with her nonsense . . ."

Judith looked mollified and stopped, saying, "Yes, I met Routrude this morning. She gabbled all manner of foolishness to me, too. Something about water, white ladies, or was it white arms, I can't remember. Well, no matter . . . but I wanted to give you a message for the Lady Elin about Reynald."

"About Reynald?" several of them chorused together.

"About the curse?" Siefert asked.

"Just so," Judith said, drawing herself up and fixing them with an imperious stare. "I know exactly what happened. I have it," she said, her voice dropping lower, "from an unimpeachable source."

They all crowded around her.

"Judith," Gunter said urgently, "tell us quickly, we must know."

"Oh, you must, *must* you?" Judith said disdainfully. "When women talk among themselves of others, it's gossip. When men do the same, it's a matter of grave import."

"Judith, please," Gunter said, raising his hands, fists clenched in frustration.

Judith drew even closer and spoke again in a low voice. "Reynald sat down to his meat last night, very much as usual. Everyone present swears there was nothing amiss, no signs or portents of what was to come. Not even so much as a guest in the hall. Elspeth set a cup of wine before him, one she swears she drew with her own hand. He had only eaten a few bites when, seized with a sudden inexplicable thirst, he drained the cup."

Judith's voice was so low it was nearly a whisper. Everyone leaned closer to her. "Something banged against his lips, so he rose and examined it by the light of a taper. It was the head of a serpent. Just then a voice cried out, no one knows from whence it came, 'You have drunk the blood of the witch, now die, traitor!' Reynald was seized with the sickness then."

Siefert drew back, saying, "Yes, Judith, if I found a snake's head in my wine, I believe I'd puke, too." He looked a little pale just at the thought.

"Puke!" Judith said. "That's nothing, a tiny part of it. He shivers, freezing, cries for the fire to be built up, and more blankets. Then he burns and begs for snow to fall and cover his flesh, strips himself naked and runs about the room screaming that fiery insects are tormenting him. Elspeth is in terror." There was a certain chop-licking enjoyment in Judith's tone. "In terror, I tell you." Judith bent down again, everyone else's head followed. "She led two oxen to the grove. You know the grove?" They did, several having visited it on one occasion or another and for no better purpose than Elspeth's. "She went this morning before sunrise."

"Did it do any good?" Osbert whispered.

Judith shook her head. "No. And now," Judith whispered, a stage whisper so they could hear her clearly. "All the slaves are running away, afraid next time Elspeth visits the grove it will be a man she brings. What think you of that!"

Gunter looked at Judith sideways. "How do you know . . ."

But Siefert frowned and with a wave of his hand warned Gunter to be quiet. "No," he said, "don't ask any questions. I'm satisfied Judith knows what she's talking about and the story is true."

A sound grew in Ingund's ears, louder and louder. Suddenly Gunter gave a shout, and throwing one arm around Ingund and the other around Judith, he rushed them into the safety of the doorway of Osbert's hall, just as the crowd in the square was hurled against them.

Elspeth thundered past, escorted by at least thirty mounted men. She rode sidesaddle at their head, more richly garbed even than Judith. Her headdress could easily have passed for a crown. The mantle she wore was fur, trimmed with silk damask over a gown of golden brocade so rich her body seemed plated with the metal. As she rode from the blue shadow into bright sunlight, Elspeth blazed, an ill-omened star, crossing the square at a gallop, and, turning at the church, rode up toward the fortress.

The sound of hooves on the cobbles was a deafening clatter, for Elspeth nor her escort of a double line of men paid the slightest heed to the crowd, and people on every side scrambled for safety. There were shouts of rage and screams of panic. Stalls overturned and merchandise was scattered under running feet.

Cowering beside Judith in the doorway of Osbert's hall, hands pressed to her ears against the echoing noise, Ingund's mouth dropped open in awe. "She looks a queen."

"And believes she is one," Judith spat.

Ingund looked up at her father's face and saw a bitter sadness.

He turned to the others. "She has made her decision. Now it begins."

Again Ingund felt that same sense that the men she stood among were now strangers, their faces hardened with a cold and dangerous resolve.

"Does Huda know?" Osbert asked.

"Yes," Gunter said, "we spoke together this morning. He and the priests support Owen. Alan's mother's people also. There are many young men among them. They owe Huda a lot. When he married his second wife, they were the poorest of the poor. Now, thanks to Huda, they prosper."

"What of Elfwine's brothers?" Judith said. "It's true that they are not the brightest of men, but they know which end of a cow the milk comes from. They won't want to see their sister abused or her husband lose his place."

"I hadn't thought," Osbert said, with a look of chagrin.

"Well, please do more than think," Judith said crisply. "See that they are informed that their sister's in danger and do it now!"

"What of you, Judith?" Siefert asked slyly. "Hadn't you best send your captain to the hall at once? He'll need to inform Godwin of your support and inquire as to the disposition of his men."

Her mouth dropped open in shock as she was, for once, struck speechless.

"Yes?" Siefert said, cupping his hand to his ear and bending toward her. "What was that, Judith? I didn't quite catch your answer. I can't hear you."

Judith's mouth closed with a snap, then opened again as quickly. "I have a lot to lose," she said.

"So have we," Gunter told her contemptuously, "as much as you and more."

"Hush," Judith said, "I'm thinking." Her eyes slitted, taking on a look of cold calculation. After a moment she turned to Ingund. "Bertrand will be the bishop?"

"Probably." Ingund nodded.

"That settles it. I'll throw my lot with Godwin. Bertrand hates Jews."

"Does he?" Gunter asked, surprised.

"Oh, yes," Judith said. "It's just that he has Owen to curse and rail at and he hasn't gotten around to us yet. But let the count hand him a crosier and he will. Sooner or later he will. That's the most malignant individual it's ever been my misfortune to encounter."

Judith, as usual, had two maids and three armed footmen with her. While she and the rest were talking, they had drifted away, enticed from their duties by the manifold diversions the square offered on a great market day.

"Louisa," Judith shouted in exasperation, "where are you?"

A small dark-haired girl darted out of the crowd and ran to Judith's side.

"Ah, my sweet." Judith put an arm around her shoulder and began whispering in her ear. The girl listened intently then whispered back. Judith smiled and said, "The very thing. You are invaluable. Now hurry and take one of the men with you. The streets near the dock aren't safe for a girl alone."

The girl turned to go. Judith said, "Wait," and caught her by the arm. "Before you go, pick something from the jeweler's table, mind, not too expensive, and tell him to charge it to me. Now hurry."

The girl, all smiles, dropped Judith a curtsy and darted away.

"It's a special occasion," Judith said smugly, "she's getting married soon. I've arranged it. The man's poor, but hardworking and honest. A carpenter by trade."

"You said all the slaves were running away," Siefert remarked.

Judith fixed him with a very cold eye. "I'm doing Godwin a favor. I expect his gratitude. In fact, I expect his gratitude to extend a lot further than giving a man his freedom. Now come, Ingund, I've already sent Louisa for the things I need. She'll meet us at the bishop's hall. And you, Osbert, be sure

Elfwine's brothers are appraised of her peril at once, please. I can't imagine how men ever accomplish anything!" Judith growled as she took Ingund by the elbow and began marching her off across the square.

Chapter

31

OWEN'S arms pulled Enar from the death grip on the prow and helped him into the boat. Owen embraced him, and Enar tried to fend him off. "Are you a living man?" Owen whispered, trying to raise Enar's hands to kiss them. "Oh, God, I feared you'd paid the final price of my stupidity."

Enar jerked his hands away from Owen, embarrassed, and hid them behind his back.

Owen seized him by the shoulders. "I had no idea that he would dream of such treachery. I saw you with an arrow in your heart. How did you live?"

"Arrow?" Enar said, mystified. He'd forgotten the slight wound. "Oh that! It was nothing, my lord." Then sat down hurriedly on one of the rowing benches because Owen showed imminent signs of kissing his face and because he realized that his knees were shaking very badly. "Don't, please, Lord Christ Priest, humble yourself to me."

"Who better?" Owen asked.

Enar pointed to the people of the forest. Owen turned. They were already lounging on the benches astern, enjoying the novelty of the big comfortable boat that afforded them a new view of their wooded kingdom, and making a fuss over the stallion.

"A lord among horses," Enar said.

"The horse," Owen said, raising his right hand, with the sword gripped in it, looking at the knuckles split open and still oozing blood from the battering he'd given the bars of the cage. Then looked at the left with the raw gash on the back. "I'm alive," he said in disbelief. "I'm alive," he said, looking at Enar, "you're alive." He was turning deathly pale.

"Yes, Lord Christ Priest," Enar said, standing quickly and

catching Owen by the shoulders, easing him to a sitting position on one of the rowing benches. "Yes," Enar repeated in a soothing tone of voice, "yes, we are both alive."

"No!" Owen shouted, trying to stand again and being held down by Enar's big hands on his shoulders. "I promised I would die, my blood wipe out my sin, my stupidity. . . . He was right to mock me about fine words. . . . I have nothing but fine words . . ." Owen babbled, tears pouring down his cheeks. "Oh God, I'm a fool. Why did You make me such a fool. . . . Why couldn't You have given Your people into the hand of one wiser . . . braver than I am. . . ."

Enar, alarmed, yelled at the forest people. "Throw me the wineskin." They did. He fielded it one-handed, still holding Owen to the bench with the other, and shook it, hoping for some left. There was. "Play the man now," Enar said harshly. "Drink."

Owen did, at first unwillingly, then thirstily. At last Enar had to pull it away from his lips.

"You see before you," Enar said, glaring into Owen's eyes, "one who has this past night endured captivity, mockery, and a small run of twenty or so miles upriver. Then a ride downriver on a log, which so harrowed my soul that almost I turned Christian on the spot. And the culminating event of my night was a high climb over a wooden fence into a camp filled with desperate criminals all more than happy to slit my throat on sight."

"All," Enar said, baring his teeth, "with the objective of saving your life. Tell me again, Lord Christ Priest, how unhappy you are to be alive and I will take that sword from your hand, make you eat it, and then dunk your head in the river so that the cold water will wash some sense into your brain. Do you believe that I can do this?" he asked softly.

Owen, dizzy from the wine and weak with reaction, knew he was helpless as a kitten. "Yes, I believe you could," he said.

"Good," Enar said, patting his cheek gently with one hand.

"It was just that I wanted to kill Hakon," Owen said. "Dump the burning roof on his head."

"Too bad," Enar said, "but the world is filled with men I haven't killed. I hate the thought, but don't let it disturb me overmuch. It shouldn't disturb you either. Besides, if you set out to kill all the Hakons who flourish and prosper everywhere, you will find it as bottomless a task as Thor found in the drinking horn of the giants. Most men are like Hakon. Kill him and tomorrow another as bad or worse rises to take his place. It's not the death of men like Hakon the world needs, but more men in it like you," Enar finished harshly.

Owen set the sword across his knees, unclasping his fingers with difficulty from around the hilt, and looked, for the first time, at the river and the forest people sitting in the stern. "Forgive my ingratitude," Owen said with a gentle smile, extending his hand to Enar.

Seeing its condition, he accepted it carefully. "I never took that foolishness for ingratitude," Enar said wearily, "but"—he indicated the forest people—"you owe more to them than to me."

Owen turned, straddled the bench, and spoke to the forest people. "My thanks to you also. But I . . . don't know you," he said.

"Alshan sent us," Sybilla said, "and your wife . . . the Lady Elin. I am Sybilla, this is my husband, Imry." She indicated the man sitting beside her on the bench. "This is Ilo." She pointed to a small creature stretched out lengthwise on the rowing bench, dabbling its fingers in the water.

Boy or girl, Owen thought. Then the little one turned her head and Owen was surprised to see she was a tiny girl no more than ten or at the most twelve. She, too, smiled.

The other man nodded to Owen. "I am Tigg."

"Just four of you," Owen asked. "You did all that?" He pointed back at the camp.

"Five," Enar growled, "five. I was among them."

"I stand corrected," Owen said, "five. How?"

"You did some of it yourself when you burned the hall," Tigg said.

"The rest," Enar said, "was smudge fires set in the ditch below the palisade." He began to chuckle, then clapped his hands. "God, it was wonderful, the confusion. They thought the end of the world had come upon them. It will take a year to sort that mess out. Such screaming, howling, trying to run away in all directions at once. I saw two start to kill each other by mistake. I swear, it was better than finding Gowen lying on the rafters of the hall. Keep friends with the Lady Elin, Lord Christ Priest. These people of hers are the best tricksters in the world. It wouldn't do to have them against you."

"The cut is to the bone," the one called Tigg frowned and said. He seemed, though it was difficult to tell because their dark skins and identical hide clothing made them look alike, to be a little older and more responsible than the rest. "By now, the camp is not a broth of confusion but a cauldron of fury. We made sport of them and our laughter is worse than death to those proud outlaws. Don't be too sure of your escape just yet. They are behind us."

Enar snickered. "And in a killing mood no doubt. They admire a successful deceiver among themselves, but when the tables are turned, that's another thing. This story will follow them home, and because this time the joke went the other way, you will become famous and Osric and Hakon will hear . . ."

"Osric," Owen said coldly, "will hear nothing unless his ears are very long. I killed him in the hall."

"What, Lord Christ Priest?" Enar cried. "And you reproached yourself for failure. A better deed was never done by the hand of man. Tell me, did he know?"

"He did," Owen answered, his face set like a stone. "He looked into my eyes and knew. I gutted him," he said between his teeth.

"Better and better, Lord Christ Priest. I will become a Christian and offer sacrifices to Christ that he stoke the fires of hell hotter to receive him." Enar jumped up, dancing with delight, round and round, in the prow of the ship, then he stopped as a thought struck him. "Or is hell cold, Lord Christ Priest? I cannot remember. I have heard both. But what's the official version? As a bishop you would be conversant with that."

Owen looked at him from the corner of his eye. "You are going to be a very difficult Christian. I don't know either."

"Never mind," Enar shouted, "fry or freeze, Osric deserved it. What do you think Christ will want? What does he ask for?"

Sunlight was beginning to burn away the mist now, striking long corridors of light down into the drifting vapor. The boat, rounding a bend in the river, slowed as the bottom began to scrape lightly over the shallows of a ford.

Enar stretched himself like a big cat and smiled up at the interplay of sun and cloud, light and shadow that warmed him. The forest people laughed, lifting their hands, palms up, as if to catch the sunbeams.

"How beautiful," Owen whispered softly.

"Is it not, Lord Christ Priest?" Enar answered. "What can God, Who does all this, want from such as I?"

"Only give Him your brave heart as you have given it to me," Owen answered quietly.

Enar looked down at his ragged clothing, his big battle-scarred body. "No," he answered, almost inaudibly, his voice soft, "no, but if you think that's what He wishes, I will try." Suddenly his face froze. "Behind us," he shouted, pointing over Owen's shoulder astern.

Rearing from the fog, high, much higher than the figurehead on their own small craft, was the head of a dragon ship. Scarlet teeth gleamed, yellow eyes glared against the pale billows of mist as it bore down on them, swift as death. Owen looked around wildly for something, anything to hasten the boat's progress through the ford, but there was nothing. They all stood frozen as the boat bumped slowly over the sands of the bottom.

Owen snatched up his sword from the bench and pointed to the forest, shouting at Tigg, "Can we make a run for it?"

"No," Tigg said, "wait. They have not reached the ford yet. It will slow them more than it slows us."

It did. Owen saw the dragon head vanish, lost in the mist as the long ship struck the sand and their smaller craft pulled away. Then he heard the shouts and splashes as men jumped out, running in the shallow waters, to ease the larger ship's bottom over the sandbars.

The river narrowed, deepened as they swept around another bend and the current picked up speed. Owen turned to Tigg. "They'll catch us at the next ford."

The little man nodded. "Yes, they have oars. We must take to the woods before they get there."

Owen saw behind them the dragon head poke itself around the bend they'd just passed. She must still be in the shallows. He saw men running beside her. Then the dragon ship was closer. Arrows splashed into the water all around them.

"Good," Enar said, "every hand on the bow is one less on the sweeps."

Owen could see the tall figure of Hakon now, standing on the deck between the long lines of men straining at the oars. "Our speed is nothing," he said. "They will catch us." His fingers tightened on the hilt of his sword.

"No," Tigg said. "Just around the next bend the river widens. At this season, they'll go aground. Not for long, but it gives us a little time." Tigg pointed ahead to where a thick growth of willows stretched out into the river, their long leaves still green despite the chill of autumn.

The boat drifted into them, its bottom grinding against the submerged roots of the trees, and was screened for a second from the ship behind. The river was broad and very shallow here, and they were only a few yards from the bank.

The forest people were over the side in an instant, the horse following like a dog. Owen and Enar leaped after them. Then they were through the willows and into the forest, running. And how, Owen thought, they could run, seeming to fly along the ground like deer. Enar matched their pace easily. Tigg led, the rest following single file as they took a winding path among the trees. Owen kept up at first and then, in spite of himself, began to drop back. He was in pain from a stitch in his side, and the night of struggle in the cage had sapped his strength. He was exhausted and had no reserves to draw on.

Outraged and infuriated that he should give way to such weakness, he gritted his teeth and willed his legs to move faster. But the stitch grew worse, until every breath was agony.

Owen heard a savage shout from behind, and knew he'd been sighted by his pursuers. He cursed his luck. No doubt they were hot on his heels, Hakon leading the pack. He could shout for help. *But what would that accomplish?* he thought. *They would die with me, for they are, except for Enar, defenseless.* The horse was running ahead near Tigg, too far ahead.

He spurred himself to one last burst of speed, but knew it was the last. A little more and he would fall and be taken, but not alive. He still held his sword, and as he fell he would drive it through his own body. When they laid hands on him, they would have a dead man.

He glanced quickly back over his shoulder and, through the trees, saw Hakon following the narrow track behind him, drawn sword in hand, well ahead of his men and gaining. Owen's vision was blurred by sweat running into his eyes, but there was no mistaking the man.

They were running uphill. Just over the crest there was a boulder and a thick clump of bushes. If he could duck behind it, there was strength in his arm for one swing. It would lend some meaning to his death to take the Viking chief with him.

Something brushed his left shoulder. Owen turned and looked into Enar's grin. He'd dropped back and was pacing him. "Trouble keeping up, my lord?" he asked.

Owen managed a nod. He wanted to say a number of things but didn't have breath for any of them. He pointed ahead to the rock and bushes and gasped, "Spent," even as he slowed. "Save yourselves."

Enar, in one smooth movement and without breaking stride, swept him up over his shoulder and, even with the extra weight, increased his speed until he caught the rest. The horse was galloping along just behind Tigg. In a second, Owen was on its back with Enar running behind. Owen felt what the effort cost him and was afraid.

"How long?" he gasped out.

Enar laughed, then shouted over his shoulder at Hakon, something to do with his paternity, then picked up his pace and ran beside the horse. "Till sunset if necessary." He grinned.

He didn't have to run that long. Tigg had a few tricks up his rawhide sleeve. The rising ground that had added to Owen's difficulties now sloped downward. It looked as though Tigg was leading them into the open. Then Owen realized that the soft green surface he saw ahead was a bog. He thought with dismay of the stallion.

But Enar moved up beside the horse, catching his mane and slapping his neck, saying, "Come, big brother," and guided him between two sucking pools along the safe path Tigg picked out into deeper water, where the horse, swimming, held him up. They plunged over small islands, overgrown with willows, then down into and through masses of reeds and cattails taller than a man's head, following streams that ran, clear open spaces of water, between hummocks of muddy ground, pushing their way past big clumps of cress and water lilies.

From behind him, Owen heard sounds of disputation. "Follow them into that?" he heard Hakon's voice roar. "Is your brain, like the ground, turned to muck, too?"

Someone else yelled, "Are you afraid?" The sound of a blow and a screech followed. Then the voices died away behind them.

Tigg slowed his pace and everyone began to catch their breath.

"Hakon is no fool," Enar grunted, looking around at the sodden land with dislike. "Men have vanished into these swamps and never come out again."

The horse was breaking tangles of floating water-weed that thrust up stems blazoned with yellow flowers, his hooves churning mud and water. Then they came to another clear channel between two islands big enough to support a few oaks, beeches, and many willows.

The stallion staggered as his feet sank into the soft bottom, floundered, then climbed up on a muddy hillock. Tigg and the rest of the forest people followed.

The land they were standing on was the highest ground for many miles. From it, Owen could look out across the fen country.

Owen checked the horizon for signs of pursuit by Hakon and his men, saw none, and relaxed. The wild beauty of the land around edged its way into his soul. As far as his eye could see, there were only islands of reeds and, between and around them, quiet pools that reflected the steady march of clouds across the sky, flying as if driven by strong winds aloft.

"It is as though they have a rendezvous," Owen said, looking at the flying shapes of the clouds above.

"They do," Tigg said. "Today your lady defends your city. Today she will try to take it from the count. Godwin is her champion."

Owen looked away in the direction of the river and the city. "I must return to my people."

"No." Tigg shook his head. "You can't. Hakon will hunt you along the river and everyone who still survives there will help him. Not because they love him." Tigg shook his head again. "But out of fear. They exist only because he suffers them."

"But I must return," Owen said frantically, "and return now. Reynald is bought and sold. He'll open the gates to Hakon. All they need do is agree on the price."

"No," Tigg disagreed. "He won't. The Lady Elin has cursed him, dangled his sin before his face. She spent flesh and blood in the curse, her own. She may die of it, but he'll die first."

"And the count?" Owen asked.

"He's left to Godwin to deal with. It's to be hoped he can," Tigg said. "But what she's done, she's done in your name. If you die now or Hakon captures you again . . . She's told Godwin that you yet live and he believes her, and we must at all cost preserve you alive, so that you may return and face Hakon."

"With all due respect," Enar said, "he's right. You'll gain nothing by spending your life foolishly now. As long as you're alive, Elin and Godwin can hold their place, but with you dead . . ."

They were right and Owen knew it. "It seems," he said, "I've become a symbol."

"Don't let it go to your head, Lord Christ Priest. These things pass. Soon you'll be only a man again and people will be criticizing you. That's why heroes die young, Lord Christ Priest, so that lesser men may endow them with the splendor of imagined triumph. Living men, with all their errors, obstinance, petty grievances, and small meanness, are boring."

"You've made your point," Owen said, giving him a cold look.

"Here, have a drink," Enar said, passing him the wineskin. "A little humility goes down better with wine."

Owen did, a long one. "I don't fear for my virtue, in that respect, while you're at my side."

"That's good," Enar said, "because if you tried to go rushing away to your death, I planned to bind you hand and foot and take you with us anyway." He upended the wineskin and squirted the remainder into his mouth, then, giving it a look of regret, threw the strap over his shoulder. "Who knows," he said, "I may get a chance to refill it sometime."

They left the island, following Tigg into the water.

Chapter

32

*E*LIN sat by the fire in the hall with Elfwine watching her, the way she might watch a tethered wild animal. Elin closed her eyes. Elfwine's stare was burdensome and there was nothing they could talk about. Elin feared even to mention the baby, lest Elfwine think she might do it some harm. Elin shared Elfwine's fear. What she had chosen to do was a dreadful thing and one who walked, as she did now, in such an aura of evil, might inadvertently do some harm, even where none was intended. For the darkness she'd summoned cloaked and clung to her. And she feared, lest the outer edges of that enveloping malevolence brush against and tarnish youth and innocence. No, the very mention of the child would be dangerous.

The madness induced by the drugs in the potion she'd taken the night before was gone, but the despair, the sickness of the spirit she felt over having turned good powers to evil uses, gnawed at her mind and heart.

She feared also to even think of Owen lest the memory of his face, the warm dark eyes, the loving hands, drive the rage, the coldness of hatred, from her flesh, from her body, from her soul.

So she sat, a stone woman, not feeling the heat of the fire burning on the hearth, powerless to warm herself in thought or deed. For that was the heart of a curse and its real malice, that she be tethered to her victim, then enter hell, counting her own anguish cheap if he but shared her torment. He did, she was sure of it. Nothing else mattered for the time being. Her disciplined will would let nothing else matter. So she trembled, but was sure of herself, remembering the crown of roses and thorns pressed into her forehead by Abreka. I am Abreka's daughter, she told herself, and will not yield.

Elin opened her eyes. Alfric was sitting where Elfwine had been a few moments before. His clear, calm eyes studied her quietly.

Elin looked away. If he had only threatened, condemned, or told her to fear for her immortal soul, he would only have strengthened her resolve. But he didn't and instinctively she knew he wouldn't stoop to such tricks. Somewhere in his long life, the little man had emptied himself of hatred, or perhaps the love of God had so filled him that it drove out everything else. Now even the worst of men, looking into Alfric's face, would see only that love, that dark mysterious compassion for God's fractious children, shining in his eyes.

Elin stared at the floor.

The thunder of Elspeth's passage echoed in the room.

Godwin jumped up and ran to the door. He stood watching through the archers' slit while the column of men passed, then strode to the stairs and called to the knights to arm themselves.

"Who is it?" Alfric asked.

"Elspeth," Godwin answered, "dressed like a queen, Bertrand, and about thirty men."

"In spite of all I've done?" Elin looked up at him, despair darkening her blue eyes.

It came to Godwin, how young Elin was, how little she understood the savagery that was about to engulf them.

Edgar opened his mouth as if to speak, and Alfric leaned forward in the chair. "Be silent, both of you," Godwin said with ringing authority in his voice. He was the commander, the leader of men now, standing tall, legs apart, hand on the hilt of his sword. "Courageous lady," he spoke gently, "you have done well, but surely you knew it must come to this."

"I didn't," Elin said, twisting her hands in her lap. "I hoped . . ."

"So did I," Godwin said, "but it's not to be. Yet, take heart. Reynald's lady is not such a one as you. Her men won't look to her as lord able to reward and punish, as one day I think men will look to you, and they may hang back while others decide the issue."

"We're badly outnumbered, Godwin," Edgar said.

Godwin shrugged. "Edgar, I never fought a battle where I wasn't outnumbered. It means nothing and you know it.

Now, get upstairs and arm yourself. The time for speech is past."

Judith and Ingund entered just then, Judith still spitting with impatience at Ingund's stolid progress. Yet she left off berating Ingund to stare at Rosamund, who had followed the knights down the stairs. "Good heavens," she said in a shocked whisper.

Rosamund wore quite a lot of jewelry now. She was disheveled and her face was painted. It was plain the three men shared her favors. Whether together or separately was a matter of prurient speculation among the more conventional members of the household.

"I heard tales of this," Judith said, outraged, "but I didn't believe them. My girl, if you can't act like the servant of a noble house, try to look like one. Go at once, wash your face! Comb your hair! Put on a modest dress! I never saw the like."

Judith's orders, rapped out, snapped at Rosamund like a series of whip cracks.

Godwin said nothing, but his face registered the purest, most aristocratic disgust Elin had ever seen.

Rosamund's cheeks flushed as much under the impact of Godwin's stare as under Judith's words. She looked as though she'd been slapped across the face.

Elin, in the act of crossing the room to go climb the stairs, paused by her side. She stretched out her hand to Rosamund and smiled, a terrible smile, one that leaped out of the desolation in her eyes. "I understand you better. And when this is ended, be it ended in my favor, ask what you wish of me and it will be granted."

Then Elin looked at Edgar, that glance a demand.

"She did what was necessary, and risked her life in the service of this house," he said.

The look of disgust on Godwin's face faded. Judith was taken aback. "She's right," Godwin said to Judith. "All that holds us together is loyalty, and by God, she knows how to win and keep it."

"I have something for you myself. Six of my men are coming," Judith told Godwin in an undertone. "I can spare no more, but they're the best I have, the most experienced and hardened fighters. I'll be with Elin. I must dress her properly to face Elspeth. She and that brother of hers mustn't overawe the child." She followed Elin up the stairs, shouting at Anna and Ingund to heat water for a bath.

Within minutes Elin stood in the hip bath in her room, Ingund holding up her hair while the impatient Judith scrubbed her with a sponge, and told her of Reynald's sufferings.

"But how can you know?" Elin asked then, her eyes widened in shock, and she gave a sharp intake of breath as Judith washed her wounded breast.

Judith examined the ugly gash closely for a second, then drew back her face, wrinkling with revulsion. "Something has been done to that so it won't heal."

"It's not necessary," Elin replied quietly. "Such things are under my control now. The wound goes to my heart. It won't bleed or close until Owen is free or Reynald dies." There was a cold ferocity in her voice.

"I see," Judith said, busying herself on Elin's back with the sponge, "and don't see at all. Did my people ever do such things . . . I don't know . . . I suppose they did. Certain stories in Scripture—" Judith broke off and brushed her hand in front of her eyes. "The room is dim."

"It's growing darker outside," Ingund said. "I'll close the shutters and light a lamp. A storm is coming."

"More than one," Elin said.

Ingund paused to stare out, astonished. "Jesus," she whispered, signing herself with the cross, then pulling the heavy wooden shutters in and pushing the iron bar across them. "How the clouds fly past, and it grows blacker by the minute. Did you summon this, my lady?"

"No." Elin shook her head. "I've heard tell of such sorceries, but I think it's mostly talk. Storms come as God pleases." Then she yelped as Judith washed vigorously between her legs. "Judith! I can do that myself!"

"Too late," Judith snapped, "it's done."

Elin gave a grunting gasp as Ingund poured a bucket of ice water over her body to rinse.

"I only do as she orders," Ingund said, directing an accusing glance at Judith.

"It brings a nice flush to the skin," Judith said, then pulled hard several times on Elin's hair, explaining, "it loosens the scalp and draws wrinkles from the brow. There, that's nice."

Elin made a sort of strangling sound. Between the ice water and hair pulling, she was speechless.

Judith turned to Ingund and spoke softly into her ear. A moment later Ingund jerked her head back and said, "I wouldn't set that mixture in front of a hog. He would run away and return to the woods to root for acorns."

Judith stomped her foot. "Do it, I tell you, and do it now! Will you give me advice in the art of making an impression?" Judith's arm swept out in a theatrical gesture. "She goes before her people."

Ingund scurried as she went.

Judith grabbed the comb and began to ply it vigorously, admonishing Elin, "Stop squeaking. You must suffer a bit for the sake of beauty."

She began dressing Elin's long black hair in two coils at the sides that, suddenly and surprisingly, gently narrowed her rather broad cheekbones, and gave her face a look of exquisite grace, all the while muttering, "Where is Louisa, I need the sapphire combs for this."

"Judith," Elin asked, "how do you know Reynald truly suffers . . . ?"

"I heard it from one who saw it with his own eyes." She looked around quickly. They were alone, the only sound the rhythmic thud of the storm wind banging the closed shutters. "I told you, Elspeth sacrificed oxen at the grove."

"Yes," Elin said.

"She had meant to use a man. He fled to me. Elspeth locked him up and placed a guard at the door. But the man, a fine, strong, young fellow, forced his way out through the roof."

"But why to you, Judith?"

"He's the liegeman of one of my maids. His terror was pitiful. He really believed she meant to lead him to the grove, and bind the ligature about his neck. But when he was found gone, she took the oxen. For me, Elin, I don't know. I hope . . . I think she might have faltered at the last moment. I detest Elspeth, but this goes beyond the mere spitefulness of ordinary women's gossip. So keep it to yourself. I'll say no more about it."

Louisa entered, carrying a small box and two large bun-

dles. Ingund followed her, frown on her face, cup in her
hand.

"Thank heavens," Judith exclaimed, seizing the bundles
from Louisa, rattling away while she manhandled Elin into
the dress. "That ruby necklace is beautiful, my dear, but
with your eyes, you must be careful of reds."

Judith had chosen a white dress of heavy pure silk that
hung in soft folds around Elin's body.

"You want her to be beautiful," Louisa said, "but not too
beautiful!"

"I know," Judith said, "that's why I chose the heavy silk.
But it does no harm for men to feel a little, just the merest,
touch of desire toward a woman they're defending. Wait until I add the mantle."

It was blue, a silk and linen weave, very simple, but it
brought out the color of Elin's eyes. Ingund gasped in admiration. Elin was a figure of elegant simplicity. The white silk
clung, but not too tightly, to her slender form.

Judith belted it with a golden chain drawn only just tightly
enough to emphasize the slenderness of her waist and the
upthrust of her breasts under the silk. The blue mantle
framed the picture she made, flowing in long straight folds
from her shoulders to the floor. Judith stepped forward and
fastened it at her shoulder with a large brooch of baroque
pearls set in silver, then stepped back and placed a finger
against her cheek and said, "Enough," then turned to Louisa.
"Just the merest touch of color in her cheeks and lips and
only a little above the eyes. It mustn't be noticeable."

When Louisa finished Elin's face, the illusion was complete. Elin was a picture of serene purity. Yet the movement
of the silken folds of her gown over the flesh beneath whispered all but inaudibly of the temptress.

"A whiff of musk," Judith told Elin. "It does no harm.
Now"—she snapped her fingers at the awestruck Ingund,
who was still gazing at Elin in openmouthed admiration—
"the cup."

Elin shook her head. "No food or drink."

"You needn't fear you will enjoy it," Ingund said, "the
taste alone is penance."

"It can't be as bad as that," Elin said, accepting the cup

pressed into her fingers by Judith. She took a sip, clutched at her throat. "Good God, Judith!"

"Drink it down," Judith commanded sternly. "If not for yourself, for the child. There's much virtue in that mixture."

"I hope so," Elin said, "for there is none in the taste."

"Drink it, I say," Judith said, stamping her foot. "No more of your nonsense. Drink it!"

Elin drank, gagged, but emptied the cup gamely.

Godwin came to the door. Elin stood in the lamplight surrounded by the women. The room, shutters closed and storm clouds thickening outside, was dark. He stood transfixed, as Ingund had been, by Elin's beauty.

She stepped toward him, palms up. "Well?" she said.

"Incomparable," he answered and looked at Judith. "Also, not the least bit obvious. A lily blooming against the sky. All the men in the church will be willing to lie down at your feet and let you mount the altar using their bodies as steps, and none of them will know quite why. Are you ready?" he said, offering her his arm. "The church is filled with people."

Elin took his arm, but stretched the other out to Judith and clutched her hand. "Stand with me," she whispered, "for I'm terribly afraid."

"We all will," Ingund said, lifting a lamp to light them to the stairwell. "We all will."

In the church, Ranulf, with Gunter's help, lit the lamps.

The largest, suspended from the ceiling, was an enormous heavy structure of wood and iron chain. It was constructed in the shape of three giant cart wheels, the largest at the top, a second slightly smaller in circumference suspended by the iron chain just below the first, and then yet a third still below the second. In the center hung, by more chain, an enormous lantern. It held four candles, a reflector behind bull's-eye glass, all encased in heavy wrought iron.

Ranulf hated the thing, and lighting it was a task he approached with both trepidation and loathing. It required at least two men's arms on the length of chain that secured it to the church wall. Three were better for safety's sake, though it had a built-in brake on the rope that prevented its crashing to the floor in the only too likely event that the hands lowering it lost their grip on the chain.

Once down, it swayed like a giant, delicate pendulum in every vagrant breath of air. Over a hundred candles had to be set in the holders, and then lighted quickly so that they would all burn with some degree of evenness.

"It's a brute of a thing," the smith said, steadying the largest wheel as Ranulf went from candle to candle with the rushlight as quickly as possible, "but fully lighted and hanging high, it's a wondrous sight."

Ranulf assented grudgingly. "That's may well be, but I'd rather someone else had the task of lighting it."

"What will you do?" Gunter asked.

"Do?" Ranulf said, pausing between candles to look up at Gunter.

"Do when you're finished with the church, when the fight starts?"

Ranulf looked down and began lighting candles again. "I'll do as Godwin tells me," he said, "though I don't imagine he'll have any important task for me. I can carry a crossbow with the rest." A crease appeared between the boy's brows and his eyes looked sadly into the light of the candles as he passed from one to another, the flames darting to each wick. "I wish . . ." He sighed and didn't express his wish aloud, but Gunter saw it, burning bright as the lights he kindled, in the young blue eyes. It was known that Ranulf followed Godwin everywhere at a discreet distance.

"He's a great man, Godwin is, isn't he?" Gunter asked slyly.

"Oh, yes." Ranulf paused again and looked up at Gunter with an expression of pure adoration for his hero. "It's said," Ranulf whispered, "that he was at Paris and served Count Odo during the siege."

The heroic defense of the city by Count Odo and the bishop was the stuff of legend. Confronted by one of the largest and most dangerous armies of Vikings ever assembled, they held them at bay for over a year and in the end were not defeated, but betrayed by their own cowardly king. The men who survived were heroes.

"It is also said," Ranulf continued, "that Godwin was part of the cabal that deposed the king, and that when Charles was returned to the throne, Godwin was among those he feared too much to try to deprive him of his lands and honors."

"Ha," Gunter said with a snort, "I don't see him enjoying any vast wealth now. How the mighty have fallen. The tale I heard, boy, was a little more disreputable, something about him abducting his brother's wife."

Ranulf straightened up, facing the smith, ready to leap to the defense of his hero. "That's a lie. Besides, if he did, she probably asked for it."

Gunter smiled indulgently down at him with the tolerance born of his six-foot height and two hundred plus pounds. "Stop waving that rushlight at me, boy, and finish with the candles. It may be a lie. And you're right. Even if it's true, she may have asked for it. He strikes me as the kind of wild man who might take her up on the invitation. But that's not the question. A more important one for us of the town is, was he at Paris or, in other words, will he fight till the end?"

"I think he was," Ranulf said, bending over the candles again, his face still tight with anger.

"Why do you believe that?" Gunter asked.

Ranulf lit the last candle and extinguished the rushlight with his foot, then confronted Gunter. "Because he doesn't boast of it. Because he backed Gowen down. I saw him," Ranulf said.

The smith whistled between his teeth. "Backed Gowen down, did he!" Gunter's eyebrows rose. "Indeed!"

"A man who doesn't boast," Ranulf continued, "is a man with nothing to prove. And a man who was at Paris and stood beside Odo would have nothing to prove to anyone."

Gunter nodded and stood quietly for a moment, thumbs hooked in his belt, deep in thought. "I hope you're right, boy. I hope for all our sakes you're right. But the proof of the pudding is in the eating. Let's see what he does when the battle starts."

"He won't disappoint you," Ranulf said confidently.

"I hope not," Gunter said. "Come"—he gestured at the lamp—"let's get this thing up."

People were already drifting into the church. Gunter saw Elfwine's brothers and called to them to come help him on the chains. They were three grown men, large, young, and strong. Between the five of them, they made short work of lifting the big ceiling fixture into place.

Huda entered, accompanied by ten of the younger priests. He smiled pleasantly at the smith and Ranulf as he passed, but the men with him were grim-faced and wore heavy mantles even though the weather outside was warm. The bulges under them suggested weapons and armor. Osbert and Siefert entered, surrounded by the men of their households, a good dozen in all. They followed the priests and Elfwine's brothers, taking up positions on the left-hand side of the altar.

Martin, the priest who'd helped Owen at the battle, led his own contingent into the church. A tough-looking lot of fishermen and farmers.

"They all lost relatives when the village burned," Gunter explained to Ranulf, "and they blame the count for allowing it to happen. The Lord Bishop is the only one they've seen who dared to stand up to the misbegotten Viking sons of hell. I think they're here to express their appreciation."

Ranulf had felt anger, rage when he faced Gerlos with the crossbow in the square, but he'd been sure Gerlos would back down, and the next time they met, Gerlos would bully him as before. He might not be so forceful about it or willing to push Ranulf as far as he had been in the past, but their positions in the scheme of things would be unchanged. Ranulf would still be a servant, and Gerlos still the privileged heir to wealth and power.

By tonight, Gerlos might not have the wherewithal to bully anyone. Or, if it went the other way, he, Ranulf, might be dead or a hunted fugitive, with a price on his head.

"What's wrong, boy?" Gunter's voice broke into his reverie. "Afraid?"

"No," Ranulf answered and surprised himself by realizing that it was true, "I was just thinking—" He broke off, helpless to put his thoughts into words and then realizing it wasn't necessary, judging by the expression on the big blacksmith's face. He understood the situation at least as well or better than Ranulf himself. "I was thinking," he continued more strongly, "that I'd best go tell Godwin what's happening, what he can expect."

"Yes," Gunter said, gripping Ranulf's arm, "and . . . good luck, boy!"

Ranulf took in a shaky breath and turned to the blacksmith. "Same to you, Gunter," he said with an uncertain smile, then strode away toward the hall door near the sanctuary.

He entered the hall at the same time Judith's captain did and so Ranulf hung back watching, while the captain and Godwin greeted one another.

They were both old soldiers and recognized the fact at first glance. Judith's captain, a grizzled veteran, with the build and a face like a granite boulder, bowed to Godwin and said, "My lord."

"Sir," Godwin replied and returned the bow, "I won't deny you're a welcome sight."

"I imagine so," the veteran replied.

"It's true," Godwin answered, "we are beset by greater numbers. But sit down, relax and refresh yourselves. Have some beer, or wine if you prefer."

"We might as well," he said, turning to his men. "The fun hasn't started yet, boys. Don't worry, my lord, they're all good men. None of them will get so pissing, shitting drunk they can't fight," he said as they took their seats at the table. "A flask of beer would go down nicely. My name is Rieulf."

He didn't bother to introduce the five men with him and they didn't seem to expect it. They were already applying themselves thirstily to the beer Anna and Rosamund brought to the table.

"How will it be?" Rieulf asked.

"The crossbowmen will let go first," Godwin said, "then it's close quarters, hand to hand, and every man for himself."

Rieulf nodded.

"But," Godwin continued, "we hope to avoid a fight."

"Naturally." Rieulf nodded again. "But you won't. It's now or never for the count, it's a small army. If he lets this opportunity slip through his fingers, he's done for. Begging your pardon, my lord, I'm a blunt-spoken man. I wouldn't venture to offer advice to a commander of your ability and experience."

"Not at all," Godwin said courteously, "I'm inclined to agree."

"How will I know your signal, if a fight's to start?" Rieulf asked Godwin.

"It will be ... unmistakable," Godwin said slowly, meeting Rieulf's eyes.

"I see," Rieulf answered, returning Godwin's look with perfect understanding. "We've met before, my lord, though you won't remember, on the quay at Paris. I helped pull you from the river."

Godwin's face stiffened, he half turned from the table, hand on his sword hilt.

At the word "Paris" conversation died everywhere in the hall, everyone was silent. The old soldier went on. "Oh, you won't like it spoken of, you're not the kind. You weren't the kind then either. But the city should know who stands before them." Rieulf gave a rasping chuckle. "I remember still, too, what you said when you puked the water out of your guts. But not to worry, I won't repeat it here."

"From the river," Godwin said, remembering the light of torches, the hands on his arms, lifting him to crouch, vomiting blood and water on the stones of the quay, and the curses vomited like the vomit from his belly. "They were yet living, many, when those bastards put them under the earth."

The Vikings, in trying to fill the ditch and take the tower that blocked their passage of the Seine, had thrown the living prisoners down with the dead as fill so they could bridge the hole. Godwin had lain, surrounded by the bodies of his dead and dying comrades, tormented by their cries, as they slowly suffocated around him. With his face sheltered in an air pocket created by a heavy beam, he'd lain for one long day while the battle raged above.

When darkness fell, he'd undertaken the nightmarish effort of digging his way out. He'd done it, though he didn't remember the last of the struggle. There had been a sentry. He remembered that and the man's neck snapping like a rotten branch under his fingers. Then he'd thrown himself into the river.

His condition was such that when they pulled him from the water, his rescuers believed he was dying. The priest summoned to administer the sacraments was horrified by his fury, saying a man should not die with such words on his lips. "Die?" Godwin shrieked. "I won't die. I'll live. I'll live to shit on their graves. I'll live to shit on all their graves." And so he had.

The room swam back into focus. The old soldier was still talking. "I was but a boy, not quite fifteen years, when that happened but I remember you and it well."

"I can't say I was much more than a boy myself when I rode to Paris," Godwin said, "not more than seventeen."

The lines and seams in the old soldier's granite face shifted into something that might have been a smile. The faded hazel eyes buried in the scar tissue of his face sparkled with chilly mirth. "Boys, yes, when we came there, but not in the end. We were men, weren't we, men, when we rode away?"

Godwin smiled the savage smile of a wolf. "That we were, my friend, that we were. Glad to have you with me again."

"The pleasure is all mine," Rieulf said, lifting his cup to Godwin.

The amenities thus disposed of, Godwin walked over to the fireplace where Ingund was mixing Judith's posset for Elin, and Anna, Rosamund, and Ranulf were trying to throw some kind of meal together for the men at the table. They all stopped what they were doing when he approached and stood waiting for him to speak, a strange mixture of awe and homage in their faces. Ranulf's eyes in particular shone with a look that was almost adoration.

Godwin put a hand on his shoulder. "Ranulf, go to the scriptorium and wait for me there. I have something special I want you to do."

Godwin turned to Anna and Ingund. "You two will accompany the Lady Elin into the church. Is there any extra armor about?"

"Yes," Ingund answered, "Anna and I are wearing it under our dresses, mail shirts."

Godwin stepped back and studied them. The dresses looked a little more bulky than usual but that was all. The flowing female attire was well and easily adapted to conceal anything under it.

"Excellent," Godwin said. "Take crossbows under your mantles."

"I plan to carry an axe and knife," Ingund said.

Godwin sucked in on his cheeks slightly, and stared at her eye to eye. She was as tall as he was and had much of her father's powerful build. "Female attire doesn't give the protection battle dress does, and an axe won't give you much range," he said.

"I know," Ingund answered. "I won't try to engage, but one or more of the men will go down. I can act as support and I may be able to deal with any that break through toward Lady Elin."

This assessment was so coolly professional that Godwin couldn't find any way to quarrel with it. "Ingund, many women who fight don't fully understand exactly what they're risking," Godwin said in a low voice.

Ingund continued to meet his eyes directly. "Godwin, my father will be there, along with many others. I understand perfectly what will happen to me if you fail. I don't intend to suffer it tamely. The count's men would give no thought at all to killing a woman, only it would be after they're finished with us, not before. But me," she said with a lift of her eyebrows and a light touch at her breast, "me, they'll have to kill first, before they begin their vileness."

He touched her shoulder lightly, giving it a slight squeeze. "Do as you like then, but take care."

He turned to Anna. "I have a special charge for you. If and when the fight starts, pull Lady Elin down and get on top of her."

Anna nodded and sniffed in derision. "Ha! I'd planned to do that anyway. I don't need your lordship's instructions to do that. My poor little lady, she won't be wearing any iron shirt. Don't make a hash of this, Godwin," she warned sternly, then turned away and began to fuss with the porridge.

It was Rosamund's turn next. "Rosamund," he said, "you'll remain here with Elfwine and the baby and ..."

Rosamund stared up at him mutinously, blue eyes defiant. "I won't, I'll stand with my Lady Elin. You said it yourself. You said I was free and I could do as I liked."

For the space of a few breaths Godwin stared at Rosamund, face impassive, his large dark eyes opaque. When he did move, it was with such blinding speed that it shocked everyone in the room. There was a loud crack as flesh met flesh, and Rosamund staggered back a step and fell sprawling. She lay on the stones of the floor, face pale, one hand pressed to her cheek, gazing at Godwin in terror.

"Up," Godwin roared. "You're not hurt, I never touched you!"

It was true. Rosamund lowered her hand from her cheek. It was plain to see there was no mark on her anywhere.

"On your feet, girl. Now!"

Rosamund scrambled to her feet very quickly.

"Freedom," Godwin said quietly, "implies a willingness to accept responsibility and take orders when necessary. Do you understand that?"

Rosamund nodded, plainly now too terrified to speak.

"Very well," Godwin said, "that's better. Elfwine is still weak and moreover not been churched yet. We'll observe the proprieties in this if nothing else. You will remain here with her. All the doors and windows will be bolted. If anything untoward or unusual occurs, or if anyone tries to break in, you'll raise an alarm at once. Do you understand?"

Rosamund nodded again.

"Don't wave your head at me," Godwin thundered. "Answer properly."

"Yes, my lord," Rosamund managed in a squeaky whisper.

"That's much better," Godwin said. "Now, go comb your hair and wash that paint off your face. Not because it's tawdry, though it's certainly that, but because you're too young and lovely to need to smear your cheeks with such filth. Do it! Move!" he shouted, though Rosamund was already moving and very fast, running upstairs to wash her face.

Anna, bending over the fire, cackled with glee. "Young and lovely, eh!"

Godwin didn't reply. He simply strolled off to the scriptorium to talk to Ranulf.

He found the boy waiting at the foot of the stairs near the door. He immediately began excusing himself. "I'm sorry, I meant to go but I wanted to see ... I mean ..."

"You mean you were too busy eavesdropping to follow my orders," Godwin said coldly.

Ranulf stopped talking, his gaze fell to the floor. He said, "Yes, sir."

Godwin smiled. "Truthful at least. Come," and he led Ranulf into the scriptorium. This room also was dim and the high windows showed only the billowing shapes of racing clouds. The light here was gray as the shapes moving and changing beyond the windows.

Godwin drew the scramsax from his belt. It was, as Ranulf had already noted, like all the rest of Godwin's arms, very simple, unadorned, with a hilt of pearl and horn wrapped with fine cord to give its holder a better grip. But the moment Ranulf glimpsed the mat sheen of the metal blade, he knew it was the very finest steel obtainable and probably razor sharp.

Godwin caught Ranulf's wrist, raised his right hand and pressed the hilt into his palm, then closed the fingers around it. "I want you to drop the big lamp on the count's men when the fight starts."

Ranulf stared up into Godwin's face past the length of the blade. His lips parted and his eyes widened. "Christ!" Ranulf breathed. "It would kill at least a half dozen, perhaps more."

Godwin smiled, a wintry smile that was only a slight movement of his lips. "That's the idea. Can you do it?"

Ranulf's eyes turned inward and Godwin knew he was thinking. Then he turned abruptly away from Godwin and began to pace rapidly back and forth, still clutching the knife. Suddenly he spun around and faced Godwin, his eyes alight with courage and confidence. "Yes," he said strongly, "yes, I can. It's not as easy as it sounds, for it will have to be done quickly to be effective."

Godwin nodded.

"It's held by two ropes, thick as your wrist, Godwin, and no knife, not even a sword, would cut them quickly. But, up high," Ranulf continued excitedly, "just at the point where the two ropes are spliced to the chain, the fisherman—it was a fisherman who rigged it with a splice fishermen use—the fisherman unraveled the ropes to weave them back into a splice so they close around the last link in the chain like fingers, many, but each thin. Run the blade along them there and . . ."

"But," Godwin said, "can you reach that spot up on the roof out on a beam?"

"Child's play. The church is my responsibility and Owen gets furious if the roof leaks. I've crawled up around there many times." Then abruptly the excitement and confidence faded from his face and eyes, leaving it shadowed by doubt. "You choose me for this because most think me beneath notice, only a servant and not worth bothering about."

"Yes," Godwin said harshly, "and those are advantages, if you learn to use them."

"Godwin," Ranulf said bitterly, "I don't think those are advantages most men would want to possess. I know I'm not—"

Godwin took one quick step toward him, seizing the hand that still held the knife. His fingers curled around Ranulf's in a tight grip. He shook it in the boy's startled face.

"Damn it," he roared, "don't think about what you're not, think about what you are!" Then dropping Ranulf's hand, he drew back. "I've noticed both Bertrand and Gerlos held you in contempt. You taught them better, didn't you?"

Ranulf stared at him, blinking in amazement, then said slowly, thoughtfully, "Yes, I suppose I did."

"Very well," Godwin said. "Now, go, serve me well, and you may ask for what you like. Don't anticipate the fight. Cut those ropes only when it starts. But when it does, cut them immediately."

"Yes, sir, before our men get in the way."

"Exactly," Godwin said. "I knew you were intelligent. That's why I chose you for this task."

Ranulf turned toward the door to the bell tower, saying, "I'd best go now. The more quickly I get up there, the better. The count's men might spot me if I try later. But . . ." He paused, then emboldened by Godwin's compliment, asked eagerly, "If I succeed, may I keep the knife?"

Godwin pulled the sheath from his belt and extended it to Ranulf. "You may keep the knife no matter what happens. Take the sheath, you'll need it. The thing's sharp. Have care for your fingers, carrying it that way."

Ranulf took it, but still stood, folding the leather nervously in his hand. "Please, if I succeed, would you . . ." Ranulf paused, then the words came tumbling out, one behind the other, in a rush. "Would you sometime tell me about Paris?"

Godwin half turned away from Ranulf, his face in deep shadow.

Ranulf, thinking he'd angered him, began backing very quickly away in the direction of the bell tower, apologizing as he went. "I'm sorry, I shouldn't have asked. Edgar said not to ask. He said if I asked you'd like as not cut me off at the knees. So I know I shouldn't have—"

"Ranulf," Godwin's voice checked the flow abruptly, "if you succeed, I will bore you to tears about Paris or any other incident in my long and inglorious career, I promise. Now, get up there, and be ready to cut that rope!"

Ranulf exited at a run and Godwin heard him singing as he began to climb the ladder in the bell tower.

Before he returned to the hall, Godwin paused. Ranulf's request had inspired him to both laughter and tears. He hadn't wanted to show either one to the boy, knowing he would likely be offended by the first and bewildered by the second. So he stood for a moment in the silent dim room alone, his shoulders slumped, then whispered, "I sent him off to risk his neck for me and all he asks for in return are old soldier's tales. Dear God, I hope I'm half as good as that boy thinks I am."

As he entered the hall, he passed the foot of the stairs. He saw a pale shape hanging there in the darkness. He started slightly, then the shape resolved itself into a face, and he realized it was Rosamund sitting on the bottom step, weeping.

"What's wrong now?" he asked impatiently.

"You played a trick on me. Now they will all be jeering and making fun."

"What?" Godwin laughed. "Would you rather I'd hit you?"

"Yes," she replied sullenly, "then I'd at least know what you mean. You're a terrible man, a tyrant. I can never tell what you're thinking," and burst into a fresh shower of tears.

Godwin was now having a great deal of difficulty keeping a straight face, but he did, and even managed a little kindness. "I'm thinking that I need you, Rosamund, and have no time for these childish hysterics."

Rosamund's head snapped up. The tears stopped. No one like Godwin had ever said they needed her.

"Suppose," he went on, "the count tries to outflank me?"

"Outflank you?" Rosamund asked, bewildered.

"Get a party of men in here behind my back."

"Oh, no!" Rosamund cried. "No! It's just that I didn't understand what was wanted. That won't happen! I'll see to the locks and doors. Don't worry," she said, springing to her feet. "If anyone tries to get in, I'll run to the church, and scream the place down!" Then she was off, up the stairs, taking the steps three at a time, to check all the windows and doors.

Godwin felt a vast shadow loom over his spirit, a great weariness. "The bastard will fight me. Why the hell not?" he whispered into the darkness. "All the rest always have."

The strength seemed to drain from his body. His knees buckled. He clung to the stair rail for support, listening to the scrape of breathing in his lungs, the ebb and flow of the pulse in his ears, and yielded himself to the embrace of his dark mistress. Knowing that one day she would close her cold arms about him and not let go, her grip tightening until that pulsation in his ears faltered, struggled, and ceased, and the breath in his lungs sighed its way to silence.

But this time, as all other times in the past, as quickly as it had come, the shadow passed. Strength flowed back into his body. He straightened his shoulders and climbed the stairs to fetch Elin.

Gunter stood among his companions near the altar. The crowd was still gathering as more men entered the church.

Even indoors he felt the strange oppression of spirit that an oncoming storm brings to some people. Outside, in the now rapidly clearing square, the sky grew darker and darker.

"Judith was right," Siefert remarked, "the whole town will be here."

"Not the women," Osbert said quietly. "Most left their wives at home."

"I hadn't realized there were so many who had scores to settle with the count," Gunter whispered.

The crowd around him seemed to grow larger every minute. All were men and all were dressed much as the smith was, in their oldest clothes, wearing heavy mantles wrapped around their bodies. All were grim-faced, and silent, and though not a weapon, not even so much as a knife hilt, was visible among them, all were most certainly armed. Some nodded to Gunter as they took up their positions. A few greeted him softly by name.

Had they, Gunter thought, spent hours arguing over it, the battle lines couldn't have been more clearly drawn.

The silence among these men was to Gunter's ears more dreadful than any curse, any shout of rage. Through the big doors of the cathedral, he looked out at the deserted square, at the building rain clouds. The church seemed to be growing brighter around him as the storm gathered outside, the glow of the gigantic lamp suspended from the ceiling, the bright flare of torches set in brackets on the wall, and the splendor of the altar decked in wax candles; all a magnificent deception, a forbidding brilliance as the chimerical overlay of sunlight on the black water of a swamp, or the glow of the sun on the steel blade of an axe just before it falls.

If Gunter down below could see the storm, Ranulf high above near the roof could feel the intensity of its rising strength. He crawled on the dusty ledge formed by the stone shell of the cathedral just below the roof. The drafts created by the wind outside swirled around him and sucked at his body.

He knew overwhelmingly, as he had known when he told Godwin that it would be child's play to reach the big ceiling fixture, that it wouldn't be that easy. The builders had set the roof on heavy beams that spanned the church below, and then cross braced it with timbers, rising from the stone walls to the rafters above, to give extra support to the weight of the big lead plates that formed the outer skin of the roof.

The lamp itself was suspended by a short chain from its own separate beam nailed to two of the big cross braces. To reach it, he had to shinny up the cross brace out over the cathedral floor. Looking at it, Ranulf wasn't tempted to sing as he had while climbing the belfry ladder. He was sorry he'd been so glib when he made his promise to Godwin.

Though the church below was bright, it was dark up here. The lead sheathing of the roof snapped and popped with metallic, distant pinging sounds as it cooled under the cloudy sky, and the draft created by the wind outside was now a steady flow of chilly air drying the sweat on his body.

To compound his difficulties, the cross brace rose from the stone well below the spot where he crouched, and he would have to lower himself by his hands and feel with his toes to find it. So telling himself not to be so craven, he did, and found himself stretched on the narrow ledge above standing on tiptoe on the cross brace. Luckily, the builders who raised the church hadn't been so careful as the Roman masons who laid the lower courses of its walls and the uneven stonework near the roof offered plenty of good handholds.

Ranulf let himself down slowly, straddled the beam and, once down, faced the wall. He managed a turn that set him to shaking like a leaf and his heart to leaping violently in his chest. He embraced the wood, clutching it tightly with both arms and legs. He made the mistake of looking down once, then resolutely closed his eyes and began the climb.

It wasn't as difficult as he'd supposed it would be at first. The rough, unfinished surface of the heavy studding gave some purchase to his heels and hands, and his own woolen breeches and leather leggings protected him from the worst of the splinters.

He was halfway to the crossbeam that held the lamp, when he realized he wasn't getting anywhere any longer. His feet slipped on the surface of the wood. Hard as he tried, he couldn't gain another inch.

He opened his eyes. The second time was worse than the first. The church seemed to spin below him. He was hanging dead level with the lamp, its light blinding him. The floor, so far below, now seemed to tilt and sway. Then he realized that it was not the floor that tilted and swayed but his own body. He was sliding down around and under the cross brace.

His arms and legs snapped into a clutch so tight, he could hear his joints crack with the strain. He clenched his teeth to bite back the scream that rose from his lips as he hung paralyzed by the fear of falling. The squared beam he'd begun his climb on was now almost round.

He slipped back a few inches and caught. It took him

some time to realize that he hadn't fallen and wouldn't, if he hung on. Only a few seconds, but long enough for an eternity of terror. It took a little more time for him to realize what had happened.

The cross brace had once been a pine tree, and the church builders, noting that it was about the right size and shape for their purposes, hadn't bothered trimming the wood above a certain point. Beyond that point it was almost a pole.

So Ranulf, still hugging the beam, hung there above the church. His mouth filled with the ashy taste of failure and self-hatred, feeling the full, sickening measure of defeat.

But Godwin had told him what he needed to know, that most of us have an edge. Nature or God gives us something we do just a little bit better than others. Ranulf's edge was that he thought well and clearly under pressure, so he began to think.

He turned his eyes away from the drop below and looked up at the curved surface of the cross brace stretching above him, faintly reflecting the light of the candles. He thought of the knife.

It took only a few minutes to cut the first notch, then he carefully sheathed the knife. He was in terror lest he drop it and fail in his mission. The heavy edge of his oxhide boot fitted neatly into the notch.

He pushed himself up, his arms aching from the strain on them and his chest from the pressure of the beam against his ribs.

Now, he thought, his forehead pressed against the beam, eyes closed, feeling the strain in his right leg, the pull on his calf muscle as he pushed upward. *Now, for the left side. First wipe that sweaty hand on the rough cloth of your shirt, then draw the knife slowly. Dear God! Dear God, don't let me drop it.*

Then he cut the second notch, slowly, more clumsily, with his left hand. *Now sheath the knife.* His eyes were open. He was just above the blazing candles in the silvery reflector of the lamp. A moment of terror while his left foot felt for the notch, then found it. Up, up, only a little more. His left foot slipped from the notch.

His stomach gave a lurch. His body did slide halfway

around the cross brace, but he was clear of the candlelight, and the beam that held the lamp within reach.

A second later the fingers of his right hand closed around it, and a minute later, he sat on top of it, his back leaning against the cross brace while he tried to master the almost uncontrollable tremors that racked his whole body.

Below him he heard a babble of voices and the tramp of many feet as the count's men entered the church.

Gunter, standing near the altar, watched them come. *A show of force,* he thought. The count had stripped the garrison of most of its men, then added those Elspeth brought with her.

He and Elspeth led them into the church, she leaning on the count's arm, Bertrand following, surrounded by the count's personal guard, the elite fighters of his garrison. They shouldered aside the curious onlookers at the door arrogantly and crowded in, followed by Reynald's men. These didn't look nearly so sure of themselves as the count's did. Here and there Gunter saw in their faces fear, uncertainty, and, sometimes, downright disapproval, as the count's men turned and raising their shields, used them to shove the smith and his friends back closer to the wall, until they cleared for themselves the largest part of the space facing the altar and the sanctuary.

The men they pushed aside so contemptuously were quiet, yielding their places to the count's men in apparent meekness as they always had. Yet, almost as if by common, unspoken, agreement, they allowed themselves to be pushed so far, then no farther.

The smith simply raised one hand, placed it against the shield of the nearest of the count's mercenaries, and looking over it directly into the soldier's eyes, stood his ground. The man heaved against the shield, but Gunter stayed where he was, and the soldier's feet slipped on the stone floor. Others, smaller than Gunter, crowded together against each of the count's knights and had similar success. If the count's men pushed harder, they would begin knocking people down. In a moment, it would come to blows.

Count Anton saw this and spoke sharply. "Enough! We have room to be comfortable."

He doesn't want to begin the fight now, Gunter thought,

relieved. He had been feeling with his free hand for the hammer in his belt.

High up, straddling the beam, Ranulf, in terror of being discovered, hitched himself along on his backside—he couldn't get up the nerve to crawl and walking wasn't to be thought of—toward the place where the ropes were anchored to the chain that suspended the lamp from the beam. He looked down at the giant candelabrum burning below him.

The fates that seemed to have conspired against him before now seemed to have turned in his favor. A dozen links of heavy iron chain held the candles of the lamp away from the wood of the roof. The splice was held tight by the ropes tied below to the eyebolt that guided them.

The last link of the chain was within easy reach of his hand, and the ropes unraveled to pass around the ring were as thin as he remembered, thin enough to part easily with one slash of his knife. He lay down, resting the length of his body against the beam, hoping to be taken for part of the rafters by anyone giving the ceiling a casual glance.

Outside the wind was rising and the heavy studding of the roof above him creaked and sometimes moaned softly as the sucking draft coursed in from under the pitch of the eaves. It wasn't strong enough to put out the candles burning below him, only seeming to make them burn faster, more brightly, in the increasing gloom of the oncoming storm.

From where he lay, Ranulf could see the church was filled. The crowd blocked the door open. The town's folk formed a loose crescent to the left of the count's men, leaving a space clear before the altar.

Outside the wind suddenly died down, succeeding it that breathless hush that presages the full unleashed fury of the elements.

Ranulf saw a stir pass through the crowd below and knew without needing to turn his head to look that Godwin and Elin had arrived.

Elin entered the hall on Godwin's arm and saw approval of Judith's handiwork reflected in all of their eyes. The men rose from around the table and surrounded them. Gowen looked her up and down, then down and up, saying, "She won't shame us with her plainness, I was afraid she would."

Then he turned away, clapped his helmet on his head, and lifted his shield. "A man likes to think he fights for something," he said in response to Edgar's frosty look.

Edgar bowed to her. "No lovelier or more gentle lady ever lived."

Alfric came from the church, carrying the processional cross. "The count is here," he said.

Godwin turned to the knights. Gowen laughed. "Don't bother, old man, we know your mind well enough. I hope the devil whispers good counsel in your ear this day."

Godwin smiled, a smile without warmth or mirth in it. "He hasn't failed me yet."

"I don't see why he should," Edgar said quietly, "he's had many poor damned souls at your hands."

"And if I survive this day," Godwin answered, looking down at Elin, "he will have a few more."

"Kneel then for my absolution," Alfric sighed, "lest you chance to join them."

Somewhere in the distance thunder rumbled.

Elin looked into Godwin's face. She felt as though she'd never really seen him before. The harsh deep lines around the mouth, the high cheekbones, straight nose, flat dark eyes—black now in the shadows of the hall but reflecting, in their depths, the glow of the firelight. The rest wore their arms with swagger or assurance. Godwin wore his as though they were a part of his body, the rough mail that brushed her sleeve and the sword belted around his waist, hand resting lightly on its hilt. The cold face above hers promised her the deaths of her enemies. Then he was assisting her to kneel and receive Alfric's blessing.

Gowen laughed. "At last he comes over to our side."

"I am not a judge, but a priest. I'll see no one go into battle unshriven," Alfric said softly. "But think what you do, Godwin—"

"Have done!" Godwin said. "The count is in my debt for Owen's blood and many insults to his wife. We break the man or he us. Now stop preaching. It's time we went."

Alfric raised his hand and signed them with the cross. Then he turned and sent his blessing to the cathedral. "For any who wish to accept it, may God go with you."

As if in answer Godwin drew his sword. Elin heard the

whisper as it cleared the sheath, sounding incongruously like a sigh of grief.

Alfric turned and raised the processional cross. A small brave figure dressed in his best brown and black robes, he led them forth.

Chapter
33

*E*LIN and the rest entered through the vestry. They walked along the altar rail past Gunter and the men crowded around him. Then she stopped before the high altar. The knights took up their positions, flanking Godwin and Elin. The archers fanned out on either side, bows raised, the heavy bolts pointed upward. The only unsheathed weapon was the naked sword in Godwin's hand, but he held that down, pointed at the floor.

For a moment no one spoke. There was no sound at all.

The count stood well back among his men. They gathered around him protectively. Elspeth stood a little apart, Bertrand by her side.

A gust of wind swirled in the square outside, raising the dust and sending its breath among the candles in the church. They flickered, scattering quick shadows that passed suddenly among the throng like vagrant ghosts, and then were gone. Outside the light had a greenish cast.

Then Elspeth raised her arm and pointed at Elin. "Look at her, harlot that she is, draped in silk, perfumed scarlet whore," she screamed, then looked at the count. "She is a witch, her servants demons. I demand her life."

Elin almost cringed before the fury in Elspeth's face. She knew that, given the opportunity, Elspeth would take that life she claimed so furiously. The woman's face was terrible, drawn and pale with fear and fury, perfectly white, above the stiff cloth-of-gold dress, with only two, living, hating eyes.

"Gutter wench," Elspeth screeched, "you came to me and I, in my mistaken charity, put on your body the first decent dress you ever owned. And bitterly do you now make me regret my kindness. I have seen, seen with these, my own two eyes." Elspeth stepped forward, the outstretched finger still pointing at Elin. "She bears the marks of a slave. Her back is scored with the lash, her wrists and ankles with the scars of chains and fetters."

Elspeth turned to the count. "I demand you take this degraded creature and return her to her former state. How dare she present herself before you as an honest wife, a free woman, this black sorceress?"

Elin's breath hissed between her teeth as she stepped forward to confront Elspeth. It was no use to deny Elspeth's words. Too many in the town knew of the scars on her body. Judith had seen her naked and Gynnor, too, when she tended to Elin after the quarrel with Owen. When she spoke, her voice was mild, almost a plea for understanding. "I am freeborn, my birth as noble as your own, Elspeth. Many now bear such marks, yes, even the nobly born, and honest wives and mothers. Someday, Elspeth, you may bear the very marks you chide me with, should chances go ill with you."

She stretched out her arms slightly, in mute appeal to Elspeth, and then turned slightly to Gunter and his friends standing near the altar. "I say, if any here claim that I have ever proven false or disloyal to my husband"—Elin's voice rose to a shout—"or to his people, that one lies and slanders me."

Elspeth shook her head. "Oh, you clever, scheming bitch. It's not even the work of a decent servant to summon the powers of darkness and lay your curse on an honest man."

"An honest man, Elspeth?" Elin spat. "Do you stand before the altar of your God and call Reynald an honest man?"

The two women stood alone, facing each other now, about ten feet apart in the clear space before the sanctuary.

Then Elin stepped forward a pace or two. Again she half turned toward Gunter and the men with him. "Have you come here to defend that traitor husband of yours as an honest man? One who has sold my husband"—she turned fully—"and promised to open the city gates to the Viking chief, Hakon, if his price be met."

There was an audible stir and murmur among the crowd at these words. Even the men with Gunter stared at each other in consternation. They all believed Reynald treacherous, but none realized his treachery extended this far.

"You lie!" Bertrand shouted at Elin, striding forward to

join Elspeth. "She is the servant of the arch deceiver, the father of lies."

"Do I lie, Bertrand?" Elin shouted. "Do I lie?"

"Creature of hell," Bertrand screeched back at Elin. "Daughter of the archfiend himself. Be silent. Don't sully the name of an honest man with your rotting foulness."

"You shut your mouth, priest." The voice was Gunter's. He'd stepped forward beside Elin. His mantle was cast aside and the largest of the hammers from his belt was in his hand. "I and the rest of us would hear what the woman has to say."

Bertrand quailed back before what he saw in the big man's face, and the men with Gunter now shifted their positions and ranged themselves with Godwin and his knights at the altar.

"Shall I recount to you," Elin hissed, "how Reynald caressed the gold, how he described to this robber, Hakon, the wealth of the city, the beauty of its women, the high prices your"—Elin turned toward Gunter—"your wives and daughters would fetch."

The count roared. "Enough! I am the master here!" He still had sufficient prestige, with that, and the threat of men at his back, to command silence.

Elin felt a hand on her arm and realized Godwin stood beside her, the pressure of his fingers drawing her slowly, imperceptibly, back to his side. His eyes were fixed on the count. They glittered, the eyes of a hawk watching a rabbit moving through the grass. She followed his lead.

"This will be settled between men as it should be," the count said. "I appeal to you, Godwin, as an honest man, the bishop having met with some evil chance or having fled away, I know not and will not hazard a guess," he said smoothly, edging a bit forward toward Godwin. "It is my right, and my right alone, to appoint his successor. So put the keys to his house in my hand, and his lady into my wardship, and you and your men may ride out safely, having done all that honor requires."

He moved forward slowly and Elin saw Godwin watching, not only the man, but the ranks behind him very carefully.

"Neither in law or custom have the kin of any churchman a claim on his property," Anton said. "This is a thing you well know, that I am in the right and the guardian of the Holy Church in this city."

Godwin smiled. The count returned the smile blandly. "Indeed," Godwin said. "We leave, then ride into your quiet little ambush on the road."

"No, no," the count said softly, "I will swear any oath you like that you may depart in peace and unmolested." He stood beside Elspeth and Bertrand, thumbs hooked into his belt of golden plates, watching them calmly.

"What of the Lady Elin's charges against your cousin?" Gunter broke in.

The count glanced at him from under lowered eyelids. "What of them?" He shrugged. "Poor man"—he shook his head sadly—"how can she know? You are deceived by all this superstitious talk of witchcraft. My cousin is ill, and the ladies' senses are disordered by grief. Now, what say you, Godwin?"

"No," Godwin answered, in an amiable and conciliatory tone. "We will remain until spring or until we have some firm assurance that the Lord Bishop is dead. You will keep your men in order and I mine. We are well provisioned. If necessary, we can both defend the city. That is my offer. Take it and we can live together in peace. And, as for Reynald, you will forbid him to enter the city, at least with any considerable force of men. My Lady Elin grieves for her husband, but I cannot think her so distraught as to be mistaken in matters of fact.

"I find it understandable, even"—Godwin smiled with an oily unctuousness that matched the count's—"laudable that you defend your kinsman, but the fact is that, if he took a golden opportunity to betray the bishop, he might be only too happy to take another, and deliver the city into the hands of its enemies. Especially if the weight of that gold exceeded the price of the bishop's life. He might even find the offer irresistible, if it carried with it a guarantee of his own safety."

The count turned slightly and looked at the men behind him. They stood firm. "I see," he said softly, "you would stay and give me orders about who I do and do not allow into the city."

"Not orders, my Lord Count," Godwin said amiably, "merely strong suggestions. I suggest we take no chances."

"What," Elspeth screamed, "you cannot mean to do this. She is a witch and deserves to die like one. She will work her arts and kill my husband, then sit here like a queen, preening herself in her triumph. You promised me her life when I brought my men and put them at your disposal, promised that she would die and the curse be lifted."

The count rounded on Elspeth. "Damnation on it. Can't you see that your loose talk lends credence to her follies?"

Elin stepped forward again, desperate to convince all those watching faces of the truth of her words. The count hadn't quite discredited her by his slighting indifference, but she'd seen the doubt planted in the eyes of the townsfolk by his contemptuous dismissal of her charges. Now she groped for a way to make them believe.

"My follies?" Elin said. "Is that what you call them, my follies? Hear me," she shouted, stepping toward the count, her arms raised. "Among all the treasure Reynald was offered for my lord's life, the greatest was a golden cup, ancient and of very soft, pure metal, protected by a filigree of silver set with pearls, a thing of great beauty." She extended her arm toward Elspeth. "Have you seen such a thing among your husband's possessions?" She was astonished by the effect of her words.

Elspeth's face crumbled. "No!" she whispered. "No. It's impossible. It can't be . . ."

Bertrand shrieked, "Unclean hag, hell vomited you forth, no Christian eyes could know . . ."

The murmur that swept through the crowd this time was a snarl of rage.

"This passed from the Viking chief's hand to Reynald?" Gunter asked.

"Yes," Elin said, turning toward him. "He held it up and admired its beauty."

"Often I have seen that chalice lifted high in consecration at the abbey church. It was stolen away when the monastery was destroyed."

"No," Elspeth whispered brokenly, "it's a lie, a lie." But no one believed her now.

"But," Gunter continued, his voice filled with astonishment, "it's been years since the monastery burned. Its treasures were all but forgotten."

Elin backed away toward the altar, one hand on her breast over the wound. "My death won't lift the curse, Elspeth. It is rooted in the blackness of Reynald's own treacherous heart."

Blackness, Elin thought. Beyond the doors of the cathedral the sky over the square looked as though night had fallen. The air around Elin was charged with violence, the violence of the coming storm, the violence among the townspeople in the church, pressing in around the count's men.

Godwin and the count looked at each other like two wolves circling, waiting to attack.

"She is a witch," Elspeth screamed, pointing at Elin. "She has known things no proper Christian—"

"Be silent, I tell you," the count shouted, "and I tell you for the last time, or kinswoman or no, you will conceal your face forever to hide its lack of a nose."

Elspeth turned from him with an expression of terror, toward Bertrand. "You dare threaten my sister," he screeched.

"Another word from you," the count thundered, "and your heels kick from a gibbet in the square."

Bertrand drew back, Elspeth in his arms.

The count came forward and paused a moment, a few paces from Elin. His face was a mask of power, power gone rotten and falling into decay. His flesh sagged with the weight of the years of debauchery, pale as corpse tallow, only here and there did it have the color of life, and as he drew closer, Elin saw that those were open, running sores where his flesh was rotted by drunkenness. The piglike bloodshot eyes glared into hers with an insane fury. When he spoke, it was a low guttural whisper and she knew the words were for her alone.

"How could you have known about that cup, what Reynald said to Hakon? How did your eyes see that, your ears hear it? Harlot and witch they call you, and that is what you are. When this ends, I will make a present of you to the widow, and my men will form lines at the door and each one, I vow, will climb the stairs to visit you. Each one will have you as long and as often as he likes."

Elin drew back, her face white under the paint Judith had put on her face. She saw the count's arm rise, pointing, not at her, but at Godwin.

Godwin smiled, and still smiling, killed him. As with Rosamund, Godwin moved so fast the watching eyes could scarcely credit his speed. His shield crashed into Elin, sending her to the floor. Then he threw his arm around the count and pulled him against the point of his sword. Godwin had expected a mail shirt under the white silk dalmatic and there was, he felt the metal rings grate against the sword point. The blade bowed slightly and Elin, staring up at them, eyes wide with horror, feared it might break, but it didn't. Instead, it straightened as it punched through iron rings and passed into the softer body of the man behind them.

Then Godwin and the count stood locked together before the astonished throng, breast to breast in a last deadly embrace, Godwin still smiling dreadfully. The count's eyes, only a few inches from his own, bulging, blood running from his slack jaw, splashing scarlet froth on the breast of the white silk dalmatic, the crossbow bolt, intended for Godwin, quivering in his back.

Elin was on her feet, mouth open, not even conscious that she was screaming. Anna, catching her around the waist, sent her back against the rail. She saw the church spread before her, the crowd blocking the great open doors, beyond them the town square. The light was green, the sky above black. *The storm,* she thought, *is breaking.* Bows were rising in the hands of the count's men, cocked and, she thought in terror, all pointed at her.

Then Godwin, with dreamlike slowness or so it seemed, raised his foot and sent the count's body spinning back into the raised bows of the archers.

Above, on the beam, Ranulf drew the knife. He hadn't known he could move with so much speed and decisiveness.

For one split second the giant cart wheel hung suspended by a few strands unsevered by the knife, then it fell away from him with dizzying speed, exploding into the packed multitude of the count and Elspeth's men.

Godwin raised his shield and arrows thudded into it. "Close with them," he howled above the screams of pain and fury rising all around.

An explosion of thunder cracked above the church. Lightning danced over the square outside, lighting the church like day. Wind screamed through the open doors, extinguishing the last candles.

Elin saw Ingund shove Alfric aside and snatch the processional cross, as her own archers let go their bolts with a whistling hiss and the thrum of bow strings.

Men were down everywhere, writhing under the fallen lamp or, near the altar, howling, clawing at arrows and crossbow bolts in their bodies.

The sky outside, veined with lightning, was one continuous string of blinding flashes. The wind rose above a scream and danced with the thunder in one long, deafening roar.

In the green darkness, Elin saw Godwin lead the charge. The townsmen near the altar hung back for a second, stunned at the execution done by the archers among their ranks. Then they, too, lunged forward, following Godwin and the knights.

The line of struggling men swayed back and forth in the gloom, falling over the dying on the floor, slipping in blood amidst the clangor of iron on iron, the shrieks of anger and despair.

Elin saw Elspeth's golden dress tossed to and fro by the whirlpool of savagery all around her. Then the count's men broke and ran. Elspeth, dragged along by Bertrand, was swept out through the church doors into the wind and rain outside.

Godwin plunged after them, rallying the knights with a yell, his voice a bellow, audible above the fury of the storm. "We have the dogs! Cut them down! Don't let them gain the safety of the fortress!"

The hail hit. Lashed by the wind, it crashed into the narrow windows of the cathedral like so many mailed fists. The windows shattered into flying fragments, driving into the bodies of pursued and pursuers alike. Both were seized with ultimate terror. Godwin's men scattered, pushing toward the safety of the wall sheltered from the wind. The count's men ran, following Elspeth and Bertrand as though the very hounds of hell were snapping at their heels.

Elin, trying to get to her feet, using the altar rail for support, and wondering why her knees didn't seem to want to hold her up, became conscious that there was a light behind her. Alfric stood on the steps of the altar, a lantern in his hand. He raised the lantern and in its flickering illumination a look of almost infinite weariness spread across his face, followed by a look of equally weary compassion.

Elin's knees gave way again, and she sat on the step, face buried in her hands, head against the rail. The wound in her breast was bleeding now, and tears coursed down her cheeks.

Outside, the wind fell below gale force. Hail and rain both poured straight down in sheets, hammering, blowing through the broken windows, puddling on the stone floor.

Fallen men were scattered about, the living entangled with the dead and moans and cries of pain rising everywhere as the rage of the storm outside ceased.

Alfric came down the steps of the altar and knelt beside the nearest of the wounded. He examined his face, then closed the staring eyes and signed his forehead with a cross, then rose and went on to the next. To the dead he offered absolution, in the hope that some faint light of the spirit still hovered near and would take comfort or find salvation in it. The wounded he assisted as best he could. After a time, the rest joined him in his labors.

Wolf the Tall died in his brother's arms, strangely less disturbed by his life running out in red streams around the two spears through his body, than by his despairing brother's anguished grief.

Huda lost an eye, cleanly plucked out by the head of a glancing crossbow bolt, and was in great pain.

Ingund's arm had been badly cut by flying glass.

Judith was unhurt. She tried swooning away after the battle, but was dissuaded by Anna's grim taunt, "What, my fine lady. Now that the excitement is over and the work begins, you find yourself ready for a nap?" So Judith pulled herself together and was, along with Elin, the most help to Alfric in binding up the wounds of the living.

Ranulf missed the fight, having found the trip down from his perch above the cathedral nearly as hair-raising as the way up had been. He crouched for a long time at the foot of the ladder into the bell tower, nauseated and shivering, until he was forced to run and empty his bowels and his stomach at the same time.

He arrived pale and unsteady, just in time to find Alan and Gowen lifting the wheel of the lamp to peer at what was under it. None of the broken bodies pinned beneath the mass of wood and chain showed even a slight flicker of life.

He turned such an ashen color when he looked at them that Godwin, without further ado, sent him in the company of Alan to stand near one of the shattered windows and breathe the fresh air that filtered in. After a few minutes the color returned to Ranulf's cheeks but he still stood there for a long time, letting the mist of rain dampen his face, miserably certain he'd lowered himself in Godwin's regard by his show of weakness.

Godwin walked over to the body of the count, lying facedown near the fallen lamp, and turned it over with his foot. The mouth, still open, was a clot of blood, and the eyes stared up at him. But now the pupils were hazy and the eyeballs slimed over with the film of death.

Ingund, still holding the processional cross, joined him. "That's a fine piece of silk you ruined, Godwin," she said, pointing to the count's dalmatic. "It's a shame."

Godwin eyed the processional cross in her hand. The crucifix was bloody. He'd caught a glimpse of her during the fight swinging it like a club. "I see you got yourself some range," he said admiringly.

"I believe I let a man or two's brains out with it," she told him dully, still looking down at the count.

Alfric knelt beside the body and tried to push the eyelids down over the ghastly stare. "He died in his sins," Alfric said. "May God grant him mercy and peace."

"How else should he have died?" Gunter said. "He thought of little else. Sin was his delight."

Godwin cleaned his sword carefully on the count's linen shirt. "He planned to kill me first,". he said, examining his blade for any remaining traces of blood that might cause rust, then, satisfied there was none, sheathing it. "He was giving the signal to his crossbowmen when I put the sword through his body. Lull us with soft words and promises of safety and freedom, all the while his men with bows under their cloaks."

Rieulf joined him, along with his men. He gave a grating chuckle. "You said your signal would be unmistakable—it was."

Godwin prodded the count's body with the toe of his boot. "My thanks for your help. I give you leave to despoil his corpse in token of my gratitude, except for this." He drew the count's scramsax from his belt and handed it to Ingund. "A weapon for a warrior," he said.

"You rule here now," Judith said, as Rieulf and his men fell to with a will. The count's weapons and jewelry were a rich prize. "We all want something."

"You have it even as you speak," Godwin said.

She whispered a few words into his ear.

Godwin snorted. "That presents no problem. If he has a beard, tell him to shave it off, if he hasn't, tell him to grow one. And I will personally swear that I've known him since he drew his only nourishment from his mother's breast and he was always a free man."

"You will defend the city," Gunter asked, "as you swore in this very church at the altar?"

Godwin bared his teeth in that same savage smile he'd worn when he stabbed the count. "Gunter, I have made sending those unlovely, unwashed, unbaptized shit-fuckers to their own blood-soaked paradise my life's work. It needs no oath to persuade me to continue it. They will pass the gates only over my dead body. Even were all my companions fallen and my arms ripped away from me by battle, I would tear the hearts from their bodies with my teeth even as I died."

Gunter studied him over the count's naked corpse. "Words," he said.

"You've had more than words from me this day," Godwin answered, looking down at the body sprawled on the floor, "but that's all the assurance I can give you at present."

"We'll want our organization, our prayer society, accepted as lawful and our right of assembly respected."

Godwin nodded. "Done and easily done. I need your help now."

"For what?" Gunter asked.

"To keep Gerlos and his remaining men pinned in the fortress. As for Elspeth, she and her men may leave, but with their swords sheathed, suitably accompanied by your people and my knights, all carrying drawn swords as far as the gates."

Gunter nodded. All this met with his approval.

There was more light in the church now. Though the rain hadn't slackened, it was turning to sleet, thick and bitterly cold. The sound of hooves echoed on the cobbles outside.

Godwin ran to the door, sword in hand, crouched, and looked. "She has forestalled us," he said.

Elspeth and Bertrand rode past, dim figures hooded and cloaked against the growing cold. About ten men were with her, all looking beaten and tightly wrapped, only dimly seen amid the screen of blowing ice.

"It's done." Godwin sighed wearily, sheathing the sword. "I feared she and Gerlos might stand together and make a fight of it. But without her support, Gerlos will probably accept our terms and leave quietly, in the end."

They stretched out the bodies of the dead near the church door. Godwin methodically saw to it that each of the count's men was stripped naked.

Alfric objected, saying, "Leave them something for decency's sake."

"What they had belongs to me," Godwin told him. "I have conquered. Had the victory fallen to them they would have taken all I had. Now stop preaching and help me, for this one is growing stiff and I can't get his arms up to pull off his shirt."

Godwin respected the men of the city who died in the battle. He went out of his way to compose their bodies decently for the sake of the grieving families arriving to claim them, praising their valor and steadfastness.

"A small lie," he answered, when Alfric pointed out that one of them had an arrow in his back. "It hurts nothing, the dead are always valiant. How else would they have been present to die?"

Wolf the Tall belonged to them and the household. By common agreement, they carried him to the hall, no one wanting to leave his body in the church. The temperature outside was dropping fast and by nightfall the cathedral would be freezing, a terrifying, grisly, blood-splattered cavern, the unclaimed dead its only tenants.

Alfric removed the body of Christ from the altar and brought it to the scriptorium, improvising a small altar on one of the shelves, placing the presence in the great monstrance and setting the sanctuary lamp before it to keep watch. The church would have to be repaired and reconsecrated before it could be used as a place of worship again.

They stretched the young knight's body out on the table and placed his weapons at his feet where, to everyone's surprise, Rosamund wept over him.

Actually what she did was faint and, being revived by unwatered wine, she screamed, tore her hair, pulling some of it out, scratched her face till it bled, beating her breast and wailing loudly and lifting her arms to heaven, shed floods of tears.

Wolf the Short approved. He stood beside his brother's body, clasping the cold hand in his, looking down at the bearded face filled now with the ivory dignity of the final mystery.

"It shows respect," he told Godwin, his face lined with simple sorrow, deep loneliness in his eyes. "I cannot yet truly believe he is gone from me, but in days to come, I will know it and remember she was kind."

"We'll bury him in the church crypt," Godwin said gently. "His bones will rest safe and in peace there in the kind embrace of God."

"Arm him," Wolf the Short said, "in his best. But send some extra along, piled at his feet. He was always given to hazard his property in games of chance. He may lose what he has and need more. It pains me that I was so often unkind to him about it." Then the tears began running down his cheeks.

Gowen, who had tapped a keg of Anna's beer and found some bread and cheese, looked at Wolf the Short solemnly. "I can't see why you reproach yourself with that. He didn't pay any attention to your grumbling, but diced and drank at every opportunity. He was never happier than when he held a dice box in one hand and a tankard in the other. Between the two, he led a full life." Gowen shook his head. "I will miss him."

If Wolf the Short didn't look cheered by these observations, he seemed at least comforted. He sat down on the bench by the table, still clasping his brother's hand. "Yes," he said softly, "so will I. He was very dear to me."

Godwin turned away, shielding his eyes, in obvious pain. "All they had in life was each other. I would not have had this happen for the world."

Alfric came in, bringing a basin of water and clean linen cloth. "We'll take him to the scriptorium, I and his brother, wash him, and compose his flesh for its last rest. His soul is with Christ."

"What will Christ make of Wolf the Tall, I wonder?" Godwin asked Alfric with sad cynicism.

"No less than you did, Godwin," Alfric answered serenely. "You found some love for his brave, simple soul in your heart. I think Christ is generous enough to find some in his."

Godwin was very tired but there remained yet one more thing to do. He paused near Alan, Huda's son. The boy was on one knee before the hearth staring into the flames, his face somber. Godwin rested a hand on his shoulder. "Come with me, I'm going to make Ranulf a knight. His courage deserves to be honored."

Alfric looked both saddened and dismayed. "He's a gentle young man."

"Yes," Godwin said, walking over to the corner where some of the looted arms were piled, "and he's shown me he'd rather be hung for a wolf than a sheep. I plan to teach him how to use his teeth."

Alfric followed him. Godwin held up a mail shirt, a leather cap reinforced with steel, and a sword. "Here, bless these," he said, "for you are the only Christian priest I know. Come to think of it, one of the few true Christians I have ever met."

"I thank you for the compliment," Alfric said, raising his hand in blessing, "though I think you might save your own soul if you but put a little effort into it."

"No, I'd rather create dissension among the damned."

"You are not doing the boy a favor, Godwin," Alfric said caustically, "and he is of no great lineage."

"I know who his parents were," Godwin said, "slaves in the household of Gestric, Owen's father. He was a tiny child, a crawler, when Gestric gave him to Owen as he might a puppy. But I will do it, Alfric." Godwin smiled with ferocious enjoyment. "I would do it just to see his eyes when he takes the oath. Help me cudgel my weak brain to invent some respectable ancestors for him."

"Hmmmmm, not difficult." Alfric's eyes rolled upward. "Now, let me see. Ah, I have it. As he, Ranulf, grew to manhood Owen noticed in his demeanor and inclinations things that did not accord with his station in life. His proud bearing, courage, and instinctive skill in the handling of arms. In fact, he showed great powers in all manly pursuits—horsemanship, hunting, and fighting, as well as courtesy and intelligence, surprising in one of his humble birth.

"Owen loved him like a brother, and taking pride in his accomplishments, encouraged him to further himself, until he became such a paragon of all the aristocratic virtues that Owen began to wonder if he truly were the son of a slave.

"So he summoned Ranulf's mother and questioned her. Thus confronted, with many sighs and tears she confessed that in her youth, Lord ..." Alfric paused. "Godwin, you will have to supply a name. Lord so-and-so, while visiting Owen's father, having slaked his thirst too well one night, seized her as she attended him to his chamber and forthwith had her maidenhood.

"Please pick for the role of ravisher someone either dead or so intemperate that he cannot remember if it be true or false, preferably both dead and intemperate. So," Alfric continued, "Lord Owen, out of respect for his great sire, freed him and admitted him to the company of his knights. There, how's that?"

"Excellent," Godwin said, "if a bit grandiose. It sets me to pondering how many of our noble pedigrees began with just such an imaginative fiction."

"Oh, quite a lot of them, I should think," Alfric answered with one of his sweeter and more innocent smiles. "Probably yours had a similar origin."

"Chances are it did," Godwin said. "Polish the story, don't go too far, make it believable and repeat it to Judith and Routrude. As for the lord, I know at least a dozen who are now dead and were intemperate. Most visited Gestric at one time or another. I'll wager in a few years Ranulf will be the king's champion."

"My mother was an honest woman and you mock me." Ranulf was standing behind them with a look of almost unbearable hurt in his eyes. "I fall off a horse if it sneezes, am but an indifferent bowman, know one end of a sword from the other only because I have had a few thrust at me, and as for hunting, I have never shot so much as a pigeon. I have deserved better of you, my lord." He spat the last two words at Godwin, his voice hoarse with rage, white to the lips with fury. "Better than to be the butt of your . . ."

Godwin caught him by the arm and forced him to his knees. "Be quiet, we're not making sport of you, but planning your future. Alfric is a wag, but an expert fabricator. Do you wish to become one of my company?"

The anger faded from Ranulf's face and was succeeded by a look of complete bewilderment. "It's not possible," Ranulf said, "as I told you . . ."

"I know what you told me," Godwin said. "Do you wish it? If so, say yes, and leave the rest to me."

"Yes," Ranulf said.

Godwin laid the mail shirt over his shoulder and put the sword in his hands. "Do you swear to follow me in battle and obey me in the hall? Say 'I do.' "

"I do," Ranulf repeated, a stunned look in his eyes.

"Protect and defend the Holy Church?" Alfric added.

Godwin gave him an icy look, but repeated, "Protect and defend the Holy Church? Say 'I do.' "

Ranulf said, "Yes."

"Respect all good priests and nuns," Alfric interjected.

Godwin sighed and added, "Respect all good priests and nuns?"

Ranulf said, "I do."

Alfric opened his mouth.

"Enough," Godwin said, "he pledges himself to me, not the pope."

"Put your hands in mine," Godwin ordered.

The entire household was now gathered around them. Alan, Denis, the crossbowmen, Gowen, Edgar, and Wolf the Short. Little Rosamund peered between the big bodies of the knights, and over Godwin's shoulder Ranulf could see his wife, Elfwine, clutching the baby, standing on the stairs looking down at them. Ine stood beside her, contentedly munching a loaf of bread.

Even when he said yes to Godwin, Ranulf had half believed this was some kind of a trick. Now he knew it wasn't. There were too many witnesses. Godwin really meant to do it. Ranulf, kneeling, clutched at the sheath of the sword, his sweat dampening the leather, his mouth dry, looking up at Godwin.

"Your hands," Godwin repeated, stretching out his own, still wearing his iron-sheathed gauntlets.

Ranulf rested the sword against his shoulder and raised his joined palms toward Godwin, as if in a dream.

Godwin's fingers closed around them, tightening in a powerful grip.

Ranulf looked up helplessly into the long-lidded, dark eyes above, and the room and the world faded into nothingness. The lean face with its hollow cheeks and beaked nose, a hawk's visage, gazed down at him, and the terrible voice rang in his ears.

"As you offer yourself, so do I accept you then, in the truth of that oath. In battle and in the hall, you are my son and my brother."

Ranulf hardly knew his hands had been released from that clawlike grip when the blow fell, knocking him spinning. And he hardly knew he was down and looking up into the blackened rafters of the ceiling when Gowen lifted him by the scruff of the neck and set him on his feet gently.

"Did ... did ... did I say something wrong?" Ranulf quavered.

"No," Godwin said, "that's part of the oath taking."

Gowen, who still had him by the collar, raised him to his toes then set him back down, saying, "He is small and light."

"No matter," Godwin answered. "I need a few men who don't leave all their brains in the pot when they squat down in the morning."

"My ears are still ringing," Ranulf said. "What brains I had are clean knocked out of my head."

"They'll come back," Alan said, "at least mine did when he administered the same treatment to me this morning."

"You, Alan, take him," Godwin said. "Huda didn't stint

you where trainers were concerned. Teach him to stay on a horse even if it sneezes, and enough of the sword not to be killed on the first pass."

"He has talent," Alan said, coming to Ranulf's defense, "I've seen him with Enar at the crossbow and throwing the axe. He learns quickly and has reflexes like a cat. Nor is he small, it's just that Gowen . . ."

"Excellent," Godwin said, "he's made a friend already." He drew off his gloves, a tall, deceptively thin figure silhouetted against the fire. "He has the will, and often in life, I've found that's what is most important."

"The will and how much else?" Ranulf said, his eyes sliding to Gowen slouching in a chair by the fire engulfing a hunk of bread and cheese.

"If strength were everything, the ox would walk behind the plow not before it," Godwin answered. "Now, go to bed and present yourself properly armed and attired to me in the morning." He gestured toward the stairs. "Your wife awaits you."

Elfwine was still standing on the stairs and Ranulf, forgetting all the rest, basked in a smile that was pure adoration. He went to join her.

Godwin stood watching them climb the stairs together. "Oh Christ!" he whispered. "Youth."

"Complaining again, ready to complain again." Gowen laughed. "The battle's over so now you remember your aches and pains, eh, old man? I always know I'm safe when you start bitching about your joints, or is it your bowels, or the sniffles?"

"All three," Godwin snarled, making for the chair opposite Gowen and the wine. "My stomach's queasy and I've noticed of late sharp stabbing pains near my groin . . ."

"Get yourself a woman," Edgar suggested. "I've noticed a woman nearly always cures those particular pains."

"Women, my ass." Godwin sighed dolefully. "I probably ruptured myself killing the count." He was just settling into his chair when he heard a loud shout.

Gunter dashed past the men at the fire and ran toward the doors that opened into the square.

Godwin swore imaginatively about having his rest disturbed, but then leaped to his feet and followed.

Gunter had reached the door and was unbarring it.

Godwin slammed his hand down on the heavy oak beam and stopped him from opening it. "Before you let in the winter night," he snarled, "tell me what in the name of hell's seven red-hot gates is the matter?"

"It's Gerlos," the blacksmith panted. "I think he's fleeing the way Elspeth did. We were carrying the dead out of the church when we saw him from the windows."

They let down the bar together, cracked the door, and peered into the darkness outside.

The torches in the hands of Gerlos's men glowed like blurred stars in the continuous fall of frozen rain and sleet.

As he watched, something flared at the corner of Godwin's eye. He extended his head farther out of the door. He looked up and saw a murky red glow above the fortress inside the walls.

"It seems," Godwin said, "that he left the fortress burning behind him."

"What do you think?" Gunter asked. "Should we pursue?"

"To what end?" Godwin asked as his expert eye counted the men with Gerlos. "Unless he's a bigger fool than I think he is, Gerlos has given every man with him a generous amount from the late count's store of gold and they'll fight like demons to protect that, if nothing else. We can't afford any more dead. Every man killed is one less to defend the city when the Vikings come."

"Not when, if," Gunter said.

"When!" Godwin repeated in a voice cold as the ice flowing into their faces. "You have a taste for fighting a roaring blaze in this?" Godwin gestured toward the tiny balls of frozen rain bouncing off the steps at their feet.

Gunter was jolted a little by the old warlord's common sense. He really didn't expect common sense from such as Godwin. The old soldier was right. There was nothing to be done about a building well and truly aflame except stand back and watch it burn. "I suppose not," Gunter said slowly. "But though the walls are stone and will stand, the hall inside and the walkways along the battlements are wood. Until they can be rebuilt, the fortress is useless."

"That may be just as well," Godwin said, closing the door, and dropping the bar into place. "No one will be tempted to flee into it and escape the fury when all hell breaks loose below. The fortress is too small to hold the whole town, much less the people of the countryside. Too many would have to be left behind."

Godwin seized the blacksmith's shoulders with his fingers and looked him full in the face. "Possibly, just possibly Gerlos has done us a favor in destroying the fortress," he said. "One of the most potent weapons the Vikings have always had against us is our own divisiveness—our tendency to distrust one another and quarrel among ourselves. It may be, now, that everyone here will understand fully that live or die, stand or fall, everything we do, we must do together."

Chapter

34

*I*T was the flatness of everything that tortured him most. He had no desire for anything any longer. Even his wife, Elspeth, seemed a distant figure with her contemptible tears and hysterics. As were the old women she summoned to his bedside to whisper spells, or try to persuade him to drink nauseating mixtures in the hope that his torments would abate. He had no faith in them, or in Elspeth's fooleries in the grove.

The witch had picked the strongest adversary of all to set upon him, himself.

Food tasted foul in his mouth; the stench of it was so disgusting to him that he couldn't bear the sight of it. Water quenched none of his thirst. That thirst returned to rage in his vitals as soon as the moisture left his mouth, until at last the bother of stilling that particular agony seemed futile.

Elspeth was gone for now, he couldn't remember where. He was alone. He sat naked on the edge of the bed and drew the box of treasure from under it. The things in it were his life's work.

A life of fear, of cunning, of self-interested duplicity. He'd looked after himself and his own well. Wasn't that what a man was supposed to do?

His fingers scrabbled through the box, counting, touching, seeking. The windowless bedchamber was dark and the gem-encrusted, golden objects glowed, glittering in the light of the one tiny lamp that burned on the table. It eased his pain to know his wealth was near him. He lifted the chalice and placed it against his cheek. The metal was cool.

Lately he'd been hot, very hot, his skin burning. He couldn't remember why, then was afraid because he knew he should remember. It was very important.

In a wave of cold, it all came back. He twisted the soft silver of the cup with his fingers. The boy was a fool and deserved to pay the price of such obstinacy. Suddenly, Owen's face was before him. Between the first blow he struck, and the second, the look on his friend's face had changed from a look of trust and eager expectation to one of heart-struck sorrow and disbelief.

He'd loved Owen, no man better, and wanted to send his son to be brought up in his household. The bishop was a well-conducted young man. In every way a proper lord.

The silver cup bent under his fingers. He closed his eyes to shut out the memory, but the face still hung in the darkness of his brain. "I'm sorry," he said, "but don't you see it had to be done? There is no way to fight them. They rule here now. They are too strong."

The cup crumpled in his hand, pearls falling from the ornamented golden shell and scattering on the floor. He dropped the bent cup back into the box among the other golden baubles, and began crawling around on the bare planks, seeking the odd-shaped freshwater pearls in the dim light.

Osric. He had given his friend to Osric. That had sickened him at the time. It sickened him even more now. Why had he not run his own sword through Owen's body? The answer mocked him as he crouched, prying one of the pearls from a crack in the raw wood, mocking him in Owen's voice.

You drive a harder bargain than Judas. The boy had spoken the truth in the end. There would have been no profit in simply slitting his throat.

How would Osric kill him? Reynald wondered, shivering in a chill that seemed to emanate from some dark center in his own body. He remembered Osric's work at the monastery. The men's bodies tied to spits like animals, roasted over the fires. Blackened bodies, mouths gaping in final screams. Dead faces transfixed in a rictus of final, unendurable agony.

Osric and Hakon.

Osric was too evil even to carry the name of an animal of the forest. But Hakon could be trusted, a man of his word and all the more dangerous thereby.

Hakon came to him whispering, tempting, "We will leave

you alone, and when we are gone, what's left will fall to you. The labor of killing them would be too much, and only a few will be worth shipping out as slaves; the rest will be easy prey. Why should we make war, pay in blood for what we can both gain by craft? But make no mistake, Reynald," the terrible Viking chieftain had promised, "we will have the city; stand in our way and we will destroy you too."

The threat and the promise; Reynald had believed both. Fear or ambition, he'd never really known which moved him the most. Fear of Hakon's battle-hardened warriors or the chance of holding in his hands the glittering prize of the city. Even a city plundered and half destroyed, its people terrified and demoralized, would be an acquisition beyond his wildest dreams. As for the suffering and death inflicted by the raiders—what of it? The citizens would be all the more meek and biddable once exposed to the ferocity of rapine and pillage. All the more willing to kiss the hand that delivered and protected them from its ever happening again.

He looked down at his hands. Hope flowered within him, brightening for a moment the cold that clutched at his heart. It might still work. The witch; Elspeth had gone to kill her. Perhaps she would succeed. But surely in time, no matter what happened to the witch, he would shake off this strange illness. This weakness on his part was only, after all, a temporary thing. Tomorrow he would be better.

He was crouching on the floor and he'd forgotten why, forgotten the cup and pearls, forgotten the open box filled with gold and precious stones that flamed in the lamplight by his side.

He sat up and leaned back against the heavy bedframe, looking down at his naked body. His paunch hung down over the soft mass of his genitals, the thick strong legs covered with curling dark hair. Two tears started at the corners of his eyes and ran slowly down each side of his nose until they reached his mouth. He thought of those smooth wet tracks against his skin, then reached out and licked the salt drops from his lips.

The witch had a mighty geas. She must hate him very much.

It grew colder and colder in the room, but it was too much

trouble to get up and crawl under the covers. Besides, usually the cold followed him even there.

"My lord?"

Reynald looked up. Someone was in the room, one of his wife's maids, putting a tray on the table.

"My lord, will you eat?" she asked timidly.

He looked up at her. Strange, the servants usually avoided him when Elspeth wasn't present to punish them if they didn't attend to his needs. This must be some girl more afraid of Elspeth than she was of him. He would cure that. He stood up and walked over to the table.

The girl stepped back quickly but not far enough. He seized her with both hands. One hand sent her spinning toward the bed, the other tore her dress away.

She landed on her back silently, one hand pressed to her mouth. She didn't scream.

He was used to having the women of his household, those that he wanted, when and where he wanted. She feared to make any outcry. The wide dark eyes stared up at him, as he bent over her, looking at him in the same way Owen's dark eyes once looked into his, helpless, mutely suffering, asking why.

It was unbearable. A wordless voice in his brain shrieked on and on. He punched her hard in the body and then she did begin to scream. He hit her again and again, just to stop the screaming. It was when he stopped punching her and put his thumbs over her eyeballs to extinguish their accusation forever that she began to fight.

She twisted out of his grip in pure animal terror, clawing at his face and hands with her nails. One ripped his cheek, another, one of his eyelids. She got her knees up under his belly and her feet tore at his groin.

He let her go, having forgotten why he had been hitting her in the first place, and looked down at his body. His penis was torn almost in half.

The girl made a retching sound and rolled from the bed to the floor.

He stood looking down at his ruined manhood, fascinated, the blood pulsing out, each red spurt keeping time to the hammering of his heart.

The girl was crawling away from him, making tiny whimpering sounds.

Two of his men were standing in the doorway. He could see the shock in their faces, and the dark shapes of others crowding behind them. The two in the doorway began to approach him cautiously.

He was cold, and the screaming in his brain never stopped, it went on unceasingly even though the girl, facedown on the floor, was silent now. The long streams of blood running down his legs were the only heat in an icy universe. They warmed his legs and even the soles of his feet. He dabbled his toes in the sticky stuff. "You are remiss," he screeched at the two men easing cautiously closer and closer to him. They seemed unmoved.

"I am cold, bring me fire. Do you hear me?" he screamed, snatching up the lamp and throwing it into his blankets. "Bring me fire." It blossomed in the bed.

Reynald crawled into it, through it, and curled his body, knees under his chin, still screaming, "Bring me fire," as the bed curtains caught and fell on his body and the mattress and bolster burst into flame. He still screamed, "Bring me fire," again and again and again.

Chapter

35

OWEN had his wind back and they weren't traveling as fast now, so he took to the water with Tigg and the rest, leaving Enar the horse. Tigg picked out another channel between two islands and followed it, leading them deeper and deeper into the marsh.

Enar clung to the stallion's mane and looked around nervously. "Friend Tigg," Enar said, "men have entered these swamps and not come out again, as I said before."

"Yes," Sybilla said, "we do know where we're going. Chatter, chatter, chatter. How does your wife stand it?"

"I'm a great lover," Enar said.

"It would be better if you were a great swimmer, then your lord wouldn't be fainting with exhaustion in the water behind you."

Owen was about to deny this when he realized he didn't have the breath and that it was true.

"Stand up," Tigg said, "it's shallow here."

Owen did. His chest was heaving, streams of dirty water poured down from his hair over his body. His legs felt leaden, as though he couldn't force them to another step. Enar jumped down from the stallion and splashed toward him, leading the horse by the forelock.

"I can't understand," Owen gasped out, "what's wrong with me. I had a rest. I should be able to swim."

"No!" Enar said angrily. "You have been tortured for a day and a night, fought a battle, and now have been running hard for another day. You need food and sleep." He caught Owen by the arm and began to lead him toward a nearby muddy hummock. Tigg looked at Enar and shook his head. "Why not?" Enar asked.

Tigg threw a stick at it. Snakes wiggled away in all directions. Enar shuddered. "The marsh has a secret," Tigg said. "But bear with us a little longer," he said gently to Owen, "and we will come to it. Put him on the horse." He said to Enar, "You can wade the rest of the way."

True to his word, a few rods farther on, Tigg pointed to what looked like another island. When they scrambled through the wiry undergrowth at its margin and climbed to the top, Owen realized that it was stone, a road.

"The Romans?" Owen said, looking up and down the overgrown trace way.

"Yes," Tigg answered, "the swordsmen."

"Why here of all places?" Enar asked.

Tigg raised his shoulders and spread his hands in a gesture of noncomprehension. "They came here. Wherever they went they built these, and many died doing it. Ghosts cry all along the path at night, and blue lights flicker in the darkness of the marshes. It's safe enough by day. Come."

Even the stubborn Romans hadn't been able to construct a perfectly straight roadbed here or lay the big stone blocks they preferred. For long distances the deeper pools of the marsh had to be bridged by causeways of timber and rammed earth surfaced with cobbles and gravel. The marsh was slowly reclaiming its own. In places the water crept in until it was only a slimy footpath.

"The footing gets better up ahead," Tigg told Enar. "This is the deepest part of the swamp. When the road turns out to higher ground, the going gets easier."

Enar, walking along beside the stallion, grunted out a noncommittal reply. In truth, he was worried about Owen, sitting slumped on the horse's back.

Fearing Owen would drop his sword, Enar eased the hilt from his hand and thrust the long blade into his belt. Owen released the weapon without protest, and this frightened Enar. Only a man far gone in exhaustion would relinquish his weapon, even to a friend.

The boy was young, but even the strongest body and spirit can be broken. He'd been cruelly used in the camp. His swollen, battered hands twined in the horse's mane were covered with wounds, their edges an angry red. Blood and serum trickled from the sores on his back and his hair was still matted with blood from the gashes inflicted by

Reynald's blows. One eye and cheek were swollen. Blisters had risen in places on his arms and chest, burns from the falling thatch in the hall.

Enar hadn't needed to be told with what expectation Owen had entered that hall or with what berserk fury he'd fought, once inside. Men like Owen went into battle driven, ridden by an almost divine madness, counting their lives as nothing, if they achieved their objective—the destruction of the enemy. Plunging forward, surrounded by a cloud of fire, they often carried the day when others faltered and drew back, breaking their hearts, burning out their lives in one overwhelming flash of insane courage.

If Enar was a craftsman of his own death-dealing trade, Owen was its genius. So he looked up in pity at Owen, pity and fear. He had also seen such men die breathing their last, though they came seemingly unmarked from the battlefield. Yet they died in the arms of their comrades, yielding up their lives as if they no longer had the strength to continue them, broken by forces too strong to be contained in the muscle, blood, and bone of frail human flesh.

Owen, drained of the last vestiges of his madness, might fall from the horse and drown simply because he had not strength enough to lift his head above the water, or couldn't care enough to bother. Finally, as Tigg promised, they'd come to a higher stretch of road, one that overlooked the surrounding marsh.

"How does the Christ Priést?" asked Tigg.

Enar looked up at Owen. His eyes were closed and his hands rested quietly on the horse's withers. He seemed content to doze, lulled by the silken flow of motion under his calves and thighs as the stallion walked along the roadway. Enar answered tersely, "Better now, he rests." Then he turned to Tigg. "Think they stand any chance of catching us?"

Tigg shook his head. "No. Few know of this road and none take it willingly, for it leads nowhere. They say, in the time of the swordsmen there was a town at the end, now lost beneath the sea. It's an old story and I can't say if it's true or not."

Enar asked, "Why do you call them the swordsmen?"

"The Romans, you call them after their city," Tigg said.

"They carried swords everywhere they went and used them. It is said among us that it was from these swordsmen that we really learned to run and hide skillfully. Before that it was only play."

"Before that the whole world was ours," Sybilla corrected him.

"No," Tigg said, "first came the housemen. They made gardens in the open country beyond the forests, and raised stone tombs to enclose their dead. We were not troubled by them, and at times almost forgot they were there."

"After them came the chariotmen," the little girl Ilo said. "Those are my favorites. There are many stories of their songs and deeds. I wish I could have seen their chariots coming in clouds of dust across the plain, the thunder of their turning wheels shaking the earth. And the beautiful warriors standing in them, clad in jewels with gold rings around their necks."

"I don't think I would have liked it so much, or you either," Sybilla remarked, her cheeks flushed and her eyes bright with anger. "The rivers ran red with the blood of the slain. For those housemen were not as we are, free, skimming over the earth as birds or the clouds in the sky, but bound to the soil of their gardens and the tombs of their ancestors. They defended their homes against those beautiful warriors, to the death. We fled from them as men flee fire, and hid in the deep woods as we do now."

"But," Tigg said, shrugging, "all that thunder and fury came to nothing. The chariotmen settled among the housemen and, because sometimes the housemen prevailed, married their sons and daughters to them, and in time they forgot they had ever been different peoples."

"Maybe for them, it came to nothing," Sybilla said, "but not for us." There was bitterness in her voice. "They brought kings with them, and iron. They cut the trees to pasture their cattle and horses. We were driven from our best hunting grounds."

"But they made offerings to us," Tigg said, "and we traded and lived in peace. They had their songs, they knew who they were. Until the time of the swordsmen. That was worst of all."

They all fell silent. There was only the piping of the wind

over the water and the crunch of their feet in the gravel of the road.

"That was a sad time," Imry, Sybilla's husband, said.

"A long time," Tigg said.

"The swordsmen, the Romans, had no songs." Sybilla spoke quietly. "They understood only power and submission to that power, and it seemed they ruled the whole world. Their words were hammered into the stones, that all might obey them, and the songs died. They killed the songs by turning them to stone."

"I don't know," Enar said. "The Romans did many wonderful things. Look at the road. Who could build such a road now?"

"Who would want to?" Sybilla flared back at him. "And I don't see that there's anything remarkable about building this muddy track, if you have a thousand slaves to do the work, a thousand lives, as many as the leaves on a tall tree to spend as fuel in the furnace of your desire."

"Now the Romans are gone, and I don't see how we are any better off," the little girl Ilo complained. "The horsemen have come and they, too, have steel axes and still we run and hide. It's very complicated." She shook her head. "And I don't understand it."

"No one understands it. That's why Alshan climbed the tree. When he returned, he told us we should seek a father among the horsemen. So we searched," Tigg said, then threw a thoroughly skeptical glance at Owen. "This is what we have found."

Ilo piped up, "Alshan is growing old. Maybe he dreamed badly or it was not a true dream."

Sybilla snorted. "Wait until you are old enough to dream before you pronounce judgment on those of others."

"He has needed more help of us than we of him," Ilo said.

"Alshan was right," Enar said, "and he dreamed a true dream. My people have their own songs, many of them, and they, too, know who and what they are and are not afraid."

He looked up at Owen, who seemed still to be sleeping. "I'm not a learned man, but I am far traveled. I have walked the streets of Rome and I agree with Sybilla. I'm not as impressed with those conquerors, at least," he said, grinning, "not as much as they were with themselves. Perhaps they destroyed as much as they built, perhaps more. The Christ Priest is not cut to their pattern, but is something more. I knew this when I saw him in the church. He stood before his people and laid his life at their feet. A power was in him, the power of all songs and dreams, the power filled him and he embraced it.

"I'm not like him. I fear that power. I respect it. I will offer sacrifices to it, but I cannot love it." Enar shook his head. "No! I will not do as these foolish Christians do, let a god demand my love. But," he continued, "the Christ Priest loves Him."

He turned to the rest and spread his arms wide. "Did you hear him revile me when we escaped the camp? I understood why he cursed me. I denied him his death, the offering of himself to that terrible truth.

"No," Enar said, shaking his head again, "you may be sure Alshan is not wrong. If he lives . . ." Enar glanced up again at Owen. His eyes were open and, though he appeared a little fogged with sleep, he was looking at Enar with a penetrating stare. "If he lives, he will be a gentle father, and lead you well." He spoke almost defiantly, knowing Owen was listening.

"Thank you," Owen said, "but I didn't like 'if he lives.' "

"I didn't think you would," Enar said, "but with respect, you are not the most cautious of men. Thank God, Osric— actually I think you probably received the intervention of several gods and powerful ones—that Osric and Hakon bargained with Reynald for a living man. Otherwise he would have stuck a knife in your throat and ended the matter right there."

"I believed Reynald was my friend. I had no reason to believe otherwise," Owen said. "Have you ever trusted someone who proved false?"

Enar opened his mouth, shut it, and then sighed.

"That for you, Saxon!" Sybilla said, snapping her fingers. "Even we believed Reynald was a friend. He took us by surprise and that is difficult to do."

Imry said something to Tigg in their own language and pointed at the sky. It was growing darker.

Igg gave Owen a worried look and shook his head. "He's

asking if you're strong enough for a run. It's beginning to rain."

"Yes," Owen said and realized that he was. He felt refreshed by the short sleep on the horse's back, and the pangs of hunger had subsided. He no longer felt the terrible dragging weakness that had attacked him when he tried to swim in the marsh. The stiff breeze was cool. He felt lightheaded, almost euphoric. Slowly, all around him the dry land was increasing in area. The trees it supported were bigger, as the marsh gave way to oak forest. He could feel the rain on his face. The drops were too fine to be seen yet, but they brushed his lips, cheeks, and eyelids with their feathery touch.

Here the Romans came into their own again and the road stretched out straight ahead, a tunnel of gray and green under the lowering sky. The road was surfaced with big cobbles and, though the forest was encroaching upon it, the center seemed as clear and smooth as when the builders dropped their tools and departed.

"How about you? Are you strong enough for another run, Saxon?" Sybilla asked Enar.

"I can run you off your legs," he replied.

She laughed and broke into a jogging run. Enar followed.

Tigg and Imry looked at each other, shrugged, smiled, and joined them. The horse's pace increased until it became a trot. Ilo ran alongside. "Give me a ride," she pleaded.

Enar laughed, shouted, "Why not?"

He lifted her easily and set her in front of Owen. She screamed with delight and buried her fists in the horse's mane. The stallion seemed to take this for encouragement and shifted smoothly into a canter.

For a second Owen was terrified the child might fall, then he had her around the waist and leaned forward over the withers. The stallion raised his head, neighed, and extended its body into a gallop. The horse's gait was swift and smooth. It seemed to float over the rocky surface. The arching branches of the trees above flashed past, then ahead, abruptly ended. The road disappeared into sand, and the stallion was carrying them like the wind over the open beach of a cove.

Rocks, like two strong arms, stretched out on either side,

and the thunder of the surf roared in Owen's ears. The stallion flew straight for the ocean. It leaped the first wave with the agility of a deer, then breasted the second, the jade-green water foaming white around its body. The third wave caught all three of them in the face, and Owen and the child were thrown into the sea.

The raw skin on Owen's back dealt him one flashing instant of blinding pain, then numbed. He grew cold, then warm as his body reacted to the chill water. He came up swimming and saw Ilo standing on the beach already pulling off her clothes. The crest of another wave lifted him high for one thrilling instant, then dumped him, laughing, on the sand.

The stallion danced with the ocean, jumping in and out of the surf over the cresting waves, mane and tail flying. Owen stood up, plunged through the breakers, swimming out to let the waves carry him in. The salt water cleansed him, washing away not only the filth of the camp and the marsh, but the bitterness and humiliation of his captivity.

The sting of his wounds was not pain, but purification, cleansing his soul of the hatred and fury he'd felt, wiping out the torment of Reynald's betrayal, his shame at his failure to kill Hakon.

Only now did he realize that, by some series of miracles, he was alive, alive and free. The journey back from death to life had been a hard one, but he'd made it. One miracle had been Enar's fidelity; another, Elin's strange people; and a third, the stallion standing between him and Hakon. Even the sea that tumbled and tossed him was like a strong father who lifts a child high into the air, but whose powerful arms always carry him to safety in the end. He heard yells and exclamations at the cold water and realized the forest people had joined him. Only they stripped before they jumped in.

"Look!" Ilo cried, pointing at him as he rode the high swells offshore until he was caught up, laughing, in the breaking waves. "He is like us," she shouted, "and can set his heart free." She swam toward him, threw her arms around his neck, and kissed him impulsively.

She was very young, her body unformed, yet the kiss filled his heart with a great tenderness. She made him think of the child growing in Elin's womb, then of Hakon and

Osric. The hate burning in his heart had been only partially quenched by the joy of killing Osric. He would have liked to have had him back to kill several more times.

Then he looked at the child. She was riding the swells joyously into the beach again. Her white body was a glimmer of ivory against the dark water.

Suppose Elin's child were a girl, Owen thought, innocent and trusting like this one. God, his or not, he would love it desperately. Yet either one of those two men might be its father.

The child was being pulled from the surf by Sybilla and towed, protesting, behind a rock to be dressed. He couldn't hear her protests, both the wind and surf were too loud, but he could imagine them from the stiffened, reluctant attitude of the small body.

He hadn't thought of love in connection with Elin's child, but only of protection and possession. But a child emerges from a woman's womb as Ilo emerged, cleaned by the sea, naked, unmarked and unknowing, sharing only whatever sin all men inherit by being sons of Adam and daughters of Eve. Would he, must he, burden the child with his hate?

Enar was now standing on the beach, shouting at him. He couldn't hear the words, any more than he could hear Ilo's childish protests, above the wild thunder of the surf. But he didn't want to return to shore yet, to the exile and uncertainty that were his fate. He wanted a few moments adrift in the violent, yet dispassionate, tumbling of the waves. So he threw himself on his back and the swells cradled him.

Osric and Hakon had both tried to bind him with chains of iron, but worse, far worse, were the chains of hate. "He can set his heart free," the child had said, and he understood the message of Christ as he'd never understood it before. Even Christ couldn't break the chains of iron men forged for each other, but He could set their hearts free.

And he set his free and abandoned hatred, casting off those chains, even as he abandoned himself to the sea.

The waves were mountainous, lifting him high, then pitching him down the green glassy surface of a trough, then up again, at the wild, churning beauty of the stormy sky. He rode them as easily as he had ridden the stallion, his buoyancy another miracle, another delight. Then the crash and boom of the surf thundered around him and the last wave carried him into shore and sent him sprawling, still laughing, at Enar's feet.

Enar stood shivering, teeth chattering, looking down at a smiling Owen. "Have you gone mad! It's freezing! I'm freezing! The rain is falling!"

Owen looked out over the ocean. The sky was gray-black toward the horizon. Short bursts of rain troubled the water, and the rising wind lashed the waves to a foaming boil.

As if in answer to Enar's complaint, a figure appeared out of the mist of rain and beckoned. "Come, we are waiting."

"The horse?" Owen shouted.

The figure standing in the rain laughed. "He is already warm and dry, enjoying his supper."

Ilo and Sybilla came from the shelter of the big rocks and they all took off running again. The rain was coming down harder and harder. They moved away from the beach. The grass of a meadow was soft under Owen's feet, and suddenly all around him tall gray standing stones loomed high out of the sheeting rain.

"Come," the voice ahead shouted, "we are almost there!"

The ground sloped upward abruptly and Owen realized they were climbing a green mound, thickly overgrown with tall grass and small trees. The rain was so heavy now it obscured everything. A hand caught Owen's and led him to the top. Enar, running just ahead, a misty shape in the torrential downpour, vanished into the earth.

"Agaaaaah!" he roared from below.

A hand was on Owen's back, urging him on, but Enar's cry froze him. Then he heard Ilo's silvery child's laughter and Sybilla's voice. "You wanted shelter, a warm fire, and something to eat. Now you have them and are screeching with fear of a few old bones."

"It is a very charnel house," Enar howled. "Their ghosts must be everywhere about me."

"Stop bellowing," Sybilla shouted. "Your howling shakes the very stones of the roof. Do you want it to fall down on you?"

"Yah," the little girl said contemptuously, "what if their ghosts are here? We don't disturb them and they suffer us for a time."

"They were good people," Sybilla said gently, "and would give even strangers shelter from a storm."

Enar moaned more softly. "I should not have made jokes about a god. They have no sense of humor."

The voices from below moved away, seeming to go deeper into the earth. Owen heard a chorus of laughter, some from behind him, and even through the curtain of gray rain he saw his companion's shoulders shaking.

He was looking down into a hole that appeared almost too small to admit a human being. But Enar sounded well in body, if not in spirit. So he shrugged and let his feet down through it. Hands grasped his legs and assisted his descent. He found himself in near total darkness, but Sybilla stood before him, smiling in the flickering light of a torch she held high in her hand. She extended a clean linen cloth toward him.

"Here, dry off and come comfort your friend. He's afraid," she said, grinning.

Owen wiped his face and dried his hair. As his eyes adjusted to the dim light of the torch, he realized he was standing in a long passage whose ends stretched away into darkness. It was floored, walled, and roofed by stone.

The slabs were crudely worked, but huge, almost as though boulders had been rolled down a mountainside and placed in a double row. Another row of stones, equally large and heavy, had been set lengthwise on top of them, forming the roof.

"It's a strange place, I know." Sybilla spoke reassuringly. "But it's safe, warm, and dry. Be careful," she said, turning to lead him toward the end of the passage. "Disturb none of the sleepers. They offer us their hospitality and this place belongs to them."

Owen looked around and saw the first of those Sybilla called "the sleepers." He or perhaps she, for the bones were small and slender, lay on its side near the wall only a few feet away.

It was difficult to distinguish the bones from the rough surface of the stone around them. They were old, not white as newly cleaned skeletons are, but as dark brown as something that has rested long in the keeping of the earth. A few fragments of wood, the decaying remnants of a bier lay under the body. A pitcher of earthenware and a few cups were scattered near the head.

Owen studied the corridor. Now that he knew what to look for, he could distinguish others. Some, much more fragmentary than this one, lay scattered. A few on their backs, prone, others in the attitude of sleep, they rested all along the walls, but the center of the corridor was clear, leaving a path for the living's feet.

"This is a tomb," he whispered. His voice echoed back, a softer stir from the walls around him.

"Not for a long time," Sybilla said. "Besides, they feasted them here and sent their spirits on their way. Come," she said, "there's a larger chamber beyond."

Owen followed the light of Sybilla's torch along the corridor. Twice they passed side chambers, the entrances simply formed by leaving gaps in the cyclopean blocks of the wall. At the first of these Owen paused, and Sybilla thrust her torch through the opening.

Owen recoiled slightly as he looked into the empty eyesockets of a dozen skulls. The small chamber was piled high with bones to a depth of several feet. The ceiling of this chamber was domed with flat rocks, the ends of each course slightly overlapping the rest, until they formed a corbel vault. Then Owen realized the builders had covered the whole with earth even as they must have covered the corridor, holding the giant rocks in place.

"This is what frightened your friend and made him cry out so loudly," Sybilla said.

"Coming on this suddenly with no warning," Owen said, "I think I might cry out too."

The walls of this chamber were covered with designs, carved out in low relief, long serpentine shapes, spirals, some still showing tracks of bright paint. Owen's curiosity overcame his fear and he made as if to enter and look more closely, but Sybilla barred his way. "No, it's not safe. Look."

She pointed at the overlapping courses of the roof and Owen felt a cold chill of fear. Trickles of moisture were making their way between the roughly dressed slabs of granite and flowing down the walls or dripping on the bones below. Owen drew back quickly, casting an apprehensive glance at the roof of the corridor above.

"That will stand till doom's day," Sybilla said, "but these . . ." She walked on a few paces and thrust her torch at another opening in the corridor wall. Stones and dirt met Owen's eyes. The roof had fallen and the chamber and its contents were buried under tons of soil.

"These were ossuaries, I think," she said, "and the builders were not so careful with them as with the main chambers."

She walked on, Owen following. Just ahead were the jamb and lintel of a door carved with the same spirals and meanders as the walls of the ossuary. Owen ducked down slightly and stood in the main chamber. It was walled with the high stone slabs of the corridor, but above it lifted the same lofty corbel vault as the ossuary. He cringed, thinking of the vast weight above him.

"No," Sybilla said, raising her torch high to illuminate the roof, "they were very careful here."

They had been. By the light of the torch, Owen could see that the slabs were more tightly fitted, the overlapping edges smaller and, though they were moist with the pervasive damp, no water entered between them. More skeletons lay scattered across the floor of this central chamber, some seeming newer than those in the corridor. The bones of a few were still articulated.

Across the chamber, in a corner near the entrance to another passage and well away from the nearest of the skeletons, a fire was burning. A joint of meat was cooking on a spit over it and a smell of food rose from a pot in the coals. Enar and a half dozen of the forest people were gathered around the flames.

It was clear that Enar, in spite of his loud expostulations, was partaking of a hearty meal. He held a joint of meat in one hand and a bowl in the other. He hailed Owen, shaking his head and saying, "I like this not, no, no, not at all. What think you of it, Lord Christ Priest?"

"Oh, give the poor man some rest!" Sybilla said tartly, seating Owen on a pile of soft skins near the fire.

Alshan rose from his place near the still-chomping Enar and came to bend over Owen.

Owen simply sat staring into the flames, conscious now that his long fight was over, that he rested safely among friends, and that he was utterly exhausted, footsore, and weary to the bone.

Alshan and Sybilla held a soft-voiced consultation about his wounds. Osric's lead-tipped whip had scored his back deeply. Parts of his scalp still had raw gashes from Reynald's blows, and his hands were swollen, the back of one laid open by his own clawing nails as he sought blood to loosen the knots of the cage.

"He bathed in the sea?" Alshan asked Sybilla as he examined Owen's back.

"Yes," she answered, raising his hands to look at the damage done there.

Owen accepted their ministrations numbly, grateful for the warmth of the fire. The heat from the small glowing pile of oak knots, with the bright flames leaping in transparent blue and gold above them, seemed to soak through his flesh, wrapping itself around his very bones, driving out the chill of the ocean and the rain. Two tears formed in his eyes and trickled down his cheeks because he had not known before how beautiful and kindly a thing fire was.

Enar glanced at him, saw the tears, then looked quickly away.

Alshan straightened up. "He's healing already."

Sybilla nodded. "I see no reason to do anything to his hurts. A few days' rest and he'll be as strong as before." She lifted a linen shirt from a pile of gear near the wall, raised Owen's arms and slipped it over his head. The shirt was old and ragged, but it had the fine fresh smell of washed, sunbleached cloth. His breeches and leggings steamed, drying in the heat of the fire.

Ilo put a bowl of broth and some bread in Owen's hands and Sybilla cautioned, "Go slowly. Your stomach has been empty for a long time."

Owen nodded, dipped the bread into the broth. It had an odd taste, coarse, bitter, and sweet at the same time.

"Acorn flour, hazel nuts, and honey," Sybilla explained with a smile.

It fell to pieces in the broth. He drank the mixture. Sybilla ladled more of the contents of the pot into the bowl, this time some of the stew. It was rabbit, wild onion, and dark greens. Delicious. Owen drank, ate the meat and vegetables

with his fingers, and cleaned the bowl with the bread. So
good, he thought, no, more than good! As it entered his
stomach, it seemed to run at once into his veins, filling his
body with life.

Owen still felt that same lightheaded sense of clarity, of
quiet peace, that had come upon him when he had awakened
on the horse and realized they were approaching the sea.

He felt the place. It was oddly empty. "They are gone," he
said, "leaving only a few moldering tokens behind." He was
at once contradicted, a presence brushed his mind, then ignored him as though beneath notice. "Well," Owen qualified
his statement, "most are gone."

Enar stopped chewing. "Most of what?"

"How do you know they are still here?" Alshan asked,
smiling a little and fingering the stoat skull at his neck, as
he stared at Owen over the fire.

Owen frowned and searched his memory. "I have always
known when a place is empty."

Ilo looked at Alshan. "Maybe it was not a foolish dream.
He can free his heart and his mind."

Owen looked around at the high-domed roof above, only
faintly illuminated by the leaping flames of the fire, and
down the passage at Alshan's back. Past the lintel and jamb
lay only darkness. "Where are they?" he asked.

Alshan gestured at the darkness behind him.

Owen stood. A strange suspension of thought took place.
His body seemed to move of its own volition and he walked
into that darkness. The rest, including Enar, scrambled to
their feet and followed him, torches glimmering on the wet
stone of the walls, footsteps echoing strangely, the sound of
the few feet making that pilgrimage were multiplied into
many.

This passage was narrower than the first and more dangerous. Only a few inches separated Owen's shoulders from the
stone of the walls, and here earth was sliding, leaking in past
the heavy slabs and muddying the floor. At the end of the
passage, a big fall of earth from the roof nearly blocked off
the last chamber from the rest. But it was secure. A cyst of
roughly dressed granite, a box. One of the walls had a slit
carved into it, a slit that looked out on daylight and a curtain
of falling rain.

Alshan spoke softly from behind Owen. "The midsummer sun and only the midsummer sun shines on his face."

"He" lay in the center of the chamber, resting on his side, knees slightly flexed as though sleeping. The couch he'd been placed on must have been more sturdy than those others Owen had seen because it had outlasted the years. A bed of planks with carrying poles at both ends, and held up by four stubs of legs. He faced away from Owen. The black hollows of the eyes looked out through the slit in the wall at the rain.

"So long," Owen whispered, "so long you have lain here, watching the seasons come and go. Through all the years of sunshine, heat, and cold, of morning fog rolling in from the ocean, only to burn away in the sun. Through long nights when the armies of stars make their tireless march across the heavens, and through the days of how many lives of men. Always hearing in the distance the unchanging, eternal sound of the sea. Is it all the same to you, all one?"

"I beg you," Enar said from somewhere behind Owen, "don't ask him ... things. He may answer."

His wealth lay piled about him, paltry by the standards of Owen's world. A few swords, some brooches, scraps of leather armor decorated with bronze, lay at his feet. A funeral feast was spread beside the bier—cups, bowls, platters with the long-dried remnants of food in them.

Alshan pointed to the floor. "They chose to follow him."

At least a half dozen skeletons lay scattered around his body, a cup near each hand. One rested, stretched out, head pillowed on the bones of his upper arm. Another curled on his side. It did look like choice. They'd emptied their cups and lay down beside him.

Owen took his sword from Enar and stepped over the fall of rock into the chamber, being careful as he did to disturb none of the sleepers, as Sybilla called them, and as he, too, thought of them now. He walked around the bier to the side near the faint shaft of light from the opening in the wall, and looked into the eye holes of the skull. The skeleton held a sword in his hand, the bones of his fingers curved around the hilt.

"We are kin," Owen said, "I live as you did, and will die the same." Owen raised his own sword point up and kissed the handguard in salute. "I thank you for shelter from the rain and would make you a gift, but my enemies left me nothing."

"An offering," Alshan said, his voice soft, but filled with chagrin, "but why do we need to be told?" He spoke and a moment later Ilo clambered over the rock fall and put the wineskin in Owen's hand.

Owen reached down and filled the cup nearest the face of the skull. As he drew close to it he realized that it was of pure gold, untarnished by time, with a very simple design, but one completely strange to him, fluted, tapering upward, wider at the mouth than at the base.

For a fleeting instant Owen was surprised at himself, at his own feeling. The beautiful cup was there for the taking and it represented immeasurable wealth. He was alone, poor, stripped of everything he owned and might never be able to regain his former position in the world. Yet he could not have disturbed the dignity of what lay before him. No, not even to save his own life.

He felt grief and a strange pride well up from the deepest part of his being. "No," he said, speaking into the empty eyes before him, "my enemies have not taken everything; they left me my sword and my honor. My sword I recaptured, my honor they could not touch."

The wood of the bier was old and rotten, that might explain it. But for whatever reason, one of the legs near the foot chose that moment to crumble. It shifted and settled a little, but only a little, because the legs were short and the frame almost flush with the ground. But something slid from among the armor and fell with a clatter to the floor.

Enar and most of the forest people gasped and pushed back from the door, taking the torches with them. Alshan and Owen stood their ground, alone in the dim light from the opening in the wall, alone with the dead.

Alshan said quietly, "He is not to be outdone in generosity." The thing was a mass of chain, glimmering faintly in the uncertain light. Alshan reached down and picked it up. The links resolved themselves into a sword belt, baldric and sheath attached.

Owen pushed his own sword blade into the sheath, and

though it seemed made for a longer, wider-bladed weapon, the sword fit well enough.

Alshan handed the belt to Owen. He slung it over his shoulder. "Would it be right to take it?" he asked.

"We are all one," Alshan said quietly. "You will bear it to the same destiny that was his. It will lie beside your bones."

The presence was an unchanging certainty in the tiny stone room, the crackle of the torches, the seething hiss of the rain through the opening in the wall, the only sound.

Owen bowed his head. "I cherish the gift and thank the giver," he said.

Ilo returned with bread, meat, and more wine in her hands.

Owen filled the plates and bowls with food. "Who was he?" he whispered to Alshan. "What did he do that they honored him so?"

"His name is not even a memory," Alshan answered, "and they that honored him lie among the others in this place. But we are his sons."

"His sons?" Owen asked, as he stepped out of the stone crypt and crowded in among the forest people in the doorway.

"His people looked long at the heavens and were the first to understand the changes in the sky that make the seasons. They followed those beacons set by the gods that guide us in our journeys. They understood that in an eternal consistency, gods keep faith with men. That's why his people set the midsummer sun to watch over him, because they could, because they knew how."

"He needs no name then," Owen said. "His monument is in the ordering of our days, our assurance of the sun and stars."

"Yes," Alshan said simply, then turned, lowering his torch, and began to walk away. The rest followed.

Owen looked back into the chamber, into the faint light that suffused it, turning blue with the shadow of oncoming night. The skeletons were only shapes clustered together in the gloom. He felt a chill of awe, of reverence creep slowly over his flesh, a sense of timelessness on holy ground.

His sons. I am his son, Owen thought. He made me heir to his knowledge. We are all the children of passion, desires that dim the storm of the flesh to sparks, fragile as the last embers of a dying fire. Enduring, unending passions of the mind and the will that outlasts death and time, remaining young as morning, forever. The dream to create, the mind to think, the heart to give. And when the long spiral of the years those bones had marked and numbered at last uncoiled to its final ending, Owen wondered, would those gods of certainty who taught them to number the days keep their covenant and the bones be clothed in flesh, to rise in the first light of some unimaginable daybreak to stride out and walk the earth again?

Chapter
36

GODWIN awakened before daylight. The house was freezing. With a muffled sigh he rolled over in the bed and tried to withdraw into the warm cocoon of darkness. But his bladder was full, his stomach empty, and his mouth tasted as if it had been invaded by mold. The tip of his nose stung from the room's chill.

Massaging the tip of his nose gently with his thumb and forefinger, he sat up on the side of the bed. His nose began to run. "Shit," he said.

As his feet hit the floor, his ankles cracked and popped, sending brief, dull shafts of pain up his legs. His calves throbbed in return. The chill quickly invaded the ragged woolen tunic he wore as a nightshirt. "Jesus Christ," he muttered as he shambled over to the pot to relieve the pressure in his bladder.

A few yet live coals set in a brazier in the corner glowed up at him malevolently. He swung his stream away from the pot and pissed into them, and was immediately rewarded by a hiss and a stink. Then at once he regretted the ill-tempered gesture when he realized he'd managed to extinguish the only light in the room.

He felt his way back to the bed, managing to stub his toe only once in the process, and found a candle. The coals still had enough life left to stimulate the wick. He set the holder by the bed, shivering as he began to shed the warmth of sleep.

He thought with revulsion of donning the clothes he'd worn yesterday, stiff with sweat, blood, and if the truth be known . . . "Why do a man's bowels and bladder always pick times like that to . . ." he muttered. "Jesus! For a minute I thought the son of a bitch had me. But I'll bet he didn't even see me coming," he said in self-satisfied congratulations, then shivered violently again, thinking that the few clean things he had left were shabby beyond belief. But worn or not ... He dressed quickly and wrapped himself in a heavy woolen mantle.

Christ, he was growing old. Even through all the layers of clothing he still felt the penetrating chill, and thought with longing of the kitchen fire.

A small linen-wrapped packet, trapped by the folds of the mantle, fell with a plop to the floor at his feet. He picked it up to toss it back into the clothes chest, then paused and thought of Rosamund. He'd carried the damned thing for years. Perhaps now was the time to be rid of it.

It was the one thing Richilda had forgot when she left him. An oversight certainly, he reflected cynically. She'd carefully gathered up all her other possessions, including those he'd given her. He'd escorted her to the bishop's house with a string of sumpter mules. In that house, God knows, she'd managed to strip him of everything else he had. Playing the wronged woman with consummate skill, she'd taken honor, reputation, family, and even self-respect. Leaving him despised by others, and hating himself for being such a fool as to love her. Love her too much to kill her, and avenge himself for such a monstrous lie.

Gestric had suggested he do just that, kill her.

"It's beneath me," he'd answered, "to avenge myself on a woman," and tasted the lie in the words even as he'd spoken them. Love doesn't go away because we want it to, but remains even when it becomes a searing pain, leaving the heart a desert of bitter remorse and grief for a joy, a happiness that once has been and now never could return.

There had been a time when simply to touch this little bit of linen he held now so casually brought every aching moment of that love back. The sense of desolate pain-drenched loss traveled up his arm, enclosing his heart like a set of icy fingers. A time when to look upon what it held was unbearable.

He shook the thing out into his hand and examined it by the light of the candle. A chain of heavy gold spaced with pink roses carved of coral.

"Just the thing for Rosamund"—he smiled a bit unpleasantly—"to go around the little hellion's perfectly white neck." The more the pity he couldn't tell Richilda where it went, to a whore. He'd gotten more from the little whore than he'd ever gotten from Richilda. When he'd asked for Rosamund's help, she'd given it willingly, eagerly, not to mention acting as a decoy for Edgar. The chick was due something, and besides, she might prove useful in the future. God knows, he needed all the help he could get now from anyone.

He took the candle, wondering gloomily if his early rising of late was one of the signs of approaching old age, and went down the stairs into the hall.

Gowen was sprawled in a chair, his feet near the coals of the hearth. He was fully armed, down to his shield propped against the side of the chair. One of Elin's big iron kettles lay half buried in the glowing ashes of the fire.

Godwin asked, "Has anything happened?"

"Much, but nothing of note," Gowen answered with a yawn.

By nothing of note, Godwin knew the big knight meant he hadn't been subjected to assault with intent to kill. Gowen considered all other events of only marginal interest. Still, he had best gather any information the handsome head contained. He'd once nearly been killed because he failed to ask Gowen the right question. "What?"

"Judith left, very angry, saying she had been insulted. She told me this and much else I didn't want to know."

Godwin chuckled under his breath. He could imagine Judith's rapid-fire harangue being hurled against Gowen's stolid disinterest. "Such as?" he asked, easing the kettle out of the fire onto the hearth stones.

"Ingund slapped her, and accused her of stealing the pillow from under her head and all the covers, leaving she and Lady Elin to lie uneasy in the cold. Further, she told me that Ingund called her most foul and insulting names, names she would not repeat and said she had the conscience of a murderer to be so unquiet and contentious a sleeper."

Godwin tried to lift the lid of the kettle and found the metal was almost red hot. He snatched his fingers away with a curse and stuck them in his mouth.

"There was much else she told me, but I can't remember any of it," Gowen said, scratching his head.

"No matter," Godwin said, wrapping the tail of his mantle around the lid of the kettle. He succeeded in getting it off.

"She went home," Gowen said. "I offered her an escort, but she took Rieulf and her own men." He stood up, stretched, yawned, and asked, "Where is Rosamund?"

"Probably with Wolf the Short," Godwin answered, investigating the contents of the kettle.

"It finally got soft," Gowen said, "and very tasty. I had some not an hour ago, but it is not so tasty as the Lady Elin's roast or so soft either."

The chunk of beef that rose like a mountain peak above the broth in the pot was nearly as big as the kettle itself.

"You might try cutting it into small pieces," Godwin suggested acidly, "it cooks more quickly that way."

"I didn't know that," Gowen answered. "What do you think Rosamund would do if I awakened her?"

"It would depend on what she was offered in the next breath," Godwin said, fishing for a piece of meat.

Gowen scratched his chest and smiled. "It's true, she's a most loose and mercenary girl."

Godwin said, "She is in company sympathetic to her inclinations. You offer her every inducement to continue in her present habits."

"It's different for a woman," Gowen complained self-righteously.

Godwin was annoyed. The liquid in the pot scalded his fingers, and the meat kept diving down below the turnips and disappearing. "Why?" he snapped.

"My father said so," Gowen replied.

"Your father had two wives and seven concubines. He set no limits on his own desires," Godwin said, licking his sore fingers and going to the sideboard for ladle and a bowl.

Gowen burped. "That's true, and he must have loved them frequently, for his tokens were all about the house screeching, howling, making puddles on the floor, or in his women pushing out their bellies. He sent me away because I ate so much. He tore his hair and said he couldn't feed the rest. But Rosamund doesn't conceive. Why is that?"

Godwin shot him a dark look. "I think because the widow taught her girls more than how to collect their pay." Then acting on a thoroughly malicious impulse, he asked, "What would you do if she did?"

Gowen looked appalled. "I hadn't thought of that! One of us would have to marry her. The Lord Bishop would demand it. He's a most strict righteous man, keeping only to one woman himself. And Rosamund has done us much service, and couldn't be sent away."

Godwin was hacking at the meat with his knife now, thinking that Gowen's definition of soft was not his.

"You wouldn't make me take her?" Gowen asked, looking horrified.

Godwin stood up, knife in hand, glaring at him with the murderous hostility that early morning frustration rouses in those who don't greet each new day with cheerful optimism.

Gowen stepped back two paces. He wasn't afraid, but Godwin, in a rage, was as dangerous an adversary as he'd ever encountered, and it was best to give him room.

Godwin took a deep breath. He'd learned over the years not to start quarrels in the morning. "No! I would not be so unkind. Now stop thinking about it and go to bed. I command you, I entreat you, and take Rosamund with you, if she's willing, but start no disturbance that will rouse the household. Go!"

Gowen smiled, picked up the shield, twice as big as those carried by ordinary men, and ambled up the stairs.

"No," Godwin whispered to himself, returning to the pot, and considering using his sword on the meat. "No," he snarled under his breath, "I would not be so unkind . . . to the girl."

Finally, he did draw on the roast. He squired it with his sword and lifting it to the table top, he searched for some area tender enough to eat. Eventually he was partially successful and settled down to his usual dismal morning meditations with a half loaf of bread, some watered wine, and the meat floating in a bowl of broth with a few turnips.

Elin appeared on the stairs. Seeing the roast still sitting on the table steaming, with Godwin's sword sticking in it, she gave a horrified gasp. "Good heavens, what's that?"

"It is some part of some animal," Godwin said. "I know

not what part of what animal. Gowen attempted to cook it last night."

"It looks like something Gowen would cook," Elin said, approaching the huge chunk of meat cautiously.

"Ah, yes," Godwin said, "but the problem is that he didn't succeed."

"It's tough?" Elin asked.

"It would defy the teeth and jaws of a wolf," Godwin said.

Elin peered into the kettle. "The turnips are all right."

"They did cook," Godwin nodded, "that I grant, unpeeled, unwashed, but cooked."

Elin strained the broth, removed the sword from the roast, wiping it carefully and placing it near Godwin's hand. Tasting a small piece of the meat, she said, "Beef," then cut it into small pieces, and discarded the turnips.

Ine came out from under the table and looked at them. Godwin gave a start. "What were you doing there?"

"Asleep," Ine explained.

"Do you just sleep anywhere?" Godwin asked.

"Anywhere," Ine said.

Elin sent Ine to fill the wood box, then seasoned the meat with a few things from the cupboard, added a log to the fire, and hung the kettle up to simmer above the flames.

Upstairs Rosamund came out of the knights' room. She swayed as she walked and jingled a bit. Gowen had awakened her but he didn't trouble her for very long, as Gowen firmly believed that the magnificence of his person was such that any woman encountering him must be instantly and totally gratified. He was soon snoring peacefully beside her.

Rosamund sported a brand-new bracelet of twisted silver wire. This, in addition to a pair of dangling earrings, four silver chains, three chokers—two of silver, one of gold— fifteen or so assorted bracelets, and a couple of anklets, accounted for the tinkling noise.

Her face was powdered to a corpselike whiteness, setting off the bright circles of scarlet rouge on both cheeks. This same substance was smeared liberally on and around her lips. All of this was accented by a mixture of lampblack and fat copiously applied to her eyelids, eyebrows, and eye-lashes. Her hair hung in sweaty rat tails around her face.

Anna confronted her, hands on her hips, blocking the hall-way.

Rosamund stopped dead.

"My!" Anna said. "And don't you look the perfect hussy." She pointed to the open door of a room at her side. "Get in here."

Rosamund crouched, and looking for an escape route, glanced back over her shoulder at the closed door to the knights' room.

"Ah," Anna said with a nasty smile, "would you rather be beaten by me or Gowen?"

Rosamund began edging into the room, back against the wall, still crouching, fists clenched, talking rapidly. "I only did what Lady Elin wanted. She'll be angry if you beat me. I made her magic work better. Love makes it stronger. I had them all after me."

Anna nodded. "Like a bitch in heat."

"I had to," Rosamund said desperately. "Suppose they'd gone, then what would we have done? She needed them to fight for her. So I thought if they're happy getting all they want, they won't go. They didn't need to give me presents. I just made them think they did. The count would have killed us all or put me back in the widow's house. I couldn't stand to go back there, not after being free. Please, Anna . . ." Rosamund wailed.

The tall, grim old woman followed her into the room and kicked the door shut behind her.

Rosamund was talking faster and faster now, breathless, trying to find something that would soften the ferocity of Anna's stare. "I'll wash my face, I promise. I'll be good. . . . I'll work hard. . . . I won't . . ." Rosamund's eyes rolled while she tried to think of something she wouldn't do. "I have to sleep with Gowen, but I won't take any more pre-sents. . . ." She moved along the wall, followed by Anna.

She concluded that Anna wouldn't believe this last and decided on bribery. "I'll give you half of any presents I get . . ." Rosamund, fetched up in a corner, realized she could get no farther, gave a low shriek, crouched down, and covered her face with her arms. "Go ahead, beat me. The

widow beat me ... but," she spat defiantly at Anna, "I still
didn't do half the things she told me to do. That's why she
sold me to Gowen so cheap. She told me that ..."
Rosamund peeked out between the upraised arms shielding
her face.

Anna was sitting on the edge of the bed, helpless with
laughter. At length she raised her head and wiped her eyes.
"Yes, I can see why the widow would sell you cheap."

"Oh, please," Rosamund trilled with pure terror, "oh,
please don't tell Lady Elin those things I just said. I didn't
mention what the widow thought of me when I came here.
I was afraid ..."

"Don't worry," Anna said, "I think Elin probably knows
what the widow thought of you. I won't beat you. And
you're right, it would displease Lady Elin if I did. She said
be kind to you. But ... kindness is sometimes ..."

Rosamund was standing up again, a little of her confidence back.

"Here, I have a present for you," Anna said, extending a
box toward her.

Rosamund took it gingerly and opened it at arm's length,
looking as if afraid something unpleasant might jump out at
her. But when she looked inside, her face registered delight.
It was a bone-handled mirror, brush, and comb set, new and
beautifully carved with long sprays of flowers.

A few minutes later, Rosamund arrived in the hall just as
Elin finished putting the meat into the pot. She approached
Elin, head bowed, and tried to curtsy, but she nearly cracked
her head on the sideboard.

Elin caught her and set her on her feet. "My heavens,"
Elin said, "what's gotten into you!"

Rosamund's hair was neatly combed, washed, and braided
into a coronet on top of her head, her face scrubbed clean
and shining. "Did ... did ..." Rosamund looked as though
she might begin to cry at any moment, tears swimming in
the blue eyes. "Did you tell Anna to play that mean trick on
me?"

"What mean trick? No," Elin said kindly, "I haven't ordered any mean tricks lately. What happened?"

Rosamund explained.

Elin turned away, sucking in on her cheeks.

"I knew it," Rosamund said, looking deeply wounded, "you think it's funny, too."

Elin threw her arms around Rosamund and kissed her. It had been so long since Rosamund had had any real affection from anyone that she stood astonished for a second; then she embraced Elin in return and rested her cheek against her shoulder with a little sigh.

"I suppose it was a mean trick," Elin said, "but, my, you look so nice now, so pretty."

"Do you really think so?" Rosamund said, instantly consoled.

Elin nodded and kissed her on the forehead. "I certainly do. Now go and see if Godwin wants anything else to eat."

Rosamund glanced at him from under her eyelashes. "I don't think he likes me," she said in a low voice to Elin. "When he first saw me, he said I was too short. I can't be much taller, even if I stand on my tiptoes. Then he cursed at me because I burned his bread. Yesterday he played a trick on me that set everyone to laughing. Now he sits there looking like a big wet eagle . . . and he seems in a bad humor."

Elin stifled a smile. Godwin usually did resemble a bird of prey. Sitting at the table, worn black mantle wrapped around his shoulders, eating sops of bread and wine, his resemblance to a hawk caught out in a rainstorm and feeling particularly vile tempered because his feathers weren't completely dry was uncanny.

"Well," Elin said, "I don't think he'd object if you bring him another cup of wine."

Rosamund, carrying the wine pitcher, sidled carefully around the table toward Godwin. Determined to create the best impression possible, she decided to offer him the wine and curtsy on tiptoe. A mistake. She hadn't mastered the art flat-footed. He didn't realize she was there until he saw the wine jug flying at his face and Rosamund going down, looking for all the world as if she were likely to fracture her skull on the stones of the floor.

With one arm he fended off the wine jug, with the other he caught Rosamund just before her head hit the tiles. The wine jug upended in the air, and a second later the entire contents were soaking into his mantle.

He opened his mouth to give vent to a roar of fury, then

choked it off because Rosamund's face was so pale it terrified him. He thought she had hit her head. In a moment, he had her sitting on the bench, and was exploring the back of her skull with what she realized were surprisingly gentle and competent fingers.

Rosamund's mouth opened in a wide "O" even as she was trying to decide whether to screech, wail, or just burst into tears.

Godwin, who'd ascertained she wasn't hurt, said in a terrible voice, "Don't do that! Not at this hour of the morning. Don't!"

Rosamund didn't.

"Now," he asked, "not that it's a matter of any great importance, but what the hell were you trying to do?"

"Wine," Rosamund gasped.

"I know!" Godwin said, with a dreadful smile. "I'm wearing it."

Rosamund's chin began to quiver.

"Don't do that either," Godwin said in a voice of iron. "Explain."

Rosamund gabbled, "Lady Elin said give you some wine, Anna said I should curtsy, she's teaching me how, she says it shows respect, you said I was short . . . and I wanted to please you."

Godwin shook his head. "I didn't quite follow that."

"I curtsied on tiptoe so I'd be taller."

Godwin made a strangled sound.

Rosamund's chin began to quiver again.

Godwin said, "Don't—you—dare! Pick up the wine pitcher." He pointed to where it lay on its side in the center of the table. "And go fill it. Then bring it back and pour me another cup of wine."

Rosamund jumped up.

"No," Godwin said, "slowly, calmly."

Rosamund walked around the table, showing only a slight stiffness as she consciously controlled her movements.

Elin stood beside Godwin. She'd rushed over when Rosamund fell. "Godwin," she said, "you're dripping wet."

He shook his head. "It doesn't matter. She's trying hard and must regain her confidence." Rosamund returned, carrying the pitcher carefully in front of her. "Slowly," Godwin said, "we have the whole day before us."

Slowly Rosamund filled his cup.

"Now"—he spoke firmly, taking her free hand—"you may curtsy." Then he steadied her as she dropped into a graceful, if slightly unsteady, bow. "Very nice, very ladylike, very prettily done. I thank you for the wine."

Rosamund colored at the compliment, and hung her head in embarrassment.

Godwin dropped the necklace of gold over her head.

"Oh! For me? But why? You never want me to do anything for you. I thought you and Edgar were friends ..."

"Rosamund," Elin said sharply.

Rosamund clapped her hand over her mouth and shot an alarmed glance at Elin.

"It's all right," Godwin said, "Edgar and I are friends, but it isn't that kind of friendship. No, you protected the house last night as I asked you to."

Rosamund fingered the gold chain with innocent delight. It seemed to her the prettiest thing she'd ever seen. The presents the knights gave her had a certain bullion value, but this finely crafted ornament wasn't the sort of thing she'd ever hoped to own. A pretty trinket that might adorn the neck of a highborn lady. "But I don't deserve anything," she said. "No one tried to break in."

"That doesn't matter," Godwin said quietly, "you did as I asked and would have given me ample warning if they had."

Quickly Rosamund began pushing the chain down the neck of her dress.

"Rosamund," Godwin asked, "why hide it?"

"Oh," she said, "so Anna won't see. She made me take off my other things, she said I clanked when I walked. I don't want her to see this because she'll make me take it off and I don't want to take it off. I want to wear it always ..."

"Rosamund?" Anna called from the stairs. "Stop bothering the Lord Godwin with your chatter. Go make a pot of gruel. Elfwine needs something to eat and so do I."

Rosamund gave a start and ran to the fireplace.

Elin began unwinding the wet mantle from around Godwin's shoulders.

"How old is she?" Godwin asked, looking at Rosamund bustling around the fireplace.

"Of years," Elin answered, "sixteen."

"Sixteen," Godwin sighed. "How long was she in the widow's house?"

"Since she was twelve," Elin answered grimly. "Sold to her by a slaver docked on the river, and where she came from no one knows, except that it was far away, since she spoke not one word of our language when the widow bought her or so Judith tells me."

"She is a child," Godwin said, with a sad shake of his head. Then in a still lower voice he asked, "How is it with you, Elin?"

Elin paused. She was spreading Godwin's mantle on the table, checking the extent of the wine stain. She answered softly, eyes downcast. "I feel ... bruised. Please, I don't want to talk about it now."

Suddenly, the door burst open and Judith entered with a scream and fell to her knees.

"Judith ..." Godwin said in a strangled voice.

"Reynald is dead ..."

A gasp flowed through the room.

"And," she said, her voice dropping, "the manner of his taking off was most horrible."

Elin spun around and covered her face with her hands. Anna hurried and embraced her. "Oh, God," Elin whispered, "Oh, God, no!"

Judith pushed open both doors to the hall. A crowd stood outside surrounding a litter with someone on it. Two of Judith's men picked up the litter, carried it up the steps, and set it down in the open doorway.

Light poured in from the square outside and Godwin saw more than he wanted of the figure on the stretcher.

She had been a young girl, but now the face was purple and swollen to twice its normal size, both eyes closed by the swelling. Her mouth was bloody and red froth oozed out around the battered lips and broken teeth.

Elin turned away from Anna and toward the door, her face ashen. "Don't," Godwin said, resting a hand on Elin's arm. "Stay here."

More and more people were pushing into the room from

the square. Among them were Routrude, Helvese, Gynnor, and other women Elin didn't recognize. Arn the tavern keeper and his patrons and even the widow and her women hovered on the outer fringes of the crowd, accompanied by most of the merchants and shopkeepers.

Gynnor left her place by the side of the litter and walked toward Elin. When she reached her, she kissed her on the cheek, then embraced her quickly, saying, "My friend," then turned and stood beside her.

No one spoke, the only sound was the faint whisper of the breeze blowing through the open door, and the distant cry of the town's unending commerce.

Elin looked at the people and felt every eye upon her, all accusing her of this that lay before her. She pulled away from Godwin and Anna and stood alone. Something in her heart rose and took a mighty leap over the pain and guilt in her breast, and she began to walk forward on legs that didn't feel as though they belonged to her, toward the shattered body by the door.

Godwin followed, inwardly cursing Judith's flair for the dramatic. Elin knelt on one side of the litter, Godwin on the other. Godwin examined the injuries with a professional eye. In spite of Elin's skill, he had more experience with those seriously wounded than anyone she'd ever known. He ignored the battered face and lifted the blanket that covered the girl's body, ran his fingers down her ribs on both sides. Her belly was flat and not swollen.

"Can you speak?" he asked.

The girl made a little whimpering sound and more blood poured from the side of her mouth. "Yes, but I'm blind." It was a barely intelligible cry of distress.

"No," he said gently, "you are not blind. When the swelling in your face goes down, you'll be able to see again." He looked over at Elin. Her lips were white and her hands shaking. Then rising to his feet, he nailed Judith with a heavy-lidded glare and said in a voice that crackled with fury, "You had no need to do this!" Then he called Ingund, who pushed her way through the crowd. "Take her upstairs and put her to bed," he said. He made a sign to the men. They picked up the litter and followed Ingund.

Elin, still on her knees, head bowed, forehead resting on her clasped hands, asked, "Will she live?" her voice shaking.

Godwin took her by the elbows and raised her to her feet, saying, "Yes, it's not as bad as it looks."

Judith led an old woman out of the crowd and presented her to Godwin. "This is Begga, daughter of Fodard."

The woman glanced nervously at Judith, then quickly at Godwin. What she saw didn't seem to reassure her, since her gaze dropped to the floor and she tried to shrink back among the people packed at the door. But Judith's arm was around her shoulders and she held her, whispering comforting words in her ear.

Godwin inspected the woman closely and realized she gave the impression of greater age than was actually the case. She was toil-worn, long hair shot with gray, with a weatherbeaten face and callused, roughened hands that protruded from the sleeves of the single woolen garment she wore. Twisting those hands together, the woman eyed him fearfully, as she listened to Judith's whispered flow of reassurance.

Godwin wished he could sit the poor creature down alone, give her some food and wine, and have a quiet conversation. He would then be able to extract all the information he needed and maybe even send her back suitably rewarded to gather more. He'd often won battles on the strength of knowledge given to him by similar humble folk whose lives were so callously trampled and destroyed by the great and powerful.

He spoke very gently and carefully to Begga. "Tell us how this came to be. No one here will harm you. I give you my personal assurance of that."

"They say she killed him," Begga spoke, staring wildly around at the crowd. "Her own kinsmen turned from her and cast her out. I couldn't, she is my sister's child, and I have none living of my own. My man and I fled with her to the woods—" She broke off, sobbing and clinging to Judith.

Judith then gave Godwin cause to admire her again, for it was she who drew from the frightened, half-hysterical woman a coherent narrative of the events leading to Reynald's death, and what happened afterward, of a long night when the girl, crippled and very ill from the beating, dragged herself from house to house seeking shelter from the storm, but none would allow her to lie even on the straw in a barn among the animals.

"They begrudged the poor child even the shelter offered freely to the beasts of the field," Judith said in outrage.

Begga said, "She came to me. Oh, how could I turn her away? She grew up at my knee, in place of those little ones I lost. I love her." Begga wiped the tears from her cheeks with swollen-knuckled hands, twisted by a lifetime of labor, and continued. "She dragged herself to my door. Not for my life's sake or my very soul's sake could I refuse her. My man and I took her in. He did so for love of me. We tended her, hoping that no more evil would come to us." The woman's shoulders slumped, and she stood staring at the floor, arms hanging at her sides as if in final defeat. "But," she continued, "Bertrand ran mad. He vowed to kill her as soon as she was found."

"Bertrand is not loved," Judith said grimly, "and they were warned."

"We fled to the woods," Begga continued, "and when we could travel no farther, I saw a fisherman on the river and hailed him. He brought us to Judith." Begga turned quickly in a circle, staring at the mass of people surrounding her. "But," she said, "that is not the worst."

She stood mute, seemingly afraid to go on, then turned helplessly to Judith, and it was she who spoke. "Reynald's people believe Elspeth has gone to Hakon."

"The devil," Godwin said, slamming his fist into his palm with a crack. "Judith, are you sure?"

She nodded.

"You are not the bearer of good tidings, woman," Godwin said to Begga, "but you have nothing to fear from me. Speak out and tell us what you know."

"We are Nithard's people," she said. "His kinswoman, Elspeth, rode to his manor before dawn and Hakon, with a large part of his men, came there just after sunup. If Elspeth didn't go to him of her own will, Nithard delivered her into his hands."

Godwin had to raise his arms to quell the babble of voices, curses from the men, some of them aimed at him, for allowing this to happen, and the loud outcries of the women, who now began beating their breasts and wailing in earnest.

The crowd was larger now, spreading out around the steps, overflowing to the porch of the cathedral, out in front of the tavern and under the arcade that held the shops. More and more latecomers arrived every moment, swelling the throng. Godwin looked at their faces and saw fear, hatred, bitterness, anger, and here and there, the terrible vacant exhaustion of despair.

He was unhappily conscious of what they saw: a thin middle-aged man. The merciless light of morning picked out the deep, bitter lines in his face, the thinning hair, threaded with gray, clad in a borrowed dalmatic, and that not new. The velvet worn to threads in places, with ratty gaps in the fur trim at the hem and sleeves. *Here I stand, the magnificent commander of six knights. What hope have I to offer them?* he thought.

He felt a hand on his arm, looked down, and saw Elin at his side. She stared up at him, her blue eyes vivid as gemstones in the sunlight. "Rally them!" she said in a low urgent voice. "They need you!"

Routrude pushed her way through the milling mass of humanity around the steps, pointed at Elin and screamed accusingly, "See, this is what comes of curses. She has destroyed one who stood between us and our enemies. Now black misfortune is upon us. Ahaeeeiii!" she screeched.

"Oh, shut your mouth, you stupid blabber-mouthed old beldam!"

Godwin looked around in surprise and realized the speaker was Begga. Routrude stopped screaming.

"Reynald was never your friend," Begga continued. She stepped forward, fists clenched at her sides, glaring down at Routrude. Then she fell to her knees before the crowd, extending her arms in a plea for mercy. "Hakon, the raider chief, came often to Nithard's house to meet with Reynald. I served them at table and worked in the kitchen. I heard them plot to deliver the city to the Northmen." Begga shuddered violently, the tears flowing from her eyes a glistening sheen on her wrinkled cheeks. "I was afraid," she moaned. "Though I have kin here and friends, I feared to speak. I was afraid to warn them. Reynald said he would have the wagging tongue from any mouth that betrayed his secrets. He's had men hanged or their tongues torn out for less. I dared

not warn anyone of his evil plotting. Have pity on me. I am
but a weak woman and not young. Oh, have pity." She collapsed in a sobbing heap on the stones.

Godwin did pity her. He gathered up the fragile old body
and thrust her into Judith's arms, saying quickly, "Don't torment yourself so, mother. No one expected you to defy
Reynald. Judith, take her away, get some food into her belly,
and let her rest."

Gunter roared at the crowd, "Are there any here who still
doubt Reynald's guilt?"

The crowd cursed Reynald fervently, loudly, and at length.

"The traitor had long commerce with the men of the
camp," Gunter shouted. "It's well he's dead."

The assenting shout from the mob was deafening.
"Aheeiieee," Routrude screamed, "the Northmen are upon
us."

Other women in the crowd took up her cry, wailing and
raising their arms to heaven. Elfwine outdid them all. Reel-
ing against Anna, she seemed to Godwin's fascinated eye to
have more than two arms, all plucking destructively at some
part of her anatomy. Elfwine had a wonderful pair of lungs,
Godwin thought in annoyance, not to mention immense en-
durance.

The crowd at the steps now nearly filled the square.
Women ran up and down screeching, distracted with grief.
Men yelled, cursed, and gesticulated at each other as latecomers demanded and got a full account of the previous
events from those already present.

In the doorway, Anna supported Elfwine's slumped body
by the armpits while the girl, half kneeling, half standing,
gave a performance worthy—at least to Godwin's jaundiced
eye—of Hecuba mourning the fall of Troy.

Routrude, still on the steps, competed with Elfwine for the
attention of the crowd with a graphic and, Godwin thought,
entirely too lovingly detailed depiction of the fate of women
in a captured city at the hands of the conquerors. She led off
with gang rape, and proceeded from there to assault, mutila-
tion, slavery, and murder, punctuating each description with
an ear-splitting shriek.

Rosamund, standing wide-eyed next to Elfwine, held the
baby, and found the energy for a full-throated yowl.

"Do that again," Anna snapped at her, "and I'll slap you! Someone has to hold the baby."

The infant in Rosamund's arms slumbered peacefully, sucking on one tiny fist. Godwin envied him.

"Rally them?" Godwin said under his breath to Elin, standing beside him. "What need have I to rally them? The women are driving them into a frenzy."

Elfwine, completely carried away, rent her garments a bit too enthusiastically, ripping her gown open from neck to waist. Obviously an experienced hysteric, she contrived to show enough skin to get the attention of every man in the crowd, while preserving her modesty by holding the two sides of the torn dress together. She then gave vent to a sound that reminded Godwin of nothing he'd ever heard uttered by any living thing, a sound supremely horrible and awe-inspiringly loud. Then she keened, "The Northmen are upon us. To the walls! To the walls!"

Other voices in the crowd took up her cry, shouting exuberantly, "To the walls! To the walls!"

Godwin's head throbbed, and his stomach seemed to be trying with persistent and vicious illogic to digest itself. "Shit," he whispered, "and all this before breakfast."

"To the walls!" the mob before him roared in one voice.

Godwin's sword cleared the sheath and glittered above the heads of the gathering at the steps. "Enough!" His voice was a thunderclap.

Complete silence fell.

"I see," he shouted, "that Chantalon has no lack of valiant defenders."

He was answered by a cheer. Godwin smiled benignly.

Elin, seeing the smile, whispered, "Oh, dear."

"However," he continued, "if you run to the walls now, the cows being driven to market will be very surprised to see you, for the Northmen are still some distance away."

A faint titter of embarrassed laughter swept the throng.

"Nevertheless, I'm pleased you answered this material call to arms"—he flourished the sword, which glittered wickedly in the sunlight—"and assembled here ready to face the foe unflinchingly, with high hearts and courageous mien, because," he shouted with vengeful delight, "I have work for everyone!"

Chapter

37

OWEN'S dreams in the tomb were strange images that seemed to flit across his consciousness like shadows, each leaving only a tantalizing trace of memory behind.

It seemed to him he drifted across stormy seas in a boat, no larger than a big coracle. The waves glittering, shifting green mountains around him. At other times he stood and looked down into open river valleys where the grass was long and green and the sunlight transfigured the landscape with its golden glow. Virgin lands opening before him with rich black soil below the lush grass. Earth that had never known the touch of a plow.

His heart yearned toward them, those valleys mantled in forests of thick-trunked trees whose branches were so tightly meshed the sky itself seemed an inlay of lapis fragments and the sun a distant thousand-rayed star.

He blessed the earth in those valleys, loving it and it alone, with all his heart in yielding innocence. Pouring the sweat of his brow into it and sometimes the warm crimson rush of his blood. For the shadows that surrounded him demanded incomprehensible rites lest they call back the threnody of such beauty and he be bereft.

At other times he fought. Whether his struggles ended in victory or defeat he couldn't say, not even knowing if victory or defeat existed in this strange world, because he wandered in a mist, or strode along by night toward unguessable encounters while the pale moon herself was only a specter concealed among glowing clouds.

Once, for an instant, he seemed to stand in bright sunlight gazing at a scarlet and gold host arrayed before him. His valley, no longer green, was blackened by the fires of a conquest that regarded neither man nor nature as sacred. In the distance his forest burned. The smoke stung his eyes, the grit of ashes was in his mouth, grief was a dagger of ice through his heart.

But the moment was only a moment and it passed. He drifted on, tumbled and tossed by the seas of time until he plumbed the deep wells of sleep. There, drowned in the profound cool enclaves of silence, his spirit renewed itself.

He woke looking up into Alshan's face, and a voice that seemed to come from within him, but was not his own, said, "I am only a man."

"Yes," Alshan answered, seeming unsurprised, then added, "and you like all men are more than one thing."

"Riddles, riddles," Enar said as he stamped out the fire.

Alshan held a torch, the only light in the huge dim room.

"Lord Christ Priest," Enar complained, "you have a penchant for finding friends who speak in riddles."

"No riddle that," Alshan said. "It has an easy answer."

"I must have been dreaming," Owen said. "The voice that spoke didn't seem to come from me."

"Perhaps. Perhaps not," Alshan said.

"Lord Christ Priest," Enar said insistently, "are you able to travel?"

Owen got to his feet slowly, ignoring the protests of his bones and muscles. He found he felt almost unaccountably strong and refreshed. "Yes," he said, "I think I can if it's necessary."

"It is," Alshan replied. "Tomorrow the Vikings will be at your gates."

Alshan took Owen on his own road through the forest. At first Owen thought it a plunge into trackless wilderness. It took him some time to realize he was on a trail. An ancient path marked by dense woodland groves, springs that bubbled into clear pools, and, here and there, standing stones.

It seemed to Owen an oddly timeless journey. The forest was so thick he could barely make out the movement of the sun across the sky, and there were so many twists, turns, and switchbacks that Owen wondered at times if they were getting anywhere.

They traveled through mountainous country filled with

steep, thickly forested slopes, high cliffs, and deep gorges. Yet, every time some seemingly impenetrable obstacle presented itself, Alshan knew a way across, around, or sometimes through it. Twice they scrambled into caves, running along by torchlight until they reached the other side.

Despite the fact that the sun was half-hidden, Owen estimated it was near noon when they stopped to rest for the first time.

"We are safe here," Alshan said, as the group paused beside a spring that gushed from a limestone crack in the rockface of a deep valley. Its water poured like a fan of fine lace over a stepped rock formation into a deep pool at the base, then flowed on to join the stream that hurried, bubbling and gurgling, over a stony bed toward the river.

Sybilla walked toward the pool at the base of the falls and poured a little wine into the water. For a brief second it seemed to Owen the rush of water from above seemed to intensify as if in a cry of welcome. Then they all advanced to the pool, drank, and washed their faces. Sybilla sat down on the grass and shared the bread, cheese, and wine among them.

Owen was restless and afraid for the city. He ate quickly and was up on his feet again in a few moments. He strolled away into the forest. He had only walked a few rods from the spring when he was struck by a sudden sense of familiarity.

He knew no axe had ever touched these trees. They were a mixture of oak and pine, towering giants among their kind with trunks so thick the arms of two or even three men could not have spanned them. The forest floor was a mass of deadfalls, leaf litter, and broken limbs all covered by a carpet of living green moss glowing with an emerald beauty in the diffused, dappled light that filtered down from above.

"All is silence here," he whispered, "but it is not empty."

"No," another voice answered.

Owen turned his head slightly and realized Alshan stood at his side. The small, brown-clad man seemed so much a part of the forest and the earth itself, he hadn't noticed him before.

Owen stepped deeper into the stillness and silence around him. "I remember this place," he said. "I walked here with the God. Elin sent him to me in the cage. She's a strong woman. She reached out her hands into the darkness of my despair and would not let me die."

Alshan nodded. "Stronger than you think. She has killed Reynald."

"What?" Owen's voice broke the silence like the snapping of a twig. He turned toward Alshan. "How could she? Elin is but a woman, he a strong man!"

Alshan crouched down on his heels near a log twined with ferns. "She cursed him. I helped her."

"You helped her!" Owen shouted, his face scarlet with anger.

"Yes," Alshan said. He met Owen's eyes, his stare flat black and uncompromising. "I put the token, a serpent's head, into his cup and announced his doom to him in his hall. He was taken with the madness that follows such an affliction. He set fire to his bedding and so perished."

"He was my friend!" Owen shouted, his voice echoing among the trees.

Alshan's gaze still held his. "Reynald was no one's friend. His loyalty was only to the red gold at his feet that night. I know. Ilo was high in the tree when he sold you. But for your own cunning, and Viking greed, you would now be a blind slave chained in the hold of a ship, being carried off to a lifetime of servitude."

Owen shivered. He'd almost managed to forget the horrible moment when Osric had placed the sword in the fire. Above all things he feared darkness. Reynald had almost condemned him to a lifetime of unendurable pain.

"Had she not destroyed Reynald," Alshan continued, "he would have used his men to help the count defeat the Lord Godwin. As it is, Godwin won and Count Anton also is dead."

"The count and Reynald, too?" Owen gasped.

"They fought in the church," Alshan explained. "I have eyes and ears in the town. The Lady Elin and her champion won."

"What means did Elin use to get Godwin to stay?" Owen asked, torn by both fury and jealousy.

"I cannot say," Alshan answered. "It may be she promised Godwin Reynald's life. It may be she promised him something else, but whatever she said, your chair sits empty at the head of the table and she sleeps alone."

Owen's left hand fell to his sword and tightened on the hilt. "How quickly can we get to the city?"

"Tomorrow night."

"Not soon enough," Owen replied.

"My lord," Alshan said firmly, "Hakon's men are still out scouring the countryside for you. If you're captured, all your friends' efforts will have been in vain."

"Godwin is old," Owen said, "and Elin, a netted bird. I know because I hold the meshes of the net. Her struggles, each wingbeat only drives her deeper into the trap of her own lechery."

"Lechery, you speak of lechery." Alshan laughed in derisive fury. "As though the fire that burns in her did not sear your flesh also. What is it, young wolf? Do you fear the old gray warrior? A bird for your net, indeed! A woman of my people? Rather say she is a falcon content to rest on your fist for a little time. But to the heavens born, whom you fear will one day fly free."

Owen had to turn away from the contempt he saw in the small man's eyes. He looked out into the mottled light and shadow of the green wilderness. Alshan's words struck at his deepest fears. "I have," he said, "spun a strange alliance of cobweb and shadow between a bishop, an outcast warrior, a witch, and a . . ." He turned back to Alshan. "I don't know what you and your friends are. Now you twit me for wondering if it will hold."

Alshan rose to his feet. "Cobweb and shadow," he murmured. "Perhaps! But even the weakest alliance is secure if all parties keep faith, while the strongest can be broken if the heart of one member is rotten with treachery and greed. My lord, don't let one man's betrayal cause you to doubt those who have proven loyal."

"Still," he said, "she is only a woman."

Alshan gave a sharp snort of laughter. "She has taken the path of defiance as you have. She took it long ago when she fled her family and joined us. This is a sad journey, I think," he said pensively, "but I trust her heart. She will not yield."

Owen stumbled away from Alshan. The sense of presence under the trees was overpowering. He needed the sky, some open space above him. In a few moments he found himself on the rocky bank of the stream and fell to his knees. He looked up.

Serried ranks of trees marched away on either side—all tremendous giants, some of them bending so low they almost touched the water. They formed an arch over the torrent that tumbled and gurgled beneath them. The chill water iced his knees and he felt the smooth, rounded shapes in the streambed press against his flesh.

Owen wondered at his God, the God of the marshes who had sent him on his long journey. The God whose arms, like the sea and this valley, were stretched out to embrace him.

A God who did not care how life began. A love so all-encompassing, it did not fret about who it belonged to, knowing only that it was life, and reached out to all those who struggled upward from the dust toward it. A God to whom all his anxious questions, his terrors, his anxieties were as the flash of a dew-covered grass blade in the sun.

Owen cupped the water in his hands and stared down at the cool transparency between his fingers, knowing that to drink and accept such a God would be the ultimate blasphemy and the most perfect sacrament.

As his lips touched the coolness between his fingers, he said, "I will . . ." and drank.

Chapter
38

GODWIN dozed over his wine. He sat near the fire, aware that even though his feet were warm, his back and shoulders were cold. The chill struck through the threadbare material of his old shirt and tunic.

He knew it was worse than pointless to seek the comfort of his bed upstairs. Once under the covers, his eyes would fly open and he would lie staring at the ceiling, a prey to every possible horrible image his imagination could conjure up. His imagination had plenty of material, grisly material garnered through a lifetime of war, images it used to torment him with fiendish originality and skill. Still, even sitting upright before the fire, when he dozed he dreamed. The worst always came first.

Godwin was resigned to this dream. He'd had it so often before battles, he'd come to expect it, the way the mind expects pain to follow when the knife slips and you see blood dripping from your fingers.

He was always glad when the dream came, and relieved when it was over. As always, he'd dreamed of Paris, of the brief time he'd been a captive. He'd been hit twice in the head. He remembered the excruciating pain-tinged explosions of light when the sword hilt cracked twice into the side of his skull—and the darkness. He realized later that the blood running into his eyes must have blinded him. Then he was falling into the hole to land painfully, his body draped across a pile of rubble.

He'd still been struggling, his fingers and toes scrabbling among dirt and broken stone, when the beam that pinned and protected him landed across his back. He'd screamed. The dirt began falling, wet and cold all around him. The weight of the wood on his back pressed the breath out of his lungs and he was silenced. Silenced, so he could hear the other screams and the horrible, low wheezing rattle of death by suffocation. He'd lain there taking, miraculously, one shallow breath after another, his face in the air pocket created by the beam and the broken body of a man, wondering as he took each breath, if that breath would be his last.

The darkness of sleep pushed him down as the beam had pushed him down, down to confront his survival, a survival so terrible that, by comparison, death seemed a kind of mercy. Except this time his imagination seemed to have added another refinement of cruelty. He couldn't understand why in the world someone could have seen fit to set his feet on fire. He came to full alertness with a jerk and realized that the soles of his hobnailed boots were smoldering.

"Christ!" he shouted and sat upright in the chair. There wasn't a hell of a lot he could do. He held his feet up, trying to keep the tender flesh against the uppers and away from the hot leather of the soles.

Anna was standing near the table. "What in the world?" she asked.

"I almost set my boots on fire," Godwin said. She hurried over and reached for the laces. "No," Godwin said, "they'll cool off in a minute." He held his feet about six inches from the floor, his knees in the air.

"I'll get some water," she said.

Godwin shook his head. "Let me see." He bent a toe down. The leather the toe came in contact with was hot, but not intolerably so. He lowered his feet to the floor with a sigh of relief, keeping them well away from the flames.

"I came to bring you your mantle, the one Rosamund soaked," she said. "When I realized you were asleep, I didn't want to disturb you, but then you began making the strangest noises. Men are a wonder, experts at making themselves miserable. Why don't you go upstairs and get into bed?"

"Why don't you—" Godwin bit off the rest of the reply and stared away from Anna into the flames on the hearth.

"Mind my own business," Anna finished the sentence for him.

"I didn't mean to be rude," Godwin said softly, "but . . . I'd just as soon not get too comfortable tonight."

"Of course," Anna said, lifting the mantle from the table. She settled it around his shoulders, tucking it in between the back of the chair and the arms so he'd be warm. "You've fought too many battles, haven't you?" she said.

"Yes." The word came out as a sigh of infinitely weary regret. He fingered the thick woolen fabric and examined the garment closely by the light of the flames on the hearth. "What did you do to it?" he asked. "It looks almost new again."

"I refreshed the dye," Anna said, "and tacked down the broken threads in the embroidery. It needed a bit of mending, but the cloth is very fine and well woven. The embroidery's done in gold thread, such fine stuff doesn't tarnish." The embroidery she spoke of was a broad border of golden fleur-de-lis edging the mantle.

"I wore it once," Godwin spoke softly, "when I stood before a king. A gift from my father. I was proud of it then."

"You can be proud of it still," Anna said. "A thing of high quality retains its luster even when time and chance have done their worst."

Something in her voice suddenly suggested to Godwin she wasn't speaking only of the mantle. He looked up quickly at her face, at a gentle motherliness that shone amidst the lines and wrinkles of a lifetime.

"Thank you," Godwin said, "now you should get to bed. . . ."

"Oh, I will, and rest as well as the old ever do." She placed a hand on his forehead. "You try to get a nap, too," she said, "and may God chase away all your bad dreams. Captain of the Lilies, sleep well."

He didn't quite realize what she'd said until she was already up the stairs and gone. "Captain of the Lilies?" he muttered and sighed deeply, staring into the mesmerizing glow of the ever-changing flames.

For a time he did sleep and had no dreams, good or bad. He was awakened by noise and a blast of cold air when Elin entered the front door of the hall. Outside, the town was still awake and the tavern doing a thriving business. A steady stream of carts rumbled through the square, bringing people and provisions to the homes of their kinfolk in the city. Elin closed the door on the noise and the cold wind.

"What is the hour?" Godwin asked.

"A little after midnight," Elin answered.

"I hope you didn't go out alone, Elin," Godwin said.

Elin yawned and smiled. "No, Godwin, I took Edgar and Ingund. I've been at Osbert's house with Judith. The woman is utterly unprincipled, a shrew and a scold."

"Invaluable, in other words," Godwin said.

"Oh, absolutely!" Elin answered. "Half the town owes her money, the other half favors. She's finding places for those in the countryside who have no kinfolk they can shelter with. Before dawn she'll have someone tucked into every nook and cranny of the city." Elin walked toward him. "Are you comfortable by the fire?"

"Yes, as comfortable as I'd be anywhere."

She paused beside his chair. "Do you think they'll come tomorrow?"

"Yes," Godwin said. He didn't look up at her. All he could see beside him were the scarlet folds of her mantle and the drape of her gray linen dress. "Elin," Godwin asked, "how strong a hold has Hakon on the minds of his minor chiefs?"

She didn't answer for a second. He saw the folds of cloth at his elbow sway, and wondered if she'd swept past him up the stairs without answering. But answer she did, and with a crisp objectivity he found almost appalling.

"His hold on the minds of his minor chiefs is very strong. He has always been . . . successful. He picks his targets carefully . . . pays his spies well, and always knows exactly what he's facing. He chooses his followers with equal skill. They can all pull their weight but, individually, none is powerful enough to challenge him. Does any of this come as a surprise to you?"

"No." He shook his head. "A man doesn't rise to command an army of freebooters unless he's a competent soldier."

"He's more than that," Elin said. "Hakon is farsighted and very clever. There's policy in what he's doing now. I'm sure he'll throw all his men at our walls, trying to break us. They'll want to be rewarded with gifts of land, and if he spends them freely in destroying us, he achieves supreme power and has many fewer to provide for."

"Elin," Godwin said—he still wouldn't look at her. He

stared at the fire and his fingers played with the sword hilt at his side. "I don't want to ask this but I must . . . the child . . ."

"I see," she said, "you are looking for something, anything you can use against him. I'm sorry, no. The closest I ever came to Hakon was the length of his boot. It seems one morning I'd chosen an inconvenient place to sleep. I'll grant Hakon this, though little more, he doesn't take women by force, but then he doesn't need to. Sometimes I hate my own sex. . . . They . . . they flaunted themselves before him. Why should he bother with a captive who is all claws and teeth?" Elin was silent for a moment. Godwin could hear her ragged breathing. "Never," she continued, "did I yield except to force until I met Owen. I don't sell myself for bread, or gold, or even pleasure."

"Only love?" Godwin asked.

"No!" Elin's voice hissed. "Not even love."

"Why, then?" Godwin asked, his eyes still on the heap of coals on the hearth, the flames dancing far above them now as they turned to white ash.

She replied with a question of her own. She spoke quietly, but there was something in her voice that raised the hackles on Godwin's neck. "Godwin, what do you call someone who is weak, who cannot avenge their kin, or punish their enemies? Say the word, Godwin, say the word and answer me."

"A woman," Godwin said, "a woman. But, Elin, certain conventions protect women."

"No, Godwin," Elin said as she continued on toward the stairs, "not really. Nothing protects women from anything. Live or die, Godwin, whether I live or die tomorrow, they will taste my wrath."

The back door of the hall opened. Godwin's hand snatched at his sword hilt. Edgar was standing there, two fingers in his mouth. He took them out. They were bleeding. "That damned stable cat. She has taken a fortified position in the loft and I had a devil of a time dislodging her." He gestured with his mauled fingers. "She did not suffer this tamely."

Elin and Godwin both smiled.

"Godwin, what's the disposition of our forces tomorrow?" Edgar asked. "My friend is waiting for me and . . ."

Godwin glanced toward the door. A young man was standing in the shadows, tapping his foot impatiently.

"Very simple," Godwin said, "I walked over the whole city yesterday looking for weak spots. There aren't any. The city is a half circle on the bend of the river. Its flanks are protected by the low muddy ground of the riverbank. He won't attack there. He couldn't concentrate his forces. They'd have to attack piecemeal, in small groups, and that's how they'd die, floundering in the mud, sitting targets for our archers, or in the ditch under the palisade, filled by spears and slingstones from above."

"Suppose he could get a ship to the docks?" Elin asked.

"Yes, Elin, he could send a ship to the docks," Godwin said, "but Judith and the merchants will protect their property, and even should he succeed in landing, his men would have to force their way into the city, up streets barely wide enough for two to walk abreast. The citizens would fall on them like wolves."

"I almost wish the illegitimate sow's whelp would try to be clever. But"—Godwin shook his head—"he won't. He'll mass his forces in front of the gate and try to overrun our positions on the first assault. He'll aim a killing thrust at the city's heart."

"Will he succeed, Godwin?" Edgar asked, already walking toward his friend at the door.

"I don't know," Godwin said, folding the length of his body into his chair. He stretched his feet out toward the flames. "I don't know if Hakon will succeed or not, but that's what makes the sport of kings interesting, isn't it?"

"Interesting?" Elin asked with a small, sad smile. "Is it really interesting?"

"Yes, Elin," Godwin said, "terrible, ghastly, grim, even unbearable at times, but always interesting."

She lingered, still beside the hearth. "I almost wish . . ." she began.

"No, Elin," Godwin said heavily. "No, you don't. What you want is to be held, caressed, loved, and told everything will be all right. Owen could do that. I can't."

"It won't be all right," Elin said, "not for many here, and perhaps not for you and me."

"No, it won't," Godwin said, nodding his agreement, "but

I'll say one thing, if there's any chance to beat Hakon, I will. In me he faces a born soldier. All my life I have triumphed amidst misery and despair, even as I failed completely at ordinary human happiness. I was born to war, and if I live I will win." He didn't know if she heard his last words or not. She made no reply and the only sound was the rustle of her gown and her footsteps on the stairs.

Godwin dozed, then slept deeply for a time. He awoke feeling someone staring at him. The fire on the hearth burned low and the hall was dark. The silence was loud, almost a ringing in Godwin's ears.

He knew it must be close to dawn. The city outside was silent. Even the wind that earlier stirred the drafts in the hall had dropped as the world slept in the chill grip of the winter morning.

Godwin's hand moved, reaching for his sword, then he realized the eyes he felt belonged to the cat. She was sitting on the table, her eyes glowing in the darkness beyond the circle of firelight.

Godwin rose and poured some wine from a jug on the sideboard. He watered it well and returned to his chair. The cat leaped from the table and climbed into his lap. "So you've forgiven me," he said, scratching her ears. She licked his hand. The cat stretched herself lengthwise on one of his thighs.

Godwin took a sip of the watered wine and prepared to slip back into his half doze. Denis and the archers were positioned at the walls. They would warn him of any movement in the countryside. The cat's claws dug into his leg. His hand had come up to shove her off his lap when he saw where the yellow eyes were staring, not at him but over his shoulder at something moving behind him.

His whole body went cold with fear. Godwin lunged forward, turning as he did toward the door and the square behind him. The axe whistled through the air where his head had been a second before. Losing his balance as the swing missed, the axeman staggered into the chair.

Godwin dashed the wine into his eyes. Behind him another was raising his sword to strike. There wasn't even time for Godwin to draw his sword. He slammed the back of the chair up, catching the axeman under the chin. Blinded for a second by the wine and dazed by the blow from the chair, the axeman staggered into the swordsman. The vicious swing missed.

Godwin caught the sword arm as the blade flashed past his face. He twisted the wrist hard. The man's body turned, but not fast enough. The swordsman's arm broke at the elbow. Godwin tore the sword from his hand. He screamed and crashed into the others. Six of them. Godwin saw six shadows closing in. Gripping the sword two-handed, Godwin let fly with a savage roundhouse swing. The men closing with him hesitated, not long, but lóng enough.

"He's but one man," a voice among them said. "All together now."

Godwin ran, leaping the table that stretched the length of the hall. He threw it over on its side with a crash. They were right behind him. Godwin's only thought was to stay alive long enough to rouse the household. He lifted the table one-handed and drove it toward his attackers like a shield. He felt the thud of bodies smash into it.

One of them aimed a blow at Godwin over the top with a mace. He missed Godwin's head. The spikes of the mace thudded into the wood of the table and stuck fast. Godwin didn't miss, as he sent the sword blade upward through the mace wielder's throat.

Something struck Godwin's left shoulder, numbing his left arm. The table fell from his fingers to the floor. Godwin struck into the darkness, in the direction the blow had come from. He heard a shriek as the man fell.

His attackers were shadows between him and the fire. He didn't know how badly his arm was injured. It might be, for all he knew, amputated at the shoulder. They had control of the big table now and were using it to shove him backward toward the wall. He knew he mustn't be caught like that. Once pinned, he'd be finished in seconds. He dropped to his knees, ready to roll under the table. One of his antagonists vaulted the edge of the table. As he did, the rest stopped pushing and Godwin heard him shout, "He's down, I'll finish the bastard."

His attacker had no shield, only an axe and sword. Godwin saw their dark shapes glimmering in the dim firelight. The sword flashed toward Godwin's head. He dropped

flat to avoid the swing and rolled desperately toward his an-
tagonist. His shoulder slammed into the man's knees. He
went down over Godwin's body. Godwin twisted into a
crouch and with one reaching blow severed his enemy's
spine at the neck.

Still in a crouch, he slammed his back against the table,
sending the rest flying as he shouted, "I take a lot of finishing." Godwin was on his feet. His left arm still wouldn't
move. He had only seconds to live. His attackers gathered
themselves up, and Godwin saw more pressing in through
the open doorway.

"A thousand pieces of gold to the man who takes his head
to Hakon," someone shouted.

But Godwin observed a noticeable lack of enthusiasm for
the proposition among the remaining warriors, and Rosamund was on the stairs now, torch in hand, screeching at the
top of her lungs.

They lunged toward Godwin, bunched together, spears
and shields up. Godwin sprinted for the stairs. As he did,
something large and white came over the stair rail with a
roar of fury and landed behind them.

It was Gowen, newly awakened, naked, and in a bad humor. He seized one of the spearmen and broke his neck. A
second had barely time to turn before the spear Gowen had
ripped from the hand of the first was through his body.
Chain mail troubled Gowen's arm not at all. The rest broke
and ran. Then it seemed, the whole household joined
Rosamund on the stairs, screaming.

Gowen ran to the table. He lifted the whole thing at once,
and using it like a battering ram, charged the figures in the
doorway, howling, "To arms, to arms, they are among us."

Beyond the door, lights were springing to life everywhere
in the town. The Vikings in the square didn't seem disposed
to make a fight of it. Instead they turned and rushed up the
narrow street to the gates. Gowen stood in the door, still bellowing, "To arms! To arms!"

The room was a swirl of noise. Rosamund and Elfwine
screaming. Anna and Elin armed with knives from the sideboard, checking the fallen Vikings for signs of life, quite
ready to extinguish any they found. Wolf the Short, standing
near the stairs, arming himself methodically, pulling his mail

shirt over his head and belting on his sword, as he shouted, "The tocsin, someone ring the bell!"

Godwin reeled against the fallen table as a shock of absolute pain tore through his left shoulder. The room faded before his eyes.

Alan was standing on the steps of the hall with a half dozen of the crossbowmen beside him. The street leading to the gates was packed with the bodies of the raiders and the square was filled by a mob of citizens, all arms and screaming for blood.

Godwin went to one knee on the floor, clutching his left arm. "Stop them! Kill them!" he shouted at Alan.

Alan nodded. Godwin heard the crossbows thrum as they fired and, beyond them in the square, the roar of the mob as they charged. Godwin reached the door in time to see a heaving mass of men force their way past the gates. The mob in the street and square separated into squirming groups as the citizens fell on the stragglers, slaughtering them, and stripping the bodies where they lay. Godwin slumped down, still clutching his left arm. Anna and Elin half led, half carried him back into the hall and put him in the chair.

"Move the fingers of your left hand," Anna said.

Godwin obeyed, the fingers moved.

"Not broken," Anna said. "You're going to have a bruise, Godwin, but the mail saved your arm."

"To hell with my arm," Godwin said. "Alan, mass your archers at the gate. Get the townspeople to the walls. Ring the tocsin."

"No, no, no!" Routrude forced her way past Anna and Elin. "Show yourself to the people, Godwin! Show them you're alive and unharmed. Already they're saying you're dead, that Hakon himself killed you. I was saying so myself until I saw you just now. Are you sure you're not killed? I don't see any blood, but sometimes you don't see blood. They say blood doesn't flow from a corpse—"

Anna slapped Routrude. Routrude slapped Anna back.

Elin grabbed Godwin's wrist. "Your shoulder's dislocated," she said. "It's easily fixed, but it will hurt."

Godwin gripped the edge of the overturned table with his right hand as Elin planted a foot on his ribs and pulled on the left. The shoulder returned to position with a grinding click. A white-light sheet of pain flashed through his body. He leaned over the table, his stomach heaved, and he spewed wine, water, and bile on the floor of the hall.

"Elin," Routrude said, "your skirt's up."

"Not anymore, Routrude," Elin said.

Her foot dropped from Godwin's ribs. Godwin found he could move his arm freely and most of the pain was gone.

"Get him to the door, Routrude," Elin said. "She's right, Anna, they must see him."

"He can't go this way," Routrude said, "he's pale as a corpse."

Elin pushed a cup of wine into Godwin's hand as Anna began washing his face vigorously with a cold wet rag, saying, "We must get some color in his cheeks."

Godwin moaned, "Elin, never has any man made me cry for mercy but . . ."

Judith appeared behind Routrude. She pinched Godwin's cheeks vigorously and pulled his hair.

"Christ!" Godwin shouted.

"There, he has color in his face now!" she said, as she and Routrude marched Godwin to the door of the hall.

Cheers rang out from the square. Godwin stared out at the people. The sky was growing lighter. The cheers that greeted his appearance died away.

Godwin raised his arms. "As you see," he said, "I am well. The raider chief's plot failed and cost him many lives." His shoulder ached. There was a vile taste in his mouth. He wondered what he could say to them. The faces of the townspeople looked up at him, a sea of uncertainty in the yellow torchlight. He had nothing to give but the truth.

He raised his arms again. "Hakon, the raider's chief, is coming. Even now he's beaching his ships. He will reach the wall at daybreak. I thank you for the love you bear me, but the fate of the city rests not in my hands but in yours. The pirate chief will try to break your bodies, your hearts, your wills on the first charge, pitting every man he can muster against you on the first assault. If you withstand him, victory will be yours, not mine, not any distant king's, but yours. You will have preserved all you hold dear, and triumphed over a mighty foe. So stand fast, stand together, and the palm of honor will rest in your hands, and laurels of the conqueror on each of your brows." They were silent still, the torch flames twisting and blowing in the dawn wind. "If I perish, fear not," he continued, "your lady will lead you."

Judith pushed Elin to the top of the steps beside him and Godwin rested a hand on Elin's shoulder. "Don't be misled," he shouted, "don't be misled into thinking she who stands before you is only what she seems, a small, weak woman. The heart that beats in her breast is that of a warrior, fierce and proud, filled with unyielding courage." He raised Elin's arm and the cheers came.

Godwin backed into the hall and barred the doors behind them.

"Thank you, Godwin," Elin said, "but . . ."

"Don't thank me, Elin, they'll need someone to lead them if I fall. If that happens, follow Gowen."

"Gowen?" Elin exclaimed.

"Yes," Godwin said, "he's an abysmal brute, but an angel in battle. The big son of a bitch never makes a mistake. I know, I've watched him for years. I hate the bastard, but he's as efficient a killer as you'll ever find. Keep him supplied with beer, with women, sober the whoreson up when you need him, and point him at the enemy. Even if I die and Owen never returns, you can hold the valley for years. You have the brains, the resolution, and, much as I hate to say it, the balls. Gowen's a shit but God's perfect fighting machine. Use him till he drops dead. He'll probably grow to love you. Now, assemble the household right away. We have to get to the wall."

Martin and Anna were setting the table on its legs. Rosamund was scurrying around the sideboard, trying to find some food for everyone.

"Ingund," Godwin said, "fetch Ine."

Alfric, helping Rosamund at the sideboard, looked up suddenly. "Oh, no!" he said to Godwin. "Heavens above, Ine's a simpleton."

"Yes," Godwin said, "but I think he understands the sound of silver, thirty pieces of silver." Elin started to turn away. "No, Elin," Godwin said, "I want you here. You need to know what to do, how these things are managed."

Wolf the Short entered the hall. There was a sad, worried

look on his face. He tugged at his cinnamon beard and took up a position near Godwin's elbow.

"You've been to see her?" Godwin asked.

Wolf nodded. "I meant to kill her myself, but when I saw her . . ." He broke off and spread his hands helplessly.

"You couldn't do it?" Godwin said.

Wolf nodded again. "They hid in her house. They were very clever."

"How so?" Godwin asked.

"They never told her what they intended to do to you. Instead, they picked a girl, no brighter than Ine. She was instructed to lure Ine to the cellar, make him happy for as long as possible, and leave the door open. It was as simple as that. They told her they wanted to do something nice for Ine. As I said, the girl herself is thick as rock. She believed them. I know, I talked to her. They told her when Ine was finished, he'd want to sleep, and she could slip out through the open door. Clea is getting drunk as fast as possible. She's sure you'll want to hang her. She's terrified. All she asks is to please leave the girls alone. They had no part in her plotting. She took Hakon's gold, not them."

"Clea?" Elin asked.

"The widow," Wolf said. He turned to Godwin. "Well?"

Godwin turned to Elin. He was smiling. "Well?" he asked.

Elin stared at the household. Anna and Rosamund had put bread, wine, and cheese on the table. The men ate, standing, gobbling the food quickly. "Well, what?" Elin asked. "Is this a test?"

"Yes," Godwin said, "I'll let you decide. Do we hang the widow or not?"

"No," Elin said.

"Ah," Godwin breathed, "why?"

Elin's mouth tightened. "Godwin, I don't suppose it's lost on you that the luminaries of this town are all related to one another by blood or marriage. We are outsiders. It behooves us to tread carefully among them."

"Very well," he asked, "what would you do?"

Elin looked at Wolf the Short. "You're friends with the widow, are you not?"

"Yes." He nodded.

"Very well," she said, "you're responsible for her behavior in the future. Are you willing?"

"Yes," he said, "Clea and I, we . . ." He floundered. "She has a fine establishment . . ."—he colored—"I had hopes . . ."

"You could be very comfortable together," Elin said.

"Yes," he answered simply.

"Good," Elin said, "I imagine when she hears you've pleaded her case with Godwin successfully, she'll be more than willing. What about Ine?"

Ingund arrived, towing Ine along by the ear. "I found him hiding behind the jars of oil in the cellar. I can't imagine what's wrong with him."

Ine dropped to a crouch at Godwin's feet, whining like a whipped dog. Elin covered her eyes with her hands. "No, Godwin," she whispered, "no!"

"So many of them are like this, Elin, so many," he said to her. "You'll get to know."

"Please!" she said. "No!"

"Stand up," Godwin roared at Ine.

Ine stood. The sheer animal terror in his eyes was sickening to Elin. Godwin backhanded him across the face. The sound of the blow silenced the voices around the table. Everyone stared at Godwin and Ine.

"Did the girl offer you money?" Godwin asked, his face terrible.

"No," he whispered. He sniffled at the blood flowing from his nose.

Godwin hit him again. "When did you realize?" he asked.

"After," Ine whispered.

Alfric drew closer to Ine and put his arm around Ine's shoulder. "Please, Godwin!" Alfric pleaded.

Godwin shoved Alfric away. Ine stood alone before him.

"Was she worth it?" Godwin asked in a low voice, a voice crackling with rage.

Ine didn't answer. He stood shaking his head, staring in terror at Godwin as though he saw death in his eyes.

"Was the one you betrayed all you lived for worth it, Godwin?" Alfric asked. Godwin's eyes shifted to Alfric's face. "He's a simpleton," Alfric said, "he didn't know."

The rage in Godwin's face reached a peak of raw passion

that terrified Elin, then drained away, leaving him oddly emptied and weary looking. "Get out!" he said to Ine. "Get out, you've been punished. You won't be hurt anymore."

Ine backed away from Godwin toward the food on the table, wiping the blood from his face, seeming unconcerned that he had a split lip and a bloody nose.

"Let he who is without sin cast the first stone, eh, Alfric?" Godwin said.

"A woman, a night of pleasure, a few coins, is much to many of these people, Godwin. Better I should have said, 'Father forgive them, for they know not what they do.'" Smiling, he raised his hand and blessed Godwin.

Godwin's mouth twisted into a bitter line. "Better than a blessing, I hope you and Judith got everyone not ready to fight out of the lower town."

"We—Gunter, Judith, Osbert, and I—went house to house near the gates last night. I believe we succeeded. It's likely to burn isn't it?"

Godwin didn't get a chance to answer. One of the young crossbowmen arrived at the door. "My Lord Godwin," the young man panted, "I have a message for you. Alan says they are on the march and there are still a few latecomers on the road to the city. They are burning everything in their path."

"Be ready to ride," Godwin shouted at the men clustered around the table. "Ranulf, secure the upper town. Why the hell isn't that damn bell ringing? Rosamund, get in there, sound the tocsin. Alfric, Elin, get the women to form a bucket line. Wet down the palisade and the houses nearest to it. Move! God's curse on you, move!" he shouted.

Chapter

39

ROSAMUND stood under the bell rope, tugging. Nothing happened since she was under five feet tall and weighed ninety pounds. The bell above, not to mention its giant carriage, weighed more than she did. She thought of returning to the hall and asking someone to help her, but realized there was no one there. Elin, Anna, and the rest of the women were in the square, forming a bucket line at the fountain. Godwin and the men were gone. She knew they must, even now, be passing the town gates, riding toward the enemy.

Rosamund seized the bell rope and pulled down with all her strength. She almost panicked. Someone had to alert the people of the countryside, hurry along the last few hardy souls in flight before the invaders. All her pulling and tugging accomplished nothing. There was still no sound from above. She backed away from the rope and stared up at it in frustration and fury. She was not about to be defeated by a big bell.

She shook off her shoes and climbed the knotted rope, and getting her toes around the last knot, she pumped, knees going up and down, the way a child pumps a swing; thinking as she did that if this didn't do it, nothing would. The great bell above sang its first satisfying note, then, to her delight, another.

She laughed, overjoyed by the success of her efforts, and threw her whole body into the pumping. The bell above rang wildly, its notes sounding out over the city, into the countryside, carrying the cry of alarm with the wind under the stars, louder and louder.

It was, for a time, difficult to tell if Rosamund rang the bell or if the bell rang Rosamund. She whipped about at the end of the rope. With each cry from the giant iron throat above, she was tossed in the air, skirts flying. Twice she nearly fell as the rope snapped like a whip, her body at the end of it. Her hands and feet were almost torn loose from the knots. Then she achieved a rhythm, swinging like a pendulum, pumping at the apex of each swing, before the movement of the giant carriage sent the rope and its rider flying through the air toward the other corner of the bell tower. Happy and preoccupied with the thrill of flight, Rosamund almost didn't see the warrior until it was too late.

He was one Godwin and the townsfolk had somehow overlooked. He'd found his way into a side street near the fortress and hidden in darkness. He slashed at her with his sword.

Rosamund shrieked and clambered higher on the rope, screaming as she climbed, wondering desperately if she could be heard above the booming of the bell.

Ranulf put a few guards at the stairs to the Lady Well. Arn and some of his waterlogged patrons volunteered immediately for the duty. At best, the stairs were steep and dangerous, at worst a deathtrap easily defended by a few bowmen. Whereas the walls ... what was going to happen there in a few hours didn't bear thinking of.

Ranulf groused a little to himself at being posted by Godwin so far from the main assault. But he was intelligent enough to understand Godwin's mind. Even a feint here by Hakon at the height of the battle might prove a disastrous distraction to the defenders on the walls. He was determined to hold his position and not allow that to happen. There were yet a few weapons at the hall. He planned to gather them up and pass them out to his sentries.

Ranulf entered the doors. He said a word, a short nasty word, as he realized he had one more unpleasant task ahead of him. Even in their haste, the knights hadn't neglected to strip the corpses of the fallen men. Their nude bodies lay in a tangle of arms and legs against the wall.

Ranulf was about to put aside his sword and shield and do something about them when he suddenly froze, listening. Faint though it was, over the clamor of the bell, Ranulf heard a scream of terror. *Dear God!* he thought and sprinted toward the bell tower, drawing his sword as he ran.

The marauder had Rosamund by the ankle. She clung to the bell rope, kicking ineffectually at the warrior's face with the other foot.

Ranulf froze in the doorway. Later he realized he should have used those few seconds of surprise to kill his opponent. But his instinctive decency kept him from skewering his unwary foe. The raider saw him. He let go of Rosamund's foot.

Ranulf's enemy was a tall, powerful man, his clean-shaven face bloody and smeared with the filth of the street. He had an arrow sticking out of his leg, surrounded by a bloody ring. The eyes that looked from the begrimed face into Ranulf's were those of a killer and someone wholly mad.

The first sword cut landed on Ranulf's shield, driving him backward. He retreated into the hall, shield up under a rain of blows. Mad or not, Ranulf knew the warrior understood what he was doing, using his size and weight to his advantage. Ranulf's shield began disintegrating under the onslaught. The hide cover hung in strips from the wooden frame. When it was gone, Ranulf would be almost defenseless before the stronger man.

Rosamund came at the raider, a little bundle of fury. She threw herself rolling at the backs of his knees. The warrior staggered and kicked backward savagely. Rosamund scuttled away screaming, this time not in fury, but in pain.

Ranulf remembered a piece of advice given him by Enar. "If overmatched, look for a weak spot and step in, but make it work, for you will get no second chance." The man wore a leather cuirass. Ranulf stepped hard left and drove his sword in at the armpit. He felt the blade skid on the ribs and bite at the shoulder joint. The raider screamed as the blade slid past the joint and entered his neck at the base of the skull.

Ranulf heard, rather than saw, the next blow coming. The raider's sword came hard at him in a swing that started almost at the floor. It hit what remained of his shield, smashed its way through leather and wood, and landed with rib-shattering force on the left side of Ranulf's body.

He and the raider both spun around with the force of the

blow. Ranulf clutched at his opponent's armor. They went down together. Ranulf's sword was torn from his hand, and his head landed with a crack on the stone floor.

A sheet of white light flashed before his eyes. Stunned for a moment, he couldn't see, then his vision cleared. He twisted, half mad with terror. The raider was up. His face was blue-black, and blood pulsed from the shoulder wound. But he held the sword hilt up, ready to drive the point down through Ranulf's body.

Ranulf twisted again. His arms and legs wouldn't move. The raider moved slowly, stiffly. The tip of Ranulf's sword had injured his spine, but he wouldn't die until he drove his sword down through Ranulf's heart.

Ranulf, half paralyzed by the blow on his head, found though his mouth opened and his jaws stretched painfully, he couldn't even scream.

Rosamund landed on the raider's back, her nails clawing for his eyes. The man's upflung arm caught her across the face, his forearm breaking her nose. She hit the floor with a thud that sickened Ranulf. But the raider, overbalanced by her weight, went down again.

Rosamund came back, crawling. She lunged at the man's belt, snatched his knife, and with a screech of absolute fury, plunged the point down into his throat.

From his position on the floor, all Ranulf could see was the man's feet. They scrabbled, kicked one time, and then lay still. Ranulf found he was able to move. He rolled onto his side and rose to his knees, his body shaking all over.

"I had," he whispered, "not known it was so difficult to kill a man." Then he fell back on to his side, his face gray with shock and nausea.

Rosamund scrambled toward him, her nose streaming blood. "My nose," she screamed at Ranulf. She caught his hair in both fists, shaking him. "My nose, he cut it off?"

Ranulf managed to shake his head. "No," he croaked.

She let go of Ranulf, reached up, and feeling it was still there, relaxed, reassured. She was covered with bruises, both her elbows and knees were skinned, but she paid no attention to her other injuries. Still on her knees, she crawled toward the warrior. Stripping the rings from the warrior's fingers, she found more gold in the pouch on his belt and a pair of earrings that made her gasp with joy and forget her broken nose—two strands of filigreed golden balls encrusted with rubies. In a moment she had them in her earlobes. They dangled almost to her shoulders.

She then relieved him of a small stack of silver coins. His brooch was a disappointment, lead plated with gold, but she pinned it to her dress anyway. His helmet was a fine one, embossed silver with a noseguard of wrought gold. She jumped to her feet and clapped it on Ranulf's head over his boiled leather cap.

Ranulf, who had gotten up to wash out his mouth with some wine, found her greed both astonished and sickened him. He removed the helmet from his head and stared at her, disgust in his eyes.

Rosamund backed away, thinking he was angry because she was helping herself to spoils rightfully his. Her mind went to the earrings ... calculating. She might give up the coins, certainly the brooch, but not those beautiful earrings. So she came forward and kissed Ranulf on the mouth.

He was shocked to find he returned the kiss greedily. Then he was in the grip of a storm of sexual desire. His breeches were down around his thighs and Rosamund's dress was up.

She screeched with pleasure when his manhood drove into her, curling her legs around him, straining to drive him in deeper. He slammed his hips against hers while her fingers clawed at his face and mail-covered shoulders. She sank her teeth into his earlobe and moaned. "Do it to me. Do it to me. Do it to me." She pounded his back with her fists.

Then his loins exploded with pleasure, not once but twice, while she writhed and moaned under him. Her cries and striving slowed and stopped at the same time his did. He found himself lying on top of her, his face in a pool of blood left over from the morning's fight, at eye level with the man he'd just killed. But he lay motionless, his body still inside Rosamund for a little while longer, because she clung to him with her legs.

Then abruptly she wiggled free, saying, "Now, may I keep the earrings?"

"Yes," Ranulf answered dully, "those and everything else you wish."

Rosamund put the helmet on his head again. "You should get half," she said. "It's only fair. We both killed him." Then she kissed Ranulf on the mouth again. "If you don't look out for yourself, who will?" she added bleakly. "No one else cares for us, not as we ourselves do.

"Everyone wants to love me," she continued, with a shake of her head, "but no one loves me. Only Lady Elin. She freed me with tablet and taper. I can't think why she did it ..." Her voice trailed off as she added, "She didn't have to ... I have been so happy to be part of a decent household. I'd have served gladly."

They were on their knees, facing each other. "It may be," Ranulf said, "she knows what is forced is not worth having. She keeps a kindly house."

Rosamund rested her head forward on his shoulder. "I'm glad you were here to defend me. There are some who'd say I'm not worth defending. I don't know what the man intended. It may be he wouldn't have hurt me."

Ranulf remembered the raider's eyes. He did not believe this. "He would have killed you, not at first, but after he was finished."

"I'll come to you any time you like, but don't let Elfwine know, she would poison me," Rosamund whispered.

Ranulf tried to see his wife in the role of a poisoner and succeeded. Elfwine had a strong will, a hard head, and a violent temper. "I thank you," he said, "but no, I'll try to remain a good and faithful husband. I don't know what happened to me a little while ago, but it is my child she carries in her arms."

Looking rebuffed, Rosamund scrambled to her feet.

"Where are you going?" Ranulf asked.

"If they're all like this, the ones at the wall are going to get rich," Rosamund said excitedly.

"If they don't get dead," Ranulf said, standing up.

Rosamund snatched the purse from her belt and poured the coins into her hand. She extended them toward Ranulf. They gleamed, gold mixed with silver. "See, see these!" she said. "And this!" She flipped one dangling earring with her forefinger. The coins were streaked with blood. "For this much money the widow would have let the man have me, let him do anything he wanted to me for as long as he wanted.

But they're mine now! Someday I'm going to have a house of my own, with a bar on the door, and no one can come in unless I want them to. And when they're inside, I won't let them do anything they please. Anyone who passes my door will do what I say."

She paused, breathing hard through her broken nose. "Or," she continued, "I'll get dead. But I don't care because the dead don't feel, they only remember. Or at least that's what my people say. I don't care what happens to me so long as I don't feel it."

"Good luck, Rosamund," Ranulf said.

She flashed a brief smile at him, then she ran from the hall, the long earrings dangling, their splendor somehow pathetic in contrast to her bruised face, worn dress, and dusty bare feet.

Ranulf stood alone, watching her run past the line of women toiling at the fountain. Then he glanced back at the corpse sprawled on the floor of the hall. For a moment he wondered who the man had been, not just his name, but what he was like, what his hopes and dreams might have been. Then he pushed these thoughts out of his mind, knowing instinctively they led nowhere except to a swamp of useless guilt and grief. But he understood the expression he saw sometimes on Godwin's face much better now.

Just for a moment, in the graying light, Ranulf's face was the face of a man. Not yet what he was, but the man he was going to become. The face was intelligent and decisive, the mouth set and determined, but a little bit hard. The eyes under the silver helmet steady, but remote and almost cold.

Then he turned back into the hall, thinking he could use another set of arms and weapons. He'd been assigned to guard the square and secure Godwin's rear. Considering dispassionately what he'd need to do if he had to mount a counterattack by himself, if it chanced Godwin was too occupied on the walls to help him, he hurried toward the body on the floor.

Chapter
40

GODWIN rode through the gates into darkness. He had, including the knights, twenty men. The fires, beginning to cast a noose around the town, were still distant. The sky was brightening in the east. A few bands of high, thin clouds stretched across the horizon. Otherwise, it looked to be a clear day—a wonderful day for a battle.

Godwin shivered. Even in his mail-covered linen shirt he was cold. The morning air was icy and smelled of raw earth and the river. The clop of the horse's hooves was loud on the dusty road.

Godwin's column split to let a dozen carts go by. He could barely see the faces of the men and women in them. He reined in his horse. The rest pulled to a stop behind him.

Godwin was counting the fires. They spread out in an unbelievably big arc along the river and were moving inland fast. "He has a great many men," Godwin said. "God help any caught outside the city now. He'll send an advance party up this road to close the gates and cut off any escape for the laggards. We'll try to keep the road open as long as we can."

He rode forward, but then he and his men had to leave the road to let a flock of sheep go by. More fugitives straggled past, most on foot. They were hurrying toward the sparks of light on the palisade, the glow of the city beyond them.

In the distance, piercingly clear in the still morning air, Godwin could hear the outcry of the cathedral bell. A few more carts passed them, the drivers pushing the stolid farm horses to their fastest pace. Then, because the road seemed clear ahead, Godwin kicked his horse into a trot.

Ahead Godwin saw a solitary point of light. A cart had lost a wheel. It was blocking half a dozen others. A knot of men stood by the broken wheel, arguing and gesticulating.

Godwin halted his party. "Get that thing out of the road," he shouted.

The cart's owner, a tall, dark man who looked nearly as stubborn as the mules pulling the cart, began cursing Godwin while the women began screaming.

Godwin jerked his head at Gowen. "Get it out of the road."

Gowen laid the flat of his sword across the rumps of the mules with a loud crack. Braying and squealing, they lunged forward, tipping the cart into the ditch. Whips snapping, the drivers howling imprecations at the owner of the cart in the ditch, the others hurried along on their way to the city.

The owner of the cart sat down at the edge of the road and began weeping. A tall, rawboned woman who must have been his wife clutched Godwin's stirrup and refused to let go. "Help me," she said, gesturing toward her husband. "I can do nothing with him!"

In the distance, a half mile ahead, a village along the road burst into flame. The woman screamed.

"That will be Hakon's advance guard," Edgar said.

The woman let go of Godwin's stirrup and ran toward the cart. In the dim light Godwin could see the frightened faces of three children peering up at him. The woman began snatching up the children.

"Abandon it, mount your wife and children on the mules and flee," Godwin shouted down at the man by the road.

The man ignored Godwin.

"Madam!" Godwin said. "Have you collected all your children?"

She nodded wordlessly.

"Free those cattle," Godwin shouted at Gowen. He snatched the torch mounted by the driver's perch and thrust it into the bedding in the cart. The bedding went up with a roar of flame as a few slashes of Gowen's sword freed the mules from their harness.

The woman put the children on the mules. The man scrambled to his feet and followed his wife, running in the direction of the city.

Godwin put spurs to his horse and raced toward the burning village. The village was a straggle of houses bordering the road. It had a tavern. The raiders had gotten into the stock. Flames were pouring from every window and door of the few houses. The tavern was the only building not burning. The raiders were gathered at its door.

Godwin yelled, "God bless Bacchus! Kill them!"

The rest was slaughter. Taken by surprise and already half drunk, the Northmen fell to the swords of Godwin's men in a few minutes. When it was over, Godwin pulled his men together. "We must get away from the light," he shouted, "or we'll be caught as they were."

He led his men back into the night, but it was no longer night, instead the pale light that spreads over the earth before dawn. Silken wraiths of mist lay in the hollows and rested in the furrows of the plowland.

Edgar gasped and pointed. It seemed that every village and farmstead between Chantalon and the forest was burning now. A great arc, its span delineated by points of fire, stretched out, encircling the city. A net whose meshes still lay in darkness, drawing tighter and tighter, closing in.

The light was glowing and the horizon flushed with the salmon color of a beautiful sunrise. Godwin was not aware he was able to see until he did see. The progress of Hakon's army resembled that of a giant crab, pincers extended. The main body was marching down the road, skirmish lines stretched out far on either side.

He turned with the rest and joined the carts in a run for the city gates. He pulled to a stop behind the last cart and the big gates swung shut. The army of Northmen came to a halt just out of bowshot.

Godwin lifted the helmet from his head and dried his face with his sleeve. The morning breeze brushed his face and chilled his scalp as it dried the dampness in his hair. Far away he could hear the cry of birds as they darted and swooped over the fallow fields beyond the city.

It was very quiet. No one spoke or even coughed.

For a moment, Godwin was glad he wasn't leading an army of soldiers. At least these people didn't really know what they were looking at. Hakon's force was one of the best armed Godwin had ever seen. Their ranks bristled with steel, swords, chain mail, spears, and axes. Every man wore some sort of armor—leather or iron—and they looked fresh, strong, well fed, and eager.

Next to him, Edgar whispered in a shaken voice, "Godwin ..."

"Be quiet," Godwin said. His voice was a low savage snarl as he ran his eyes over his own ragged troops at the wall. Thanks to the efforts of Judith and the tanner, they all carried some sort of shield. Their lines were spiked with the long ash-pole spears Wolf the Short had made. Bows and arrows, knives, and above all, axes of the powerful tree-felling kind bristled among the throng. Denis had, as Godwin ordered, massed his archers at the gate. He had around sixty good crossbows and he'd divided them into two groups, one to fire as the other section reloaded. The women stood behind the men, tending fires over which boiled water or oil. The wooden uprights of the palisade glistened in the morning light and the street behind, running along the wall, was wet and muddy. Godwin reached out and touched one of the stakes—sopping wet.

"We're ready," Elin said softly, as though even she were afraid to break the strange, ominous silence. She was standing with the other women. She wore a leather cuirass and a boiled-leather cap. Her skirt was belted to calf-length over her stockings and leggings. The rest of the household was with her. Anna was armed with knife, axe, and sling. Ingund, dressed like a man, was carrying the sword she'd taken from the Viking she'd killed in the street.

A man was riding along the serrated ranks of the warriors facing them. He was outstanding, even among the richly dressed chieftains. He wore a scarlet mantle over golden armor and a helmet crowned by a rearing dragon. The creature's claws curved down over his cheekbones, then up to shield his eyes.

"Hakon," Godwin whispered.

"Yes," Elin said. "Do you think he wants to parlay?" she asked softly.

Godwin showed his teeth. It was nothing like a smile. "He's looking for the softest place to sink the knife." He felt a brief wave of dizziness and nausea. "We will take the brunt of his attack," he said, "here!"

A sound like a vast sigh swept the people on the walls as Hakon began very deliberately massing his forces at the gate. Godwin knew he'd been wrong earlier. He could see it in their faces and hear it in their voices as they gave vent to the strange sad sound. They understood what they were looking at as well as he. They were here for the same reason he was, because the alternative, surrender, was as unthinkable to them as it was to him.

The sun lifted over the rim of the hills beyond the city. Its first rays turned the weapons of the attacking army to flame. All along the wall Godwin heard the soft rustle as the archers stepped forward to meet the charge.

Hakon reined in his horse, drew his sword, and raised it—a dazzle of white fire in the morning sun. The reflected light flashed in Godwin's eyes. He stood in deep shadow, compared with the great Hakon, a slender, rather shabby-looking man dressed in worn armor, helmetless, gray streaks in his dark hair.

"Don't waste bolts," he grumbled to Denis.

Denis smiled quietly. "I haven't wasted one yet," he said.

Godwin put his helmet back on and drew his sword almost absentmindedly. "I apologize," he said. "You understand these things as well as I do. Whenever you wish."

Hakon's sword fell.

For a second Godwin closed his eyes. He didn't need to see the charge begin, he could feel it as one does a storm surf, in the quivering of the earth itself pounded by so many feet.

Behind him Gowen drew his word and bellowed, "Look you, my friends, these well-dressed strangers are coming to call. Maybe they will leave some of their wealth behind when they leave, booty for us all." His last words were a shriek heard above the charge.

The scream that echoed Gowen's cry from the townsfolk on the wall seemed to rise from one vast enraged throat—an inarticulate cry of blind fury. The crossbows let go, whistling like the sound of the reapers' scythe slicing through the stems of ripe wheat. Everything in front of them died.

The men charging the gates went down by the dozen, but Godwin knew it wouldn't be enough. The massed forces struck the wall like a battering ram. The thick posts shook with the impact.

Godwin ran forward to meet the first wave as the attackers leaped the ditch and seized the posts in their hands.

Then there was no science, only savagery, raw, naked fury
unleashed. All along the wall the townsfolk and the raiders
clashed, hand to hand, breast to breast. No one in the melee
could hear or think or see.

Godwin hacked viciously at everything that tried to come
over the wall, screaming as insanely as the rest. He saw
Gowen next to him drag one man up and impale him on the
posts, then kill another behind him by driving his sword between stakes impenetrable to ordinary mortals. Rosamund
brushed past him swinging a kettle of boiling oil that looked
near as big as she was and hurled its contents into the faces
of the men below.

Near him Ingund drove her spear through the eye of one
man and sank her axe into the skull of another. Gunter, defending the gate itself with Denis and the archers, swung his
hammers like Thor.

Godwin didn't know when the fires began, only that it
seemed after an endless time the living men in the ditch
were scrambling away, leaving the dead and wounded in
screaming heaps at the foot of the posts.

He heard Elin's shout behind him. "They are breaking
through!"

He looked around. The wall was burning in half a dozen
places and the attack was concentrated at these. She pointed
to the most serious breach, about a dozen yards away.

The stakes were down, blazing, and attackers were pouring in. Without waiting for Godwin's reply, Elin snatched up
a kettle of boiling water and ran toward them. A wedge of
warriors had forced their way past the broken stakes. The
citizens, no match for the heavily armed men, gave ground
before them. Elin hurled the contents of the kettle full into
the face of the foremost man. He shrieked, his body bucking, his fall taking a half dozen others down into the ditch
with him.

But at least a dozen of the raiders had broken in and Elin
found herself among them. A hand snatched at her hair. She
raised her shield and it took a sword cut that drove her to her
knees.

"Kill the witch," someone screamed.

Then there was a terrible howl and Gowen was upon

them. "Come, my beauties," he roared at the citizens, "will you have it said your women fight better than you do?"

The men at the breach were mobbed. Gowen was the devil incarnate. He fought laughing, and killed with a smile. He didn't bother with killing at first. He picked up three of Elin's assailants in rapid succession and threw them back over the wall, yelling gleefully, "They were not invited. It may be they won't return."

One of the invaders tried to drive a spear under his arm where the mail gave way to leather. Gowen sliced the spear in half before it could penetrate. He then amputated the arm holding it, as another aimed an axe cut at his head. The axe landed a glancing blow, tearing a flap of skin loose on the side of Gowen's head. He slapped it back in place with one hand while killing the axeman with the other.

Elin staggered away from the wall, her whole body shaking so badly she could barely stand. Her left arm and hand had been cut to the bone by the strap and hand grip of the shield.

The whistle of the crossbows was a steady, dreadful keening in her ears. Alan and Denis held their men to the walls, firing without respite. Everyone who could draw one of the heavy bows backed them up. They found the bows pressed into their hands as quickly as they could fire.

"As God loves you," Godwin screamed, "keep the pressure on them. They fail. They fly before you."

Edgar fought at another opening in the walls, and Wolf the Short at yet another. Edgar's sword flashed like a living flame. Men facing him seemed to die before the eye could make out the cut that killed them. Arms, legs, and heads fell at Edgar's feet with a dreadful spontaneity.

Wolf the Short went forward into the breach, accompanied by Osbert and his stockmen. They were all armed with the long spears. In a moment they seemed to be landing warriors hooked to the poles, wiggling like gaffed fish.

The thatched roof of the house behind Elin caught fire with a roar. At the same moment Routrude grabbed her, screaming, "I'm shot!" She fell at Elin's feet, a burning arrow in her side.

Elin went to her knees, trying to beat out the flames of Routrude's blazing dress with her bare hands. Suddenly it seemed a rain of fire poured from the sky. The men at the walls didn't break. They raised their shields and took the fiery assault without flinching. Elin, scrambling in the mud, tried to cover both herself and Routrude with her shield.

The bucket line down the steep street to the gates was still in operation, Rosamund at the end of it. The flaming arrows thudding into the palisade were extinguished as quickly as they landed.

Alfric joined Elin, trying to calm the terrified Routrude. Godwin ran over and added his shield to Elin's cover. The smoke grew thick around them. Elin's eyes filled with animal panic and they teared from the smoke.

"We're winning," Godwin said, "hold fast."

"Winning," Elin repeated in a strangled voice, her eyes darting about wildly. More and more roofs seemed to catch fire.

"Yes," Alfric said, pressing her hand, "at a fearful cost, but still the victory is ours. He will not try another attack on the walls."

The rain of fiery arrows was thinning. More and more people ran past with buckets in their hands to drench the palisade. It smoked, hissed, and smoldered in places, but it did not burn.

Still others ran about collecting spent arrows for Alan and the bowmen. They were returning the deadly fire with interest.

Alfric was tearing strips of Routrude's skirt to bandage her wounded side. "Am I killed?" she asked, clutching at his sleeve.

"No, Routrude," Alfric said, "it was into the meat." She sat up and smiled. Then she lifted the arrow Alfric had drawn from her body and held it out to one of the bowmen. "Take this for me and send it back"—she spat on the tip—"with my curse."

The crossbows were deadly, and wherever their bolts flew, men died. The Vikings drew back out of range. The smoke grew thicker and thicker. A dozen houses smoldered, fires inside the rooms lighting the windows of oiled parchment. Timber and thatch, as yet too wet to burn, poured out rivers of smoke into the air.

Houses on the edge of the street leading up to the Roman

gate were catching. This was serious. The narrow alleyways between the tall houses lining the palisade were already impassable. If the houses along the street went up, the defenders at the gate might be cut off.

Godwin and some of the men ran to the bucket line in the street and began sluicing down the housefronts.

Gunter was at the gate with Elin and Ingund. "They are massing again," he said.

Just then the tall house nearest the gate exploded. Elin crouched down, arms covering her face, screaming. She hadn't known fire could explode.

The house behind her was a torch. Every beam and joist was ablaze, furniture—blackened hulks in the empty rooms—could be seen, all swept by fire. Flame ripped through another house with a boom that seemed to shake the ground, then a third turned into an inferno with a flash and a roar. Houses on both sides of the street were burning.

Elin saw Godwin go down, blown off his feet by the fierce updraft of the fire in the narrow street. The men and women fighting the blaze fled toward the Roman gate above.

Elin, back pressed against the gate, watched helplessly as the house nearest Godwin caught, and flames clawed from the doors and windows at Godwin's prostrate body. Edgar and Wolf the Short reached him. Edgar soaked him with a bucket of water, and Wolf the Short dragged him up the street and into the square to safety.

Elin and the defenders at the gate stared at each other in terror. They were cut off now. Rosamund, clinging to the top of the gate screamed, "They're bringing up a battering ram."

Gunter lifted his bloodied hammer. "The devil," he said, as if in answer.

Gowen appeared out of the smoke behind him. "If they want to get in so badly," Gowen said, "why don't we let them?"

Gunter looked shocked for a moment, then he stared at the inferno behind him and slowly he smiled. Every house on the street, the whole lower town near the gates, was on fire. The street leading to the square was a roaring tunnel of flame, the houses lining the palisade a pyre.

"Now, let them come." Gowen laughed with enjoyment. The houses were too tightly packed here to save any of them. It would be all they could do to prevent its spread beyond the inner wall. The heat was intense. Elin's whole body was streaming with sweat, sweat that evaporated as quickly as it reached the surface of her skin.

Anna plucked at her throat. "I can't breathe," she whispered, falling to her knees.

This heat will kill us, Elin thought. *We'll open the gates to them just to escape it.* But the street along the palisade was a sea of mud and water, spilled when the stakes were wetted down. Elin seized Anna around the waist and threw her into a puddle, drenching her.

"Follow your lady's lead," Gunter yelled, "she has the right idea." He was used to dealing with heat. In seconds, all around her people were rolling in the filth, blood, and mud. Anything, anything, to escape the sheer radiant fury of the fire behind them.

Elin cowered with the rest along the palisade, shivering in terror, her ears deafened by the din of explosions as fire swept like a storm through every yet unburned building and roared up furiously toward the sky.

Alfric used the last few buckets of water to cool the wounded and, with the help of the rest, dragged them to the shelter of the palisade.

They waited then to see if they would live or die. They could have retreated, following the wall until they reached safety at the river end of the palisade, but to do so would have been to abandon the whole lower town to Hakon. No one tried to flee.

Routrude sat in front of Elin, sobbing with terror and pain. Her back was blistered, she'd been too close to one of the houses when it went up.

Ingund threw aside her mail shirt, the metal grown so hot it seared her flesh.

Anna crouched behind Elin, gray-faced, breathing openmouthed, each breath a shallow wheezing gasp.

Gunter lay in a puddle near the gate until the water itself got too hot and he rose and hung his arms over the uprights to let the breeze cool him.

No one tried to flee.

Not the young archers, or Siefert, crouched near them.

The tanner was nursing a bad leg wound and was one of the ones wet down by Alfric.

Gowen rolled Rosamund in the mud and covered her with his body.

For what seemed an eternity they waited, thanking God for the steady breeze that flowed along the river delta. It blew the flames and smoke away. It cooled their bodies.

Elin felt a pain in her right shoulder, the one closest to the fire. She looked down. The woolen sleeve of her dress was smoking. She slapped wet mud on the smoldering cloth and bit into her lower lip to keep from screaming.

That was the hottest the fire got. A few minutes later she realized the heat had begun to abate and Rosamund, freeing herself from Gowen, was shouting again. "They're on the march!"

They were. This time in a wedge-shaped mass, battering ram at the apex. It seemed to Elin's streaming eyes to be studded with nails. Then she realized these were the heads of the warriors pushing it.

Gowen and the smith lifted the bar from the gate. Gowen turned to the people and bellowed, "Let's invite them in, so they may join us here in hell!"

The smaller houses lining the palisade street were burning out, roofs and walls collapsing inward, the unburned timbers of the upper stories falling, showering charred rubble and clouds of embers everywhere.

Elin ran to the nearest, found the biggest unburned beam she could, and began dragging it toward the gate. The rest joined her, dragging the still smoldering timbers out to form barricades on either side of the gate, to funnel the invaders up into the inferno of the street above. In the tall houses that lined it, the fire raged on unabated. The very stones forming the housefronts glowed bloodred, incandescent with the fury of the conflagration.

Gowen's plan was so simple, it was immediately grasped by everyone. Gowen's plan was so simple, it worked perfectly. The ram struck the gate with a crash. It flew open and the raiders poured through, following the ram.

Denis and Alan had the young archers poised at the barricade. They fired point-blank into the mass of men as they stumbled forward, surprised by the barrier's easy yielding.

Elin watched as the surprise in their faces turned to terror as they were pushed forward, upward into the red maw of the fire beyond. They began to scream, trying to claw their way backward toward the gate. Most were too slow, the press of the men behind them too much and so, screaming, they died.

Hakon saw the trap from his horse outside, and raising his horn, frantically blew retreat.

It was too late.

The barricade Elin was standing on dissolved under her feet as the raiders, trapped between Denis's crossbows and the fire, sought to escape searing death in the street above. Attackers and defenders both swirled together in a savage whirlpool of destruction.

Elin struck out with a spear until it was torn from her hand, then drew her knife and used it until it was left sheathed in a human body. She saw Ingund and Gunter carried by in the thick of the fighting, Ingund beside her father using her axe and shield like a man.

Gowen waded into the melee, sword in one hand and axe in the other, arms bloody to the elbow, his body splattered with gore. He slaughtered everything in his path.

Screams of rage and agony deafened her and, above the sounds of human carnage, her ears rang with a constant rolling thunder as the walls of houses caved in, falling to earth, sometimes bringing each other down as they collapsed. Elin was thrust against the palisade as the townspeople, in a frenzy of hatred, fought each other to get at the raiders.

Four of the flaming houses on the main street collapsed, one into the other, sending a torrent of fire down the street into those locked in mortal combat at the gates. The Northmen broke and fled. Not an orderly retreat but a rout, an utter rout.

Elin helped Gunter lift the bar back into position on the gate, then crouched down, retching.

"You are a mighty fighter, my lady," Gowen said.

Elin glanced around. The dead were piled in heaps on the bloody, trampled ground, and the mound heaved and stirred as the living wounded screamed and struggled, trying to escape the heat of the charred, smoldering timbers, and the weight of the dead. Gowen strode among them, pulling the townsfolk to their feet and delivering death strokes to any of the still-living Vikings he found.

Higher up, the flaming battering ram stood surrounded by the warriors who'd driven it. Elin could see the contorted bodies, caught in grotesque attitudes of struggle, black, all veiled by flame. The street was the mouth of a furnace. The timbers of the broken houses, piled on the cobbles, fed a fire boiling and twisting up toward the cloudless sky.

Elin's dry retching stopped. The women were beginning to wail and scream. Many had lost all they owned in the flaming houses. Now their menfolk lay dead at their feet.

But Gowen wouldn't have it. He seized Elin around the waist and set her on his shoulder. One hand was still locked into the shield she'd chosen, her hand frozen to the leather by the rigor of terror. She caught at his hair with her free hand, fingers slipping in the blood and sweat covering his head, and finally steadied herself with a grip on his hair.

A wave of smoke blew into her eyes. They prickled angrily for a moment and tears poured down her cheeks. Then her vision cleared and she was able to see. The city had withstood the storming of its attackers. Hakon and his men were still retiring in defeat. The fire, which seemed so universal from the gates, was confined to the main street and the area around it. The inner keep was untouched.

Godwin and his men fought it on the Roman wall and she knew the fire wouldn't leap that wall.

She raised her shield and shouted, "The city stands!"

Gowen wrapped one arm around her knees and roared, "Do not weep. You are the victors!" He slapped her shield with one big paw. The hide-covered wood boomed like a drum. "You have saved the city." He slapped the shield again. "Women, do not weep, for you will be sought after by all men, as the mothers of valiant sons."

Around Elin the chorus rose as hands and swords slapped shields and incoherent shouts of savage rejoicing burst from the parched throats of the defenders.

Gowen began his dance of victory, leaping and whirling among the dead with Elin still on his shoulders, howling, "You are the victors. You are rich. Look at the spoil around you!"

"It is yours," Elin screamed, her long black hair streaming and whipping in the wind from the river.

Hakon heard them from afar, and saw Elin borne high on Gowen's shoulder.

"The witch queen rejoices," he said, turning his horse to look back at the city. He wasn't the only one. Others were staring at Elin. The few Christians among Hakon's men made the sign of the cross. Others touched amulets or made gestures to avert the evil eye. Then as if by common, unspoken agreement, they turned and continued walking toward the spot where they'd made camp near the forest.

Hakon knew better than to order another assault. To give an order that might not be obeyed could very well be the end of him. The men he commanded weren't a disciplined army, but a mob of greedy individuals. The first two attacks had been an unmitigated disaster. Even his own personal followers might not forgive him for a third.

As things stood, they were happy. Glutted with the plunder of the countryside, footsore and weary, his men looked forward to a nightlong orgy of eating and drinking. They considered it a just reward for their efforts, and if he tried to deny it to them, he wouldn't last another day.

Hakon alone turned back and stared up at the city. It rose above the countryside, secure on the limestone outcrop, a jumble of walls and rooftops. It looked almost placid, basking in the warm sunlight—as it might well have looked on any other clear winter day. The only signs of conflict were a pall of smoke and the blackened scar near the gate.

Always a realist, Hakon thought, *I've lost.* He tried the words on his tongue. They were bitter. "I've lost," he whispered. Then he said, "No!"

They were defenseless, a rabble. Women and children had fought him. He held Elspeth's stronghold and the fortress in the river. Eight great longships did he command. "No." Nothing stood between him and control over the countryside but the city, and it would fall in time. It must. This was a setback, no more. In time, he would prevail. Holding the thought, he turned, set spurs to his horse, and galloped toward the camp.

* * *

If he'd known how thirsty and exhausted the defenders were and how few, Hakon might have rallied his men and broken their will. But he didn't. Thanks to Gowen all he heard were screams of triumph and shouts of rejoicing.

The fire was burning itself out when Judith reached them. She was driving a cart filled with water barrels.

As the fires died down, it became clear to the defenders that much of the city had escaped harm and the fire was confined to the crowded quarter near the gate. Other dwellings were set on their own plots of land surrounded by gardens and sometimes orchards. Though a few were damaged, the fires were isolated and easily contained.

The street running along the palisade followed the wall to where it ended at the river. Judith had taken the road at the height of the fire, knowing Godwin couldn't reach the people at the gate from the upper town.

Everyone who could run, Elin included, ran for the cart. Gowen reached it first. He stood in front of Judith and flourished his sword. This alone was enough to stop the rush. All had seen him in action. "I love you like brothers," he said, "but I would kill you with my own hands rather than see you die screaming with the cramp. We will all, for the love of God, drink slowly." Ignoring his own thirst, he thrust the first dipper at Elin.

Elin took it with shaking hands. In the sudden silence, she could hear the moaning of the wounded still lying beside the palisade. She turned to Alfric and pushed the dipper into his hands. "For them." The words rasped out of a throat that felt choked with sand.

The wounded drank first. There were other containers on the cart, but none of the people gathered around it would touch a drop until the men and women lying prone by the wall slaked their thirsts. Then they drank as Gowen said, slowly, sometimes with their arms around each other, each restraining his companion's excess.

Gowen's lips were cracked and bloody, but he stood near Elin beside the cart, a model of restraint until everyone was satisfied. Then he slapped his chest and said, "My thirst is of such an intensity that it were a shame to waste it on water. I'll save it for a draft of beer."

"I thought of you," Judith said. "There's beer in the back." She pointed over the water barrels.

He howled with joy. In seconds he had one of the casks in his hands. He pulled the bung out with his teeth.

Elin had her arm around Rosamund and was slowly giving her a dipper of water. She was faint and her tongue was swollen. She had yet to take a drop of water herself. She felt she couldn't let Gowen outdo her.

He lifted the cask to her lips with a nod of approval, saying, "You are like the women of my people . . . strong!"

Judith sniffed. "What a compliment!" she said.

"It's the greatest he can give," Rosamund said.

The beer burned Elin's mouth, but her body welcomed it the way a desert welcomes rain, seeming to soak it up. She shuddered with the pleasure of satisfying her thirst, at least until Gowen pulled away, laughing and shouting, "Save some for me!" Then he lifted it to his lips and drained the barrel dry.

Judith began to pass out bread and cheese. It went from hand to blackened hand.

Gowen helped himself to another of the small barrels and shouted, "Hoy! Let's look at what we've won."

Everyone scattered to plunder the dead. The fights that broke out over loot were quickly broken up by Gowen. He strolled around, the beer barrel under one arm, and drank and robbed to his heart's content.

Judith and Rosamund helped Elin to a seat by the cart wheel, where even the noon sun cast a little shadow. Elin was half drunk and completely exhausted. Rosamund and Judith joined her. Judith, glancing at Rosamund, caught her by the chin and turned her head from side to side. "Your nose is crooked," Judith said.

Rosamund fingered her nose. "I think it's broken," she replied.

Then, keeping a firm grip on Rosamund's chin with one hand, Judith reached over and quickly and brutally straightened it.

Rosamund screeched. The nose bled a little.

"There," Judith said, "when the swelling goes down, you'll be as pretty as ever."

Rosamund looked as though she didn't know whether to say thank you or be angry.

Elin supported Judith, saying, "My brother did the same for me after I fell from a horse once. It's sometimes necessary."

Rosamund said, "Thank you."

"A woman's face is her fortune," Judith said, "but it's not the only fortune you'll have if this keeps up."

Elin looked at Rosamund. The girl's fingers glittered with rings, gold and silver, some set with precious stones. She wore several braided circlets of silver around her neck, others on her wrists. Ruby earrings dangled from her ears. "It behooves a woman alone not to waste her time," Rosamund said primly. She patted her belt. Two daggers, one hilted with gold, the other with silver, protruded from the leather strap around her waist.

The fire was almost burned out. The sun crept past the zenith and the shadow of the wagon grew longer. A man came up and dumped a heap of armor in front of Judith. "How much for the lot?" he asked.

She sorted through it and named a price. There was no haggling. The man nodded and accepted Judith's word in lieu of cash.

The filthiest individual Elin had ever seen plucked at Judith's sleeve and offered her an intricately worked brooch of pure gold. She weighed it in her hand and named a price, then added, "Ah, Fortunatus, you'll be drunk for a month."

Fortunatus shouted with joy, "More than a month, Judith. Pay Arn. I'd only lose it the first night out."

"Move downwind, Fortunatus," Judith commanded, motioning with her finger. "Now," she asked sternly, "who's next?"

Elin walked to a space on the wall, well away from the corpses, and stared out over the countryside. She could see the fires of Hakon's camp near the forest. She felt stronger, but not refreshed by her brief rest beside the wagon. She leaned forward against the post in front of her and closed her eyes. Hakon was not leaving. She thought of Owen, wishing for him to be there, for the simple and infinitely sweet comfort of his arms. "Return," she whispered, "return and love me. These burdens are too heavy for me to carry alone. I have given myself to you and your city. I had no choice, for you and your people are one. What more can I do? Only give me some tenderness that I may rest from my labors."

Then she found herself wondering if there was any tenderness in their love, in the fierce, perhaps transitory thing between them. Even Owen's love was a kind of combat, a thing he used to try to club her into submission, a battle in itself.

Elin turned. Godwin was picking his way down the rubble-strewn street toward the gates. Heavens, he looked ten years younger than he had last night. He'd thrown aside his mail shirt, was wearing only his breeches and an old linen shirt. He looked the horseman he was. His hips and legs were slender, but under the thin shirt the length and power of his bare arms were striking, and the axe-handle's breadth of his shoulders apparent. She watched him turn aside to acknowledge greetings, many greetings from the citizens. He smiled often and the smiles were genuine, warm and kind. He seemed to have a pleasant word and a friendly handclasp for everyone.

"Why are you laughing?" he asked when he reached her.

"You look so different."

"Do I?" he said, taking her arm. They walked together toward the street to the upper town. "Perhaps," he said, "that's because I'm a coward, Elin. When a battle's over I know I'm not going to die right away, hence I'm relieved and it shows. Was it bad down here?"

"Very bad," Elin answered, "and we're still in danger."

Godwin laughed mirthlessly and glanced over the wall at the Viking camp. "If Hakon had anything like a disciplined army and not a pack of brigands, we'd all be dead. What happened? I couldn't see through the flames and smoke."

"Gowen," Elin answered. "He ambushed them at the gate. You said he was an angel in battle. He is—an angel of death."

"That's the idea," Godwin answered.

"But could we withstand another attack?" Elin asked.

"I don't know," Godwin said. "I can't answer that any more than I could answer Edgar's question last night. We meet each thing as it happens and hope for the best."

They walked past the ram and its grisly escort. Elin turned

her face away. Godwin studied the blackened bodies. "I believe you've had your revenge," he said.

"Oh," Elin said, "my revenge. I've gone beyond revenge."

"Yes," Godwin answered, "I thought you might."

They reached the Roman gate leading into the square. Elin turned. She looked back over the charred rubble of the houses and out into the countryside. The blue curve of the river flowed past the city and through pasturelands, the brown winter grass a shimmer of gold in the afternoon sun. Her eyes sought the cool benediction of the rolling forested hills beyond. She rested her hand against the gray stone of the gate post. Her perspiration left a faint wet stain on the granite. "What's going to happen now?" she asked.

He paused beside her, his gaze fixed on the distant activity in the Viking camp. "I don't know, Elin. He's failed. That won't sit well with his men. But no doubt he'll be able to content them with the spoil already taken. My guess is he'll try some trick, a night attack, or"—Godwin glanced briefly at the buildings surrounding the square—"fire. He'll try to find some way to burn the city. We've had a warm autumn and it's been dry. But my guess is tonight he'll do nothing. His men will expect a rest, a chance to feast on the plunder of the countryside, but after tomorrow . . ."

Godwin gave a start and peered into the distance. "Sometimes," he said thoughtfully, "I hate being right."

"What is it?" Elin asked.

"Have you ever heard of a catapult?" Godwin asked.

"I've read of some such," Elin said, "but never seen one."

Godwin pointed to a frame of logs in the distance near Hakon's camp. "I believe you may be looking at one now," he said.

"Oh, no," Elin whispered, horrified.

"I think," Godwin said very softly, looking around carefully to be sure no one was within earshot, "I think sometime soon, not tonight, but perhaps tomorrow, we may be faced with a rain of fire."

Chapter
41

*T*HEY were all footsore and weary when they approached the river on the second afternoon. The party stopped on a hill crowned with a circle of standing stones, a bleak place covered with sear brown grass. Just beyond, screened by a few trees and bushes, Owen heard the sound of waves thundering against a rocky shore.

Owen set his back to one of the standing stones and sat down cross-legged on the ground. A steady sea breeze whistled across the dead grass, chilling all of them. The little girl, Ilo, shivered, then hurried over to Owen and climbed into his lap.

He hesitated for a second, then put his arms around her. She sighed wearily, rested her head against his shoulder, and fell asleep. The small body in his arms seemed to radiate warmth. Owen felt a strange contentment and a sense of acceptance he hadn't felt before among her people.

Far away across a sea of treetops, he watched Sybilla cross a barren, weed-grown field toward a tumbledown village. Nearby, hidden by tall grass, he could just make out the remains of a burned-out manor house.

"What can she want there?" he asked idly. "Surely the place is abandoned."

"Not quite," Alshan replied. He hunkered down near another of the standing stones, his back to the wind. "There are a few people still living among the ruins. The young ones are all gone, but their elders remember us. When the Vikings come, they hide in the woods. Since they are too poor to be worth robbing and too old to be worth taking as slaves, Hakon leaves them alone."

Enar, finished with hiding the stallion in the woods below, entered the stone circle. He gave Owen a look of grim disapproval as he, too, settled himself into a sheltered spot away from the wind. He cleared his throat loudly. "With respect, Lord Christ Priest."

Owen rolled his eyes toward him. "Yes?" he asked.

"With all due respect," Enar said, glaring at the child sleeping in Owen's lap.

"Get to the point," Owen said.

"I have learned a great deal from these people," Enar said, "but you are in danger of becoming one of them."

Laughter erupted from the men all around Owen.

Owen didn't laugh. He stroked the sleeping child's cheek gently with his fingers, and the clearing between the standing stones blurred away for a moment as tears filled his eyes. "Can you see the city from here?" he asked Alshan.

"No," Alshan said. "We are too near the coast. When Sybilla returns, I'll send her to see how the city fares."

"I'd like to go with her," Owen said.

Alshan studied him for a moment while his fingers played with the amber jewel he wore. "My lord? Can you move as swiftly, as silently, as fearlessly as she?"

Owen knew the answer was no. Compared to Sybilla even some of her own people were clumsy in the forest. Once she'd saved him from almost certain capture while they were scouting ahead on a mountain road. They blundered into a party of armed men—Hakon's men. She'd been quick-witted enough to be up the trunk of a tree like a squirrel and Owen followed. Even as the warriors passed below, her bird calls warned Alshan and the rest in time for them to seek hiding places. So far the wiry old man had kept them safe on his journey. It was only proper Owen accept his judgment now.

A few minutes later Sybilla returned with the food— several loaves of coarse brown bread and two big jugs of beer. They gathered in a circle around Owen, their knees almost touching his, and Sybilla put the provender before him.

"My lord, will you bless the bread after the manner of your own people?" Alshan asked.

Bless the bread. Owen had never exercised his priestly office. He left this to Ranulf, or lately, Alfric. Bertrand had anointed him bishop and Bertrand's touch had seemed more of a contamination than a blessing by then. He had felt, he realized, unworthy to bring God's flesh and blood to his own people, but here among these lonely, secretive outcasts, he felt more a priest of God than he ever had.

Bertrand had hurled the words of consecration at him like a curse, but priest he was. Presiding over an offering given by the poor to the poor. He stared at the circle of faces surrounding him. Alshan and Elin's people were like no others he had ever known before. No law ruled them. They were a family and they were all here, even Enar, because of love. What stood between them was a covenant of love. Owen lifted his hand and made the sign of the cross, then broke the bread and shared it out among them.

It was plain as they ate that however poor the villagers were, they had given of their best. The bread though dark and coarse was filled with sausage and onions. The beer was a ripe, rich brew. When they finished eating, Sybilla set out for the city. After she left, Owen like the rest relaxed, with the child in his arms.

The stones in the circle were small and rather crudely wrought with the exception of one—a tall menhir carved in loops and spirals that reminded Owen of the tomb where they'd spent the night. Alshan stood in front of it, his fingers touching the strange markings carved into the rock.

"What are you doing?" Owen asked.

"I am speaking with the ancients," Alshan said.

Owen smiled. "What do they say?"

"They speak of this hill and where their village was. They talk of the forest and the sea. One needs food, water, and shelter to live. They tell us where all of these things may be found. And still more, where places of power like this one are."

"Is this a place of power?" Owen asked.

"Of course," Alshan answered. "Did you not feel it when you blessed the bread?"

Owen nodded. He had, realizing he had been set free of the shame and guilt of his priesthood. He understood now that the consecration that made him God's man had not been Bertrand's, but another, much higher power.

He clasped the child close to him and drifted away into a gentle sleep. He dreamed as he had in the tomb, of times and places he could not possibly remember or have known.

He awakened when Sybilla returned. It was near sunset, a lowering sunset darkened by a rising storm.

She hurried into the stone circle and addressed Owen. "The city stands. Twice the Northmen broke against your gates the way a wave breaks against a rocky cliff."

Owen heaved a deep sigh of relief.

But Sybilla frowned. She hunched down and began to refresh herself with the remaining bread and beer as she told her story. "Hakon has suffered one setback, but he is not gone. I found my way into the city and heard Godwin speak to the people in the square. I didn't understand all that he said, but it seems Hakon plans to burn the city."

"No!" Owen shouted as he set Ilo aside and leaped to his feet.

Sybilla shook her head. "I don't think he can succeed," she said. "Elin will summon a storm."

"Then she will die," Alshan said flatly. "Between the curse and the storm she will have done too much."

"No," Owen said. "I'll set out for the city now, Hakon or no Hakon, and stop her."

"It's too late," Sybilla said. "You would never reach it in time."

"There is a way," Alshan said glancing at the tall carved stone ablaze with the afternoon light.

"Show me how," Owen demanded.

"I don't know if you are ready," Alshan said, "and there will be much pain."

"I have endured pain before," Owen said, "and there will never be a better time to find out if I am ready than now with Elin in danger."

"Lord Christ Priest," Enar said. It wasn't a form of address, but a statement of fact or perhaps a mild reproach.

"I'm not sure whose priest I am tonight," Owen said.

"If the tide catches us on the way out to that rock," Enar replied, "you won't be anyone's priest, but a corpse. I hope our good friend Alshan knows when to start running. The hands that placed the grooves in that stone are ages ago gone to dust and things may have changed."

The rock protruded from a vast expanse of sand like the top of a buried mountain. Beyond it the sea shimmered like a mirror in the evening light. High above, a wall of cloud was blotting out the last rays of the setting sun. It towered over them like a gigantic tidal wave of darkness.

Alshan pointed to the thunderheads, still crowned with light. "Her spirit summons it," he said. "She will break her heart against the heavens to call down their wrath on the Vikings."

"I won't let her go alone," Owen said.

"Be careful, Lord Christ Priest," Enar warned. "I have heard stories of men and women who made vows that bound them in this world and the next. They were not happy ones."

"They were heroes," Alshan said.

Owen knew Bertrand and the Church would condemn what he was about to do. Had he been asked, he might condemn it himself, but he couldn't leave Elin to enter a struggle she might lose alone. They were heroes, Alshan had said.

Your life for my people, Elin, Owen thought. *My soul for your life.*

"If I die will my liege Lord damn me for this?" Owen asked the question aloud, not of Enar and Alshan, but the sea and sky.

"My lord," Enar said, "you worry too much about what your Lord thinks and believes. If this transcendent one exists, He judges men's hearts, not their follies and mistakes, and your heart has ever belonged to Him."

"It's time," Alshan said, and the three started out as fast as they could across the sand.

The first waves of the returning tide licked at their feet as they reached the rock and began their climb. The top was nearly as barren and desolate as the slope had been. Only the tumbledown ruins of the small monastery once planted here remained. Owen could look out through the broken arches on the sea beyond.

The stones of the ancient circle lay fallen, scattered in the grass except for one tall menhir that stood near the land's end, bleeding with the fire of the setting sun. Near it stood a few stunted trees permanently deformed, bent by the endless lash of wind from the sea.

Alshan led Owen toward one of them.

Owen paused before the twisted tree. It was an ancient, stunted oak, lightning blasted long ago. Only two branches were left with a scattering of leaves. They stuck out at right angles to the trunk like the arms of a cross.

Beyond the island over an almost mirror-still ocean, the cloud wall seemed to rise higher and higher, lightning twisting in and out of the murky billows sparkling like starlight on a winter night. The clouds seemed to carry the fires of Elin's wrath within.

Owen turned his face away from the tree and looked at Enar. "I don't . . ." He faltered.

Enar's face was somber and cold in the greenish light. His week-old beard stood out against his pale skin.

"Then don't," Enar said, glancing at the tree. "I have always hated him, refused to serve him. Perhaps that's why I've never had any luck, though I am the son of a Jarl. But you knew what I was from the beginning, didn't you, my lord? I came from among your enemies."

Owen nodded. "It was of no moment," he said. "A free man chooses where his loyalties lie and you have abided by your choice. I cannot find any fault in you."

"If that is a farewell," Enar said, "then it is a better one than I deserve. But I beg you, my lord, Lord Owen Christ Priest, don't do this in his name. The one-eyed is a cruel god, and the only one who still takes men."

Alshan, standing on the other side of Owen, spoke. "He must take men, for they are what he uses."

A gust of wind struck, one so strong it seemed to shake the island. The low bushes and trees writhed and twisted in the blast, but the broken oak before Owen never moved, though the low leaves on its branches rattled with a strange whispering sound.

"You may know a god by what he takes," Alshan continued, "and those he takes are the best among us. Into his hands go the sacrificial victim, the warrior fallen fighting in the heat of battle, and the woman doomed in failed childbirth. Those who have spent every drop of their heart's blood that the rest may live. He calls them because he needs them. He is lord of the brave dead and gained his power by showing courage. For nine days and nights he hung on the tree whose roots are the world, and plucked out one eye that the other might see clearly."

Enar shivered. The steady breeze that buffeted the island was cold, but a look of longing was on his face.

"They say," Alshan continued, "that he fought the greatest battle of all against evil. But then," he added slyly, "you know the story."

Owen bowed his head, knowing what was in their minds. He'd heard it, too.

The memories were dim, silent, and secret because Gestric, Owen's father, thought he'd banished the old gods from his hall. But the stories were still told by the dim firelight of a winter's night when the icy wind shrieked around the eaves, and the trees were naked poles against the orange flare of a winter sunset.

Once, the story went, all the world lay captive in the grip of a winter that would not end. Snow lay deep over the land, life fled from the fields, and at last even the rivers and streams ceased to flow as they lay locked in ice. The whole earth lay barren and desolate. Men cried out in fear and wept with the pain of hunger in their bellies. Even the gods themselves were powerless before the icy demonic furies of the northern wastes. All but the one-eyed.

He strode forth into the snow and blew his horn and called out to the dead. For the living were too weak to struggle any longer.

His women, the choosers of the slain, armed the men, steadied their stirrups as they mounted, and handed them the cup, the cup with the mead of immortality. They rode out across the clouds against the night and the cold. Against the darkness that enveloped the world. Their battle was a cloud of fire among the stars.

The grip of the northern demons was broken and the earth knew again its green mantle. The flowers bloomed and birds sang in every tree.

Tears stung Owen's eyes as they had long ago when he heard the story whispered among his father's warriors. And he remembered thinking, what man who called himself a man would not want to ride with such heroes, even if it meant death.

"The dead ride hard," Enar said, "even the brave dead. The Christ Priest's God doesn't take men, but bread and wine. He was the son of a god. He, too, hung on the tree as

the one-eyed did. He, too, journeyed among the dead and returned. His bread and wine are tokens that we are free of the
quest. He did it once and for all men, and no one ever need
make the journey again."

"Come," Alshan said with an impatient shrug. "We have
not much time. If you don't seek the woman's soul in the
storm and find her, she will die. What is this silly talk of
gods as though they were rivals. It may be that the one-eyed
was, after all, only a man."

Owen turned to Alshan. He felt something hard and tight
in his chest begin to unknit itself. "Only a man," he echoed.

Alshan nodded. "To us, as I said, a man is much, all who
came before him and all the get of his seed. So it may be
true of the one-eyed, that he was only a man who was willing to yield more of himself than the rest in search of truth.
So he is remembered. You need not make the journey in his
name, or even in the name of Christ. You may, as a man, undertake it alone."

The last rays of the sun were gone, blue shadows covered
the island, except for the tall, gray cloud, closer now, looming over the island like a cliff. Far out over the water Owen
saw the clouds trailing long, gray veils of rain.

Owen went to his knees and stripped off his shirt. He
heard Enar give a sigh that was almost a sound of pain.
"You and the woman," Enar said.

"Yes," Owen answered and bowed his head. "Only a
man." The words brought him peace. He was not betraying
his God. He was going alone. But are we ever really alone?
Something deep in his being whispered, "No, never."

So Owen questioned his heart and found within it the
same peace he'd found when he touched his lips to the living water deep in the forest—when he'd realized his God
was forever incomprehensible to him, but decided to love
him anyway.

Perhaps, as Enar said, God had made the great journey
from death and back again once and for all time, but he still
had not forbidden it to mankind.

And, as for the one-eyed, had he, the old man of song and
story, been only someone like him? Someone who saw evil
and went out to do battle with it. Descending into the
shadow of the grave to find wisdom. Torturing his flesh to

free his spirit, so that it could search among the stars. Yielding his eye so that the remaining one could look beyond time into eternity.

Owen took a deep breath of the clean wind from the sea. He felt a strange stillness as though he'd been emptied of both fear and desire. Then he rose and walked toward the tree.

"I'll hold you," Enar said, "and when Alshan ties your wrists, I'll let you down gently so your arms aren't plucked from the sockets."

Enar's hard embrace was like a father's. Owen closed his eyes, stretched out his arms and felt the bite of ropes at his wrists. Enar, true to his word, did let him down gently, though Owen felt his friend's whole body tremble with the strain.

Then the pain came, engulfing Owen like a black tide. His head swam and he understood he was about to faint. The sensation passed, leaving him in agony but in command of himself.

Owen whispered, "Elin," and opened his eyes. The clouds boiled above him. It was nearly dark and the last daylight was only a faint shimmer on the horizon's edge. Raindrops began to sting his face and body.

Chapter
42

E LIN awakened to see Edgar dozing in the chair opposite her and Judith standing in the door.

"Well," Judith said, and managed to make the "well" sound like the scratching of a pen signing a death warrant. "Things have come to a pretty pass," she continued. "Elin, why didn't you tell me you needed my servants? Good heavens, I could have sent over two or three. But as it is, I come here and what do I find: that lazy Elfwine lounging in bed, Rosamund sobbing on the stairs, Anna delivering a baby, Ine sleeping under the widow's bed, Ingund trying to turn herself into a man, Godwin buying rats, and you being compromised. Edgar, I know he's of great family, but, tell me, does his distinguished ancestry ever give rise to any eccentric or peculiar behavior on his part?"

Elin opened her mouth, but Judith forestalled her. "Now, hush," she said, "of course you can depend on me to set things to rights at once." She clapped her hands. "Elfwine . . . here, now!"

Elfwine scurried in, carrying the baby.

"Attend my lady," Judith said.

Elfwine sat on the bed and began to nurse the baby.

"Edgar, go find something for Godwin to wear," and Judith added with the sternness of a judge, "something befitting his rank. Do you have something in scarlet?"

"What?" Edgar and Elin said at the same time.

"A dalmatic for Godwin," she explained patiently to Edgar. Then seizing him by the elbow, she said, "Show me what you have." She paused in the doorway. "A posset will arrive in a few moments. Drink it," she commanded Elin, then departed with Edgar.

A few moments later the posset arrived, carried by

Rosamund. Elin drank. When she handed the cup back though, Rosamund didn't leave. She lingered, her eyes downcast as though she wanted to say something, something she lacked the courage to put into words.

"Rosamund," Elfwine said, "I'm hungry. Go downstairs and fetch me . . ."

Rosamund turned toward her, eyes blazing with fury. "I'm sick of waiting on you. I see legs under your gown. If you want something to eat stand up and—"

"You little trollop," Elfwine spat, "how dare you speak to me like—"

"Stop it, both of you!" Elin said. "Be silent. Elfwine, Rosamund is right. The child is now some days old. You've regained your strength. If you want something to eat, you can go downstairs and get it. And don't call names."

"Judith charged me—" Elfwine began.

"Judith doesn't govern this household," Elin said. "I do. If you're hungry, go and eat. Besides, I think at the moment I prefer to be alone."

Elfwine shifted the child on to her hip and flounced out.

"I'm sorry," Rosamund said miserably. Her chin trembled and she showed imminent signs of bursting into tears. Elin embraced her. Rosamund clung to Elin and did begin to cry. "Please," she sobbed, "please don't die. Please don't die and leave me alone."

Elin's arms tightened around her and she thought for the first time with tenderness of the child in her womb. Rosamund's arms were soft and warm. Her smooth cheek rested against Elin's neck. Her skin had a child's fragrance. "Hush," Elin said, "hush, be still. Even if I do die, you won't be alone."

This brought a fresh shower of tears from Rosamund. "Judith is kind," she whimpered, "but she's not you. I love you."

Elin pushed Rosamund to arm's length, holding her by the shoulders. She stared down at her bruised, tearstained face. "Rosamund, I have responsibilities. Don't make what I have to do any more difficult."

Rosamund gulped, stared up at Elin, and controlled herself.

"Send Godwin to me, and I must speak to Gynnor."

Rosamund shook her head. "Godwin's already spoken to Gynnor and Judith. Everything is being made ready. Tonight the whole town will feast, eat, and drink ... but you ..." Rosamund broke down again.

Elin embraced Rosamund, murmuring, "Little one, little one, I'm sorry you love me. I pity anyone who loves me. My feet are already on the road to where ... I cannot say, but don't hold me back. Help me, Rosamund, help me do what I must."

It was evening outside. The cooking fires for the feast were being lighted, but the room was dark and growing darker as the light faded from the sky. Judith returned and Elin sent Rosamund away with her. She remained alone. The light of a solitary candle kept her company. Elin listened to the sounds of feasting and laughter in the distance, feeling now these things were no longer anything she had a part in, withdrawing deeper into herself.

She lay on the bed, watching the flickering candle. Her eyelids felt heavy and she knew her spirit was struggling to leave her body and float free. But something held her back ... Rosamund's grief, the sudden new tenderness for the child in her womb. They were all one. She struggled to sort them out.

At first her pregnancy had been insult added to injury, a dangerous encumbrance, hindering possible escape from the Viking camp. After meeting Owen ... an inconvenience, and then a tool, a means of winning her people to Owen's side. Now, thinking of Rosamund, she didn't know. Whatever kind of life Rosamund had led, she was still a child, a loving child, grief-stricken and afraid of being abandoned.

Ah, how sad, Elin thought, *I could already be holding something like that in my arms. As it is, I may never know such love.* Were they all dead, she wondered. Was her home as much a ruin as Agelf and Dominola's hall? She could have asked Alshan, her people would know. But she hadn't, hadn't wanted to know. Fearing, if they were, she would succumb to a grief so crippling she would be of no use to anyone. If she'd married, she would have died with them. Perhaps, like Dominola, unable to imagine anything powerful enough to destroy her world.

No light shone at the stone casement. Sounds of distant

revelry borne by the night wind drifted to her ears. Here the candle shed the only light, keeping its watch like a sentinel against the darkness.

If she had married, she might have held something like Rosamund in her arms, something warm and soft and all hers. But she hadn't chosen the marriage and the choice had been, as she told Godwin, hers. Right or wrong, she was as the truly free are . . . bound to abide by the consequences.

"God keep you, Rosamund."

Elin felt the trance taking her into the night, into the storm, her whole being wrapped, warped, twisted in a terrible summoning. She was taut with it, waiting, when Godwin appeared at the door.

Godwin didn't resist Judith's attempts to dress him. He knew the value of ceremony. He visited the sweat bath and dressed. Anna prepared clean linen for him. Then he climbed the bell tower. He stood, feeling refreshed by the bath, and though the air near the ground wasn't moving, here up high a stiff breeze was blowing, bringing a swift, pleasant tingle to his skin.

The sun was gone and a rose flush burst through the distant trees. One large star flamed alone on the horizon. Down below in the square, he heard the sound of singing and the stamp of dancing feet. Children were playing on the cathedral steps. Their shouts and laughter rose faintly to his ears.

The town below was filled with light; there seemed to be one behind every window. Gardens were ablaze with lanterns and candles. He could see beyond the lower town, to where Alan and the bowmen kept watch at the walls. Torches were burning all along the palisade. Light everywhere, except in the scar of this morning's conflagration. The ruins lay—a great black sword cut at the town's heart. People thronged the streets. Some visiting friends and kin, but most hurrying toward the sound of feasting in the square.

Drive out the night, Godwin thought. Godwin didn't pray. He hadn't for many years been sure there was anything to pray to. Instead, he looked down at the merrymakers in the streets, thinking Elin's death might be the culminating event of their evening. She and he were both what they were and there was no question of backing away. He knew she planned to take the drug the Berserks ate before a battle. It induced frenzy. Even now she must be as the Berserks, preparing her mind for the transformation. She would, as she had that night in the crypt, drive the soul from her body. Sometimes the soul, driven from the body by such a means, did not return. But he vowed to himself, if she went, if her strange journey took her beyond the gates of death, she would go in glory, with shouts of triumph ringing in her ears.

His fingers tightened on the balustrade. He uttered something that might have been a curse but was perilously close to a prayer, then turned and looked out to sea. Far away he saw a line of clouds and they boiled and shivered with high lightning.

Godwin returned to the hall and finished dressing. Judith gave him a scarlet velvet dalmatic trimmed with dark sable. Miracle of miracles, the magnificent garment fit. The long loose sleeves hung to his wrists, the hem came to just above his knees. He pinned the lily-trimmed mantle to his shoulders with two golden brooches.

"The Lilies of Clovis," Judith said, examining the border of the mantle.

"I have a right to wear them," Godwin said. "I am the blood relative of two kings."

He turned to Ranulf. The boy was armed and wearing his mail. His hand rested on the sword at his side. The iron links of his shirt hung straight. He wore the silver-embossed helmet he'd taken from the dead raider.

Godwin's eyes scanned him from head to toe. He nodded his approval. "Excellent," he said, "you look a soldier now. If Elin calls on me to help her, I can't wear iron. You will carry my sword."

Ranulf could see it was an old blade, very fine. The steel shimmered, a multicolored mirror in the torchlight. He stretched out his hand to take the hilt, then drew back. "I've never seen one before, but I've heard of them." He named the smith.

"I see you know your weapons," Godwin said. "Yes, it is."

"But he's long dead," Ranulf said. "The sword must be an heirloom."

Godwin nodded. "Bequeathed to me by my grandfather, and presented to him at the cutting of his first beard by a man called Charles."

Ranulf looked bewildered for a moment, then the truth hit. He jerked away. "Charlemagne!" he whispered.

"I believe he was a man called Charles," Godwin said. "I am proud to have you carry my sword," he added softly.

Ranulf flushed, tears of joy starting in his eyes, as he quietly, almost reverently, took the sword Godwin held out.

"The feasting in the square is coming to an end," Judith said. "My traveling carriage is at the door. The timing of these things is very important. We must hurry now; soon they'll start getting drunk again."

"Stop fretting," Godwin said, "I'm going to fetch Elin now. We will begin at once."

Elin was lying on her back on the bed, hands clasped the way a corpse rests on a bier. "Is it possible?" she asked.

"It is," he answered. "Are you ready?"

She rose and seemed to glide toward him, the white gown glimmering in the candlelight. When she stood before him, Godwin saw her face was serene. The struggle it had held the night she cursed Reynald was completely gone. Instead, she glowed with the force of one who, once setting their eyes on their objective, never turns aside, never will be turned aside. The eyes looked at Godwin, through him, and into the abyss of eternity beyond. He had seen her afraid the day they met the count in the church; cast into the depths of despair, of inner torment, on the night she cursed Reynald. But now she needed no one. She was alone, alone with the purity of her love.

Alfric waited for her at the foot of the stairs. He held the tall processional cross in his hand. Elin knelt at his feet. Her hair was loose, unbound, flowing in black waves over her shoulders and back. She wore a circlet of rosemary.

She looks, Alfric thought, *like a bride or a sacrifice.* The clean scent of the rosemary was sweet in his nostrils. "I bless you," Alfric said, "because I believe in a God who knows no boundaries, a God as much present in the heights of heaven as in the blackest depths of hell, a God present in the souls of saints as sinners, Christians and pagan alike, a

God of perfect and unending love. I will bless you, but I don't know if I can bless your actions."

Elin looked up at Alfric. Power burned in her blue eyes. "As you will," she said. "I'll take what you offer."

He raised his hand. "God go with you, Elin."

Elin stood. She turned and began embracing the members of the household, one by one.

Elfwine, holding the baby, was prostrate with grief. Elin thought, *Naturally, everyone is looking at her!*

Rosamund was quiet, dry-eyed, but looked desolate.

"Prepare a lantern, a low-shielded lantern," Elin told her. "Godwin may need it."

Ine knelt at her feet. Elin kissed him on the forehead, saying, "Build up the fire. We may need warm, dry clothes."

Ingund still wore the boar-tusk helmet. "I'll lead the mules, my lady," she said.

Judith kissed Elin and pressed her hand. "Gynnor is waiting outside. Don't act surprised." Elin nodded.

She reached Anna last. "My dearest," she said. Anna didn't reply, but held her tightly for a moment, pressing her cheek to her shoulder, then let her go.

Ranulf stood by the door next to Edgar, Godwin, and Wolf the Short. Elin followed them through the door into the square.

Judith's traveling carriage waited at the foot of the steps. It was no more than a large cart, but an impressive thing. The low sides were covered with the carved figures of strange beasts, curving and curling around them and back. Deer hides covered the bottom, and the bench was covered by scarlet cushions. Harnessed to it were two white mules.

The square was a sea of torches. Elin stepped from the door into a blaze of brilliance.

Gynnor stood beside the cart. She held a crown. The crown was a circle of silver set with four candles. "The crown of lights," Elin said. "I am honored."

Carrying herself with queenly grace, she descended the steps and went to one knee before Gynnor on the cobbles.

Gynnor raised the crown high, then placed it on Elin's head, and the chanting began. Gynnor shouted the first words and the whole crowd made the response.

Godwin felt the hackles rise on the back of his neck. He

didn't understand the ancient words. He wasn't sure the people in the mob understood all of them either, but their import was clear.

The woman climbing into the carriage was an offering. Louder and louder came the cry in agonized invocation with Gynnor's voice ringing out, and then being answered.

Alfric hesitated for a second beside Ranulf. "Suppose she fails?" Alfric whispered.

"She won't fail," Ranulf answered. "She can't, she's already succeeded, they are one. They . . . we, will give Hakon nothing, even if he burns the town to ashes," he whispered tautly.

"Yes," Alfric said, then hurried forward to take his place at the head of the procession.

The cart passed through the crowd, rumbling and jolting over the cobbles. Elin stood alone in the center, a slim figure, pale as her gown, the candles resting like stars over her brow, the green rosemary twined at her forehead the only color about her.

Godwin walked beside Alfric. Ranulf strode behind him, the sword resting over his arm, reflecting the fire of the torches. They went through the upper town, past the Roman gate, down the burned-out street to the palisade.

The mass of people in the square fell in behind the cart and flowed, a river of torchlight, down the sloping street toward the gate, chanting as they came. Their voices grew louder and louder until they reached the gate, coming to a halt in front of the posts on the bloody ground. The crowd was a pool around the cart. Men and women climbed into and around the ruined houses, the better to see. Silence fell like a blow, sudden and complete.

Godwin looked up at the sky. A wall of cloud was rising, blotting out the stars. He climbed into the cart with Elin.

She was drawn taut as the prod of a crossbow. Under the gown, every muscle of her body was rigid. She caught his wrists in a grip of steel. She threw back her head. He could see the long corded muscles of her throat. Her eyes stared over his shoulder beyond the blaze of the torches into the darkness. Her face, a mask of struggle, eyes black in the flickering torchlight. She spoke in a hissing whisper. "Hakon is close. I feel him, I scent his blood. I want him to know."

An arrow thudded into the palisade. Denis and his men returned fire; the crossbows sang.

"Close enough, Elin?" Godwin said.

A gust of wind took the torches, turning them into a muttering whirlpool of flame. Elin's dress fluttered. Godwin felt it on his back. Elin's jaw stiffened. Her teeth locked. She spoke next from her throat or her mind to his, he never knew how. "Now, I fly."

It was fast. Oh, God, so fast. The cart whirled, the torches a hurricane of fire, round and round. Then, up and up. The torchlight vanished. It was headlong, dizzying, fast as a fall and Elin knew the utter gut-wrenching terror of a fall, except that she was rising as if borne by a screaming wind.

But a lifetime of discipline had taught her well. She didn't cringe or flee into madness. Abruptly she was over the wall, above the Vikings clustered with Hakon. A second later the forest masses were a dark shadow below her.

Elin couldn't breathe, she was sure she was dying. And like one dying, her being began to unravel. Her life and the things that made her what she was were like so many shells torn away, one by one.

The terrible pain of leaving her home, her family, she had willed it. But it hadn't been easy to abandon her girlhood and reach out to become the sorceress Abreka wanted her to be. The death in life of the Viking camp. It seemed even in the tearing away of that bitter shame she understood how much of it had scarred her.

Last of all was the pain of separation from Owen. She realized now that if she achieved what she wanted tonight, he might be lost to her forever. She might never see him again.

But then, that was gone, too, faster, faster, higher, higher. Like a bolt shot from a crossbow, but gaining speed not losing it. As she rose she seemed borne aloft now by the tempestuous winds in the clouds above.

Intellect dissolved and, with a suffering, shuddering, last burst of pain, a nameless will-o'-the-wisp pierced the clouds and looked down on the storm.

It was a floor of vapor rolling below and she reached at last the terror of that calm which is the heart of the most violent storm.

Elin was a mote of light, a spark brighter than the sickle moon, bathing the clouds in silver radiance.

The storm rolled below, shining like a great sea, a shore-less, everlasting ocean, the same, yet forever shifting, moving, changing, throwing up columns of vapor that hovered and then melted like wraiths back into the swirling seamless glory under her. Lightning played and crackled within the billowing ocean, dancing in and out, lighting one cloud then another like great lanterns.

Elin hovered, a point of light. She poised herself over infinity.

Godwin could feel his grip on the woman's wrists and the soles of his feet on the cart. One spasm after another was shaking her body as she tried to break his grip.

Elin's wrists were ripped from his fingers by a last convulsive tremor. Her breath whistled out of her lungs past her purpling lips in a scream.

He heard her last cry and, again, never knew if it came from her throat or her mind. He didn't believe the writhing, tortured thing at his feet could speak in any human sense.

"My love, I give my all for you!"

The lightning flash, and there was only one—answered her. It shot a sheet of livid blue brilliance across the sky.

Godwin saw all in it—the city behind him, the faces of the crowd around, the pointed stakes of the wall, and beyond, Hakon on his white horse rearing against the lowering sky.

The thunderbolt struck a tree at the edge of the wood, a giant oak. Godwin saw the burst of flame in the distance. The clap of thunder exploded directly over the city, shaking the very earth under him and throwing him to the floor of the cart. And then it seemed the very floodgates of heaven opened.

The rain came straight down, a pouring rush. It doused the torches in an instant, sending the milling, screaming crowd scattering into the darkness, running for safety and shelter through streets turned into rivers by the force of the storm.

Godwin lay beside Elin. The rain, the ice-cold rain, slammed into his back, but he was too exhausted, too stunned to move.

Alfric's hands on his shoulders, shaking his body, roused him, his voice shouting above the drumming of the rain, "Up! Get up! You have all you desire. We must get her to the hall. Feel the air, man, this will kill us if we remain."

The journey back to the hall was a nightmare battle fought in darkness and cold. The narrow street between the ruined houses funneled the water down on them. The unshod mules staggered and slipped on the cobbles as they tried to pull the heavy wagon to the upper gate. The darkness was utter and absolute until Rosamund and Ine reached them. They carried horn-shielded lanterns. After that, the going was easier.

A fearful Godwin carried Elin's dripping body through the doors and, pushing aside the chairs, placed her on the floor in front of the fire. He threw propriety to the winds and began cutting away the soaked dress with his dagger. "Alfric, fetch one of your mantles," he said.

"Why mine?" Alfric said. "I wear only the coarsest of woolens."

"It must be one of yours," Godwin said. He looked up from Elin's icy body, the flames patterning his face, then, light dancing in his eyes. "Yours," he repeated hoarsely.

Alfric stared at him for a moment, then a look of pity crept into his face. He obeyed.

Ingund, outraged by Godwin's behavior, seized his dagger and made the men turn their backs while she finished stripping Elin and wrapped her in Alfric's mantle. Then she hurried upstairs and brought down the wolf skins from Owen's room, using them as an additional cover for Elin.

Rosamund pillowed Elin's head on her lap, and felt her face. "I think she's dead," she whispered softly.

Elin did look dead. Her skin was cold and so pale it appeared almost transparent, her eyelashes lay like black stains on her cheeks.

Godwin took his sword from Ranulf, wiped it dry, and held the mirrored surface to Elin's lips. Her breath stained the shining steel. The faintest dew of moisture blurred the blade.

Ranulf took the sword from Godwin's hand and set the weapon's cross hilt on Elin's breast, the blade running the length of her body. "Iron and a cross, both sovereign against evil," he said.

Alfric stared down at the sword, then up into Godwin's eyes.

"However much I may have dishonored the man," Godwin said, "I have never dishonored the weapon. And it came to my family from the hand of he who was the greatest of earthly kings."

Ingund built the fire into a roaring blaze. The flames leaped high into the chimney.

"Listen," Godwin said, "we have won! Listen!"

Outside, the rain hammered down, pounding, thundering, gurgling with an eerie laughter as it poured from the roof and spurted from the gutters.

"Yes," Alfric said, "no ordinary rain, this. So loud, a rush, a great quantity of water is falling. I saw the clouds move in. The rain must cover the whole coast."

"We have won!" Godwin said, staring up at the rafters, listening to the roar and rush from above, listening to the sound of victory.

Alfric gazed down at Elin. Her face seemed paler in the firelight, her eyes sunken, her lips blue.

"Ranulf," Godwin asked, "how many young men in the town would like to stand in your shoes?"

Ranulf sat down on the bench and began wearily to unarm himself. "A lot of them," he answered. "To have a man of your distinction and lineage take them by the hand would be a great honor."

Alfric seated himself on the bench beside Ranulf and began helping him remove his hauberk. "Godwin," he said, "you make war the way a spider spins its web, because it's part of your nature."

"Yes," Godwin answered, drawing closer to the fire, trying to dry off, "yes I do. But tell me how to live without war, Alfric, make Hakon go away, trouble us no more. When I was seven, my father came and found me. I was sitting in a peach tree in my mother's garden. I remember the moment well because I think I passed, then, my last hour of untroubled joy. I was eating a ripe peach when he found me, the juices running down my chin. He made me wash"—Godwin smiled sadly—"and led me away to the hall. He put a sword in my hand. I have never been happy since. But then . . ." He paused, glancing down at Elin. "I'm not sure we were created for happiness. I'm sure I wasn't, but I do understand responsibility, the here and now. The city is my responsibility. I will not let Hakon and his army take this place and I will do what I must to prevent it. At whatever cost to herself, Elin has given me the advantage and I mean to use it."

"And how long will your advantage last, I wonder?" Alfric asked.

"Long enough," Godwin said, a slow, cold smile spreading over his face, "long enough."

Outside, the rain sheeted down unendingly, seeming to grow harder through the long, cold night. The city, perched on the rock, welcomed it.

The fresh water gushed into drains built by the Roman garrison centuries ago. It drowned what rats had escaped the attentions of the children, flushed the ancient sewer, driving out filth that might have caused plague and disease. The rain freshened those springs that served the fountain, soaked thatched roofs, dampened walls of stucco, wattle and daub, thoroughly fireproofing the city. The cold that came with the rain killed insects, fleas, and lice, destroying another source of danger.

Hakon's men weren't so fortunate. They cowered and fled into rain and darkness, scattering, in search of shelter through the countryside. The water drowned their fires, undermined them, flooded their tents, turned the trampled earth of their camp into a sea of mud, mud into which men and animals sank knee-deep.

The Vikings had cause to regret they'd burned so many of the farms and villages in their path. They crowded into the few buildings that remained, trying to light fires under the leaky roofs of barns and cow sheds, to protect themselves against the growing cold.

The heavens had no mercy. The rain refused to let up, but fell, thundering, beating down. It soaked the soil until it was gorged with water, filled every ditch and stream. They bubbled and gushed, pouring their burden of water into the river. It rose higher, the silent rush of the sea became a threatening hiss, and then a roar as it overflowed the banks and flooded the valley.

Hakon and his men struggled with their longships, battling

to keep them from being swept out to sea by what was now a raging torrent. Blinded by rain and darkness, they were only partially successful. One ship and perhaps thirty men were swept away by the rising water and were never seen again.

Nothing would burn, neither fire nor torch, and though Hakon's men were tough, the wounded suffered from exposure and cold and many died in the night. And still the rain fell, on and on.

The pain in Owen's arms was terrible.

He hung upon the tree Alshan had said of Christ and Owen knew now Alshan's comment had been a token of respect. For he, too, had hung on the tree in search of wisdom. He, too, had hurled body and mind against the elements, against searing agony, against, finally, himself.

Now Owen hung there.

The sea boiled around the rock. Wind and rain smashed themselves as they must have time out of mind against the unyielding stone.

Owen hung in a prison of darkness and suffering. The rain blinded him and battered his bare back and chest like needles of ice. The weight of his body pulling down on his bound wrists seemed to want to dislocate his shoulders. The wind was a constant scream in his ears.

He retched and the bile poured from his mouth to be washed away by the fury surrounding him. He could not tell his tears from the rain. As his suffering grew worse and worse, he exulted in it, knowing when it became great enough, he would escape as he had escaped in the cage.

At last, after what seemed like an eternity of misery, his spirit tore free of the punished flesh. He plunged into the night, into the raging storm, into the lightless void in search of Elin.

In the hall, the household kept their vigil over Elin. There was nothing else they could do. Godwin tried forcing a little wine down her throat, but she wouldn't swallow. The wine ran from the corner of her slack mouth and he began to fear she might strangle if he tried again.

Ingund and Anna pushed more fuel into the fire until the

logs were an incandescent pyre and the heat stung their cheeks six feet away. The sword on Elin's breast flamed red, glowing as though newly forged, against the dark wolf skins.

Elfwine, holding the baby, fell asleep in Ranulf's arms. Anna knelt beside Alfric in prayer for a long time. Then her knees got stiff and she sat in one of the chairs and dozed.

Edgar and Wolf the Short stretched out on the table and fell asleep. Ine did the same under the table. Godwin, Rosamund, and Ingund kept watch.

Godwin and Ingund fed the fire. He pushed a chair behind Rosamund to support her back as she continued to cradle Elin's head on her lap.

Elin struggled in darkness trying to reach full consciousness, knowing she wouldn't make it, not ever again. She was a burned-out husk, the last ember of a dying fire, taken by the wind to be quenched in the dust.

Abruptly, she stood in a bright meadow facing a blue-eyed girl with long, dark hair. She held a hawk on her wrist.

Elin knew she saw the double-goer—herself. Not now, not a shadow, drained dry, but as she had been long ago, before she made the series of choices that brought about her doom.

A sending, a last moment of joy before the silence of eternity. *Thank you,* she thought, *for the time to say farewell to youth, to light, to life.*

The girl loosed the jesses on the hawk as though getting ready to cast off the bird. The hawk spread its wings, the feathered pinions glowing between Elin's eyes and the sun as the light shone through them.

Then the wings closed, beating at her face, and the bird was not of feathers, but of flame. Its embrace not burning, but warming her, filling her body with the heat of love and power. Pumping breath into her lungs and life into her body, chasing out the cold and the dark.

She heard Owen's voice. It thundered around her like a breaking sea and his voice said, "Wherever thou art, there am I also ... forever."

The first to know Elin would live was Rosamund. She saw Elin take a deep breath. One, then another. Color began to rise into her cheeks. Rosamund caught Godwin's eye. She began crying, her tears dripping down on Elin's face.

Godwin knelt beside her. "Now we truly have won," he said, touching Elin's cheek. He woke the rest of the household, briefly, to tell them.

"I never doubted her for a moment," Anna said. "My God, it's freezing! The only warm place in the house is near the hearth fire. She's giving those northern devils a taste of their own medicine."

Ranulf smiled and cuddled Elfwine and the baby closer.

Godwin returned to the chair behind Rosamund, her head rested against his knees.

Alfric and Ingund collapsed on the benches beside the table. They all slept.

Enar and Alshan crouched over a fire in a tiny grotto, at least partially sheltered from the wind and rain while they waited out the time of Owen's testing. Alshan dozed, arms around his legs, head on his bent knees. Enar fretted and fumed. He kept sticking his head out into the rain to see if Owen was calling him. Owen wasn't and so bitter was the night and so dark, he couldn't even see anything.

"Don't worry so much," Alshan said. "He will cry out when it is finished."

"Suppose he can't?" Enar asked fearfully.

"He will," Alshan reassured him. "He is a very strong man."

Enar grouched and grumbled, but privately he agreed with Alshan. Finally he pushed his way deeper into the grotto, folded his mantle around his shoulders and waited. His attitude was one of unhappy resignation.

For a time Alshan let him sulk and simply endured the glares of dislike Enar threw at him from time to time. However, at length, he said, "I cannot see why you trouble yourself, son. You faced an ordeal at one time. Didn't you?"

"Yes," Enar said, "I did. And many were the deeds of strength and agility it encompassed. I ran through the woods. And though I was given but a small start, none of my brother warriors could catch me. I jumped a stick level with my chest at a dead run, ducked under another the level of my knees so quickly I could not be struck with a spear.

While doing it I removed a thorn from my foot without breaking stride. Lastly, I faced the spearmen, buried up to my waist in the earth and none touched me. I did all of these things well, but when it came time to take the cup . . . I . . ." Enar paused and looked troubled, but then continued, "Well, I have small use for such things."

Alshan smiled. "Was your journey so terrible?" he asked.

"Ah, no," Enar answered. "It was, shall we say, embarrassingly brief."

"Indeed?" Alshan asked with a sly twinkle in his eye.

Enar grunted a disconsolate grunt. "Oh, well," he said, "I suppose, since you're almost a priest, I might as well talk. She was a buxom blonde. Clad as we all are when we are born. She had but one thing on her mind, which, I might add, suited me well enough since I had but one thing on mine. I had, you understand, been celibate far too long."

"How long is that?" Alshan asked.

"Now it's a week," Enar replied, "but at that age two days was more than enough. I awakened among my companions very contented with a smile on my face only a few hours later."

"You were not happy with this visitation?" Alshan asked innocently.

"No," Enar said flatly. "Many of my fellow warriors went on much longer journeys. They saw wonderful things. They . . . if their tales be true . . . received great names and walked with gods and goddesses. But when I told mine, all my family and my brother warriors said I had the soul of a peat bog and was a most single-minded inveterate lecher."

"Yet," Alshan asked, "you are singularly successful with women, are you not?"

"Yes," Enar answered. "I seldom go more than a few days, anywhere, without finding a willing companion. But what has that to do with . . ." Enar's face brightened. "I see what you mean. I received the favor I wished. I can't say," he mused, obviously leafing through his memories, "that I could have asked for a better gift."

Just at that moment he heard a loud outcry from Owen. Both Enar and Alshan bolted into the rain.

Owen was shaking all over when they led him into the grotto. Enar pulled on his shirt, then dropped his own deerskin dalmatic over his head, while Alshan built up the fire. They knelt on either side of him to keep the wind off.

There was still some of the bread and beer left. Owen bolted it like a starving man. When he finished eating, he leaned back against the rocks, warmed by the fire, and closed his eyes.

He realized now, with the pleasant heat of the rocks against his back and with food in his stomach, he felt not weakened by his ordeal, but immensely strengthened.

He felt there was nothing he could not do. It was as though he had cast off some tremendous weight he carried all his life and was set free.

"Did you find her?" Alshan asked.

"Of a certainty he did," Enar said. "He has that look."

Owen met Enar's eyes. Enar looked quietly away. He had never seen in all its perfection such absolute peace.

"First," Owen said, "I lost myself and was a fish of the waters, but I hungered and dreamed. No fish dreams. Silver-sided and scaled I leaped."

Alshan thrust another log into the fire. The wood was damp. It hissed, sputtered, then took flame. "And so?" he asked.

"And then," Owen continued, "I was a stag, fleet and powerful. The forest murmurs were in me and I fled . . . got away but toward the living waters of a spring. There was a light in the water and I followed it. I became . . . I became a bird of the air. A hawk, not on the hunt, but a falcon on a lady's wrist."

Owen shrugged under his shirt and dalmatic. The flames were licking the roof of the grotto. He felt the rising tide of strength in himself and was almost uncomfortably warm. He stared down at his wrists. He'd felt the bonds' hard bite in his skin. He had been sure they'd sawn through the flesh. But they hadn't and the ridged markings faded as he watched.

"The woman . . ." Enar prompted.

"It was Elin and I became the falcon on her wrist. I stood between her and her double, as she faced herself for the last time."

Enar shivered and turned his face away. "He who sees himself sees death. He sees his soul as it departs."

"No," Owen said, "but I think . . ." He paused, almost

gasping for breath. "I think I almost died ... almost cut whatever cord bound me to my flesh. I wanted as I embraced her, not simply to possess her, but to be one with her. To give ..." he whispered, "not only life, but myself. I felt that there was not only life against death, but that there was not death. No abyss between being and not being. At that supreme moment I was returned to my pain."

"The flesh is," Alshan said, "ecstatic pain."

Enar's face tightened and he wrapped his mantle more closely around himself. He drew away from Owen. "I had a dream of passion," he said.

Alshan smiled and played with the stoat skull at his breast. "And in return you got passion. He had a dream of selfless love."

"Yes," Enar answered angrily, "and had she toppled over into that abyss he speaks of, she would have taken him with her and she may still. I want no truck with such love. She is only a woman."

"I know what Bertrand thought of women," Owen said, bowing his head and closing his eyes.

"Only a woman," Alshan said. "I have told you what I think a man is. Would you hear what a woman is?"

"Yes," Owen said, opening his eyes and staring as the wood in front of him was transformed into the curving flames.

"In the beginning of the world, the first man slept and in his sleep he dreamed of the love he felt for the gods. These same gods looked into his mind and saw the dream. They gave it shape and substance.

"The shape and substance they gave this dream of love was ... woman. Because of this, the love between men and women is sacred. The sacred fire of creation. A sacred act.

"As the earth is mated to the sky in a sacred act and so is created every living thing. So man worships in woman's flesh the power that gives him life and she in his. And as the earth and sky are one in giving life, so are men and women one in their love."

Enar cleared his throat harshly. He still would not look at Owen. "The rain is beginning to abate."

"And the tide," Alshan said, "no longer splashes against the rocks. How do you feel?" he asked Owen.

Owen let out a long, ragged breath. "As though I'd tapped some source of unending power."

"Come then," Alshan said. "We will reach the city before dawn."

Chapter

43

OWEN returned at dawn. He came by the stairs from the Lady Well.

Gowen was on guard. Godwin had assigned him the duty not long before Elin called the storm. He was delighted to have such an easy task. A little rain troubled him not at all. As for the cold, he'd grown up in the highlands. He regarded the temperature as refreshing and, unlike the Vikings, he was able to warm himself at a fire whenever he chose.

He paid a desultory visit to Alan and his men at the gate. They were warm and comfortable, camped on the ground floor of a burned-out house. They were enjoying beer—courtesy of Owen's cellar, a rack of ribs from one of Judith's oxen, and a pot of Ingund's excellent soup. He stood at the palisade for a time, with a smile on his face, listening as the commotion as Hakon and his men fought to save their ships from the rising water.

Pleased to note the Vikings were satisfactorily occupied, he strolled to the upper town. He found the guards at the fortress and the Lady Well wet and miserable. He set up a crude shelter and built a fire, then ambled over to the tavern and terrorized Arn. He returned to his improvised guard post with a barrel of unwatered beer and an enormous platter of roast chicken.

Comfortable, his belly full, he considered paying a call on the widow, but finally, regretfully, decided against it. Gowen was an absolute egotist, but he was not a fool. Godwin would have no mercy on a derelict sentry, and Hakon might pull himself together sufficiently to attempt something, and Gowen didn't want to be caught with his pants down if Hakon did.

Gowen was sitting in the shelter, bored, watching rain pour off the roof when he heard the clicking sound of horse's hooves climbing the stairs by the Lady Well. There were three possibilities. He considered them in an orderly fashion. The Northmen? No, he didn't think so. Surely they wouldn't be such idiots as to bring horses with them.

The horned one himself, dropping in to pay a call on Godwin and Elin? A distinct possibility. If so, he would want to greet him with due honor. Whatever the priests said, Gowen felt the horned one was a valuable friend. Besides it didn't do to quarrel with him.

Owen returning home? Gowen drew his sword. He didn't feel like leaving the shelter. He peered into the murk at the head of the stairs and heard Enar's voice.

"Lord Christ Priest, I think we should call out or give some sign of our presence. They will have set a watch. I don't want my throat cut."

At the same moment he saw them, shadows entering the back garden. "Beer and a fire," Gowen called out, "over here."

When they drew near, Gowen gave the stallion an expert glance. "A fine bit of plunder." He studied Owen's sword belt. "Gold," he said, "and very pure, not the cheap stuff they make nowadays. You haven't done badly out of this adventure." He passed the platter of meat and the beer.

Owen crouched down in front of the fire, his head bowed. He was soaked to the skin, and exhausted. "How has it gone?" he asked Gowen.

"As you see," Gowen said, "the Northmen came. We welcomed them with fire and steel, not once but twice. They were most unruly but we quieted a lot of them. Greedy, but we stopped their mouths and stilled their hands with our generosity. In return they left many fine gifts behind. Enough for everyone.

"But guests, like fish, begin to stink after three days, so Godwin asked Lady Elin to call a storm. As you can see, she did. I don't know if they will have any stomach for our hospitality in the future. I think not, which is a pity. I have been well entertained and profited by knowing them. But I believe I could look upon their departure with dry eyes. My hope is, since we so well contented them, they may move on."

Chuckles all around. "Well said," Enar commented.

Owen entered the hall through the back door. The whole household was sleeping in front of the fire. Behind him he heard Enar sigh deeply, a sigh of pleasure at the warmth of the room.

"My heart," Owen whispered, "my home."

He felt an enormous warmth, a love, well up in him as he stood watching them wrapped in the helplessness of sleep. He could see the tokens of their struggle against the Vikings scattered all over the hall—the piles of weapons in the corners, the table hacked and chopped when Godwin used it to defend himself. A smell of arrow poison and dried blood lingered under the scent of wood smoke from the hearth. They had done as he asked, kept the city safe, defended it.

Then Owen saw Elin. Her head was still pillowed on Rosamund's thigh. She'd grown warm and shrugged off some of the covers. They were down around her shoulders. She'd freed one arm and her hand lay on her breast, on the hilt of Godwin's sword.

She was, he thought, as he had seen her first, her cheeks flushed by the fire's heat, her black hair down around her alabaster shoulders, pale yet warmed by the fire of life. So beautiful.

Something clutched at his heart. A joy so great it was pain. It may be that he made some sound as he approached her or perhaps a thought passed between them. For whatever reason, she opened her eyes as he stepped toward her and moved from the shadow into the light.

"Do I dream you?" she whispered, rising to one elbow and holding the wolf skins to her breast.

He knelt beside her.

"Love me," she pleaded softly, "love me. For you I called the storm. I gave myself naked into nothingness. I rode the wind and came, flung down by the rain. The lightning pierced my heart. But not all that struggle gave me so much pain as the fear you would leave me. The fear you would hate me for . . . for Reynald . . . for Reynald, that I destroyed him. My soul is emptied by that sin. Fill it with your love."

Her blue eyes looked up into his dark ones, dark, tinted golden by the firelight, beseeching.

"I thought," he said, "I hungered for the springtime. But it was you and what you bring me that I longed for. You are my springtime and I will see it returning forever in your eyes."

No one had ever looked at her with such tenderness. He set the sword aside and gathered her into his arms. The hall slept around them as he carried her up the stairs.

She sat on the bed, watching, as he barred the door and set the fire blazing on the hearth. She was patient, sure wherever they had gone together there was no time.

Time may be the endless grinding out of eons, but eternity is an instant.

They never knew when their bodies joined, they were so much one already. He was not in, but within her, and she unfolded herself to him as the petals of a flower open to the sun. They drifted together on a golden river of joy. Then the pleasure expanded like a flame. They were caught up in its fire, and warmed.

Yet still it grew, without struggle or end. Reaching into those secret places in the heart where we bury our sorrows until they fester, and rot the day. All . . . all were open to that transparent flame, and vanished into it.

For her, her sorrows were the shaming of slavery, the brutal rape in the camp, and the distrust of all men it engendered. For him, it was Bertrand's cruelty, his hatred of the forgiving flesh, and the torment of body and spirit. And for both, the secret loneliness that lies at the bottom of every human heart. The isolation that is the glory and tragedy of our kind. All gone. All swept away, less than ash before the wind.

They became for the eternal instant one. Became what God has truly joined together and nothing can ever sunder.

The flame sang, sang of the hunger of the heart satisfied and the bitter struggle of the spirit for love fulfilled. That was how it ended, amidst a great silence. A silence more eloquent than any word, in a vast stillness that is the heart at peace.

The light of eternity faded slowly and quietly as a sunset and they were returned into time. Warm against each other

... the room cold around them ... the fire blazing on the hearth ... they slept.

Ingund awakened first. She saw Elin was gone. She didn't realize Owen had returned. She thought Elin simply had gone to wash and dress, so she made a trip to the wood box. Ingund was no longer unhappy about returning to her role as cook. She derived a great deal of satisfaction from fighting, but, after all, one had to be practical and, next to battle, she loved good food and the joy of preparing it. She looked forward to giving everyone, Elin included, a good hot breakfast. Her mind was fixed on the bundle of faggots in her arms, and she didn't look up until she was close to the fireplace. She raised her head and found herself staring at the face of a horse.

Her screech and the sound of six or so sticks of firewood crashing to the floor roused everyone in the room.

Rosamund opened her eyes and looked up. The stallion's head was just above hers. His ears pricked. He lowered his muzzle toward her face and blew softly through his nostrils. "Don't take on so," she said to Ingund, "I have awakened to worse sights. Where is Elin?"

Enar sat cross-legged on the hearth, his clothes steaming. He'd found one of the stronger preparations Elin used to drive out cold and was dosing himself liberally. "Elin is with Owen upstairs," he said, "and if I were you I wouldn't go up.... I repeat, I would not go up right now to congratulate him on his safe return. What passed between them when they greeted each other was such that I crept away like a mouse and tried to stable the horse. I found four families living in the stalls and two in the loft, so I brought him here."

They all looked at the stallion. It arched its neck and stood proudly, as always ready to greet and gratify its admirers. Dutifully they admired it.

"How beautiful," Godwin said.

"Magnificent," Edgar said.

"So gentle," Rosamund said and, reaching up, she stroked the velvet nose.

Ingund said ominously, "He is a horse and doesn't belong in the hall."

"He is a horse," Enar said, "who may claim a blood debt. He saved my lord's life more than once."

"No one should put so fine an animal out in the storm," Anna said.

"Listen," Alfric said.

Godwin and the rest started fearfully and obeyed. "Am I deaf now?" Godwin asked. "What is it? I hear nothing."

"That's just it," Alfric said, "nothing. The rain's stopped."

Godwin walked to the door, and pushed it open. He looked out across the square. The thick storm clouds above were suffused with deep blue light. Alfric wasn't entirely right. It was still raining, a mist now, a heavy scatter of fine droplets that collected on Godwin's hair and face, covering them quickly with moisture. He walked across the square, his feet stirring circles in puddles reflecting the cloud-fissured sky.

Godwin stopped at the burned-out street leading to the gate beside the Roman wall. He looked out past the palisade, hung with its burden of dead men, into the valley beyond. Water drowned the ditch at the wall and stood in vast shallow lakes in the fields.

In the distance, he saw fires springing to life in the Northmen's camp. They didn't appear to be very successful fires, only a few faint sparks of light. Godwin chuckled. He considered that the Vikings were probably finding dry wood hard to come by.

He was an old soldier and knew the difference between the disorganized milling of a crowd and the more disciplined activity of an army. He smiled grimly. The camp resembled nothing so much as an overturned ant hill. The proud ships lay askew, one completely beached, resting on its side, and where yesterday there had been five ships, now there were only four.

"Damnation on it!" Godwin whispered. "If only I had an army, if only I possessed half his force." Suddenly he turned and ran, splashing through the puddles toward the hall. He burst through the doors so quickly and loudly that Ranulf jumped in front of Elfwine and the other women, hand on his sword hilt.

Godwin approved. The boy was developing the right instincts. "Ranulf," Godwin shouted, "I want Judith and her

men right now. Send them to ... to Osbert's house, then
wake Gunter."

Ranulf began arming himself quickly.

"I remember," Godwin said, "you told me many would be
glad to take the same oath you took. Gunter will know who
they are."

Ranulf nodded. "My lord," he asked, "what are you planning? I'm not questioning you but I want to know so I can
better help."

Godwin laughed savagely, his face filled with furious joy.
He wrapped the black lily mantle around himself. "I'm planning to make Hakon sorry the bitch who whelped him ever
loved the boar who was his father. Oh, you gods," Godwin
cried, raising his eyes to the ceiling and baring his teeth,
"the Viking dung is delivered into my hand."

"Godwin," Anna said, "you're not making any sense."

"It doesn't matter," Godwin shouted. "Anna, drag that
Saxon out of his wife's arms and do it now! Rosamund, stop
feeding the horse. Move, all of you, move! I want every man
in the city in the square. We ride against Hakon within the
hour. Move!"

Ranulf charged through the door at a dead run. Rosamund
went flying up the stairs.

A minute later Enar came staggering down the stairs, Ingund pushing him, Rosamund pulling him by the arm.

Godwin seized him by the shirtfront and jerked him toward the hearth. "Saxon," Godwin said, the fist on Enar's
shirt lifting him to his toes. "Saxon," Godwin whispered,
"would you have my friendship? Would you have my love?"

To Enar, Godwin looked extremely dangerous. He seemed
to be on fire. His whole body vibrated with a tremendous energy. He flamed with a mysterious madness. "Love?" Enar
said. "I beg you, consider me excused. What I want right
now is sleep."

"Saxon," Godwin said, "don't try my patience. There are
four longships drawn up at the river's edge. I want you to
make them burn."

"Godwin," Enar wailed, pawing at the hand gripping his
shirt, "we have just had a rain hard enough to quench the
fires of hell. How am I ..."

"Saxon!" Godwin hissed. Enar's nose was an inch from

his own. "I swear I will never again suggest Owen hang you, no matter what mischief you make. I will not even consider spiking your wine cup with some fine medicine, one which frees us from all earthly ills."

Enar's eyes widened, his brows rose. "Godwin!" he said. "I have my pride. It won't let me yield to threats."

"What"— Godwin shook him violently— "what do you want?"

"I want you to be polite to me."

Godwin shoved Enar away. He staggered back several feet. "Saxon," Godwin said with murderous softness, "I begin to think you a worthy opponent. Polite! You want me, the cousin of two kings, to be polite to you, be polite to one created for the express purpose of convincing those tiny creatures who crawl at our scalp, armpits, and groin that there is an all-sustaining and merciful God. Polite to the answer to a louse's prayer?"

Enar paled.

"As insults go . . ." Alfric said.

Godwin smiled. "Want more politeness, Enar?"

"The answer to a louse's prayer," Enar repeated. He was impressed. "I think I could make the ships burn. It's really important, isn't it?"

"Yes," Godwin said, "and I wouldn't entrust the task to a fool. Did I not consider you had proven your loyalty and ingenuity over and over again, I would not entrust it to you! Speak! Can you do it?"

"Yes," Enar said, "I'll need pitch and dry wood . . ."

Anna snatched up an axe. "There's plenty of furniture in the house," she shouted, "and it's dry."

Godwin's rap on the door awakened Owen.

"Presently," Owen said. He jumped out of bed and began to dress quickly. He didn't arm himself.

Elin did the same, pulling on her shift and a plain white linen dress. She opened the door for Godwin. He and Edgar were standing in the hall.

Owen didn't have to ask what Godwin wanted, he knew.

"They are wet, cold, hungry, and terrified. They saw what Elin did last night," Godwin said. "We will never have a better opportunity."

"I still say it's a gamble," Edgar said.

"There will never be a better time to gamble," Owen said. He turned to Elin and met her eyes, realizing as he did that there was no need for words between them. He took both her hands in his, lifted the fingers to his lips, and kissed them.

For a long moment they stood still, gazing at each other, as if each was seeking an image of the eternal moment they shared and trying to enshrine it so they could carry it away and keep it forever in their hearts.

Godwin broke in on them. "Hurry," he said. "We have not much time."

Owen turned and followed Godwin down the stairs.

When Owen entered the hall everyone stopped what they were doing and stared at him open-mouthed. They looked at him as they might have a ghost.

Anna paused as she was reducing a chair to splinters with an axe. Rosamund and Ingund stood gawking at him from beside the big table they were in the process of filling with bread, cheese, and wine. Ine and Denis were cocking crossbows methodically, one at a time.

At that moment Ranulf exploded through the door in a rush. "Godwin I have the men gathering in the square. Every man in the city who has a horse and can bear arms. I told them no torches, no lanterns, no lights of any kind. You want this to be as much of a surprise as possible. . . ." His voice trailed off as he saw Owen.

The two stared at each other in silence for a long moment. Owen realized everyone waited to hear what he would say.

Ranulf was armed as the knights were, mail shirt, sword, and he carried a shield on his arm.

Owen turned to Godwin. "It seems you took command in my absence."

"Who better?" Godwin answered coldly.

Owen felt a brief spasm of fury. Then his anger quieted. Ranulf stared at him, a strange helpless look in his eyes, and Owen knew the boy couldn't begin to hope for his approval. Ranulf waited for the blow to fall, and Owen knew he could crush him, perhaps forever, with a word.

He walked toward Ranulf. "Once," he said, "I almost

called you brother in the hall after your quick thinking
brought my sword to me as I fought Gerlos. I lacked both
the wisdom and the courage. Will you let me call you
brother now?"

Quicker than thought, Ranulf was on his knees, trying to
kiss his hand. Owen wouldn't let him. He caught Ranulf as
he fell to his knees and embraced him. Then the others were
all around him, weeping, laughing, thanking God for his
safety, welcoming him home.

Godwin broke up the celebration by clapping his hands.
"Open the doors and show yourself to the people."

Ranulf threw aside the big doors to the hall and Owen
stepped out. The square was filled with armed men, and
Owen realized the Vikings hadn't only left their dead behind, but their weapons, too. Now they were on the backs of
the citizens.

Godwin stood to one side with a torch in his hand, Ranulf
on the other. The two torches threw the only bright light into
the early morning gloom.

Owen and the people greeted each other in silence. Then,
very deliberately, he pulled off the old linen shirt. He turned
his back to the crowd, showing the still-open wounds made
in his flesh by the scourge. He turned to face them and
stretched out his battered hands.

A deep sigh ran through the throng.

"As you can see," he said, "I was taken, not only taken
but tortured. I did not leave of my own free will. But Hakon
failed then, as he will fail now."

They seemed about to cry out, so Owen stretched out his
arms for silence. "I beg you," he said, "raise no shout. Light
no more torches. Hakon must not know we're coming."

Elin appeared at his side, carrying his mail shirt and
sword. She armed him, slipping the mail shirt over his head
and did the laces at the back. Then, kneeling, she belted the
sword at his waist.

In the brilliant torchlight Owen could see how the king in
the tomb had honored him. The sword belt and baldric were
made of many woven gold chains secured by latch knots inlaid with rubies. The sheath was covered by a skin of beaten
gold.

Owen raised Elin to her feet and put his arms around her. He could feel her fingers tighten and knot into his hauberk.

"Oh, God," she whispered into his ear, "to find you again and then fear in the moment of finding you ... to lose you."

"Elin," Owen pleaded softly, "don't unman me."

"No," she whispered, "never!" She drew back and spoke in a loud voice. "Ride out against your foe, my lord. I pray God give you victory."

The mob in the square swore a low savage shout.

Owen mounted the bay warhorse. Ranulf and Godwin were already in the saddle. He lowered his lance, the tip resting at Elin's feet.

She lifted her arms, a lonely figure in white between the great doors. "Go," she said, "and may God ride with you."

Owen led his ragtag army through the gates, riding hard toward the Vikings' camp.

Godwin and the knights rode on his right, Ranulf and the archers on the other. Owen took the road. He knew Hakon would see him coming, so he might as well give the horses the best footing possible.

Enar, Alan, and ten of the best archers, screened by the trees and the half dark, snuck along the riverbank toward the ships beached on the shore.

In the camp Hakon stared in disbelief at the riders issuing from the city. Then he turned in horror to the disorganized and demoralized men around him. Some were trying to light fires, others sat shivering, huddled in the mud, thankful the punishing rain had at last ended.

They stood amidst the wreckage of tents and wagons. The livestock they'd collected for food had broken free in the night and were scattered all over the valley, foraging in the flooded fields.

One man near Hakon stood with his back to the wind, pissing on his fallen tent.

Godwin, Hakon thought, had men behind him, a lot of men. Fresh troops. They must have remained in the city all night.

Then Hakon realized that the man leading the attack wasn't Godwin, but a man he thought must be still in flight, hiding somewhere trembling in fear.

Hakon felt a strange sense of futility settle over him. Nothing had gone right since he met the bishop. He had thought Osric's cage could break anyone, but Owen had escaped. Not only escaped, but made a shambles of the camp and killed Osric. Then he had eluded all attempts to recapture him with almost magical skill.

But Hakon wasn't a man to be defeated easily. He ran, cursing his spies in the city, screeching at his men to arm themselves at once, thinking Owen must have had the soldiers in the city all the time. He must have been saving them, waiting until Hakon was vulnerable as he was now.

In the distance, Owen, his horse laboring on the muddy road, saw Hakon's line beginning to form. He shouted at Godwin, "Faster!" and spurred his horse to full speed, thinking he had to arrive before Hakon could fully collect his scattered wits and recover from his surprise. He had barely enough men to make a showing. He'd concentrated his best in the front ranks so Hakon would see them first and not realize he had only a handful of battle-trained men.

Hakon's camp was just ahead and Owen knew Hakon hadn't been able to fortify it as well as he would have liked. Owen gave a yell and raised his arm. The experienced men with him understood his signal.

Ahead, Hakon's men, those he'd been able to gather quickly, raised the shield wall. He'd chosen the boar's head formation.

Wise, Owen thought, he would protect his flanks. Buoyed by the better footing on the road, Owen felt borne along by the wind until they reached the Viking camp.

The boar's head Hakon had chosen was a big wedge with a flat apex. The overlapping shields, once so brightly colored, were now brown, muddy ovals. Spears and axes waved above them, showing the dark glint of wood and steel in the growing light. Hakon chose to stand his ground. The bastard was smart, Owen thought. The camp was a sea of mud. The gummy, slippery footing would slow the horses, slow Owen's charge.

With a scream of unbridled fury and hatred, Owen turned his horse from the road and across the open field toward the camp, drawing his sword as he drove the horse toward the waiting line. The wind was a raw blast in his face, stinging his cheeks, burning his open eyes. They teared quickly, but cleared. He held the horse to a punishing pace, Godwin and the rest straggling into a ragged "V" at his back. Owen's horse slowed. Hakon had dug a ditch at the edge of the camp.

Owen's horse plunged through the water, then up to the sodden ground inside the camp. The horse's neck stretched almost straight out as he labored through the mud.

"A flanking movement?" Edgar yelled, his horse's head at the withers of Godwin's mount.

"No!" Owen yelled. "He can maneuver all day on this slop. Head-on!" he shrieked.

And head-on they came. From the corner of his eye, he saw more and more men running to join Hakon, and Owen knew his first instincts had been correct.

He glanced back, his people were bunching. They would strike a flying wedge at the forefront of Hakon's line. The knights' lances dropped. Godwin rode at Owen's side, Ranulf flanking him. Owen had wondered if the boy would hang back with the green troops, but he hadn't. He was crouched over his horse's withers, lance couched in his hand. Gowen was on his left. Beyond them he could see Rieulf. Then the muddy shield wall was flying at him at terrible speed, and Owen, as he had through his life, flung himself at the enemy, giving, as Elin had, his all.

The melee exploded around him. His lance punched through a shield and was torn out of his hand, left in a man's body. His horse took an axe cut across the chest and leaped away from the shield wall, stiff-legged, then running. The screams of horses and men rent the air around him. The knights crashed into each other as the horses refused the charge. They fought the bits and tried to bolt.

Ranulf was almost thrown. He lost the stirrups and his lance as his horse bucked and then kicked at the shield wall. He fought the unfamiliar animal and brought him under control. He found himself riding beside Edgar, fifty feet from Hakon's men. There was scrambling behind the shield wall as they tried to deploy their bows and shoot at their attackers.

They had little success. Bowstrings and arrow fletchings

were sodden. They could get no tension on the bows. The arrows they loosed wavered and wouldn't fly true.

"We failed," a white-faced Ranulf said to Edgar.

"No," Edgar answered. He looked at Owen. He and Godwin gathered their men. "No!" Edgar said. "He knew the horses would refuse the first charge. They almost always do."

Ranulf glanced at the new recruits Gunter had brought. They milled farther back, a bewildered mass of horses and men. Edgar smiled quickly and savagely. "He has the bastard where he wants him. Look, they're running now!"

They ran. Not the stalwarts who stood with Hakon, they held their ground. But those who hadn't been able to reach the boar's head were in flight, led by the women and walking wounded. They streamed toward the ships beached by the river.

"What now?" Ranulf asked, pulling his horse's head up. The animal under him was quivering, its flanks coated with sweat even in the bitter wind.

"We play hunt the commander," Edgar said, "as Godwin did with the count in the church. That's a game for men, Ranulf."

Edgar kicked at his horse and rode toward Owen.

Ranulf watched him, then grasped what Owen was doing. He and the strongest knights were forming themselves into a wedge. Ranulf galloped his horse toward the green troops at the rear.

"What's happening?" one of them shouted at him.

"He's readying another assault," Ranulf said. "Be ready, it's our turn."

Then the group of frightened bewildered youngsters were all around him, their horses pressing at his horse's flanks, legs brushing his stirrups.

"You mean we haven't lost?" Martin asked. He was there with his usual contingent of fishermen's sons.

"Martin, to me!" Ranulf said.

Martin was frightened, but Ranulf saw he was willing to obey him. "Hakon is beaten," Ranulf said. "Look, he cannot get his men to go forward."

Even as he spoke the words, Ranulf realized they were true. Hakon was urging his men, but the Vikings weren't moving. Owen's wild charge and a night in the icy rain had taken the heart out of them. They were willing to hold their position but not to advance.

Exultant shouts rose all around Ranulf. He knew it wouldn't be that easy. The battle hung in the balance. He stiffened in the saddle and stood in the stirrups, looking toward the ships. Where the hell was Enar?

Enar was having problems of his own.

He and Alan had, as they had been ordered, attacked at the ships, but the men there raised the shield wall, and his contingent of ten archers was too few to force their way past to the giant hulls beyond them.

Alan and Enar pulled back into the trees. The men guarding the ships didn't try to follow. They'd seen the executions done by Denis's crossbows and wanted no more of them.

"What can we do?" Alan asked.

Enar was hugging a big bundle of dry wood—the remains of three chairs and part of a table. The wood was wrapped inside oil-soaked cloth. He was near complete exhaustion. His face was gray, his eyes, nose, and mouth lined with blue shadows.

He crouched, studying the river. A half mile away Owen charged the Viking line. Enar was trying to decide to whom to give his soul. Owen had said Christ wanted his brave heart. Enar had his doubts. But Odin was, in Enar's opinion, extremely unreliable and he was not and had never been friendly with the horned one. *Christ it is,* Enar thought.

The ships were pulled up on the shore, lying among the ruins of Martin's village. One rested on the burned-out church. The river had come over the banks in the night. That meant the water had to be shallow around the ships, and behind the ships.

"All right, Christ," Enar said. "Please, I don't want to kill anyone. I just want to burn a ship, one little ship. Please, Christ, just one ship," he muttered.

"What?" Alan said.

"Cover me," Enar said. "Make a frontal attack, then pretend to run, try to drag them off."

The trees at the river's edge were a drowned forest. The

water came halfway up the trunks of the poplars. The wandlike willows were a tangle of branches in the flood.

Enar stripped off his shoes and leggings. He forced his way through the trees, finding himself standing on the old riverbank. It was five feet under water. The water reached his chin. He held the faggots on his shoulder, keeping them dry. Anna had given him a clay jar filled with coals from the hearth fire. He held that on his other shoulder. He waded among the willows in the half-light until he heard the sound of Alan's attack, then walked through the water toward the stern of the nearest ship. He walked on his toes, his legs cracking with the strain, praying desperately he wouldn't step into a hole, or that a sudden eddy wouldn't sweep him out into deeper water. He prayed for help. He prayed, after the manner of his people, for luck.

Then he was beneath the stern post of a ship. With hands that shook violently from cold and fatigue, he poured the coals into the bundle in his hands. It smoldered for a second, then the oil caught fire with a roar. He hurled it over the stern.

The bundle landed on a bench. The wood steamed, then smoked and burst into flame. The flames licked at the furled sail. The linen began to steam, then smoke, and it, too, caught. Fanned by the high, cold wind, the blaze whipped up all along the sail, the damp cloth giving off clouds of smoke. Its black shadow wavered against the dawn sky.

Enar heard a shout from the shore. He was trapped, the river behind him. He was nearly done in, but not finished. He breasted the flood and ran for the shore, his fingers fumbling for the axe in his belt, just as Owen charged Hakon once more.

Owen's men formed a wedge around him. Hakon was at the center of the boar's head, mounted on his white horse. They charged. This time the front line of the boar's head gave. The men thrust forward, locked in savage combat with each other. Owen fought, laying about him on all sides amidst a maelstrom of blows. It was as though Owen, maddened by the fury burning in his blood, could smell Hakon's.

Two men in front of him dropped without Owen's seeming to do anything. Owen threw aside his shield and swung his sword in a wide arc, clearing a space around him. Then driving his spurs into the bay, he lunged with a scream directly at Hakon.

His first blow smashed Hakon's shield. His second didn't land. Hakon jerked his horse's head around and tried to cut Owen's throat with a backhand swing.

Hakon could hear Owen's ringing two-handed parry above the battle's tumult. He felt it, too. It nearly jerked the sword from his hand. He gave ground, backing his horse away from Owen. He gave ground instinctively because he saw in Owen's face the same thing he'd seen when Owen had trapped him in the hall—the death light surrounding a hero riding to Valhalla.

This man could be killed, but could never be conquered. Hakon remembered the horse running into the hall to save Owen. The very memory seemed to weaken his arm. This man, he knew, would never fall until the riders of the storm came to bear him away.

The Vikings at the snout of the boar's head closed the gap Owen had forced, and Owen and the knights inside were encircled, trapped.

Ranulf, farther back with the younger men, knew it was now or never. He raised his sword and shouted, "Owen! Forward, you mothers' sons, forward. Will you hang back when victory is within our grasp?" They followed him. The boar's head dissolved around Ranulf in the fury of battle.

Hakon and Owen fought, knee to knee. No one in the melee could see or think or hear. Then the two forces seemed to swirl apart as Owen's men pulled back. The boar's head was still intact, but there seemed fewer men in it.

Nearly all of Owen's force were wounded. Gowen's mail was stained with blood in a half dozen places. Edgar had a sword cut on one arm. Owen was bleeding from a gash on his forehead. Godwin's shield was hacked almost to bits. The hand holding the grip was a pulped, bloody mess. Ranulf himself was wounded. Blood ran down the outside of his thigh, puddling in one boot. But his sword was in his hand and they were all still in their saddles.

"Hakon!" Owen screamed at the raider chief. "Your ships are on fire." He pointed away toward the riverbank. The ship's masts and rigging were outlined in fire.

Enar, Ranulf thought, had done his work.

Those remaining in the Viking camp, sheltered by the boar's head, began the rout and finished Hakon. They took up the cry, "The ships are burning!" The boar's head formation dissolved around Hakon as everyone began running toward the burning ship in the distance.

But where was Enar? Ranulf wondered.

Enar swung his axe. The face of the first man to reach him vanished into a bloody mess. A dozen weapons seemed to slash at Enar at once. But he was running as only he could run. Then he was free of them and flying out across the plowed land. But eight of the Vikings guarding the ships gave chase.

In the distance, Enar could see Owen and Godwin along with the rest pursuing the fleeing Vikings. They were riding toward him, the Vikings running along the shore toward their ships.

The only thing that saved Enar was his bare feet. Mud clung to the boots and leggings of the Vikings behind him, slowing them down. Enar's bare feet splashed clean down through sludge and slime, faster and faster.

But he knew he was finished. His legs didn't seem to want to obey him. The stitch in his side stabbed raw agony at his ribs. His lungs gasped for air that wasn't there.

In the distance, Owen saw Enar running desperately. He broke off his pursuit of Hakon, shouting, "Enar!" Owen's horse was nearly blown, but he drove his spurs in to the hilt. He still wasn't fast enough. He could see blood pouring from the big man's mouth and nose. Enar ran with his head back and he looked as though every stride would be his last.

"No!" Owen shouted and flogged his horse to full speed, turning to intercept the fleeing Enar. *Gamble,* Owen thought, *gamble.* He lifted his backside out of the saddle and slashed at the girth with his sword. The saddle fell away. The horse stumbled but then, terrified by the falling saddle and freed of part of the weight on its back, it bolted ahead of the pack, straight toward Enar.

Owen reached him just as Enar pitched forward and went down. He swung his horse around and brought him to a rearing halt beside Enar, and the Saxon, with his last strength, threw his arms around Owen's waist. They galloped away together.

One of the closest Vikings, hot on Enar's track, gave a yell and tried to close the gap between himself and Enar. But another recognized Owen and shouted his name. Thereafter the remaining Vikings showed a marked lack of interest in catching up to them. A few seconds later, they turned and joined the rush to the longboats.

Owen pulled his horse to a stop and watched the Vikings run. Alan, Denis, and the archers harassed them as they embarked, speeding their progress along.

Owen leaped from his horse's back. There were several riderless horses among the pursuing crowd. He snatched the reins of one and vaulted into the saddle.

The Viking ships were on the river. Even the one Enar had burned had been pressed into service, since the fire only burned away one bench, the rigging, and the sail.

They were at midriver, every available man's hand at the oars, picking up speed against the fierce current, rowing upstream toward Hakon's island fortress or, perhaps, Reynald's stronghold.

Owen galloped his horse parallel to the fleeing ships. As he passed the archers, he snatched a crossbow from one of them.

"Stop him," Enar gasped. "He's a madman!"

Godwin nodded.

Godwin, riding behind Owen, swore. Owen was going like the wind, spurring savagely. Godwin knew, fast as he was riding, he would never catch him.

Even though Owen's eyes were locked with Hakon's, he seemed to have a sixth sense about the obstacles in front of him. Owen's horse plunged through a ditch filled with debris from the swollen river, then leaped a low stone wall.

Owen found himself in the clear, thundering alongside the fleeing warships. Everyone in them was at the oars, pulling frantically against the stiff current.

Everyone but Hakon.

He stood beside the high, carven stern post of the longship, a broad-bladed spear poised in his hand. It flashed silver in the growing light.

For a moment that seemed to last for an eternity, Owen's eyes met Hakon's. But strangely enough all he could remember was the bread and water being shoved into the cage. A moment of mercy, a moment of kindness on Hakon's part.

Owen had a second to wonder why such a memory would rise to torment him now, when he needed all his strength, all the hatred in his heart to stiffen his arm and make the crossbow bolt fly true.

Then he saw the implacable bright darkness in Hakon's eyes. A look of fury and almost supreme contempt. As though he, Owen, had denied the Northman something he felt was rightfully his. Something he felt was sure soon would be his.

With all his heart Owen wanted to wipe that look of absolute self-assurance away. Wash it away in blood.

Owen let go of the reins. The crossbow seemed to fall across his left arm with dreamlike slowness as he sighted down the arrow groove toward Hakon's breast. Owen stood in the stirrups, lifting himself clean off the saddle to negate the rocking motion of the horse. He pulled the trigger.

He saw Hakon stagger as he let fly the spear.

Owen knew instinctively Hakon's aim would be as true as his own. Owen kicked free of the stirrups and dived clear of the horse. He landed, rolling in the mud. His horse went down, floundering and screaming.

Owen raised himself to his knees and saw the spear blade had gone through the saddle and was sticking the animal's ribs.

At that very moment, he heard a wailing cry of fear and distress rise from Hakon's crew as they saw their chief stricken. But Hakon didn't fall. He stood still clutching the stern post with one hand as he freed the bolt from his mail with the other. However, even as the distance between them grew greater and greater, Owen could see the bright scarlet splash of blood on Hakon's armor. And Hakon no longer looked the confident conqueror, but shaken as any man when he takes a wound.

Then, the longboat swept around the first bend in the river and was gone.

Godwin reined in at Owen's side. The wounded horse was up on its feet, bucking away the offending spear. Godwin stepped aside a little to avoid being splashed with mud, and stared after Hakon. "A valorous chase," he said, and then pointing to the horse added, "a very near thing. Do you think it did any good?"

"I can't say," Owen answered, "but I marked him, took some of his confidence away. That's something."

Godwin nodded. "Sometimes it is much."

Owen turned. Far away he saw Elin. She was mounted on the red stallion, riding bareback easily with only a saddle blanket.

A strange sense of peace descended on Owen as he looked at her and he understood she had brought him peace and beauty, too. He had found both in her arms.

Then he glanced up at the lean man standing beside him. How long had it been really? Only a few weeks since the aging warrior had arrived, and not long before he came, Owen had taken Elin to his bed. But it seemed to Owen that they had always been there. The man in friendship. The woman in love.

Elin was closer. She and Owen looked at each other. There was, Owen sensed, sadness in both of their eyes.

Yet Owen felt again a hint of the peace that had descended on him in the church when he committed himself to Christ and his people's cause.

He still had no assurance of anything, not tomorrow or his springtime, but he had found his heart and his life. However long he lived, he would take that assurance with him.

Even if his road brought him soon into the shadow of death, he would carry that achievement, that peace with him into darkness and beyond. To whatever God waited there.

Owen sighed and took Godwin's hands. He held them, clasping them tightly until Elin reached them and pulled the horse to a stop almost, but not quite, between them.

"My Lord Count," she said to Godwin.

"Yes," Owen said, "my Lord Count Godwin."

Godwin released Owen's hands. "I thank you," he said humbly, "but it's not necessary."

"Oh, yes," Elin said, "oh, yes, it is."

The three of them stood in the bitter wind, looking out at the flooding river, the drowned fields, the vast expanse of water and sky.

A shell of cloud lay over the valley and from beneath its edge shone the first fiery light as the sun rose. The water had a smooth metallic sheen, gray and silver in the light of the new sun, cold and deadly as a sword blade burnished, filed to a razor's edge, and readied for battle.

WIN A TRIP

With American Airlines® AAdvantage® Miles!

Enter the
See How Far a Good
Book Can Take You....
Sweepstakes!

Name_____

Address_____

City_____State_____Zip_____

Mail to:
SEE HOW FAR A GOOD BOOK CAN TAKE YOU SWEEPSTAKES
P.O. Box 8012
Grand Rapids, MN 55745-8012

No purchase necessary. Details on back.

Ø Signet   ◉ Onyx   ♈ Topaz

AAdvantage